Praise for Linda Green

'Clever and compelling. This is a brave story, which is touching right down to the final word'

Dorothy Koomson, *Sunday Times* bestselling author

'A beautifully crafted novel of knife-edge suspense that held my attention to the very end. I wanted to compare the author to Gillian Flynn or Alice Sebold, but that wouldn't be right. This book is one hundred per cent Linda Green, and Linda Green is bloody brilliant!'

Amanda Prowse, #1 bestselling author

'The suspense becomes quite unbearable – and there's a final flourish in the form of a very punchy twist. A terrifyingly plausible story, that will have parents looking over their shoulders'

Sunday Mirror

'A powerful and provocative read that will get under your skin'

Sun

'This novel is fantastic. I couldn't put it down . . . I read it with my stomach fluttering the whole time'

BBC Radio Leeds Book Club

About the Author

Linda Green is a novelist and award-winning journalist who has written for the *Guardian*, the *Independent on Sunday* and the *Big Issue*. Linda lives in West Yorkshire. Her previous book, *While My Eyes Were Closed*, was a paperback bestseller and in the top five bestselling Amazon Kindle books of 2016. Visit Linda on twitter at @LindaGreenisms and on Facebook at Fans of Author Linda Green.

Also by Linda Green

While My Eyes Were Closed
The Marriage Mender
The Mummyfesto
And Then It Happened
Things I Wish I'd Known
10 Reasons NOT to Fall in Love
I Did a Bad Thing

After I've
GONE

linda green

Quercus

First published in Great Britain in 2017 by

Quercus Editions Ltd
Carmelite House
50 Victoria Embankment
London EC4Y 0DZ

An Hachette UK company

A CIP catalogue record for this book is available
from the British Library

PB ISBN 978 1 78648 303 4
EBOOK ISBN 978 1 78648 301 0

10 9 8 7 6 5 4 3 2 1

Typeset by CC Book Production

Printed and bound in Great Britain by Clays Ltd, St Ives plc

In memory of Samantha Hunt

Everybody loses their mum at some point. But your mother is supposed to be old when it happens; wrinkled and stooping and frail.

They are not supposed to be cut down in their prime. When they are still bleeding every month, haven't received any 'keep calm at forty' cards, or even started using anti-wrinkle moisturisers, for goodness sake.

When life ends so rudely, so prematurely, it makes no sense at all. The world stops turning. Your foundations have been removed. The floor beneath you could give way at any point. It's like playing one of those ball in the maze games and knowing that at any second you could fall down the hole.

Precarious. Life is precarious. And if people try to tell you otherwise, and say you are crazy for thinking that way, you have to remember that the crazy ones are those who deny it. Because the only thing which is certain in life is that we are all going to die one day. And that day could be sooner than we think.

PART ONE

JESS

Monday, 11 January 2016

I smell his bad breath a second or two before I feel his hand on my arse. That's the weird thing about public transport gropers, they always seem to have personal hygiene issues.

'What's your problem?' I shout, as I spin around to face him. Immediately, the crowd of people jostling around the ticket barriers parts. The one thing commuters hate even more than delays is a confrontation.

The guy with the dodgy breath and wandering hand obviously hadn't expected this. He looks to either side, desperate to pass the buck.

'Nope, it's definitely you, middle-aged man in the shiny grey suit. Get off on touching women's arses, do you?'

He shuffles his feet and looks at the ground then pushes his way towards the ticket barrier.

'That's it, you run along to work. I bet the women at your office can't wait to see you. Keep your mucky hands to yourself next time, OK?'

I glance behind to see Sadie looking at me with a raised eyebrow.

'What?' I say. 'He got off lightly if you ask me.'

There is now a clear path in front of me to the ticket barrier. I go straight through and wait for Sadie on the other side.

A young guy with dark hair stops in front of me. 'Nice takedown,' he says with a smile. 'Do you want me to go after him for you?'

He is wearing a plum-coloured jacket over a white T-shirt, like he's come in for dress-down Friday on a Monday by mistake.

'What I really want is for all members of the male species to go to hell and stop bothering me.'

The smile falls off his lips. 'Point taken,' he says, before walking off.

'What did you do that for?' asks Sadie, staring at me. 'He was only trying to be nice.'

'Yeah, well, it's difficult to tell sometimes.'

Sadie shakes her head. 'I don't get you. Is this national bite-someone's-head-off day or something?'

'PMT and hunger, always a bad combination. Come on, I need food.'

Breakfast (I hate the word 'brunch' so I refuse to call it that, even when it is after ten thirty) for me consists of a huge blueberry muffin (that I hope will count as one of my five a day) and a can of Tango (that possibly counts as another). Mum used to tell me that the day would come when I wouldn't be able to eat and drink all that crap without looking as if I did.

I'd taken it as a green light to have as much of it as possible while I could still get away with it.

I hear footsteps approaching as I stand waiting to pay. Sadie gives me a nudge. I look up. The guy who'd offered to go after the groper is standing there, bunch of flowers in hand. Actually, it isn't a bunch; it's a proper bouquet. Hand-tied, I think they call it, not that I've ever seen a machine tie flowers.

'An apology for earlier,' he says. 'On behalf of the male species. To show we're not all complete jerks.'

All conversation in the queue stops. I am aware my cheeks are turning the same colour as the roses in the bouquet.

'Thanks,' I say, taking them from him. 'You didn't have to do that.'

'I know, but I wanted to. I also want to ask you out to dinner but I'm not sure if that would be risking a massive public bawl-out so I've left my business card in there with the flowers. Call me if you'd like to take up the invite. And thanks for brightening my morning.'

He turns and walks away, one of those supremely confident walks that stops just short of being a full-blown swagger.

'I hate you,' says Sadie. 'I have no idea why I chose someone who strangers give flowers to as a best friend.'

'You didn't choose me,' I reply. 'I chose you, remember? Mainly because you had the best pencil case in reception.'

'Well, whatever. I still hate you. You don't even have to try. You wear a puffer jacket, leggings and DMs and you still get a gorgeous stranger asking you out.'

'I might not call him,' I say, lowering my voice, aware other people in the queue are listening.

'Then you're a bigger mug than I thought.'

'Well, I'm certainly not going to do it straight away.'

'Playing hard to get, are you?'

'No. I'm just starving and I'm not going to do anything until I've stuffed this blueberry muffin down my gob.'

Sadie smiles at me and looks down at the flowers. As well as the roses there are lilies and loads of other things I don't even know the names of. 'They must have cost him a packet,' she remarks.

'Shame he didn't know I'd have been happy with a blueberry muffin then,' I reply. She laughs. I hold the flowers a little tighter, despite myself.

Leeds city centre is its usual Monday morning self: grey, drizzly and slightly the worse for wear from the weekend. Someone presses a copy of a free magazine into my hand as I stand at the crossing. I take it, not because I want to read it but because I feel for anyone who has to get up at the crack of dawn to force magazines into the hands of grumpy commuters. I roll it up and wedge it into the side pocket of my backpack as I cross the road. The woman in front of me has her right arm turned out and a bulging tote bag hanging from it. I resist the temptation to tell her she looks like a Barbie doll that has had its arm twisted the wrong way by a little boy. I am convinced that if the female species carries on like this, baby girls will eventually be born with their right arms protruding at this weird angle, ready for the midwives to hang tote bags on them.

Sadie follows my gaze and smiles knowingly at me. We are both fully paid-up members of the backpack brigade.

'I wonder if they'll do something for Bowie at work,' Sadie says. 'Put *Labyrinth* and *Absolute Beginners* on, maybe.'

'Yeah,' I say. 'I bet a lot of people would come if they did.'

I decide not to tell Sadie, who has spent most of the train journey talking about David Bowie, that, actually, I am already fed up with it all. Every time I look at Facebook it's full of people posting tributes to him, all doing that RIP crap as if they'd actually known him, actually suffered some deep personal loss. Never stopping to think about what that must feel like to someone who had genuinely lost a loved one. The most important person in their life, even.

We turn off the road into the comparative warmth of the shopping centre. Someone had the bright idea of not putting any sides on the building, so people have to sit at the tables outside the restaurants with their coats and scarves on in winter, even though they are technically inside.

I follow Sadie up the escalator. The cinema is on the 'leisure' floor, with all the restaurants. It's a trendy independent one with squishy sofas and pizzas served in your seats. That's how I justify working there (well, that and the fact I don't have to start work before 11 a.m., even on an early shift). I could never work at a multiplex. It would be like letting the Dementors suck out your soul.

Nina, who's on a rare outing as duty manager, is on the

front desk. She looks down at my flowers and raises an eyebrow. 'I hope you're not thinking of starting a Bowie shrine here.'

'It's nothing to do with him. I was given them, actually.'

'What for?'

'Telling a guy he was an arsehole.'

'Very funny.'

'No, really,' I reply. 'Only the arsehole wasn't the guy who gave them to me.'

Nina shakes her head and sighs. 'So, basically, you bought yourself some flowers on the way into work to make it look like someone gave them to you.'

'Actually,' says Sadie, jumping in before I have the chance to say anything, 'she got them from a drop-dread gorgeous guy who came up to her in the station and asked her out. She's just too modest to admit it.'

'Oh yeah? What's his number then?' asks Nina.

I reach for the business card inside the cellophane and read it out to her. 'Call him if you like,' I say. 'I might not bother.'

Nina rolls her eyes and goes back to whatever it was she was doing on the screen. Sadie nods at me and we head off towards the staffroom. When we get there, I realise I still have the business card in my hand.

'What's his name?' asks Sadie, following my gaze.

'Lee Griffiths. It says he's an associate director at some PR firm in Leeds.'

'Woo. Big cheese. Call him.'

'Nah. It's probably a wind-up.'

'Well, if you don't want him, I'm very happy to take second-hand goods.'

I smile at her as we step back into the lobby to find Tariq and Adrian laying the new red carpet leading to screen one.

'Here you go, ladies,' says Adrian, 'just in time to try it out.'

'Me first!' cries Sadie. I laugh as she sashays up and down the red carpet, posing for imaginary photographs for the paparazzi.

'Hang on,' I say, throwing myself on the floor in front of her. 'Name the film premiere.'

'Suffragette,' she shrieks, before joining me, prostrate on the floor.

'What's all this noise?' asks Nina, sticking her head around the corner.

'Guess the film premiere!' I say. 'Do you want to have a go?'

'No. I want you two to stop treating this place like a soft-play centre and get to work.'

Sadie groans as Nina returns to the front desk. 'I bet Carey Mulligan never had to put up with this,' she says.

I wait until lunchtime to text Lee, when I am on my own in the staffroom. I want to be sure no one else is around in case the whole thing is a wind-up. I decide to keep it short and sweet.

Hi, thanks again for the flowers. Let me know a date and time to meet up. I finish work at 7pm until Wednesday, then I'm working late for a week. Jess.

I hesitate for a second, aware that I might be about to make myself look incredibly stupid, but then I decide to do it anyway. I exhale deeply and press send. It is only once I have done so that I realise how bothered I am about whether or not he responds. Fortunately, I have to wait less than thirty seconds before my phone beeps with a message. Clearly he is the sort of guy who doesn't have to worry about looking desperate.

Hi Jess. That's great. How about Wednesday @ 7.30pm, the Botanist?

The Botanist is an uber-trendy bar just along from the shopping centre. I have never been there, mainly on account of the fact that I am not uber-trendy and don't know anyone who is.

I text back to say that I'll see him there, as if it's a usual hangout of mine. He replies, Great, looking forward to it already.

I am still sitting there with a smug look on my face when Sadie comes in.

'You've called him, haven't you?' she says.

'Texted.'

'And you're going out with him.'

'Might be.'

'If you two get married, I'm going to hunt down the arse-groper guy and invite him to the wedding.'

'I don't think there's any danger of us getting married.'

'Why not?'

'Er, different leagues.'

'Bollocks. You're well up there with him.'

'I still reckon he did it for a dare. Anyway, you'll be on your own on the train home on Wednesday. Think of me surrounded by hipsters trying to order cocktails I've never heard of.'

Sadie snorts. 'I hope he's paying.'

'So do I. Otherwise we're going to Subway, I tell you.'

It's only as I'm walking home from Mytholmroyd station later that I realise Dad will ask about the flowers. I think for a second about chucking them over my head – bride-style – but a quick glance behind confirms that they are likely to be caught by a long-haired, overweight guy, who probably wouldn't appreciate it. I decide to tell Dad a censored version of what happened. He may be able to cope with a guy hitting on me but I'm pretty sure he would freak if I mentioned the arse groper.

I walk past the rows of little back-to-back terraces, lines of washing hanging across the backyards like something out of a bygone era. I bet the people down south watching the Boxing Day floods on the news couldn't believe that a place like Mytholmroyd even existed. It does my head in most of the time, the smallness and oldness of the place. Some people have lived here all their lives, have never even been to Leeds, let alone London. I think that's why I took the first job that came up in Leeds when I left college. No, it wasn't doing what I had planned to do, but at least it meant I could get out of Mytholmroyd.

Our front door opens straight onto the street and the back door onto our yard behind. If I can ever afford a flat in Leeds (which is doubtful), I've already decided I'll get one high up, so people walking past can't have a good gander inside when you open the door.

I go in the back way, as usual. Dad's in the kitchen, Monday being a rare evening off for him because the Italian restaurant where he works is closed.

'Smells good,' I say. Dad looks up from the pan he's stirring, his gaze immediately dropping from my face to the flowers.

'They're nice.'

'Yeah.' I put the flowers on the kitchen counter, knowing full well that I'm not going to get away with that answer.

'So, who are they from?' Dad is still stirring the vegetables on the back hob, trying to pretend he's not that interested.

'A guy I met at the station this morning.'

He nods slowly and puts the wooden spoon down on the chopping board.

'That was nice of him.' Dad's tone suggests he actually thinks the man in question is a serial killer. I decide to get it all out in one go.

'Yeah. I'm going for a meal with him on Wednesday.'

'Are you now?' Dad picks up the spoon again and stirs with an intensity that is entirely unnecessary.

'How old is he, this guy?'

'I'd say seventies, maybe eighty at a push.'

He turns to face me. I have the smile ready prepared for him.

'Very droll,' he says.

'Well, what do you expect? He looks like he's in his late twenties but I don't know. I'll take a questionnaire with me on Wednesday, if you like.'

'So you've never met him before?'

'Nope.'

'And he just walked up to you this morning and gave you flowers and asked you out?'

'Yep. That's pretty much how it was.'

'Doesn't that strike you as a bit weird?'

'Not really.' I was starting to think it would have been easier to tell him about the arse groper after all.

'It sounds a bit weird to me.'

'Look, you've got to let me do normal stuff like this.'

'It's not normal, though, is it? Giving flowers to someone you don't know. Maybe he does this all the time. Some kind of scam he pulls on pretty girls.'

'Dad, I can't win with you. You're the one who always used to tell me to get out more.'

'Yeah, I didn't mean with a stranger.'

'Well, he's not a stranger now, is he? He gave me flowers and asked me out. I said yes. I thought you'd be pleased.'

This is a lie. I knew he'd be exactly like this but I also know how to play him in an argument. He looks down at his feet.

'I'm happy for you. It's just that after last time I, you know, I don't want to see you get hurt.'

'Callum was an emotionally inadequate bastard.'

'Jess.'

'Well, he was! And I've grown up a lot since then – I'm not going to make the same mistake again, am I?'

'So how do you know this guy's not like that?'

'I don't yet, but he gave me flowers, which is a pretty good start, and if I don't like him on Wednesday I won't see him again. Simples.'

Dad nods. He is trying his best to be two parents rolled into one, I know that. But I still wish Mum was around to tell him to let me learn from my own mistakes.

'OK. I'll give him a chance. What's his name?'

'Voldemort.'

For the first time in the conversation, Dad manages a smile. 'Really?'

'His name is Lee and he's the associate director of a PR firm in Leeds and I don't know anything else about him – but if you submit your questions by midnight tomorrow, I'll be sure to put them to him over dinner, OK?'

I flounce out of the kitchen and up to my room. When I return ten minutes later, Dad has put the flowers in a vase. I smile at him. Sometimes he tries so hard it hurts.

Sadie Ward ▸ **Jess Mount**
2 mins

Your dad just told me. I can't believe you're gone. Can't believe you're never going to crack me up laughing again. I'm so, so sorry I couldn't save you. Love you forever. RIP Jess.

JESS

Monday, 11 January 2016

I'm in my room later when I see Sadie's post. It's the photo I see first, one of Sadie and I when we were at primary school. My socks are around my ankles and I have messy hair. We are both grinning inanely. I am about to message her when I read the words she has posted above it.

I read them again, twice more, sure I have missed something. I wait for another post to pop up from her saying it was a joke. It doesn't. I call her.

'Why did you just post that?'

'What?'

'That RIP thing on Facebook.'

'About Bowie?'

'No, about me.'

'I didn't post anything about you.'

'You did. To my timeline. Two minutes ago. A photo of us at primary school and stuff about how you can't believe that I'm gone and you're so sorry you couldn't save me. You basically said I was dead.'

'Why would I do that?'

'I don't know. That's why I called you.'

'I honestly haven't posted a thing.'

'Check Facebook now. You'll see it.'

'OK.' It goes quiet at the other end of the phone for a minute. 'There's nothing there,' she says. 'I haven't posted anything for hours and I've looked on your timeline and there's nothing there either.'

I look again at my phone and read the post out to her.

'That's really sick. I'd never do that. Not even as a joke.'

A comment comes up underneath Sadie's post from Adrian at work.

'Listen,' I say, 'Adrian's just posted this: "Oh Jess, so sad to lose you. Will miss your smile and the laughs we had together. RIP sweetie."'

'Maybe someone's hacked your account,' says Sadie. 'I wouldn't put it past Nina. She could have got hold of your phone or something.'

'But how come I can see it and you can't?'

'I dunno. Maybe there's some way you can do that.'

'Well, they must have hacked into yours as well because the post's from your account.'

'Change your password. I'll change mine too. That should put a stop to it.'

'OK. I'll call you back in a bit.'

I go into my account. I'm rubbish at remembering passwords

so I have to write down the new one as soon as I've changed it. I log out of Facebook then log in again and go back to my timeline. There are now eleven comments underneath Sadie's post, a couple of them from people I haven't seen since I left school and who I unfollowed on Facebook long ago. I have no idea how this is happening but I am going to put a stop to it straight away. I begin to type: *Ha, ha, very funny. It seems the news of my death has been greatly exaggerated* – which I seem to remember was a line from a book or a play or something. I post it. It doesn't appear. I post it again, twice more in fact. Still nothing. I don't get it. I don't get what's happening. I call Sadie back.

'I changed my password but it's still there. Lots of people have posted comments on it but I can't, it won't let me.'

'Maybe it's a virus or something.'

'And you're sure you can't see it?'

'Absolutely.'

'I don't understand how that's even possible.'

'It'll be some thirteen-year-old hacker who's bored stiff doing his maths homework and gets off on doing sick things like this.'

I sigh and shake my head.

'So what do you think I should do?'

'Do a virus scan. That should get rid of it. And if no one else can see it apart from you, there's no harm done, is there?'

'But what if the people who commented can see it? What if they think I'm actually dead?'

'Well, Adrian would have messaged me for a start, wouldn't he?'

'I guess so.' Adrian is lovely. I'm actually touched that he sounded so gutted in his comment. Which is really stupid, I know.

'But the things people have said in their comments,' I continue. 'They actually sound like the sort of thing they would say.'

'Well, nobody's going to say they're delighted you've popped your clogs, are they? Everyone says the same stuff when people die.'

'Adrian called me sweetie. How would they know he calls me sweetie?'

'Probably because he calls everybody sweetie on Facebook? There's probably some algorithm that tells you what words people use most.'

'What if you were right about Nina, though? Maybe she has got something to do with it.'

'She might have the motivation but I'm not sure she's actually bright enough to do it.'

'Well, who else hates me, then?'

'No one hates you, Jess.'

'What about Callum?'

'He's hardly super-brain league either, is he?'

'Why didn't you tell me that at the time?'

'Because you wouldn't have listened. Anyway, why don't you front Nina up in the morning and see what she says. And quit worrying. You're clearly alive. OK?'

'Yeah.'

There is a pause on the other end of the line. I have a feeling I know what Sadie is going to say next.

'You are OK, aren't you? I mean you'd say if . . .'

'I'm fine.'

'And you would tell me if you weren't?'

'You know I would.'

'Good. Now turn your phone off, do a virus scan on your laptop, zap anything that comes up and I bet when you look in the morning there'll be nothing there.'

'OK. Thanks. See you tomorrow.'

I put my phone down and open my laptop. Maybe I won't even be able to see it on there. It might only have been on my phone. I click on Facebook and scroll through everyone's posts from the past couple of hours. Nothing. The photo isn't there. I click on my timeline to double-check. Sadie's post comes up straight away. There are loads of comments now. People asking what happened. And others have started posting to my timeline. Jules from college and Tariq from work and a couple of Mum's friends. They all say the same: that they're in shock; they can't believe I've gone. That it's too much for one family to bear.

I brush the tears away from my cheeks and tell myself not to be so stupid. If it is a virus, the person who created it won't have stopped to think how upsetting it is for someone who has lost a loved one. Sadie's probably right – it'll be some kid who's bored out of his brain and thought it would be a laugh. I shouldn't take it so personally.

I can hear voices on the television drifting up from downstairs. It doesn't sound like football – maybe it's a cookery programme. They're about the only two things Dad watches.

I wonder for a moment about going down to join him, just to clear my head. Snuggling up on the sofa together like we used to do. He'd like it. He always says we don't spend enough time together. I decide against it, though. He'd probably ask me what was wrong. Either that or start quizzing me about Lee again.

I get my earphones, push them into my phone and play the first thing that comes up on the menu. But I can't stop thinking about the post. I suddenly remember the arse groper at the station. What if he's an IT nerd who has decided to get his own back on me for his public humiliation this morning? What if he's somehow managed to find my photo and track me down online?

I pull my earphones out and throw the phone across the bed. I get up, go over to the laptop and start a virus security scan. I'll leave it running overnight and by the morning the whole thing will be gone.

Joe Mount

12 July 2017 • Mytholmroyd, United Kingdom

I'm heartbroken to say that my beloved daughter Jess died yesterday following an accident. I've lost my little girl and I don't have the words to say what she meant to me. My only comfort is that she will at least be with her mum and that Deborah will take care of her for us. RIP beautiful girl.

JESS

Tuesday, 12 January 2016

I died in an accident. I screw my eyes up tight and then open them again, just to make sure that I am fully awake. The words in front of me remain the same. I go cold inside. The overnight laptop security scan came up clear. *No viruses found.* Probably the only time someone has been disappointed to hear that. Because, if it's not a virus, what the hell is it? I am about to phone Sadie when I realise there's no point – she won't be able to see it. I'll have to show her the posts on the train. That way she'll know I'm not making it up.

I read Dad's words again, tears pricking the corners of my eyes. They sound like the words he would use. I can see him sitting there, typing it with two fingers on his keyboard (he never does posts from his phone. He says his fingers are too big for the buttons and he doesn't get on with predictive text). His eyes are red. A scrunched-up tissue is poking out of the pocket of his favourite cardigan – the grey one Mum got him the Christmas before she died. This feels too real, far too real for my liking. It doesn't feel random. It doesn't feel like some hacker messing around. It feels like whoever is doing this is getting at me on purpose.

It is only when I go to read the post for a third time that I notice the date above it: 12 July 2017. I stare at it for a long time, my brain trying to process what my eyes are seeing. How can someone change the date on Facebook? That's eighteen months from now. Eighteen months exactly. I scroll down to last night's posts. At the time I read them, they just had *2 minutes ago* or *1 hour ago* above them. Now Sadie's says *11 July 2017*. My breaths are coming fast and shallow. I Google 'How to change the dates on Facebook'. There is a surge of relief when I see that you can. Apparently, you can change the dates of posts to as far back as 1 January 1905. But a second later I am reading that you can't change the dates of posts to the future. Can't. As in, impossible.

Someone is screwing with my mind. Maybe some kid I used to go to school with who knows what happened to me, who thinks it would be funny to freak me out like this. There are a few comments below Dad's post now. One from my cousin Connie in Italy. She's done a breaking-heart emoji at the end of it. And another from a chef at the restaurant where Dad works, saying how sorry he is for his loss.

Nobody has asked yet what kind of accident. I probably got run over by a bus. That's the sort of stupid thing a space cadet like me would do. Probably looking at my phone at the time. I find myself thinking that I hope it wasn't messy. That, however I died, people didn't have to scoop up parts of me from the road. I wouldn't like that. Wouldn't like it at all.

I'm not going to let them get to me like this. I'll report it to Facebook, let them find out who is doing it and have them blocked or whatever. They can get the police involved if they want, or at least threaten them with it. I just want it stopped.

I pull my dressing gown on. It's a huge purple fluffy thing; Sadie says it makes me look like an extra from *Monsters, Inc.* I pad across the landing to the bathroom. I can hear Dad downstairs in the kitchen. I try to get the image of him sitting at his laptop, crying, out of my head.

Usually, I turn the temperature in the shower down when I use it after Dad. He likes his showers hotter than me, like he drinks his tea hotter than me. But today I leave it where it is, welcoming anything that takes my mind off what is happening – even the scorching sensation as the water hits my body. My skin is decidedly pinker than usual by the time I step out. I grab my towel off the rail above the radiator and hug it around me. It's one of the things I always remember about Mum: her rubbing me dry after a bath when I was a kid and singing cheesy eighties' pop songs to me.

By the time I make it down to the kitchen, Dad is on what I suspect is his third coffee of the day. He smiles and comes over and kisses me on the forehead. Sometimes I pull away and remind him that I am no longer seven years old. Today I don't say anything, just give him a little smile back. I know he won't have checked Facebook yet. He doesn't even bother turning his phone on until he leaves for work some days. I'm pretty sure he won't be able to see the posts, though. And for that I am mightily relieved.

'You OK?' he asks.

'Yeah, not a great night's sleep, that's all.'

'Were you cold? I'll put an extra blanket in there for you if you want.'

'No. Just couldn't get to sleep for ages.'

He nods. I catch sight of the flowers, still in the same spot on the table as last night. I'd almost forgotten about Lee with everything that has been happening.

'Early night tonight then, before your big date,' Dad says, bringing over my mug and putting it down in front of me.

'It's not a big date,' I say.

'What is it then?'

'A meal. That's all.'

'Right,' he says with a wink. I look down; I can't even look him in the eye without thinking about it. What it would do to him if I died.

I meet Sadie on the platform as usual. We're not always on the same shifts, but if it's Chris or Liz doing the rota they try to make sure we are. People used to take the piss out of us at secondary school. My English teacher called us Jessadie because he said we were inseparable, like conjoined twins. I've always liked it though, having one best friend rather than being part of a big gaggle. Or a threesome. Threes were a nightmare at school because you never knew who to sit next to.

'They've done a post from my dad now,' I say, reaching

into my pocket to get my phone. 'Saying I died in an accident. And they've changed the date to make it seem like it's from next year.'

'How can they do that?' asks Sadie.

'You can't, according to Google,' I reply, clicking on Facebook and going to my timeline. 'Which is why it's freaking me out. The virus scan was clear too. Somebody's doing this on purpose.'

'Show me. I still can't see anything on mine.'

I don't respond because I'm staring at my timeline. It's back to normal. The posts aren't on there. I scroll up and down. Nothing. I look up at Sadie, phone in hand.

'They've gone.'

'Good. Maybe it just took that long for the password change to take effect.'

'But they were there just now, before I left the house. I checked again before I came out because I wanted to show you.'

Sadie looks at me. I can almost hear her choosing the right words in her head before she says anything.

'Well, at least they're gone, that's the main thing.'

'I wanted you to see them though!'

'I believe you, Jess. But it doesn't matter now, does it? They've gone and that's what you wanted.'

'Yeah. I suppose so.'

'You could always check with Facebook? Maybe they could tell you if your account was hacked.'

'But I haven't got any proof now, have I? It would just be

me saying there were some crank posts with nothing to back it up. They wouldn't bother looking into it.'

'I guess not. Anyway, like I said, it was probably some spotty thirteen-year-old lad in Hong Kong with nothing better to do.'

I hear the whistling on the tracks and a moment later see our train coming into view. Sadie's right. I should forget it, I know that. But there's a cold place deep inside me that can't. Somebody did that, knowing full well how upsetting it would be. And I can't let that go.

Nina is back with the rest of us plebs on the hosting team today. Hosting is a rather grand word for dashing in and out of different cinema screens with pizzas and burgers (posh ones that they can charge more for because they've got halloumi in). I suppose it's like the bin men now being called refuse collectors, and woodwork and metalwork being called resistant materials at school. Everyone and everything has to have a souped-up title these days.

'No flowers today then,' Nina says as I walk past her in the corridor. I turn and look at her, trying to work out if the smirk on her face is a guilty one.

'Have you been messing with my phone?' I ask.

'What kind of question is that?'

'One that I want answered. You were pretty interested in who gave me the flowers yesterday.'

'Do you honestly think I'm desperate enough to go trawling through your contacts for your supposed boyfriend?'

'Maybe you wanted to have a look at my Facebook.'

'Why would I do that?'

'I dunno. You tell me. Some people get off on that sort of thing.'

'Well, I'm not one of them. I have no interest in your private life. And I suggest,' she says, jabbing a finger towards my face, 'you don't go around making accusations like that.'

I look at her, trying to work out whether she's telling the truth. Her dyed blonde hair is scraped back into a ponytail. The whole of her face looks like it's been scraped back with it. She has one of those mean, vacant faces you see in mugshots. But, despite the smirk, I'm not sure Nina's capable of doing something as clever as hacking into my account.

'Fine. We'll leave it at that, then,' I say, walking off.

I hear a loud tut and muttered swearing behind me, but I choose to ignore it. I go to the staffroom to make myself a tea, swishing the kettle side to side to check there's enough water in it before I flick the switch. No one else is around. I know I shouldn't but I can't help myself. I get my phone out of my bag and go to my Facebook page.

The posts are back, with even more comments under them, dozens of them now. Sad emojis and RIPs by the bucketload. My fingers tense around the phone. I don't understand this. Has the hacker somehow discovered my new password? I go into my account and change it again. I check back but the posts are still there. And the dates on them are all from July next year.

The kettle has boiled, but I'm no longer bothered about the tea. I march out of the room to go and find Sadie.

'Look,' I say, hurrying into the kitchen, where I find her sorting out the ketchups and mustards. 'They're back again.'

I thrust the phone in her face. She takes a step back, stares at it then looks at me, a frown creasing her brow.

'Crazy, eh?' I say.

'There's nothing there,' she says softly. I turn the phone round to look at it. She's right. It's my usual timeline. No RIPs in sight.

'I don't understand!' I cry. 'They were there a minute ago in the staffroom. I just checked.'

Sadie gives me that look. The one she used to give me when it was at its worst. The one that says, *I really don't want to hurt your feelings but I think you should know you've lost the plot.*

'Maybe leave it for a bit, eh?'

'I know this doesn't make any sense, but it's like I'm the only one who can see them.'

Sadie nods slowly. 'Like I said, maybe stop checking all the time.'

'Yeah,' I say, putting the phone back in my pocket. 'You're right.'

She smiles at me, but even Sadie, who is experienced in these things, can't hide the concern behind her smile. She returns to organising the mustards.

'Here,' I say. 'I'll give you a hand. Pass me the ketchups.'

Sadie Ward ▸ **Jess Mount**
12 July 2017 at 8:37pm

I still keep expecting to see one of your posts on here. I see your name and I think it's going to be you, posting something stupid, and it isn't, of course. It's someone posting a tribute to you. And the daft thing is you never had any idea how many people loved you. I know you came across like a cocky sod sometimes, but you weren't, not underneath. You were as insecure as the rest of us. More so, I think. That's why you fell so hard for Lee. It was like you couldn't believe someone could actually love you. I wish you had known because look at this now, Jess Mount. Look at all the people queuing up to say how much they loved you. People who are heartbroken that you're gone. It's stupid, isn't it, that people don't tell you that until you die? Even Nina at work cried when she found out, and you thought she hated your guts. Love you, Jess. We all do. And we miss you like crazy. And don't worry about H. I promise I will find a way to look after him.

JESS

I read Sadie's post several times. And the comments below. People sending their love to her. Telling her to be strong. Saying how devastated Lee must be. And everyone thinking about 'H'.

I am lying on my bed as I read, but my head is spinning like I'm on a waltzer at a fairground. So many thoughts are ricocheting around inside, crashing into my skull. I tell myself that it is complete rubbish, but a tiny part of me doesn't want to believe that. A tiny part that can't help feeling ridiculously excited at the idea of still going out with Lee in eighteen months' time. Which means I am being doubly stupid, because if I do believe it, I'll be dead by then, so the having-a-boyfriend thing wouldn't exactly matter.

The weird thing is how whoever is doing this can know these things about me, because I'm not friends with Lee on Facebook and I only met him two days ago for a matter of minutes. The people who are sending Lee their condolences don't even know he exists.

I sit up in bed, as if hoping the mere act of being upright will stop the world spinning. Instead, it feels like I'm standing at the side of the waltzer, my legs trembling, sure I am going to throw up at any moment. And the one question rising above all the others that are competing for my attention is who is H? People are sending love to H and Sadie is telling me she's going to look after him and I don't know who the hell H is. All I can think of is that guy from Steps and I'm quite sure he has nothing to do with any of this. Maybe I'll get a kitten and call it H. I want a kitten, a tabby one, but I also know that if I got one I would call it Minerva, after McGonagall in *Harry Potter*. I would definitely not call it H.

And the other thing I can't get my head around is that the date of these posts is still in eighteen months' time. Does whoever is doing this want me to think that this is my future? That they are some kind of demonic fortune teller and I only have eighteen months left to live? It's the social media equivalent of finding a voodoo doll of yourself with a hundred pins stuck in it – next to a ticking clock. No wonder it's freaking me out. I want it to stop but I don't know how to make that happen. It's pointless ringing Sadie. I know she's already worried about me and I don't want to make things any worse. I can't show Dad because saying, 'Hey, you know how you've never got over your wife dying, well, now someone's saying I'm going to die in eighteen months too,' is clearly not an option. And I can't go to the police because they won't be able to see it. I have no proof. And if they did bother to investigate, they'd find out about my history and decide I'm a fruit loop.

I sigh and rest my head on the desk. The fact is, I wouldn't blame them. The whole thing is beyond belief. I sigh and sit up sharply, unable to believe that I haven't thought of it before. I check my laptop, making sure the post's still there, and take a screenshot. I have a little smile on my face as I do it, like I've caught someone out and they haven't realised it yet. The smile lasts for only a matter of seconds until I check the screenshot and find it's of my usual timeline, the one everyone else can see. My stomach clenches. I try it again but the same thing happens. Even if there was a way that someone could hack my account and post all this stuff, there is no way they could stop it coming up on a screenshot, no way at all.

Another idea comes to me. I get out my phone and take a photo of the laptop screen. I take three in a row, just to be sure. But when I check, the photos are of the usual timeline too. The one that isn't even on my fucking screen. I start shaking, and put my laptop down on the floor.

I lie back on my bed. Maybe Sadie's right, maybe I am cracking up. Perhaps I'm the only one who can see it because it exists only inside my head. And we all know what my head is capable of. Maybe it's just different this time, which is why I didn't recognise it at first. It makes sense, if you think about it. If you are thwarted from gaining control one way, you find another way to do it, to get past security. If my mind is playing tricks on me, it's making a bloody good job of it. I'm not even sure I'm clever enough to have a mind that could make that up. I let out a snorted laugh. It's come to something when the best-case scenario is that I am going mad.

You hear about people who have white blood cells that attack their own healthy cells. What if I'm somehow programmed to do this? What if I'm so used to being miserable that I am destroying any signs of happiness as soon as they appear?

I open my eyes, instantly surprised that I managed to drop off at some point during the night. I reach straight for my phone. More posts, more comments. More grief that only I can see. If I can see it at all, that is.

I time my entrance to the kitchen so that Dad will know I haven't got time for breakfast. He looks up from the table.

'There's a banana on the side,' he says, nodding towards the kitchen counter.

'I'm fine thanks,' I say.

'You should have something.'

'I'm fine.'

'Saving yourself for the big date tonight, are you?'

'Yeah, something like that.'

Dad is still looking at me.

'It's not too late to blow him out,' he says. 'If you're having second thoughts. Your mum blew me out on our first date. Did I tell you that?'

'I'm not having second thoughts,' I say. 'And yes, you both told me lots of times.'

I see his face and look down at my feet. 'Anyway, I've got to leave now if I'm going to make the train. Don't wait up, OK?'

'Have fun. Be careful.'

I nod and open the door. When I look through the window as I pass it, he is still sitting at the kitchen table, staring at the flowers.

I get changed in the toilets straight after work. I have no idea what you wear for a date at a swanky bar with an associate director, which is why I brought my favourite vintage dress with me and am now wriggling into it while trying to get a soggy piece of loo paper off my boot. My thinking being that if I am going to wear the 'wrong' thing, it should at least be something familiar, something I'm comfortable in and that everyone says looks great on me. I emerge from the cubicle and look at myself in the mirror. The top half looks OK. If the mirror could speak, *Snow White*-style, it would probably say, 'Not sure about the purple tights and DMs, love,' but fortunately we live in a world where mirrors can't speak, so I am saved from the humiliation.

I draw on heavier eyeliner, apply some shimmering copper tone eye shadows and top it off with two coats of mascara. A slick of lip balm and I'm done. Eyes or lips, Mum always used to say, there's no need for both. I stick my hair behind my ear on one side and ruffle the rest of it. The good thing about doing the wild, unkempt look is that my hair seems to be very good at it.

When I leave the loos, Adrian is walking towards me with the Henry vacuum cleaner.

'You're looking particularly gorgeous this evening, sweetie.'

He smiles. I smile back, but find it difficult to reply. All I can think of is what he wrote about me on Facebook.

'Is tonight your hot date?' he asks.

'How do you know about that?'

'The walls have ears in this place,' he says. 'And a few people have particularly large mouths as well.'

I shake my head. Nina, no doubt.

'Well, he's a lucky guy, whoever he is.'

'Thanks. I'd better not keep him waiting.'

'Fashionably late, darling,' says Adrian over his shoulder. 'Always be fashionably late so that people notice your entrance.'

I smile and walk off. Still unsure about the purple tights.

I have resisted looking at my phone all day. I made a promise to myself not to. But as I stand on the escalator my hand reaches for it and, in what I swear is a completely involuntary movement, clicks on Facebook.

It's like stumbling into a wake by mistake. Everyone raw with grief, grasping each other for comfort and passing on condolences to their nearest and dearest. Which, in my case, appears to include the man I am about to go on a first date with. It's like some weird time-slip movie where the main character knows she dies in the second part. I need to remember, if there is one of those awkward pauses in conversation, not to blurt out, 'By the way, everyone sends their love to you after I die.'

I arrive outside The Botanist. It's all wrought iron and rustic-looking. I go down the steps. There are outside tables but no one is sitting on them tonight. A waitress who, unlike me, is dressed sophisticatedly and doesn't smell of burgers, glides towards me, smiling. I quickly scan the room, spotting Lee at a table in the far corner. He's wearing the same plum jacket but with a different coloured T-shirt underneath. I suspect he is one of those annoying people who looks good in anything.

'Hi,' the waitress says. She's looking at me expectantly, but I have a complete mental block on Lee's surname.

'Hi, I'm, er, with him,' I say, pointing in Lee's direction. She nods, doing a very good job of hiding her surprise that someone like me has a date with someone like him.

'Great. Follow me.'

I do as I'm told. Lee looks up. He grins at me and I swear half of Leeds is being plunged into darkness; that smile can only have been powered by the national grid.

'Hi, Jess,' he says, standing up and bending to kiss me on the cheek. 'You look fantastic. I'm so glad you could make it.' He is greeting me like I'm an old friend, not someone he picked up in a train station a couple of days ago. I sit down quickly, desperately trying to put the thought of him grieving for me out of my mind.

'Thanks,' I say. 'It makes a change from grabbing something at the station and legging it for the train.'

'And at least you don't have to face the grubby commuters at close quarters.' He smiles.

'No, there is that.'

'Do you get that often?'

'Often enough.'

'There are, as you said, a lot of complete jerks out there.'

'Arseholes.'

'Sorry?'

'I said there were a lot of arseholes. Leeds appears to be full of them.'

'Well, I'm honoured that you've deemed me an honorary non-arsehole.'

He smiles at me as he says it. I'm about to say that I might change my mind by the end of the night, but then I think better of it. The waitress returns and asks what we'd like to drink. I glance at the menu on the table, all cocktails that I've never heard of. Lee is looking at me expectantly.

'You choose,' I say. 'I'm up for anything.'

He raises an eyebrow. I notice for the first time what amazing eyebrows he has: dark, thick and really rather shapely for a man.

'We'll go for the Lemon and Jasmine Collins, please,' he says. The waitress nods. He smiles at her, but not in a lechy way.

'So,' he says, once we're left alone. 'Where do you work?'

'The cinema in the shopping centre,' I reply, pointing upwards before sharply bringing my hand down as I realise how ridiculous it looks. 'I'm on the hosting team, which means I do waitressing, a bit on the front desk and whatever else needs doing.'

'Do you enjoy it?'

'It's a job, isn't it?' I shrug. 'And it means I get to watch lots of films. Well, bits of films anyway.'

'They're very lucky to have you.'

'You can tell my boss that, if you like.'

'Well, if they don't appreciate you, we're about to advertise for a receptionist.'

'I'm not sure that's my sort of thing. I can be a bit gobby, in case you hadn't noticed.'

Lee smiles again. 'Can't say I had. Anyway, I'm not going to turn this into a job interview. This evening is strictly for pleasure.'

I glance down at the menu, mainly to hide the rising colour in my cheeks. What I really fancy is a burger, but I suspect it's not what someone sophisticated like Lee would go for.

'How about we both go for the deli board?' says Lee, as if sensing my hesitation. 'It's basically a mezze and then we can mix and match.'

'Sounds good.'

'You choose the starters, though.'

'OK. It'll be the garlic mushrooms, though.'

'Are you trying to ward me off?' He smiles.

'Nope. Just don't fancy something served in a tin or on a piece of slate and I have no idea what piri-piri sauce is but I don't like the sound of it.'

'You,' Lee says, leaning over towards me, 'are a complete breath of fresh air.'

'Good,' I reply. 'Although you won't be saying that when I've eaten the garlic.'

There is no awkward pause in the conversation. Not for the entire evening. We talk about all sorts of stuff: where you can get the best pizzas in Leeds, crap films, me not owning a brolly and him not being able to ride a bike. By the time we get to the desserts all I can think about is what it would be like to spend the next eighteen months of my life with this guy. And that, even if I do die then, I suspect I will at least die happy.

'So, have I retained my non-arsehole status?' asks Lee. 'Or did I turn out to be just as bad as the rest of them?'

'You're still non-arsehole,' I say with a smile. 'What about me? Do you want your flowers back?'

'No, you can keep them,' he says. 'Though had you spent the entire evening checking your mobile phone, I'd have said otherwise.'

I swallow, wondering for a second if he somehow knows what's been going on.

'Why do you say that?'

'Just hate it, I think it's really rude. An ex-girlfriend of mine used to do it all the time. Drove me up the wall.'

'I take it she didn't last very long?'

He hesitates before replying. 'No. Bit of a deal-breaker, as far as I'm concerned.'

'But what if I needed to check it for work?'

'Yeah, but unless you're an on-call doctor or something, how many people actually need to do that? Certainly not of an evening, anyway. Most people are just obsessed by what other people are up to or watching stupid videos on Facebook.'

I clench my hands under the table and try to smile. 'You'd better not friend me on Facebook then. I'm the one sharing them.'

'Facebook's on the way out. I'm not even on it anymore. All the kids are on Instagram these days. And next year it'll be something else. It's like anything, it keeps moving. You've just got to move with it.'

'Now you're sounding like someone in PR,' I say.

'Sorry.' He grins. 'Anyway, I shouldn't be telling you what the latest thing is. How old are you?'

'Twenty-two.'

'There you go – you're ten years younger than me. You should be telling me where it's at.'

I shrug, trying not to let him see that I'm shocked he's thirty-two or think about my dad going apeshit when he finds out. 'I'm not into following the crowd; I like to do my own thing. Wear what I want, do what I want, say what I want. Not what some blogger or app tells me to.'

'Bit of a free spirit, are we?'

'I just don't like taking crap from anyone.'

'I had noticed that bit.' He smiles again.

Our baked chocolate-chip cookie dough arrives. There are two spoons with it. He passes one to me and waits to let me have the first mouthful.

'Good?' he asks. I nod, afraid to speak because I suspect I've got chocolate all over my teeth.

He picks up his spoon and tries it. 'Top choice.'

'Always go for what you would have chosen when you were twelve,' I tell him.

'You would have gone for garlic mushrooms when you were twelve?'

'Yep. My dad's a chef. We did garlic from when I was a toddler. He said he didn't want me to be one of those kids who wouldn't eat what their parents were having. He's half Italian,' I add. 'It explains a lot.'

'Have you got some sultry Italian surname then?' asks Lee.

'Nope. It's Mount. Which was great fun at school. His mum's Italian, not his dad, so I still got a lousy surname.'

'You got his Mediterranean looks though.'

'Only the eyes. Everything else is from my mum.'

'She must be one beautiful lady then,' says Lee.

I look down at the table. 'She died,' I say. 'Seven years ago. Cancer. She was beautiful, though. In every kind of way.'

'I'm sorry,' says Lee.

'It's OK.'

I reach my hand out for my glass but he takes it in his before I get there.

'I mean it. I'm really sorry. I had no idea. That must have been so tough for you.'

'Thanks,' I say, trying hard to keep myself together. 'I got through it, that's about all I can say. Still miss her.'

'Are you close to your dad?'

'Yeah, I guess so. I still live with him. It hit us both pretty hard.' I'm not going to say any more than that. I'm surprised that I've said this much. I don't usually, not when I've just met someone. Although maybe it's because I know he's an important someone. According to my Facebook page, anyway.

'What about your parents?' I ask, keen to change the subject.

'Divorced,' he says. 'Mum still lives in Horsforth, where I grew up. I see her a couple of times a week. She cooks a mean Sunday roast.'

'And your dad?'

Lee shakes his head. 'I've not really seen him since.' I want to ask more but I get the sense that Lee doesn't want to talk about it. I realise he still has hold of my hand. It feels good. It feels right.

He still has hold of my hand later, when I glance at my watch and see the time.

'Shit!' I say. 'I need to go. The last train home is in ten minutes.'

'I'll get you a taxi if you'd rather,' Lee says.

'No, honestly, it's fine. I'll get the train.'

Lee gets the bill and pays in cash before I even have the chance to offer half.

'Thanks,' I say. 'My turn next time.'

'So, you think there'll be a next time, do you?' asks Lee, his eyebrows raised.

'Yeah. It takes at least two dates to work out if someone's an arsehole or not, sometimes three. The first time, they're trying so hard to impress that they might be able to cover it up. On the second, they drop their guard a bit and usually say something stupid. And on the third they think they're in there and all sorts of crap comes out.'

'So it's kind of a three dates and you're out process, is it?'

'Possibly. Though not everyone even gets to the third date.'

'I'll count myself lucky to make it to two then.'

'Well, thanks for the first one. I'd better leg it.'

'Let me walk you to the station.'

'You'll have to run with me.'

'Fine by me.'

He follows me outside and I start running. A second later I feel his hand slip into mine.

'Wow,' he says. 'Usain Bolt has nothing on you.'

'It should be an Olympic sport, you know. The six-minute train dash.'

We go full pelt down the road and into Leeds station. I can feel my nose start to run and hope to God I won't be all snotty if he goes to kiss me. We get to the barrier and I fumble in my pocket for the ticket.

'If you can't find it you can always stay at my place,' he says. 'My flat's just opposite platform 17b.'

'That's a bit Harry Potter. Do you run through the wall to get to it?'

'Sadly not. I have to go around the long way.'

I find my ticket and hold it up for him to see. 'Sorry,' I say.

'Well, the offer's still there for another time.' He steps forward and kisses me on the lips. If I have got a snotty nose, he's too polite to say anything.

'Now go on,' he says, smiling as we pull apart. 'Before you miss your train.'

I smile and nod and hurry through the barrier. I run up the escalator and down the other side just as the Manchester Victoria train pulls into the platform.

I find a seat next to the window. My phone buzzes. I pick it up.

I don't know about you but I'm still getting my breath back. X

'Good night?' asks Dad, when I arrive back. It's nearly midnight. I thought he'd be in bed by now.

'Yeah. Great, thanks. Turns out Lord Voldemort's quite nice in real life.'

He smiles. 'And what about Lee? Would I like him?'

'Yeah,' I say. 'I think you would.'

'That's OK, then. I'll head up to bed.'

'You didn't need to wait up, you know. I'm a big girl now.'

Dad turns to look at me. 'You never stop worrying, Jess. That's the thing you learn about being a parent. However old your children get, you never stop worrying.'

Joe Mount
14 July 2017 • Mytholmroyd, United Kingdom

For all those asking, I'll post details of Jess's funeral arrangements as soon as they have been made. We've just got to wait until the coroner has finished his investigations. Apparently it's routine when there's been a sudden death. Thank you all for the sympathy cards and messages of condolence and lovely tributes to Jess. Nothing can ease my pain right now but it's good to know you all care and that Jess meant so much to so many people.

JESS

Thursday, 14 January 2016

I am glad my death is sudden. Mum told me once that her greatest pain wasn't physical; it was seeing our pain as we witnessed her slow, agonising demise. At least with a sudden death, everyone will be spared that. It's just the shock they will have to contend with. Shock that is apparent in every comment I have read so far.

I think again about what type of accident it might be. I remember once at primary school, when we were doing paint-blowing pictures, I sucked instead of blew. The paint was red. I nearly gave the teacher a heart attack when she turned around and saw the scarlet liquid dripping from my mouth. It will be something stupid like that, I am pretty sure of it. I just hope they don't put it on my gravestone. *Here lies Jess Mount, who died a really stupid death.*

I sit up in bed and shake my head, realising that I'm buying into this crap. It's what they want, I know that. But when you read a post from your dad, talking about your funeral arrangements, it is hard not to take it seriously. Very seriously indeed.

It occurs to me that it might not have been an accident. I could have meant it. Committed suicide. That could be why the coroner is involved. I don't think I'd have the guts to do it, though. Even if I had the reason. And if I'm still going out with Lee in a year, I don't see how I could possibly feel suicidal.

I allow a smile to creep over my face, remembering how good it felt to be holding hands with him as we ran for the train last night. There is going to be a second date. I know that much. And, if I am to believe what I'm reading, which I don't, there are going to be a hell of a lot of other dates too. Until the point where I get run over by a bus or something.

Actually, I'll probably fall down that gap between the train and the platform. How fitting that would be for the girl who spent her entire life running for trains. It would be messy, though. And public. And I wouldn't like it to be either of those things.

I sigh and get up off the bed. I look at my phone, charging on the chest of drawers, but I am determined not to touch it. I need to stop reading the posts. There's probably some way they can tell if I'm actually clicking on them and reading them. If I don't read them or complain or report it, they'll get bored of it in the end and pick on someone else. I can't imagine that whoever is doing this is going to keep it up much longer.

I certainly hope not. Because the thought of having Dr

fucking Who sending me post-death reports from the future for the rest of my days is enough to send me round the bend.

'Well?' says Sadie, as soon as I arrive at the station.

'It was good,' I reply, trying hard to keep the grin off my face.

'How good? On a scale of one to ten.'

'I dunno. Maybe a nine.'

'I take it he paid then.'

'He was a complete gentleman.'

'You mean he didn't offer to shag you?'

'He said I could stay the night if I wanted to.'

'So why didn't you?'

'Come on, I'm not that bad. Not on a first date.'

'Like that's ever bothered you before.'

'Yeah, well, that was a long time ago.'

'He snogged you though, right?'

'Might have.'

'Marks out of ten.'

'Nine.'

'Two nines from the girl who never gives tens! Bloody hell, I'd better go and buy a hat.'

'Piss off. It's early days. He's got plenty of chances to screw up yet. So have I, for that matter.'

I say it because it's the sort of thing I usually say. But even as I do, I'm thinking about what Sadie said on Facebook. About me falling hard for Lee because I didn't think anybody loved me.

'When you seeing him next, then?'

'He said he'd text.'

'They all say that.'

'He will do.'

'How come you're so sure?'

'He just will.'

We board the Leeds train. The second carriage, as usual. Sadie never says anything about it now. Occasionally, when it's busy and we have to get on one of the end carriages, she looks at me to see if I'm OK, but she never says anything. She knows better than that.

My phone beeps with a message. I get it out and see Lee's name on the screen. I only dared put it in my phone on the way home last night. I click on it.

When can I see you again? How about a lunchtime rendezvous if you're working lates now. Friday?

'What did I tell you?' I say to Sadie.

She whistles. 'Impressive. He's a keeper.'

I text back: Friday's good. About 12.30pm. I start work at 2

He replies quickly: Great. Same place at 12.30 then. Looking forward to it X

I put the phone back in my pocket.

'So?' asks Sadie.

'Friday lunchtime.'

'Keen.'

'Seems so.'

'Great. It's good to see you with a smile on your face. I take it all that other stuff's stopped? You know, the Facebook thing.'

I hesitate. I want to tell her, but it'll probably be the same as last time and she won't be able to see the posts. And I don't want her to give me that concerned look again. I've seen enough of those to last a lifetime.

'Yeah.' I sigh. 'All back to normal.'

Nina is the one who tells me. If I could have selected anyone to be the bearer of bad news, she would have been last but one on my list, narrowly behind Professor Umbridge.

'Have you heard about Alan Rickman?' she asks as we pass in the kitchen.

'Heard what?'

'He's dead. In real life, I mean, not as Snape at the hands of Voldemort.'

I stare at her, not wanting to believe what I am hearing.

'Are you sure?'

'Yeah. It's on the BBC news website and everything. Cancer, apparently. Only in his sixties. Who'll be next, eh? They're all popping their clogs this week.'

She makes it sound like some game of celebrity deaths bingo. I put down the plate I am holding and turn to leave the kitchen.

'Oi!' calls Nina. 'Don't leave me on my own. We've got loads of tables to clear out there.'

I'm not listening. I'm heading straight for the toilets. She has no idea, of course, how much he meant to me. I worshipped him when I was a teenager. Snape was easily the best character in *Harry Potter*, and Alan Rickman was Snape, he brought him to life perfectly – his flaws, his secrets, his internal conflicts. I watched the first five films with Mum. I can still remember how hard it was to watch *Harry Potter and the Half-Blood Prince* without her. I knew that she would have loved it almost as much as I did.

I go into the cubicle and begin to cry. I hadn't even known he was ill. Not that it would have made it any easier. It's just a shock, that's all. Mum dying, Alan Rickman dying and now me supposedly dying, it's all come as a terrible shock. I get my phone out of my pocket and go to the BBC news website. There are quotes from J. K. Rowling and Daniel Radcliffe. They say exactly what you would expect them to say: he was a brilliant actor, a lovely guy, a friend for life. I go onto Facebook. My wall is full of tributes to him. I scroll through and share a couple of the good ones. I do a Google search for the scene I am looking for, the one from the very first potions lesson, copy the link and post it with the word 'Always' above it.

I scroll down some more, seeing photos of a blur of dark hair through my tears. People are saying such nice things: how sad it is that they take the best ones first; the silly little things they will remember. I brush back damp strands of hair from my eyes. It is only then I realise that I am no longer looking at Alan Rickman's tributes; I am once more looking at my own. It is me they are mourning. Me they are expressing shock and sadness for. Me who has left a hole in their lives. The tears fall more heavily now. I'm not sure if they are for Alan or

Mum or me. Maybe for all of us. For everyone who is taken too soon.

It must be about ten minutes later when I hear the door open. 'Jess. Are you OK?'

I wipe my nose on my sleeve and open the cubicle door.

Sadie takes one look at my face and throws her arms around me. 'I'm sorry. Nina just told me. I figured you'd be in here. What a bastard week this is turning out to be. I know how much he meant to you.'

I sniff loudly in her ear. 'I'm going to be next. Dad's arranging my funeral. You're saying how much you miss me.'

Sadie pulls away and looks at me. I hold my phone up.

'You won't be able to see the posts, I know that, but they're here. I can see them. In eighteen months' time you're all saying ridiculously nice things about me, only I'm getting a bit sick of the loveliness now and I kind of wish one of you would say I was a moody cow with crap taste in clothes and a big gob.'

Sadie shakes her head and takes my phone from me. 'There's nothing there about you, Jess. It's all Alan Rickman stuff. I understand you're upset, but you mustn't let this start up again.'

'I know it sounds stupid but it is there – but only when I'm on my own. I can't even take a screenshot of it or a photo but you have to believe me that it is there.'

Sadie strokes my damp hair. 'Come on,' she says, taking my hand and leading me over to the sinks. 'Let's get you cleaned up. They'll be wondering where you've got to. I know it's been a shock, Jess, and I can understand that it's brought a whole load of stuff up, but you've got to get through today, OK? I promise you it will all seem clearer in the morning.'

I nod and put my phone back in my pocket, hoping to God that she's right.

JESS

April 2008

I stand at her grave for a long time. I am empty even of tears. Apparently, the fact that I knew this was coming is supposed to make it easier. It doesn't. And if anyone else says that at least she isn't suffering anymore, I swear I will punch them. Of course she's suffering. She's left us. And that was the thing she was dreading most.

I don't know what happens next. I'm not sure I want anything to happen. Maybe I can simply stay here next to her, feeling close to her. Because the one thing I know is that I can't bear to walk away.

I can't see how anything worthwhile can happen now Mum has gone, but she told me not to think like that. She gave me big lectures about it. About how she wanted me to go out and live my life and do all the things she never got around to doing. She told me I was her brave girl. That I was strong enough to get through this. But now she's gone, I don't feel strong at all. It is all I can do to hold myself upright. Even putting one foot in front of the other is beyond me right now.

I look down at the coffin in the ground below me. I want to jump down and sit on it. Tear open the lid and see her one more time before she goes. Before they cover her up and she's gone forever.

I feel a hand on my shoulder. I turn to see Dad standing there, his eyes rimmed red, his cheeks hollowed out, hurt and pain oozing out of every pore.

'I don't want to leave her,' I say.

'I know,' he replies. 'Me neither.'

'Can't we take her home with us? Can't we bury her in the back yard?'

He shakes his head. Wipes his eyes. 'She's inside you,' he says. 'You can carry her around with you all the time. She's in your heart.'

I look at him. He means well, I know that. But he doesn't know how to deal with this any more than I do. And I am so sick of being treated like a kid. She's not inside me. She's in the coffin in front of me. And soon she will be covered over with earth and there'll be a headstone that reads, 'Deborah Mount, much loved wife, mother and daughter', and people will walk past it and they will read it but they will have no idea, no fucking idea at all, of what she really meant to us.

ANGELA

Thursday, 14 January 2016

When people talk about putting on a brave face, I understand it's just a phrase they use. But it happens to be the best description of what I do every morning, and have done for as long as I can remember. I look in the mirror and see the real me: the worry lines etched on my face; the sadness in my eyes; the dry, sallow skin. I can't go out like that; I don't want people to know that version of me. It is too raw, too honest. Their minds will go into overdrive and they will understand too much and ask too many questions. Always questions. From people who think they already know the answers.

So I put on my brave face. It is a long, laborious process, more so than ever these days. But it is entirely necessary. I pull the make-up band up over my forehead, scraping my heavy fringe back off my face. It accentuates the fact that my roots need doing, but I try to ignore that for now. The moisturiser seeps into my pores, my skin always greedy for more. The woman behind the make-up counter in Boots once told me my skin tone was between shades for foundation, so I opted for the darker one, keen to avoid looking like death warmed up. I haven't changed it since. I wait until it has been absorbed and then apply my pressed powder, from one of those compacts with a mirror and a puff. I suppose it's old-fashioned now. I see the young women with those big brushes, applying loose powder like there's no tomorrow. It is too messy for my liking and too random. I like to know that everything has been covered, with no waste, no fuss, no flicking or flourishes of the hands required. Next, I use a brush for my blusher. Only a small one, mind, and only a touch of it. My eyes take the longest. I draw around them slowly and carefully with black eyeliner. I feel naked without it. I wouldn't even open the door to the postman. I dust a little light shadow on the lids and then apply a coat of black mascara. My brows are thin and could do with a bit of colour too, but they're mostly covered by my fringe. Finally I add a slick of pearl lipstick. The same shade I have been using for thirty years. I don't know what I'd do if they ever stopped making it.

I take off my make-up band and brush my hair so that the bottom of it curls gently around my jawline. It is my brave face. I have to be brave every day, but I do not want the world to know that. Hopefully, they will be fooled into thinking that this is me, and will not stop to ask what lies beneath, will not try to chip off the veneer. And I will keep wearing it. Smiling and saying I am fine when asked. Because it is the only way I know to cope.

I look at my watch. It is still only seven thirty. I have always been an early riser, even when there is nothing to get up for. I don't work on Thursdays. It's one of the things I like about working in a supermarket, how flexible they are for part-timers. Lee visits on a Thursday after work. He'd laugh if I told him that's why I don't work on Thursdays. Tell me not to be so daft. But I like everything to be just right for him – the house clean and tidy, dinner in the oven, me looking my best. We may move on but we do not forget. Not ever.

I go downstairs. Radio 2 is on in the kitchen. It keeps me company all day, although I sometimes put a CD on during the Jeremy Vine show because I prefer the music to the talking. Especially the politics; I have no interest in that at all.

I pull on my marigolds and start on the sink. My mother taught me how to clean a kitchen properly. You could see your face in her taps. None of this 'I'll give it a quick wipe over' for her. I breathe in the smell of the cream cleaner. It's supposed to be pine-scented, but it's the other, sharper smells that I like. The chemicals, I suppose. Whatever it is that makes it smell clean. I like the reassurance that nothing will get past it.

By the time I finish, the place is spotless. You could use it in one of the adverts on TV. It is a good way to start the day, turning something ordinary into something special.

I look at my watch. Lee will be here in ten minutes. He still likes to be punctual, as I do. Old habits die hard. It's difficult with the rush-hour traffic, of course, but he always seems to manage to get away on time. When he got this job, I worried he was going to turn into one of those workaholics who always put their career first and then wake up one day when they're fifty and realise they entirely forgot to have a family. But the fact that he's still got time for his mum gives me hope that he makes time for other things too. That it's not all work and no play. Although there's been no sign of a romance for a while now. Not since Emma – and we don't talk about her, of course.

I check the lasagne in the oven and turn it around to make sure it cooks evenly. He has lots of fancy things when he's out, I know that, but he still enjoys his mum's lasagne and Sunday roast. I give him good portions, too. More than they do in those posh restaurants he goes to. And I do try to move with the times. I did a pasta bake with tuna and chilli last week. One of those little twist things I'd seen on the Sainsbury's adverts.

Right on time, I hear Lee's key in the door. It's been almost ten years since he moved out but when he uses his key it's nice to think that it's still his house too. There's something special about coming home to the house you grew up in. At least, I imagine there is.

'Hello, love,' I say, greeting him in the hallway. He smiles and stoops to kiss me. His cheeks are cold but his eyes seem to be particularly bright this evening. He has his father's eyes, of course. Although we don't mention that either.

'Hi, Mum. Something smells good.'

'Lasagne,' I say. 'It'll be ready in a minute. Come on in and warm up.' I take his coat and hang it up on the peg, then follow him through to the kitchen. 'So how's work?'

'Yeah, good. Crazy busy as usual and Carl's off sick, which doesn't help. But we'll get there.'

He smiles again. I never ask too much about work. I understand the gist of what he does but I have no real interest in the details and he knows that. What matters to me is that he's got a good job. The sort of job I always hoped he would get. It's what every parent wants – for their child to have a better life than them, better prospects. And I know it pays well because there are not many of his age who can afford a nice city-centre flat.

'I'm sure you're managing to keep on top of it all. You always do. Anyway, sit yourself down and I'll get dished up.'

'Can I give you a hand?'

'No, thanks, love. You just relax.' He always offers and I always say no but it's still nice that he asks.

'There you go,' I say, putting his plate down in front of him. I go to pour him a glass of wine. Well, half a glass, which is all he has when he's driving.

'No, I'm fine, thanks,' he says, holding his hand over the glass.

'You haven't given it up for something, have you?' I ask as I sit down opposite him. 'One of those charity dry January things?'

'No. Just had a few last night.'

'With the crowd from work?'

'No. I was at a restaurant, with a friend.'

I start to cut up my lasagne. 'Anyone I know?'

'Nope. Someone I only met this week.'

He lowers his eyes but I still manage to catch the look in them.

'Who is she, then?'

'I can't keep anything quiet with you, can I?' he says, looking up. He is smiling as he says it, though. Smiling in a way that suggests he doesn't mind me asking. I swallow, aware of the equivalent of a pilot light going on inside me.

'Well, you obviously seem pretty happy about it, whoever she is.'

'Her name's Jess. First date last night, so it's early days, but I like her. I like her a lot.'

'Does she work at your place?' I hope not. From what I can make out, the women Lee works with are very career-focused.

'No, nearby though. I met her at the station actually, we just kind of got talking.'

'What does she do?'

'She works at the cinema in the shopping centre. Meet and greet and show them to their seat kind of thing.'

I nod. Not the sort to put a career before a family then. 'Pretty, is she?'

'Mum.'

'What, can you not ask that these days?'

'She's stunning, actually. Not in a conventional, glamorous kind of way. Just striking. But very down to earth.'

'When am I going to meet her then?'

'Give me a chance, it was only a first date.'

'Well, just you make sure that you bring her round for Sunday lunch as soon as you can.'

'So you can vet her, you mean.' He smiles again.

'No. So I can welcome her to the family.'

Lee raises an eyebrow. 'Like I said, let's just take things one step at a time. I don't want to rush things.'

'You're thirty-two, Lee. I don't think anyone could accuse you of rushing things.'

He stops eating for a moment and looks at me. For the first time this evening there seems to be a chill in the air.

'If you pressurise someone to settle down, maybe they'll make a mistake. Maybe they'll resent it for the rest of their life. Maybe they'll take it out on those around them.'

The chill has turned decidedly icy. I chew my mouthful for a long time, not sure I am physically able to swallow. The gagging feeling is distant yet familiar. Lee can do that. Can bring it all rushing back to the surface with a barbed comment, a change in tone or simply a look. Like father, like son.

'There's no pressure,' I reply. 'But if you do decide to bring her, she'll be made very welcome.'

We go back to eating. After a few minutes of silence I change the subject to Leeds United, always plenty to talk about there. And far safer ground to be on.

Afterwards, when he has gone and I've got the dishwasher going, I venture into the spare room. It's a bit chilly; I keep the radiator turned off because it seems wasteful to heat a room that isn't used.

I kneel on the floor and pull out the drawer under the double bed. They are all arranged in size order, from newborn upwards, still in their plastic bags with the labels on. I only buy new things. I like the idea of starting afresh. They are mostly in neutral shades of white and lemon, though there's a set in a lovely shade of green that I couldn't resist. It's hard these days – so much is in blue or pink. But I am still able to be quite selective about what I choose. Only the best will do for my first grandchild. I haven't been able to bring myself to open the drawer since the thing with Emma ended. But now there is a glimmer of hope, I am able to look again. And maybe start buying again too.

I reach to the back, feeling for the delicate tissue, and pull it out when I find it. My fingers tremble slightly as I unwrap the paper to reveal the christening robe inside. This is the one thing of Lee's I want my grandchild to have. I can still see Lee in it, his huge eyes looking up at me. His hands clutching the lace and giving it a good pull. I don't think you would see the tiny speck of blood unless you were looking for it. It has faded with time. Besides, I could easily pass it off for something else if anyone did notice. Nobody would know otherwise. Except *him*, of course. And he won't be there. Lee is no longer in touch with his father. I know that much.

What I haven't told Lee is that I see his father every time I look at him, hear him every time he speaks, smell him whenever he is next to me. Like father, like son, they say. It chills me to the bone.

Joe Mount

14 July 2017 • Mytholmroyd, United Kingdom

At such a difficult time, I am trying to focus on the happy memories. Like this one, Jess's wedding day. We both cried as I walked her down the aisle. I don't think I have ever seen her looking so beautiful. She made me the proudest dad on earth.

JESS

Thursday, 14 January 2016

The photo I am looking at is of me and Lee on our wedding day. I know Photoshop is good, but it is not that good. You can't play around with something that isn't there. This isn't a case of airbrushing something out, this is the creation of something that has not happened. I am wearing a tight bodice under a lace, off the shoulder, half-sleeve top, with a big sash around my waist and a full skirt. My hair is piled up on my head with two strands falling down in a style I have never worn before, and it's topped off with a tiara. A tiara, for fuck's sake. I'm wearing a pearl choker and my make-up is different. I have no idea how to make myself look like that, but it is still unmistakably me, standing next to someone who is unmis-takably Lee. He is wearing an expensive-looking suit and a purple cravat but otherwise he looks exactly the same as when I saw him on Wednesday. And he is smiling at the camera. A huge great beam, actually. I'm smiling too, but unlike Lee, it is not a smile that lights up my face. It is a slight, uncertain one. I guess I must be nervous. It is a big deal. I didn't think I would ever get married. I don't consider myself the marrying kind. I mean, you don't have to these days, do you? Anything goes and all that. And yet, I marry Lee. I am staring at the evidence. Evidence that seems impossible to disprove. Because it's not just our faces superimposed on a bridal couple. They are my shoulders and my arms and the ring I can see is on my finger.

I take another breath, my gasp for air making me realise belatedly that I had been holding the last one all this time. A chill runs through me; my whole body starts to shake. I am looking at a future in which Lee and I get married, at some point in the next eighteen months. There is no date on the photo but it appears to have been taken in the summer; the leaves are green and there are some blurry flowers in the background. Maybe I hadn't been married long when I died. How ridiculous is that? I go and land myself a husband and then pop my clogs.

A tiny little bit of me, the never-quite-stopped being-thirteen-years-old bit, is elated, is performing cartwheels inside because she marries a guy like Lee. But I manage to block her out because, really, it doesn't matter. My father has posted this photo to remind him of me after my death. That is what we are talking about here.

Except we're not, because Facebook says posts from the future are impossible. I am seeing this because I want to see it. I am so fucking needy that I want to believe Lee marries me. And as for the rest of it, well, I've been here before, haven't I?

I'm losing it. I'm getting obsessed with people dying and if I'm not careful I'm going to fuck this whole thing up because of it.

I throw myself onto my bed and cry silent tears into my pillow. I will not go back there. I tried to get Dad to promise he would never let me go back there when they let me out, but he shook his head. He couldn't make that promise. Having seen me lose it once, he knew that it could happen again. And that is the truth that has been hanging over us ever since. Mental health is a continuum. I remember them explaining that to both of us when they finally took me off the medication. There is no such thing as better, as cured. We are at one point on a line at any given time. And a few months later we could be at a different point – better or worse. That is the truth of it. The madness lies within me at all times. It is simply a matter of whether I choose to let it gain a hold.

As soon as I catch sight of Lee the following lunchtime, I feel a lurching sensation in my stomach. Here he is, my future husband. I can't tell him that, though. If I give even the tiniest inkling that I have seen one of our wedding photos, he'll probably run screaming for the hills. And I can't say I would blame him.

'Hi,' I say lamely, as I get to his table. 'Am I late?'

'No,' he says, standing up. 'I'm always early.'

He leans towards me and for an awkward second I'm not sure if we should go back to the peck on the cheek of Wednesday's greeting or the kiss on the lips from our goodbye. Lee takes the decision into his own hands. As my lips tingle afterwards, I try to stop myself thinking that I have just been kissed by my future husband.

I smile at Lee and sit down, fidgeting as I place my napkin on my lap.

'So, how are you?' he asks.

'Yeah, good, thanks,' I lie. I glance at the table, where there is a bottle of sparkling water and two glasses.

'Is that OK?' he asks, following my gaze. 'I didn't think you'd be drinking before you start work.'

'I don't, as a rule. And water's fine, thanks.'

'If I'd thought about it, we could have gone somewhere they do a late breakfast.'

'No, lunch is fine. I'm not a great fan of breakfast anyway.'

'I am,' says Lee. 'I'd eat a bowl of cereal for every meal if I could.'

'What, muesli?'

'No, not that stuff. Coco Pops and Rice Krispies – all the kids' crap that I've never grown out of.'

I smile at him as I hook my hair back behind one ear. 'I'm surprised you've still got your own teeth.'

'I haven't,' he replies, going to take his top set of teeth out and then stopping when he sees my face. 'Nearly had you there.' He smiles. My shoulders drop slightly; my body relaxes. I'm enjoying second-date territory.

I shake my head. 'At least I'm not the only one who eats crap. Are we going for the posh burgers for lunch then?'

'Absolutely,' he replies. 'You've got a long day ahead. What time do you finish?'

'Ten thirty. There's a later shift that finishes at eleven thirty, but because that would mean we miss the last train home, me and Sadie volunteer to do more ten-thirty finishes than the others.'

'Who's Sadie?'

'My best mate. She was with me at the station on Monday.' Lee still looks vacant. 'Tall girl, short, dark hair, wearing a leather jacket.'

He nods but I am not sure he even registered her. I feel a bit bad for Sadie. Not that she'd be bothered.

'And you don't mind working evenings?'

'No, not really. It means I miss all the rush-hour commuting.' I don't tell him that until this point in time I've had nothing better to do with my evenings. But it does cross my mind that it won't be easy fitting these dates in with my shifts. Maybe that's why I marry him. Maybe it's the only way I could get to see him.

'Well, just remember what I said about our receptionist vacancy. It's probably better money than you're on too.'

'Thanks, but I'm OK where I am.'

'How long have you worked there?'

'Since I left college.'

'And what course did you do there?'

'Art and design. I was going to go to uni and do a degree in it.'

'So why didn't you?'

'I didn't get the grades I'd been predicted. I was working

at the cinema in the holidays and they offered me a full-time job. I just thought it was the best thing to do at the time.'

'And now?'

I shrug. 'Like I say, it's OK, and I get to see a lot of films for free.'

The waitress comes up and asks if we're ready to order.

'Beef or chicken?' Lee asks me.

'Beef, please.' I gave up red meat for a while after Mum died. Along with quite a few other things. Maybe that's why now I eat it more than I used to *before* she died, just to prove to myself that I can.

'Great. We'll have two chargrilled beef burgers, please,' he says to the waitress. 'And some fries on the side.' She nods and smiles at him. It is the sort of smile I would give if I was taking an order from a guy like Lee: a kind of dreamy look that crashes into hopelessness as she realises she has no chance. She is no doubt wondering what the hell he's doing with me. She probably thinks I'm his kid sister or something. I can hear myself screaming inside: *Actually, I'm not only going out with him, I'm going to marry him!*

I know to keep it inside, though. I remember all too well the looks people give you when you give the madness a voice.

'So, what films are you showing this weekend?' asks Lee.

'*The Danish Girl*. The one where Eddie Redmayne has a sex change.'

'I think I'd rather stick pins in my eyes.'

'We're putting on a couple of Alan Rickman's films, as a

tribute. *Harry Potter and the Half-Blood Prince* and *Truly, Madly, Deeply*.'

'I haven't seen that one,' he says.

'Juliet Stevenson is in it. She plays his wife. It's basically about how she copes after he dies. Only he comes back and sort of watches over her until he's sure she's going to be OK.'

I break off because I know my voice is about to crack. I don't know how I'm going to cope with having this hanging over me. It's like I'm haunting myself from my grave before I'm even dead. I'm going to screw this up if I'm not careful. Maybe that's what this is all about. Maybe I'm so scared of being happy I'm inventing stuff in my head to mess things up.

'Sounds like a barrel of laughs,' says Lee. 'Think I'll give that one a miss, if you don't mind.'

I nod and smile. A weak sort of smile. Because I'm now convinced I'm on a self-destruct mission. I have to stop it. I have a serious chance of a proper relationship for the first time in ages, but for it to happen, Lee needs to fall in love with me. And I'm well aware that weepy women who obsess about death really aren't considered the best catches.

Our burgers and fries arrive.

'So,' I say, picking a fry up off the plate with my fingers. 'Where to go for the best chips in Leeds? You start.'

Sadie Ward ▸ **Jess Mount**
28 July 2017

You're going to be buried next week and I can't bear it. I failed you as a friend, I know that. I doubted you when I never should have and I wasn't there for you when it mattered. I will always regret that. But I want you to know that I will be the friend you need now. And I will not rest until you can truly rest in peace.

JESS

Sadie's remembered what I told her. Eighteen months from now she's on some massive guilt trip about all the Facebook stuff that she told me to ignore. I wish she wouldn't blame herself; it's making me feel bad for having told her. I mustn't mention it to her again, however bad it gets. Because if I do, she'll only beat herself up even more when I . . .

I stop myself just in time and put my phone back in my hoody pocket. It's not true. It's all inside my head. These posts aren't even there – no one else can see them. I look in the wardrobe mirror. I am Jess Mount and I am not going to die. Nor am I going to crack up again. I am not going to let this take hold of me. I have way too much to lose this time.

Two and a half weeks in, Lee and I are still going strong, which is pretty unusual for me. By this time, my arsehole detector has normally gone off. But Lee hasn't said or done anything to make me think he's an arsehole. If anything, my opinion of him is going up every day. And for some reason he appears to feel the same way about me. I've only seen him three more times, but that's because I've been working lates, not because I haven't wanted to. To be honest, my shifts are already starting to feel like a pain in the arse; it's so hard to find an evening or weekend when I'm not working. It's like we're in different time zones, which is stupid, because we're in the same city. Lee hasn't said anything about it but I'm sure it's starting to piss him off a bit. He makes jokes about lunch hours being the new evenings, but I kind of get the impression that he doesn't actually find it funny. I need to do something about it, but I'm not sure what.

When I arrive on the platform, Sadie is already there. I go up to her, put my arms around her and give her a big hug.

'What's that in aid of?' she asks.

'Can't I give my best mate a hug?'

'Are you after something?'

'Like what?'

'I don't know. But it's either that or you're about to apologise. You are still coming tomorrow night, aren't you?'

It's Sadie's little sister's eighteenth. Actually, I shouldn't call Maddie little anymore – she's even taller than Sadie. It's weird though, we used to babysit her while her parents went out, once a fortnight. They insisted on paying me too, even though I was only there to keep Sadie company.

'Yep,' I reply. 'Looking forward to being one of the old farts embarrassing the kids for a change. We'll probably start complaining about the music being too loud.'

'And you're still crashing at ours afterwards?'

'Yeah, why wouldn't I be?'

'Dunno, just thought you might be sneaking off early to see lover boy.'

I look down. I had thought about doing exactly that. My only Saturday evening off this month and I'm spending it with my best mate instead of Lee. He was disappointed when I told him. I explained, though, that it had been arranged for ages. That I'd known Maddie since she was a baby. That she was kind of like my own sister.

'Lee's fine about it.'

'You can still bring him if you want. It's not too late for him to change his mind.'

I feel the colour rise in my cheeks. I hadn't actually asked him. I mean, it's an eighteenth birthday disco in a church hall in Mytholmroyd. Not exactly sophisticated company director territory. And he wouldn't know anyone apart from me. Plus, Dad said he'd pop in for a bit on his way home from work; I'd have to introduce them and it would be a big deal and Dad would probably say something stupid and the whole thing would turn into one of those dreams where people you know who have never actually met are all in the same room.

No, when Lee does meet Dad, I want it to be private. Certainly not at an eighteenth birthday party in a church hall.

'No, it's fine, thanks. He's probably going to go out with his mates, somewhere in Leeds.'

Sadie nods. I know she's curious to meet him properly, but I suspect she's also quite pleased he isn't coming. I remember what it was like when she was going out with Robbie. I always felt in the way.

The train pulls into the station. We get on and she lets me choose the seats, as usual. She will probably even check on me when the train speeds up or if it judders as it goes around a bend. Old habits die hard.

I'm showing people to their seats for *Kung Fu Panda 3* when I feel my phone vibrating in my pocket. I glance at the screen and see that Lee is calling, but I know I'll have to leave it until after everyone is in. The kids always take a long time, laden down with cartons of popcorn, cups of pop and armfuls of sweets. I swear some of them consume their own body weight in sugar while they're here.

Finally, as the opening credits roll, I escape and hurry down the corridor, ducking into the staffroom, which is empty.

I call Lee back and he answers straight away.

'Hi,' I say. 'Sorry I missed you earlier.'

'No, that's OK. Look, I know this is a bit last minute, and I completely understand that you've got something on tomorrow, but Carl is off ill and he and his wife are supposed to be going to this big awards dinner thing tomorrow evening. We're up for an award for best creative company and we've got two seats on the Lord Mayor's table. Would you be able to come with me?'

I'm thrown for a second. I can't believe he's asked me, but at the same time I can picture Sadie's face if I say I'm not going to her sister's party.

'Um, I don't know. I mean, it's really nice of you to ask, but I don't want to let Sadie's sister down.'

'I know, I understand that and I wouldn't ask unless it was really important.'

'Isn't there someone else at the company who can go?'

'Unfortunately not. Amy's at a PR conference in London, Mike's at his daughter's engagement do and Scott is flying to the States for work tomorrow. We're really stuck.'

I hesitate again, wondering if I could somehow manage to do both.

'What time's it due to end?'

'I don't know. Half nine or ten? It starts at seven.'

'Well, maybe I could come and go on to Sadie's sister's party afterwards, just for the final hour or so. Would that be OK?'

There is a pause at the other end of the phone. I'm going to end up pissing both of them off if I'm not careful.

'Yeah, if that works for you, that'd be fine. I mean, I have to be there but I need to take someone and, well, I'd really like it to be you.'

I feel myself welling up. I know I need to make my mind up quickly before I either burst into tears or piss him off.

'Thanks. I'd love to come.'

'Jess, you're a complete star and I owe you big time.'

'It's OK,' I say. 'I'll get a free meal out of it.'

'It'll be nice food too. It's at the Queens Hotel. Very swanky.'

I am gripped by the sudden realisation that I have absolutely nothing I can wear to a do at the Queens Hotel.

'What's the dress code?'

'Evening wear.'

'Oh, I'm not sure I've got any of that, and I can't really afford—'

'No problem,' says Lee. 'I'll get you something on the way home this evening.'

'No, I wasn't asking you to do that.'

'I insist. I'll get it on expenses. I think it's the least we can do in the circumstances. You're putting yourself out to help our company, I think it's only right we should cover it.'

'Are you sure?'

'Positive. Absolutely no arguing. Am I looking for size eight or ten?'

'Ten.'

'OK. I might send you some photos of the possibilities and you can tell me what you think.'

'Thanks.'

'No, thank you, Jess. I'm so pleased you said yes. I'll speak to you later.'

I put the phone down. The part of me that's looking forward to it is having an internal cat fight with the part of me that feels like a complete cow for letting down Sadie and her sister.

Adrian walks into the staffroom. 'Hi, sweetie,' he says. 'Are you OK?'

'Yeah. I'm fine, thanks.'

'Only you look like someone who's working themselves up to watch *Kung Fu Panda 3* from start to finish for the fourth time.'

I smile at him. 'What's the best way to let someone down gently, Ade?'

'Man or woman?'

'Woman.'

'Tell her you know she'll understand because she's such a good friend.'

'OK,' I say.

'Let me know how it goes.'

I nod and go to walk out of the room. Adrian calls my name and I turn back to him.

'Only do it once, mind. Anything more is pushing it.'

I wait until *Kung Fu Panda 3* has finished and Sadie and I are clearing up in screen two. I still don't get how people can make so much mess in ninety minutes. Not while they're supposed to be watching a film.

I'm in the row behind Sadie, working my way along with a bin bag. I try to make my voice sound casual, even though I know it won't come out that way.

'I know I said I'll be there at the start tomorrow, but Lee rang earlier, it was a bit of an emergency.'

Sadie looks up at me, a half-eaten carton of popcorn in her hand.

'What is?'

'He's got to go to an awards dinner tomorrow evening; the director who was supposed to go is ill. He said he felt really bad asking but no one else could do it.'

'Why do you have to go too?'

'His company's got two seats on the Lord Mayor's table. It's kind of a big deal. I didn't feel I could say no and I knew you'd understand.'

My words hang heavily in the air between us. For a moment I'm not sure whether Adrian's approach is a good one – it feels too much like a threat.

'But you are still coming, right?'

'Yeah, afterwards. It should finish about ten. I'll get the train over then.'

Sadie looks doubtful.

'OK.'

'I'm really sorry, Sadie. And tell Maddie I'm sorry too.'

She nods and stuffs some cups into the bin bag with particular vigour. I think I'd have preferred a mouthful from her rather than this grudging acceptance.

My phone buzzes in my pocket. I get it out and look at the two photos Lee has sent: one of a black lace dress with long sleeves and the other of an off-the-shoulder number. I can see a Jigsaw label on the second one. I've never even been in there because it looks too expensive. I hold the phone up to Sadie.

'Which one do you think? Lee's getting me something posh to wear.'

She turns and frowns at me. 'Fucking hell, what *is* this? Is he Richard Gere in *Pretty Woman* or something?'

'It's formal evening wear. I let slip that I didn't have anything.'

'So he's buying it for you?'

'Not him. The company. He's putting it on expenses.'

She raises her eyebrows and scrambles on the floor for some rubbish that's been left under the seats.

'Which dress then?' I say.

'I dunno. It doesn't really matter what I think, does it? Why don't you ask him?'

I text back that I like them both and he can choose. Sadie goes off to get the Henry vacuum cleaner just as Adrian walks in. He looks at Sadie's face then at mine.

'Did I balls things up?' he asks.

'No,' I reply. 'I think I did that all by myself.'

Dad is pulling up outside our house when I get home.

'Hi, love,' he says, slamming the car door and fumbling in his jacket pocket for the keys. 'Good night?'

'Yeah, it was OK. You look tired.'

'Busy night. Had some big work party in. Still, better than being quiet.'

I nod as he lets us into the kitchen. It feels cold; Dad doesn't like leaving the heating on when we're both working.

'I'll make us some hot chocolate, shall I?' he says.

'Thanks. That would be great.'

I let him warm the milk before I say anything else, so that he's a tiny bit distracted.

'Change of plan for tomorrow evening. I'm going to an awards do in Leeds with Lee before I go on to Maddie's party.'

'Oh. How come?'

'The director that's supposed to be going is ill. They've got two seats on the Lord Mayor's table. Lee didn't think it would look good to have a no-show. It's at the Queens Hotel.'

Dad whistles as he pours the milk into mugs and stirs briskly. 'Wow, very posh. So what time does it finish?'

'About ten, he thinks. I'll get the train over straight afterwards.'

'It'll nearly be finished by the time you get there.'

'Yeah. I know. Best I could do really.'

'What about Maddie?'

'She'll be fine. She'll be with all her college mates anyway. She won't even notice.'

Dad raises his eyebrows as he puts the mugs down on the table. 'It's a shame to let your friends down, though.'

'I didn't want to let Lee down either.'

'You've only known him five minutes.'

'Yeah, and it's not going to last much longer if I don't actually see him at any point.'

'Just make sure your friends are still there for you too, eh?'

'What's that supposed to mean?'

'They're the ones you can count on, Jess. Long after the boyfriends have disappeared.'

'Maybe this one won't disappear, though.'

'You still need friends, Jess. Whether he disappears or not. And if he really cares about you, he'll understand that.'

'Thanks for the pep talk. Let me know when your radio agony uncle show is going to start.'

Dad manages a smile. 'I'm only looking out for you. It's my job.'

'I know, I know. But you've got to trust that I'm old enough to look after myself now.'

Dad says nothing and gives his hot chocolate a final stir before putting the spoon down on the saucer he has placed between us on the table.

'So have you got to hire something for this posh do tomorrow?'

'No. Lee's buying me a dress. On company expenses. He says it's the least they can do.'

Dad nods slowly. 'You know I'll always buy anything you need, Jess.'

'Thanks. He insisted on getting it, though. There is one thing you could help with, mind. I haven't got any shoes I can wear to something like that. Would you mind if I borrowed Mum's best pair? I'll be really careful with them.'

I see his hand shaking as he brings the mug up to his lips. I feel bad now for asking.

'Look, it doesn't matter,' I continue. 'I can nip out and get some on my lunch break tomorrow. I wasn't thinking.'

'No, it's fine. Borrow them. It's what she'd have wanted. Can't have you turning up for the Lord Mayor in DMs, can we?'

I smile and kiss him on the cheek before picking up my mug. 'Thanks. I'll go up and get them now, if that's OK? Make sure they fit.'

He nods. I go upstairs, careful not to slop the hot chocolate on the carpet. I put the mug down on the landing before going into Dad's room. I know exactly where they are. It still feels weird though: opening the wardrobe, crouching down and reaching to the back. Dad took most of Mum's things to the charity shop, but there were some he couldn't bring himself to part with. The things that seemed so much a part of her you couldn't look at them without seeing her inside them. The clothes are all at one end of the wardrobe in plastic bags. The accessories are in a large box on the floor of the wardrobe.

I pull it towards me and take the lid off. It's like opening a giant memory box. I touch the green scarf, remembering the softness of it against my face as a child. The multi-coloured woolly hat smells of Bonfire Night and frozen winter walks. I hold the purple beads in my hands, twisting them, just like she used to, without even realising she was doing it. I put them back and rummage a little further down. The black patent stilettos are at the bottom. She didn't wear them very often; most of the time she was in sensible flats. But on those rare occasions that called for a bit of glamour, these are what she wore. I remember looking at her reflection in the long mirror in the bedroom as she stood and adjusted the neckline of her purple velvet dress, which is still in the wardrobe. I told her she was beautiful. She smiled at me and said she scrubbed up OK when she had the time. She was beautiful, though. Dad said so too. She was just one of those people who never really believed it.

I put the lid back on the box and return it to the wardrobe

before taking the shoes into my room. I go back to the landing to get my hot chocolate, and when I return to my room I swear I see her standing there in the shoes, finally admiring her reflection in the mirror.

Joe Mount ▸ **Jess Mount**
29 July 2017

Burying you on Monday is going to be the hardest day of my life, harder even than when we buried your mum. I have lost the two people I love most in the world. The only thing keeping me going is this little man. Can't believe this photo was only taken three weeks ago. You were, and would have continued to be, the best mum in the world to Harrison. For those of you asking, he is fine and being looked after by Lee, with the help of Angela. But today he will be coming to see Grandad. And I will give him a special kiss and cuddle from you, Jess. And I'll make sure your precious boy never forgets you x

JESS

Saturday, 30 January 2016

I stare at the photo of the baby on the screen. He has big blue eyes and slightly surprised eyebrows – although not nearly as surprised as mine at the moment – a tiny button nose and the most beautiful little dimples. On top of his head are some tufts of dark hair. He is beyond adorable. He also looks so much like Lee it's uncanny. He is Harrison. Presumably the 'H' everyone has been talking about. He is my baby. And there, my face squashed next to his, is me. His mum. I look entirely different. I'm obviously tired, with hardly any make-up on, but the way I am looking at my baby . . . That's not my face at all. It is filled with big, grown-up stuff, things I have not experienced, that I don't understand. The nearest I can get to it is the way Mum used to look at me, and Dad still does sometimes. It is a look that is full of love and protection, hope and fear, excitement and worry.

I am not imagining this. Not even my head could conjure this up. It is real. The photo is real, the baby is real. Its chubby little fingers are pulling at my hair. I can practically feel them on me, smell that baby scent against my cheek. He may not exist at the moment, but that doesn't mean to say he isn't real. The version of me in the photo doesn't exist at the moment either – but she will do, in eighteen months' time.

The thought of it is enough to make me sit down heavily on my bed. I'm going to have to deal with all that parenting shit and I don't even feel like a grown-up myself. How am I going to cope with a baby? Clearly, I don't manage it for long. I look again at the photo. I'm no expert on babies but I'd say he's a few months old, which means I die shortly after he is born. Maybe it's to do with post-natal depression. Mum said she had it bad – perhaps it's genetic? Although I don't look depressed in the picture. I just look knackered.

I wipe the tears from my eyes. It's all too much. A massive part of me wants to carry on believing that this is purely a figment of my overactive imagination. But the truth is here in front of my eyes. I look at the photo of me and Harrison again. Maybe I am mentally unstable, but I know my own baby when I see him.

I'm not ready for this. Not for any of it. Somehow, in the next eighteen months, I get married, have a baby and die. It's like my entire life is on fast forward. How am I going to cope with that? Me, the girl who can't be arsed to get out of bed until 10 a.m. and who has blueberry muffins for breakfast. The girl who jacked in the chance of a career to work at a cinema because it's a laugh and she gets to see films for free. The girl who cracked up when her mum died; whose dad still wraps her in cotton wool. Maybe I die from the weight of responsibility. This isn't my life. This isn't who I am supposed to be.

I lie back on the bed, sobbing. I want it to stop. I want everything to be normal. I want to wonder when Lee's going to shag me for the first time and if we'll go on holiday together in the summer and whether we'll still be going out at Christmas. That's what normal girls of my age worry about. I didn't ask to have my life mapped out in front of me. I don't want to know the answers; I want to find them out as I go along, like everyone else. I want to stop the ride. My head is spinning and I want to get off. But I don't know how to.

I stare down again at my baby son. Even the words sound wrong in my head. I've never really thought about having children. It's always seemed too responsible for me. I leave stuff everywhere. The woman in the lost property office at Leeds Station knows me by my first name. I'll probably leave my baby on the train. That is the kind of crap mother I will be. I think of my mum, of everything she did for me. How can I possibly live up to that?

And now I have all this going round in my head instead of thinking about going out with Lee tonight. How can I look him in the eye when I've seen our future baby? How can I not tell him that? It's wrong. The whole thing is wrong and somehow I've got to work out how to conduct a relationship with him while watching our future son grow up on Facebook.

I bring the photo on my phone close to my chest. I know it's insane, but I want him next to me. I know I should stop looking at it, but it's too late for that now. I have a baby. I have a responsibility to make sure he's OK.

Maybe I can try to work out how I die. Perhaps I can stop it. Maybe it'll be like *Back to the Future* and I can change things, alter my own destiny, if I can only manage to get myself in the right place at the right time when lightning strikes. Maybe that's why I'm being sent this stuff. Perhaps someone from the future is trying to save my life.

I shake my head at the idea that anyone out there would give a toss and glance at Mum's shoes on the floor by the wardrobe. She would have known what to do. I could always talk to her about anything. She would have sorted all of this out and made it go away. I miss her today. I miss her more than ever.

I spend the day at work in a bit of a daze, caught between worrying about the future and looking forward to this evening. Sadie has taken the day off to help get ready for the party and I'm glad of the breathing space, sure I would crack under interrogation if she were to ask me what the matter was.

As I walk down to the station after work I feel like I'm going on a date with my future. Talk about pressure! It's a bit of luck I like him, as I don't know if I could do anything about it if I didn't. What would happen if I chucked him? Not that I want to. I just wonder if I actually could. And if everything has already been decided, how do I even conduct this relationship? Do I just lie back and think of my wedding day?

We've arranged to meet in front of the station. As I approach,

I tell myself to put it all out of my mind. It's easier said than done though. As soon as I catch sight of Lee, all I can think of is how I will leave him, quite literally, holding the baby after I've gone. Would he have anything to do with me if he knew what was going to happen? Maybe it would be kinder to walk straight past him now and spare him from all that.

Lee smiles and waves at me. I walk towards him, telling myself repeatedly that I have to carry on as if nothing has happened. That I can't let it spoil this.

'Hello, you,' he says, kissing me on the lips. 'Ready to go to the ball?'

'It's not a ball, is it?'

'No, only kidding.' The Cinderella reference isn't lost on me though. I'm standing here in leggings and my DMs and I am about to be transformed into ball-worthy material. Although it has to be said that Lee is an unlikely-looking fairy godmother.

'Good,' I reply. 'Because I can't do ballroom dancing. But I am ready to fill my face for free and whistle and whoop when you go up to get your award.'

Lee laughs. 'Are you really going to whistle?'

'Well, yeah. Isn't that what people do?'

'Nope, they clap politely and try not to look pig-sick that they didn't win.'

'Like at the Oscars, you mean. Are they going to have a camera on all of the nominees' faces?'

'I hope not. Anyway, we might not win.'

'You will. They wouldn't have sat you at the Lord Mayor's

table if you weren't going to win. He's not going to be put with a bunch of losers, is he?'

'Let's hope not. Anyway, your outfit awaits. We'd better get back to my place.'

He takes my hand and we start to walk around the front of the station.

'Shame you can't just jump over the railings on platform seventeen and three quarters.'

'It's 17b.'

'Same thing if you're a Potterhead.'

'Oh God, you haven't got one of those Deathly Hallows necklaces, have you?'

'Yep. And a tattoo of it.'

'Where?'

'That would be telling.'

'I'll have to find out, then. Just don't flash it at the Lord Mayor before you show me.'

'I promise.'

'And I'll make a mental note never to take you to a fancy dress party as I now suspect you've got the full Professor McGonagall costume at home.'

'Bellatrix Lestrange, actually. The baddies get all the best outfits. How about you, what would be your fancy dress costume of choice?'

'Han Solo from *Star Wars*.'

'Is he the one with the lightsaber?'

'No, that was Luke Skywalker. Han Solo is older. Harrison Ford played him.'

I stare at him. He likes Harrison Ford. The baby we supposedly have in the future is called Harrison. It might simply be a coincidence. Then again, it might not.

'Are you a big fan, then?'

'Yep. I loved all the *Star Wars* films and all the Indiana Jones movies too. He's class, sheer class. Even if he is knocking on a bit now.'

'So would you name your kid after him?'

Lee turns and frowns at me.

'What do you mean?'

'If you had a son at some point, would you call him Harrison?'

'I dunno. It's better than Obi-Wan Kenobi, I guess.'

I nod and smile. This is all actually going to happen. We are going to have a baby boy called Harrison. Lee will probably remind me of this conversation when we're discussing names. Maybe I should say something now. Something I can remind him of at some point in the future.

'I think I'd go for Severus,' I say.

'Well goodbye and good luck with that.'

I laugh but it's not funny. Not really. This is our life we're talking about. It's simply that Lee doesn't know it yet. And I have only just got my head around the fact that it may actually be true.

We turn right. The trendy shops make way for grubby units underneath the old railway arches and they in turn give way to new blocks of apartments clustered around the canal, all of a uniform size and design with little glass balconies.

'Here we are,' says Lee.

'Which floor?'

'The top one.'

I nod silently.

'It's OK, there's a lift, and you'll be glad to know it's usually working and it doesn't smell.'

I wasn't thinking of that. I was actually looking up at the balcony and wondering if I fall from there. Do people do that in real life or is it only in films? A chill surges through me as I realise I could be looking at the scene of my death. Maybe I'm pissed and topple over the side? Would I fall on the tow-path or into the canal? Either way, it wouldn't be pretty. Then again, presumably I wouldn't be pissed while in charge of a three-month-old baby. And we probably wouldn't live in an apartment like this if we had a baby. Maybe we will have moved somewhere entirely different by the time it happens. I realise Lee is still looking at me. I attempt to unclench my hands.

'Nice spot,' I whisper.

'Yeah, got everything I need, really. Cafe and little shop underneath. Bar just across the wharf. And ten minutes' walk to work.'

'Great,' I reply, rubbing my hands together to try to get some warmth and feeling back in my body. I follow him up to the building where he punches in an entry code and holds the door open for me. The foyer is smart and clean-smelling. He calls the lift; it opens almost instantly and I step inside. There are mirrors all the way around. I catch Lee looking at me as the doors close. I realise for the first time that I am going to be truly alone with him. He turns me around to face him and kisses me. A proper, full-on movie kiss. I think for a moment he's going to jam the lift and we'll end up doing it in here like in *Fatal Attraction*. That would be fine by me. The last time I had sex it was in a grungy little bedsit above a launderette. I'm going up in the world in more ways than one.

The lift stops and the doors open. I look up at him.

'Shame,' he says. 'I was enjoying that. Oh well, after you.'

I step out of the lift, Lee's hand firmly around my waist. He guides me towards the door on the far left and opens it. I follow him inside to a small entrance hall with closed doors surrounding us. It feels a bit like one of those adventure games where you have to crack the code to get out.

'Here, let me take your coat,' he says. I take my backpack off and hand him my coat. I bend down to take my DMs off.

'It's OK,' he says. 'You don't have to do that.'

'I don't want to muck up your floor.'

'I have a cleaner.'

'Well, I don't want to muck up her floor then.'

I take them off. What I don't want to admit is that they're rubbing me because I only have stockings on, instead of my usual thick socks. Mum's shoes are in my backpack. I wasn't sure I could manage to walk this far in them.

'Quick tour then?' Lee asks.

'Yes, please.'

He takes me through the far door to the living area. It looks like something out of an IKEA catalogue: all laminated floor, trendy furniture, rugs and lamps. It is the window I am drawn to, though.

'Wow, great view.'

'Yeah. It's not Paris, but Leeds doesn't look too rough from up here, especially at night.'

He leads me back out to the hallway and opens the kitchen door. There are two bar stools at the counter. I wonder how many mornings have seen someone sitting on the one next to him. There must have been plenty of other women. I'm surprised he's still single, to be honest. Guys like him are usually snapped up pretty fast.

'Very nice.'

'Can I get you a drink of anything before we go?' he asks.

'No, I'm fine, thanks.'

He nods and I follow him back out. 'The bathroom's across here, if you need it,' he continues, opening the door on the opposite side of the hallway. I am greeted by a sea of shining chrome and spotless white tiles. Towels are hanging neatly from the rails, the edges lined up perfectly. It feels like being in the penthouse suite of one of those swish hotels you see on the telly. I'm still trying to work out how the hell I ended up with a guy who lives in a place like this. It's as if they got the wrong person for the part. Perhaps I should check it's not a case of mistaken identity.

'I'd be too scared to go in there in case I messed it up,' I say.

'That's the beauty of having a cleaner. When I come home on a Monday it always looks like this. No matter what state I leave it in.

'But it's Saturday,' I say. 'How come it looks like she's just been?'

He shrugs. 'I guess I'm pretty tidy. And I don't like clutter around me.'

I should warn him what a shock he's in for if he does marry me. I can see I'm going to have to up my game.

'And along here,' he continues, heading back to the door nearest the front one, 'is your dressing room.'

He lets me go in first. It's straight out of one of those interior design magazines. A king-sized bed with a grey duvet with black trim and matching pillows and cushions; a laminated wooden floor with a coordinating rug; white walls and built-in mirrored wardrobes. And not forgetting the double doors leading to the balcony.

He steps forward and opens them. A rush of cold air hits me. I don't want to go out there, but at the same time I am drawn to view what could be the scene of my death. I poke my head outside, just far enough to see the canal below, and step back inside, trying desperately to stop thinking about the drop.

'Not keen on heights?' he asks.

'Just bloody freezing, that's all.'

Lee shuts the doors before opening the wardrobe and taking out a long black dress. 'This,' he says, holding it out towards me, 'is for you, madam.'

A minute ago I was thinking about where I might die. Now I am looking at the dress I shall go to the ball in. It's like being in the weirdest Disney film ever, one where you are presented with two alternative endings: the Prince Charming one, or

Bambi getting shot by the same guy who shot his mother, and that being the end of the film. I'm pretty clear about which one I will choose.

I reach out and touch the dress. He went for the off-the-shoulder one. It looks even better than it did in the photo. There are sparkles in the fabric that shimmer under the light. It's like nothing I've ever owned before.

'Oh my god. Thank you so much. It's gorgeous.'

'It's the least I can do,' he says. 'I really appreciate you putting yourself out like this.' I feel a pang of guilt as he says it. Especially because I'd actually forgotten about Sadie's sister's party.

'That's OK. I've said I'll get the last train back so I can make the end of the party.'

'Don't be daft, I'll get you a cab. You don't want to be dashing for trains in all your finery. You might leave a glass slipper on the platform.'

He glances down at my bare feet.

'Oh, was I supposed to get shoes as well?' he asks.

'Oh, no, it's OK. I've got some with me. In my backpack. I'm not very good at walking in heels, that's all.'

'Phew, for a minute there I thought you were going to be turning up in an evening dress and boots.'

'Don't worry,' I say, deciding not to admit that the shoes I brought aren't actually mine. 'I'm not that bad.'

'Right, I'd better get changed and let you do the same,' he says, taking his suit out of the wardrobe. 'I hope it fits. If you need a hand with anything, just shout.'

He smiles at me and I smile back. It feels weird, being with this man in his bedroom. I wonder if Harrison is conceived in here. And how the hell am I supposed to act normal when I've seen so much of our future together? As Lee closes the door behind him, I let out a sigh and start to undress, relieved I remembered to put my strapless bra on in case he went for the off-the-shoulder number.

I take the dress off the hanger. Lee has removed the price tag but I already know how much it cost. I looked it up on the Jigsaw website. This one was £179, the other was £159. I feel honoured that he went for the more expensive one. Even if he is claiming it back on expenses.

I wriggle into the dress and manage to zip it most of the way up at the back before turning to face the mirrors. I don't recognise the young woman who stares back at me, all glamorous and sophisticated. Well, sort of sophisticated. My hair is still a bit crazy but my brush is in my backpack in the hall. I take a deep breath and open the door.

Lee is standing in the hallway in his tuxedo, looking like he's stepped out of a James Bond film. He turns around and looks me up and down. His expression reminds me of the hotel manager in *Pretty Woman* when he sees Julia Roberts done up for the first time.

'Wow,' he says, stepping forward. 'You look incredible.'

'Thanks,' I say. 'You don't look too bad yourself. I can't quite do up my zip, though.'

He walks behind me. I feel his breath on the back of my neck as he pulls the zip to the top. His hands touch my shoulders. A second later he is kissing my neck. Soft, gentle kisses. Like he thinks I am a delicate thing of beauty. No one has ever kissed me like that before. He turns me around to face him and kisses me on the lips. More urgently this time. His hands are in my hair, pulling, squeezing. It's like he's moved up a couple of gears at once. One hand drops down to my thigh, slipping inside the slit in the dress to my stocking top, the other is on my right boob.

Our lips part for a second; both of us take a gasp of breath.

'I knew this was a bad idea,' he whispers. 'I was stupid enough to think I'd be able to control myself.'

'Are we going to be late?'

'Not if we're quick. Stay there.' He disappears into the bathroom and comes back a second later with a small square foil object in his hand.

'Can't have me messing up your dress, can we?' He smiles, putting it in his top pocket. 'Now, where were we?' He cups my breasts before hitching up my skirt and sliding his hand inside my knickers. My head drops back against the wall, my back arching. His fingers move quickly and easily. He is so fucking good at this. I let out a moan, biting on the shoulder of his jacket to stop myself screaming louder. He is smiling as he makes me come. Smiling like he is loving every second of it. He breaks off to unzip his fly and tear open the condom packet.

'You are so beautiful,' he whispers. The smile on his face has disappeared, replaced by an intensity that I haven't seen in him before. He moves forward, tilting my hips towards him, his eyes burning into me. He is going to shag me, here, against the wall. And I don't think I have ever wanted it so much.

Afterwards, we lean back against the wall, our chests heaving, both of us trying to catch our breath.

'Well, that was worth keeping the Lord Mayor waiting for,' says Lee, smiling at me as he brushes a strand of hair out of my eyes.

'We haven't missed the start, have we?'

'No. We'll be fine. But I wouldn't have minded if we had.'

'I would,' I said. 'I'm looking forward to this meal.'

'Where the hell do you put it? There's nothing of you.'

'My mum used to say I'd wake up on my fortieth birthday and all the crap I'd ever eaten would have gone to my thighs overnight.'

'I hope not,' Lee says, running his hand along my thigh. 'I rather like them as they are.'

A smile spreads over my face. I've never had a guy who makes me feel like this. I want to savour every single second of it. My stomach lets out a loud rumble.

'That,' I say, trying not to laugh, 'was my audible alert that we need to get our arses in gear and go and get some grub.'

'Come on then.' Lee smiles. 'I'm not prepared to go into battle with your stomach.' He leans over and gives me one last kiss before going to the bathroom. I stand there, still trying to take in what has just happened. I worry that he used a condom without me asking because I look like the sort of girl who sleeps around. I worry that he might have been grossed out by the fact that I am too afraid of pain to wax my bikini line. And most of all I worry that I can't stop thinking about all the stuff on Facebook instead of allowing myself to fall in love with this man.

We arrive at the hotel bang on seven o'clock. I am convinced we still smell of sex. We hurry through the foyer and Lee shows our invitations to the man on the door of the function room. He nods and points towards the far end. Everybody else is already in their seats. Lee holds my hand and leads me to the two empty places on the Lord Mayor's table. When we get there, Lee pulls out the chair for me and the Lord Mayor stands up, followed by the other men. I smile and sit down quickly, suspecting I have a huge neon light above my head that reads, 'I'm late because I just had sex with him', with an arrow pointing towards Lee.

The women at the table nod politely. I'm damn sure they know too. There is a certain colour in the cheeks that you can't get from blusher alone.

'It's an honour to meet you,' Lee says, extending his hand to the Lord Mayor. 'Lee Griffiths, Eclipse PR. And this is Jess, my girlfriend.'

Girlfriend. He said it out loud. This means it's real, not a Disney movie after all.

'Very glad you could make it,' he says, shaking each of our hands in turn. 'I was beginning to think I might have to eat three dinners.'

'Don't worry,' I say. 'I have no intention of leaving a scrap of mine.'

The Lord Mayor leans over to me. 'Quite right too,' he says with a wink. 'I only come to these things for the free food, but best not tell anyone.'

He introduces us to the Lady Mayoress. She has a glazed look in her eyes and chubby cheeks. I suspect she only comes for the food too.

Lee strokes my thigh under the table. 'Told you we'd make it in time,' he whispers.

'People are giving us weird looks. Do you think everyone knows what we've been up to?'

'I don't care if they do. They're only jealous. Well, the men are, anyway.'

He smiles at me again. When I look up, every woman at the table is looking at him. Seems like the men aren't the only ones who are jealous. I feel a swell of pride. I want to yell, *Hey, he's mine, eyes back in their sockets, please!* I don't though. But I do look incredibly smug.

When Lee's company wins the Best Small Business in Leeds award later, I do a little whoop, whistle under my breath and clap so hard my hands hurt.

'Told you!' I whisper, when Lee gets back to the table with the award.

'Seems I should listen to you,' Lee says. 'You're pretty good at predictions. If you've any idea who's going to win the three twenty at York next weekend, you might like to put a word in my ear.'

I smile at him, wishing that was the only thing about the future I did know.

'Congratulations,' the woman next to me says.

'Thanks,' says Lee.

'You too, dear.' She smiles.

'Oh, I don't work for them,' I say.

'Not yet,' says Lee. 'I'm working on her.'

I look up at him.

'I mean it,' he says. 'I want you to go for the receptionist's job.'

'I told you. I'm not interested.'

'The job's yours if you want it.'

'I can get my own jobs, thank you. Anyway, like I said, I'm not the glamorous receptionist type.'

'Says the most glamorous woman in the room.' I blush. 'You'd be amazing. Plus, I'd get to see you loads more because you wouldn't be working crazy shifts.'

'I'll try to get a night off next week.'

'The interviews are a week on Wednesday. And I'm very happy to make an exception for late applicants on this occasion.'

'Nice try. Still not interested.'

'Well, if you change your mind, the offer's still there,' he says. I glance across at him when he's not looking. He seems a bit deflated. I imagine he's the sort of guy who's used to getting what he wants. I hope he's not going to hold it against me.

*

We emerge onto the front steps of the Queen's Hotel, Lee still clutching the award. My feet are killing me. I look down at my shoes and am instantly reminded of Mum. I can't help wondering if her feet ever hurt this much when she wore them.

'What time is it?' I ask. I left my watch back at his flat.

'Just gone ten,' he says.

'I should still make it then.'

'I'll call a cab for you from the flat, if you want.'

'Thanks. Are you sure?'

'About paying? Yes. About you going? No.'

I look up at him. 'It's just that I promised.'

'I know. But I don't want the night to end here. I want to take you back home. I want you to stay over. I want to wake up next to you in the morning. I want to spend the weekend with you, take you for Sunday lunch at my mum's. Do all the stuff couples are supposed to do together. I want to be with you, Jess. It's as simple as that.'

I feel my heart quadruple in size. I fear it might burst right out of my ribcage. All those years I used to lie in my bedroom, dreaming that a guy would say stuff like that to me, and here I am about to walk away from him. I'll be fucking certifiable if I do. He'd have every right to dump me – it's not like there are a shortage of candidates to take my place.

'I haven't brought a toothbrush,' I say.

'You can share mine.'

'Or an overnight bag. Or anything to wear to Sunday lunch at your mum's.'

'It doesn't matter. You don't need anything to sleep in and we can sort an outfit tomorrow. The shops'll be open from ten.'

I look down at my feet, which are now really hurting in the heels. The thought of walking away from him to go to some crappy church hall in Mytholmroyd is ridiculous. Sadie and Maddie will understand that, surely?

'I still feel bad about letting down Sadie and her sister . . .'

'I'm sure they won't mind. They'll probably be pissed by now. They might not even remember that you didn't turn up.'

I know he's wrong – certainly about them not remembering, anyway. But I also know what I want to do. I want to leave that old life behind. I want to grasp what he is offering me with both hands. I want him. And right now I want him so badly that nothing else matters.

'Yeah. You're right,' I say.

'I know I am. Just say you missed the last train home. They'll understand.'

Lee puts his arms around my waist. I feel myself fold into him, the last twinge of guilt melting away.

'Come on, gorgeous. We've got unfinished business to attend to.'

'Have we?' I smile.

'Well, I don't know about you, but I don't usually do things quite as quickly as that. I'd like to start over, right at the beginning, if you don't mind. Take my time. I don't want to miss any inch of you.'

He pulls me closer and kisses me. I am utterly gone.

Someone up there must really like me, to give me a break like this. There is no way on earth I am going to screw this up.

I wait until Lee goes into his kitchen to make some coffee before I text Sadie and Maddie.

Really sorry, the awards thing ran late and I missed the last train. Hope you've had a good night x

It's a lame text, even by my standards. I text Dad too. Tell him the same and that I'm going to stay the night at Lee's. Which feels a bit weird because it's basically like telling your dad you're about to have sex and he should look away.

After a moment or two, my phone pings with a response from Dad.

Are you OK? I can come and get you or I'll pay for a taxi if you'd rather xx

He means well, I know that. I can hear him saying 'I'm just doing my job' before I even pick the fight with him. But he needs to face up to the fact that I am twenty-two years old.

I want to stay, Dad. I'm fine. More than fine, actually. See you tomorrow x

I feel kind of grown-up sending it, and then, as soon as I've read it again, I feel like a complete cow.

Dad sends back two kisses. I imagine him sitting there in the kitchen, grinding his elbows into the table with worry. And I see again his Facebook posts in my head, so heavy with sadness and loss, like he is going to disappear under the weight of it. I realise I haven't checked my phone once since Lee met me after work. I click on Facebook and go to my timeline. There is now a stream of comments under Dad's photo of me with Harrison.

I have just started scrolling through them when Lee comes back into the room with the coffees.

'See, I go out of the room for five minutes and you're straight on Facebook.' His tone is jovial, although there is a flash of something that looks distinctly like irritation on his face.

I manage to smile at him before glancing back down at my phone. The photo of Harrison has disappeared, as have all the comments underneath. Not that I would have been stupid enough to show them to him if they hadn't. If I want this relationship to work, which I do, it is clear there are some things about us that I am going to have to keep to myself.

JESS

July 2008

Dad knocks on my door. My first reaction is to pretend I'm asleep. I do not want to have this conversation. But he knows full well that I'm not asleep, and I can't bring myself to be mean to him. So I say, 'Yeah?' and brace myself for what I am about to hear.

He comes in and sits down on the edge of my bed. He is fiddling with the buttons on his cardigan; he can't even look me in the eye.

'Mrs Booth phoned me today,' he says. I roll my eyes and continue staring at the ceiling. 'She says she's concerned about you.'

'What she's concerned about is that I'm going to screw up my exams next year and that will look bad in the league tables.'

Dad sighs. It is his turn to look up at the ceiling.

'She does care about you, Jess. We all do. We simply want to help.'

'Well, you can't, can you? Not unless you can raise people from the dead. And I know everyone thinks I'm not coping – I see the looks they give each other – but you know what? I am coping. I'm coping the only way I know how. And I'm sorry I'm not turning cartwheels of joy, but funnily enough I don't feel like doing that right now because it's only been three months since Mum died. And you know what? I don't think I'll just snap out of it after six months or a year or whatever because I don't feel like it, OK?'

Dad looks at me for the first time. His eyes are wet with tears. I feel like such a cow.

'Your mum didn't want us to be like this, did she? And if school are concerned about your work suffering, we need to do something to help you, because that's the last thing she'd have wanted – for it to have an impact on your education.'

'But I don't care about my results. I don't care about anything. Don't you get that?'

'You told Mum you'd work hard to get into art college.'

'Yeah, well, I was trying to be positive because I knew that's what she wanted. I wasn't going to tell her that I thought I'd be a miserable cow and screw everything up after she died.'

Dad runs his fingers through what is left of his hair.

'Maybe if you got out more with your friends? It's not good, you being stuck in here by yourself all the time.'

'I don't want to go out. You don't go out.'

'I do.'

'Only to work. You don't go out partying, do you? Because you don't feel like it – and neither do I.'

'Yeah, but I'm an old git who hasn't got any friends. You're fifteen and you've got loads of them.'

He has a hint of a smile on his face as he says it. I try really hard to smile back. I think I manage to turn up one corner of my mouth.

'I see Sadie. She's the only person I need right now. She's the only one who understands.'

I let Sadie come round because she lets me be miserable and cry and say it's not fair. I know I must sound like Eeyore, but that's how I feel and I'm not going to pretend otherwise. Not to my best friend. Sometimes I wish I lived in one of those cultures where you have to be in mourning for a year, because that seems a hell of a lot more decent, more fitting, than everyone going around smiling and pretending it never happened and not talking about it because they don't want to upset me.

Dad has got his head in his hands. I know he's doing his best. I know I should go and give him a hug, but I can't. Because if I do, I'm scared all the hurt will come out, and that will freak him out. Then he really will be worried.

'Please just try, Jess. For your mum's sake,' he whispers.

'OK,' I whisper back. He gets up and leaves the room, silently closing the door behind him.

ANGELA

Sunday, 31 January 2016

Lee calls at ten, which is early for him. I wonder if he is going to cancel. I do hope not.

'Hello, love. Everything OK?' I ask.

'Yeah, fine, thanks. Just wondered if it's too late to add one extra for Sunday lunch? Only, I'd like to bring Jess, if that's all right.'

A smile creeps across my face. It is serious. I knew it.

'Of course she can come. It'll be lovely to meet her.'

'That's great. I wasn't sure if you'd have enough food in. I can bring some bits with me if it helps.'

'No, don't be daft. You know I've always got plenty.'

'Well, she's got quite an appetite on her.' I can hear giggling in the background.

'There'll be more than enough to go around. Is roast OK for her? Is there owt she doesn't like?'

'Only piri-piri sauce.'

'Sorry?' There is a muffled sound and I hear someone saying 'Oi' softly, away from the mouthpiece.

'No, don't worry. She eats anything and everything.'

'Oh, good.' And I mean it. Emma had the appetite of a sparrow. I worried she didn't like my cooking at first, but Lee said she was always like that.

'Great. We'll see you at one then.'

I put the phone down. For a second I am paralysed. There are so many things to do that I am unsure where to start. But then something takes over and I know what I must do first. Shopping. I need to go out to get some more food. The topside of beef is easily big enough for three but I'm not sure I'll have enough potatoes for the roasties now. And I'm maybe a bit short of carrots too.

I put on my boots, grab my bag and coat and pull the door behind me. It is handy to have the little M&S at the petrol station down the road. Just the thing you need in these sorts of emergencies. Not that it is an emergency, really. It's simply that I'd rather be safe than sorry.

Lee doesn't usually bring them to meet me this early. This one must be special. I can sense it in his voice. He is clearly proud of her. He wants to show her off. I suspect she will be quite a stunner.

I hurry across the garage forecourt into the shop. Normally, I would pick up the *Sunday Mirror* while I'm here, but there isn't going to be time to even glance at it today. I pop a bag of potatoes into my basket and turn to the carrots. I don't usually buy the ready prepared stuff but I am going to make an exception today. Anything to save a bit of time. I hand over the money to the girl on the till. I imagine they're good to work for, M&S. The pay's probably better than mine too. But I don't think I could ever work in a petrol station. I would worry too much about the chance of a hold-up. At least in the supermarket you know that's highly unlikely to happen.

I head straight back home and get the vacuum cleaner out of the cupboard under the stairs. It's a Miele pull-along. I'm not so keen on the upright ones, especially the see-through type. I don't like to think about the dirt that might be on the carpet and I certainly don't want to see it. I only vacuumed yesterday but I think I should give it a once-over. It's not that I think she'll be judging me – girls in their twenties probably don't even think about such things these days – but I want her to know that Lee is from a good home, one where things are done properly. The last thing in the world I want is to let Lee down. I may not always be a mother he can be proud of, but I certainly am not going to be one who embarrasses him.

The beef goes in the oven in plenty of time. I sprinkle some rosemary over it. I've done it once or twice before and Lee has said he likes it. While the roast is cooking I start work on the kitchen. I put a Robbie Williams CD on while I'm cleaning. Lee reminds me of him sometimes, when he's being cheeky. Not that Lee can sing, of course. But he could have been in one of these boy bands, with his looks. Some of them only seem be there for their looks, to be honest. Certainly a few of the ones I've heard on *The X Factor*.

I check the clock and get the roasties in with the beef. I'm just relieved Lee's never been out with one of these vegetarians who would want them done separately. There's no other way, as far as I am concerned.

Once the veg is going I get the Yorkshire pudding batter ready. Proper big Yorkshires, served as a starter with gravy. These southerners don't know what they're missing out on.

I have a final look around the kitchen before I go upstairs to make myself presentable. Everything is fine; everything is under control. Exactly the way it should be.

I start looking out the bedroom window at ten to one. Lee would hate it if he knew I was watching, but I don't think he'll see me up here. It's not that I want to spy on them, it's just that I want to see the two of them together before they arrive, when they don't think anyone is watching.

I glance at the edge of the wall next to the window. There is paint now, where the wallpaper used to be. I can still see it though, in my head. Still hear the noise as I scraped that bit off. Still feel the shame deep inside.

I pull back from the curtain as Lee's car pulls up across the road. He gets out and goes around to her side to open the door. He is a gentleman, our Lee, there has never been any doubt about that. I see her legs first – or, rather, the knee-high boots that emerge from the car with those big clunky heels all the girls seem to wear these days. She has a mustard-coloured tunic dress on and a black padded jacket. Her hair is long and a bit straggly. She is smiling at Lee. He takes her hand and shuts the car door.

I hurry downstairs, glancing in the mirror in the hall as I pass it. I've redone my face since this morning, just to freshen it up a bit without looking as if I've tried too hard. I am in the kitchen by the time I hear Lee's key in the door. I step out into the hallway as he calls out hello.

'Hi, love,' I say, giving him a kiss.

'Mum, this is Jess. Jess, Angela.'

She looks at me with wide eyes. She is probably incredibly nervous. I can still remember meeting Simon's parents for the first time. It was all very formal and I dropped a pea from my fork onto the floor at the dinner table. I was in two minds as to whether I should scrabble around to try to pick it up or pretend it never happened.

'It's lovely to meet you,' I say, giving her a peck on the cheek. 'Come in and make yourself at home, there's no standing on ceremony here.'

She smiles at me, and her shoulders appear to drop a little. Lee takes her jacket. He is right – her face is stunning. She has a slightly Mediterranean look about her and is all eyes and cheekbones. She is quite a catch – although Lee is too, of course. They would, no doubt, produce a very striking child.

They follow me through to the kitchen.

'I'll just put the Yorkshires in now you're here,' I say.

'Wait till you taste them, Jess,' says Lee. 'Best ones in the county.'

'Don't say that,' I tell him. 'I'm sure Jess's mum does a lovely Yorkshire pudding.'

They exchange a look. I get the distinct impression I have said something wrong.

'Sorry, I should have told you,' says Lee. 'Jess's mum died seven years ago.'

'Oh, I am sorry, dear. I've put my foot in it, haven't I?'

'No,' says Jess. 'You weren't to know. She was a brilliant mum but she was rubbish at Yorkshire puddings so she gave up and used a packet mix.'

She is smiling as she says it, although there is a tremor in her voice. I like her. I like her a lot.

'Well, she must have been very proud to have a beautiful daughter like you,' I say. 'That tunic looks fantastic on you. Such a lovely colour, too.'

There is a hint of pink in her cheeks. She looks down at her feet. She is not so full of herself, this one. There is almost an innocence about her, which seems to be a rare thing in girls of her age these days.

'Thanks,' she says. 'It was a present.' She looks up at Lee as she says it. She clearly adores him, it is written all over her face. We have a chance here, we really do.

'Well, I'm glad to see he's treating you right. Now, what would you like to drink? I've got red or white wine.'

'Just a coffee for me, thanks,' says Jess.

'And me,' says Lee. 'Late night last night.'

'Of course, I'd forgotten about that awards do,' I say as I put the kettle on. 'How did it go?'

'Good, thanks,' says Lee. 'We are now officially the best small company in Leeds.'

'That's fantastic! Well done you. Did you get a trophy or owt?'

'Yeah. I left it at home, mind. Nice bit of bling for the office.'

'And we sat on the Lord Mayor's table,' says Jess. 'He was dead nice, too. Not stuck up at all.'

Lee was right. She is very down to earth. She seems quite excited by the whole thing too. I suspect she's no more used to these sorts of things than I would be.

'Wow, mixing with all the right people, aren't we?'

She nods and gives a little shrug, as if she can't quite take it all in.

'And Jess was the most gorgeous one in the room, of course,' adds Lee.

She blushes again and looks down. Lee takes hold of her hand. He appears as smitten as she is.

'I'm sure she was,' I say, putting their coffees down on the table. 'Now, you two sit down and I'll see if those Yorkshires are ready.'

They are. I serve them up with my homemade gravy. One big Yorkshire each. I remember Emma frowning the first time she came. Apparently they don't do big Yorkshires down south where she came from. Jess eats every scrap. She finishes before either of us.

'Wow, that was lovely, thanks,' she says.

'Thank you. You can come again,' I joke.

'Oh, she will do,' says Lee. I catch the look in his eyes as he says it. He means it. He has no intention of letting this one go.

When we have all finished, I get the beef out of the oven

and Lee does the honours with carving. He stepped straight into the role of father of the house when it became vacant, even though he wasn't yet a teenager. My little man. That's what I used to call him. Not so little now, of course. He will make a great father, I know that. And now, for the first time in ages, I have real hope that it is going to happen.

'So, where do you live, Jess?'

'In Mytholmroyd, near Hebden Bridge, with my dad.'

'He hasn't found anyone new, then?'

She shakes her head. 'No, too devoted to Mum. I don't think there'll ever be anyone else.'

'You must be very close.'

'Yeah. I guess we are.'

It's good, of course, being close to your family. Just as long as she's not so close she won't leave him.

'I bet he'd miss you if you weren't around.'

She drops her fork on the plate with a clatter. She glances up, a slight frown on her forehead. I don't understand what I've said. Maybe she's got the wrong end of the stick.

'I mean, it will be difficult for him, when you move on. Have your own family and that. Men find it hard coping on their own sometimes.'

She opens her mouth but doesn't say anything. Lee is giving me a look.

'Jess's dad is a chef,' he says.

'Oh, well that will be a big help then. A lot of men can't cope with the cooking, you see. Not used to all those domestic duties, but it sounds like he'll be fine.'

She has her head down now, her hair hanging over one side of her face.

'Anyway,' says Lee. 'Jess might not be working at the cinema for much longer. We're interviewing at work on Wednesday.'

'Oh, what for?'

'The receptionist job. It's maternity leave cover for Beth but we're pretty sure she won't be coming back.'

'That's great,' I say, unable to keep the relief from my voice. I thought for a moment he was going to say she wanted to go into PR. That she was one of these career girls. A receptionist's job is different. It's something you do before you have a family. Not something to prevent you having one.

'That would be lovely, you two working together, wouldn't it?' I say, turning to Jess. It is only then that I notice her face. She is staring at Lee.

'I haven't actually agreed to be interviewed,' she says, her voice firmer than I've heard it since she arrived.

'But you know you will,' Lee says. 'You're just playing hard to get.' He is teasing her; I can see that by the expression on his face. I'm not sure she appreciates it, though. She turns and sees me looking at her, fidgets a bit in her seat.

'It doesn't really sound like my thing,' she says.

'And I've told her she'd be great at it,' counters Lee. 'She would, wouldn't she, Mum?'

'Now don't get me involved,' I say, holding my hands up.

'It makes perfect sense,' says Lee. 'An end to all those late shifts at work.'

'Oh, I hadn't thought about that,' I say. 'Do you have to work a lot of lates then?'

'Yeah,' she says. 'Last night was my only night off for the next fortnight.'

'Oh dear,' I say. 'That's not much fun, is it?'

'Not for her or me,' says Lee. 'I'm having to book a month in advance to see my own girlfriend.'

Jess sighs and looks up. 'Look, I'll think about it,' she says. 'But I'm not making any promises.'

'There you go,' says Lee. 'I knew you'd come around.'

I see Lee take her hand under the table.

'Well, good luck if you do go for it, Jess,' I say. 'Not that you'll need it. Sounds perfect for you. Now, can I get anyone some more roasties?'

Lee helps me load the dishwasher after lunch. I've told Jess to go and make herself at home in the living room.

'She's lovely,' I say as I hand him a plate.

'I know,' he replies.

'Look after her, won't you.'

He looks up sharply. 'What's that supposed to mean?' I see the flash of anger in his eyes. Still, it takes me by surprise sometimes, seeing my past reflected back at me like that. I feel my shoulders tense. I have to remind myself that it is my son I'm talking to.

'Nothing. I just want you to be happy. She's got spirit, this one. You mustn't push her too hard, you know.'

'I do know how to treat my girlfriend,' he says.

'Good,' I reply, before passing him another plate.

They stay for about an hour after lunch. Lee says he is going to run her home, to save her waiting around for a train on a Sunday.

I kiss her on the cheek as she leaves. 'It's been lovely meeting you, Jess. And remember, you're booked in for Sunday lunch from now on.'

'Thanks,' she says. 'I think that will keep me going all week.'

'I'll remind you of that tomorrow,' says Lee. 'When you're queuing for a blueberry muffin.' She pulls a face at him. I like that they are playful like this. It's good to be able to have a bit of banter. Simon and I never had that. Not that I can remember, anyway.

When they have gone, I go upstairs, pull out the drawer under the bed and take out Lee's christening robe once more. I do my usual thing of chasing away the darker memories it brings back in order to concentrate on the happy ones. I don't think it will be too long before I'll see it worn again. And some new happy memories will be created, which might just bury the bad ones for good.

Sadie Ward
31/07/2017 11:46am

Jess, I'm messaging you privately because I can't put this on your timeline. I know it's stupid, what with you being dead and that, but I want you to know something and at least this way it feels like I have told you.

I remembered your letter. I'd put it away somewhere safe and almost forgotten it. I read it with tears streaming down my face. It is so like you to think of others before yourself.

That is why I have decided to go to the police. Because I know now for sure what happened to you. I suspected it wasn't an accident but I didn't have any proof. Now I have your letter, they will have to listen to me. So I am going to tell them tomorrow, the day before your funeral. And if they don't listen I'm going to shout louder until they do. I am fighting for you, Jess. I know it's too late to save you but it's not too late for H. Some people won't like it and there will probably be a massive fall-out, but I will make sure the truth comes out.

I still can't bear the thought of them burying you. The only thing that keeps me going is the thought that at least you are safe now. That where you are, no one can ever hurt you again. I love you and miss you so much x

JESS

Monday, 1 February 2016

I have no idea what Sadie is talking about. No idea at all. How can it not be an accident? Is she saying someone killed me deliberately? Murdered me, even? Surely the police would have been involved already. No one has mentioned the police. If there was anything suspicious, people would have been talking about it on Facebook. And Dad said the coroner had finished his investigation. They wouldn't let me be buried if there had been anything dodgy about it.

I don't understand how a letter from me can change anything. I have no idea what letter she is talking about. Did something happen before I died that I didn't tell anyone about? And how she can say she knows what happened. Was she there? Perhaps she was a witness. But if she was, the police would have talked to her already, so it doesn't make any sense.

Maybe she feels so bad about not believing the Facebook stuff that she needs to blame someone else for my death. Though that doesn't sound like Sadie at all – at least not the

Sadie I know. The trouble is, it's going to kick off a whole load of crap. That will be the last thing Dad wants. And Lee, for that matter. Presumably my father and husband would not stand by and let me be buried if there was the slightest doubt about what happened. And now Sadie is going to say something and make a big fuss and it's going to hurt them even more. Fucking hell. Dad's only just about coping as it is. This could push him over the edge. I wish Sadie would just accept it and let me go. Let them bury me and do their grieving and get on with their lives. Not have some massive scene just before the funeral.

I stand up and run my fingers through my hair. *Move away from the laptop!* I hear a voice inside shouting at me. I know I should stop reading this stuff, but it's like finding your biography before you've even lived your life. I need to know how it's going to end. Not just for me, but for Harrison.

I go back to the laptop and scroll to the photo of Harrison. I am desperate for a new one. I want to see how he is growing. Dad says Lee is looking after him with Angela's help. She was OK, Angela, but there was something a bit weird about her. And I'm damn sure I don't want her bringing up my son. I can see she's close to Lee but I can't imagine her being much fun. That was the great thing about Mum – she could be firm when she wanted to but she was always great fun.

I allow my fingers to brush Harrison's cheek. I want to touch them for real. I want to be his mum, watch him grow up. Protect him from all the crap out there in the world. I'm going to have to try to change things. Just because I believe the beginning of this story, it doesn't mean I have to accept the ending.

I get my things together, stuff them into my backpack and go downstairs, deciding I should at least show my face before I leave for work. Dad looks up as I enter the kitchen. He didn't say much when I got in last night. To be fair, I didn't say much either. I pretty much went straight to my room in order to avoid a confrontation. I'd hoped it would feel less awkward this morning, but it doesn't.

'Morning,' he says, before glancing at his watch. 'Well, just. Good weekend, I take it?'

'Yeah, it was.'

He pushes a mug of tea on the table towards me as I sit down.

'Thanks.'

'Nice place he's got, is it?'

'Yeah, well swish apartment. Great view of Leeds too.'

He nods. He clearly knows what I got up to in the apartment, but he at least has the decency not to mention it, or give me some big lecture.

'What about the awards do, was it good?'

'Yeah. His firm won. Posh hotel, good grub. Chatted to the Lord Mayor, it was well good.'

He takes a sip of his tea.

'So where did you go yesterday?'

'To his mum's. She's in Leeds too. Well, Horsforth.'

'Is she nice?'

'She's fine, friendly and that. Does a mean Yorkshire pudding.'

'But?' He looks up as he says it. I guess he has picked up on something in my voice.

I shrug. 'She's not a patch on Mum.'

He nods slowly. 'No one is, love. That's the trouble. What about his dad?'

'They split up years back. I don't think he sees him anymore.'

'And did you find out how old he is? Lee, I mean.'

I sigh. I hadn't told him after the first date but I realise I've got to at some point.

'He's thirty-two. He looks younger than that, though.'

'Jesus, Jess.'

'What does it matter?'

'It matters if you've got a twenty-two-year-old daughter to worry about.'

'Why? It means he's more mature than the other guys I've been out with. I'd have thought that would be a good thing.'

'Yeah, well, I guess I've got a different way of looking at it.'

I know what this is about. It's about sex. He doesn't want to think of a man in his thirties taking advantage of his little girl. Although he's never going to admit that, of course.

'For your information, he's a lot more responsible than anyone else I've been out with too.'

Dad sighs and looks up at the ceiling. I suspect he knows full well what I am getting at.

'Well, what's he doing still being single at thirty-two?'

'I don't know. I'll ask him next time, shall I? Or I can bring him in and you can ask him yourself.'

'You could have brought him in when he dropped you off last night.'

'I know. And I'm glad I didn't now, if this is what he would have had to put up with.'

We sit in silence for a bit. I drink my tea, more to prevent the need to talk than anything. The truth is, I didn't invite Lee in because I didn't want him to see this place. It was bad enough just driving through Mytholmroyd without having to do the whole 'come in and see the tiny terraced hovel I live in' thing. The guy is used to swanky apartment living; if he comes here he will see that I don't belong in his world.

'I'm only trying to look out for you, Jess.'

'Are you? Or are you trying to keep me as your little girl forever?'

I stand up and head for the door. Dad glances at the clock. My train isn't for another fifteen minutes. Dad knows that but he chooses not to say anything.

There's no sign of Sadie on the platform when I arrive. It's unusual for me to be so early. I guess I am officially between awkward conversations. Though I suspect the one with Dad will seem like a breeze compared to the one I am about to have with Sadie. She did text me back on Sunday but only to say 'OK'. She could have said something to make me feel better and she chose not to.

I catch sight of her coming over the footbridge. I can tell by the way she is walking that she is still pissed off with me. Even her leather jacket appears to be bristling.

'Hi,' I say, when she gets to me. 'How was the party?'

'Yeah. Good.'

'I'm really sorry I didn't make it.'

'Are you?'

'Of course I am.'

She nods and we stand in silence for a bit. Sadie shuffles her feet. She has never been very good at being mad at me for long.

'Well, I wouldn't be,' she says.

'What do you mean?'

'If I'd had the choice between a hot guy offering to shag me senseless and going to some kid's tinpot birthday party in Mytholmroyd, I don't think I'd be sorry I missed it at all.'

I allow myself a hint of a smile, watching her closely in case it is not the right thing to do.

'Actually,' I say. 'He'd already shagged me before we even got there.'

Her mouth drops open and she grabs my jacket. 'You complete slag.'

'I thought I was going home afterwards, didn't I? I was hardly going to say no.' I am smiling properly as I say it. More in relief that she's being so cool about it than anything else.

'I bet you did it again later though, didn't you?'

'Might have,' I reply, trying not to laugh.

'Got cystitis yet?'

'Shut up,' I say, trying to pull her away from the other two people who have arrived on the platform.

'Well, you will do soon if you carry on like that. You're not used to it, girl.'

'I think I could get used to it.'

'That good, was he?'

'I'm not complaining. I am sorry, though. About not turning up, I mean. I hope Maddie didn't mind.'

'She was off her face by ten thirty.'

'Lee said she would be.'

Sadie turns to look at me, her brow furrowed slightly. 'What do you mean?'

I realise too late that I have put my foot in it. 'I was feeling really bad about not being able to come, that's all. He was trying to make me feel better.'

'Right.' She doesn't sound convinced. 'Did you stay all yesterday as well?'

'Yeah. We went to his mum's for lunch then back to his place for a bit.'

'It's a bit soon to be meeting the parents, isn't it?'

'He always goes to hers for Sunday lunch. It was no big deal.'

Sadie raises her eyebrows. 'Sounds pretty serious to me. Are you sure you weren't there for official approval?'

'No. It wasn't like that at all.'

'Remind me of that when she's your mother-in-law.'

I stare at her. She can't know, of course, what she has just said. But it still turns me cold inside. I walk a couple of steps away, hoping she won't be able to see my face. She knows me too well to get away with that, though.

'Hey, I was only joshing.'

'I know.'

'Is she that bad?'

'No. A bit weird and in your face, but nothing I can't handle.'

'So what's the problem?'

I look up at the sky. I want to tell her everything so badly, but I also know that the more I say, the worse it will be for her when I die. I can't do that to her.

'Anything to do with what might happen in the future, it reminds me of all that stuff on Facebook, that's all.'

'I thought you said that had stopped?'

'Yeah, it has. It freaked me out a bit, that's all.'

There is a pause.

'You are OK, aren't you?' asks Sadie quietly.

'Yeah. I'm fine.'

'Good. You had me worried for a bit there.'

I feel the tears pricking at the corners of my eyes. She's always been so bloody good to me. She was the only one who understood, or at least tried to understand, what I was going through. And now I'm going to saddle her with all this guilt. I have to try to make her forget it, or at least convince her that I didn't believe it either.

The train pulls slowly into the station. I turn to face Sadie as we wait for the doors to open. 'Can you forget I ever said anything about it? It's just, I feel a bit stupid about it all. A lot stupid, actually. I was being a total idiot.'

'Sure,' she says.

'Thanks,' I reply, hoping she will remember this conversation one day in the future. And that it might help her not to be so hard on herself.

The new rota for the next fortnight is up in the staffroom at work. I'm down to work both weekends and until ten thirty every night apart from tomorrow and Monday and Tuesday next week when I'm off.

'Oh great,' I say as I read it.

'What?' asks Sadie.

'I'm hardly going to be able to see Lee for the next fortnight.'

'You'll have to go for some more hot lunch dates.'

'It's not the same.'

'You mean because you can't shag him?'

'No,' I say, turning sharply back to Sadie. 'I mean I want to spend proper time with him. Last weekend was so amazing, God knows when we're going to be able to do that again.'

Sadie comes over and looks at the rota. 'I'd offer to swap with you,' she says, 'but we're on exactly the same shifts.'

'I know. Thanks anyway. I guess I have to hope he's keen enough not to mind.'

It's about an hour later when Lee texts me.

Thanks for a great weekend. Last interview slot going is midday on Wednesday. Am saving it for you. Let me know. No pressure. When can I see you again? X

I shut my eyes and sigh. I could do midday Wednesday; I'm not starting work until two. Lee wants to see me again and if I stay here it's never going to happen. He'll end up getting bored waiting around and go off with someone else. I can't risk that.

I don't want my new life to be over so soon. I'm enjoying it way too much for that. I send the text quickly, before I have a chance to change my mind.

Thanks. I'll take it, if you're sure I'm up to the job, that is. I'm off work tomorrow evening then not till Monday next week. X

I stuff the phone back in my pocket and blow out hard. I've done it now, I really have. Sadie will go mental if I leave, I know that. But I also know I can't go on working here if I want this relationship to work. And it has to work. I've seen my future and I want it. Well, apart from the end bit, obviously. And I can change that. I must be able to change that. But I have to make sure the rest of it happens first.

My phone beeps again, another text from Lee.

That's great. Carl will be interviewing you. Wear something smart but feminine. And the boots I got you. You'll knock him dead. I've got a work thing on tomorrow eve so I guess I'll have to wait till Monday. X

I'm not sure about the feminine thing. I don't even know what 'smart but feminine' means, to be honest. Although I'm pretty certain I don't possess anything that fits into that category. I'll have to go out during my break and get something. Which is a pain as I'm skint as it is. I need to do it, though. I need to look the part. I can't risk showing Lee up by going in leggings.

I take my break while Sadie is still busy in the kitchens. If I pop to somewhere in the shopping centre I can be back before she realises I've gone. I hurry down the escalator. Clearly, Primark isn't going to cut it for this one. I stare at the mannequin in the window of French Connection. She's wearing a black pencil skirt with a white blouse in a floaty, almost see-through fabric. I walk into the shop, conscious that I look rather out of place. I wait for the female assistant to sneer at me, like in *Pretty Woman*. She doesn't though. She smiles and asks if she can help. I tell her I need to look smart but feminine for a job interview. A few minutes later I'm standing in the changing room, gazing at my reflection in the mirror. I look like a fucking receptionist. Which freaks me out, even though it's what I asked for.

'I'll take them,' I say to the assistant when I get back outside. I don't even look at the figure on the card machine as I put my number in. Whatever it is, it'll be worth it if I can be with Lee.

Joe Mount ▸ **Jess Mount**
2 August 2017

I nearly didn't do it, you know. When the undertaker arrived and I saw the hearse outside, I thought about pushing him out of the way, telling the driver to get out and taking off with you. I didn't really think through where I'd go. That didn't matter. All that mattered was that it wouldn't be to a cemetery to bury you. I don't think I actually believed it until today. Until I saw your body in a coffin. I cried, Jess, great big, noisy sobs. All the way there in the hearse and all the way through the service. I wasn't the only one, of course. I think everyone there was in tears at some point. But I was the only one who was burying my daughter.

Saying goodbye to you was the hardest thing I have ever done. I know Lee was saying goodbye to his wife but it's not the same. He might find another wife one day but I'll never find another daughter.

Harrison won't ever find another mum either. One of the things that hurts most is that he won't be able to remember you. I'll tell him everything about you as he grows up, though. All the silly, crazy things you used to say and do. The things that drove me and your mum mad. And all the brilliant stuff too. The way you made a room light up just by walking into it. The way you looked at him even when you'd been up all night and had hardly got any sleep.

Goodnight, Jess. I'm so very proud to have had you as my daughter.

JESS

Wednesday, 3 February 2016

It's a long time before I stop crying and can even think about facing Dad. I splash my eyes with cold water several times, then look up at the ceiling and blow out long and hard, trying to calm myself.

When I do finally make it downstairs, I have to stop and compose myself again before I enter the kitchen. Part of me wishes I could put some sort of spell on my dad, bloody stupefy him, anything to stop him going through that. The only tiny shred of comfort I have is that whatever Sadie said to the police, it didn't stop them burying me. I don't think he could have coped with that. At least now he has put me to rest, however difficult it was for him.

I make a little noise in my throat as Dad turns and smiles at me.

'Morning, love,' he says. 'You're up early.'

'Yeah. Thought I'd have breakfast with you today before I grab a shower.'

His smile broadens. 'Great. How about poached egg on toast then?'

'Sounds good,' I say.

He starts busying himself. He is never happier than when he is in the kitchen. Mum used to sit there watching him for ages, towards the end. She told me once it made her feel better than any therapy she'd ever been offered.

'I'm going in early today,' I say.

'To meet Lee?'

'Not exactly. I've got an interview at his firm.'

The busyness stops almost as abruptly as it began. Dad takes the pan off the heat and turns to face me.

'You never said anything.'

'I only decided on Monday.'

Dad's frown gathers momentum as it races across his forehead. 'But I thought you were happy at the cinema?'

'I am, sort of. But it makes it really difficult to see Lee when I'm working late shifts all the time.'

'You'll cope. People stayed together through world wars, you know. If he's serious about you, it won't be a problem.'

'Yeah, well, there's no war on and it is a problem for me.'

He shrugs and shakes his head. This is the part where Mum would have come in and smoothed things over between us and calmed everything down. I miss her even more at these moments.

'So what's the job?' asks Dad, his voice straining to be reasonable.

'A receptionist. It's only maternity cover at the moment

but Lee's pretty sure the woman won't come back afterwards.'

'You're going to give up your job for maternity cover?'

'He says they'll find me something else if she does come back.'

'But you don't know anything about PR.'

I shake my head. 'Thanks for the confidence boost, Dad.'

'I'm being honest, that's all.'

I feel the mercury rising inside of me, pushing all the warm, fuzzy thoughts of Dad at my funeral out of the way.

'Well, like I said, I'm going for an interview for a receptionist job. I greet people, make them coffee and show them where to go. Which is kind of what I do at work, only I won't have to smell like burgers all day and scoop up people's half-eaten popcorn from the floor.'

Dad sighs and goes back to the poached egg on toast. Only this time there is a lot more clanking and scraping than before. When he does speak again, he still has his back to me.

'What if it doesn't work out with Lee?'

'You really are trying to cheer me up this morning, aren't you?'

'I mean, if you guys split up, it could get messy. Do you really want him to be your boss as well?'

'We won't split up.'

'You said that about Callum.'

'This is different. I know.'

'How can you know? You've only been going out with him a few weeks.'

He turns around to face me, the exasperation practically oozing out of his pores. I wish I could tell him why I'm so sure, but I can't without telling him all the rest. Including the fact I've just read him describe how awful it is to bury your daughter.

'Look, this is for keeps. You'll just have to trust me on this.'

He manages a half-hearted smile, plonks the plates of egg on toast on the table and sits down opposite me. I am torn between throwing it in his face and going round to give him a hug. In the end, I simply say thank you and eat my breakfast.

When I come down later, after I've had a shower and got changed into my interview clothes, he does a double take as I walk into the kitchen.

'God,' he says. 'Look at you.'

'What's wrong with me?'

'Nothing,' he replies. 'You look so different, that's all.'

'You mean I normally look such a mess that it's really obvious when I make an effort?'

He almost manages a smile. Almost but not quite. 'I mean I hardly recognise you. You look like a receptionist.'

'Bit of luck, being as I'm going for a job as one.'

He starts unloading the dishwasher. 'Did Lee buy you all these clothes as well?'

'No. I bought them myself. I'll need this sort of stuff if I get the job.'

'But you can't afford them.'

'It'll be more money than I'm on now.'

'And what about getting up in the mornings?'

I roll my eyes. 'You're doing everything you can to put me off this, aren't you?'

'I'm simply being realistic, Jess. I know how much you hate getting up early.'

'I'll manage, OK? Maybe some nights I can stay over at Lee's.'

There is a clatter as he drops a handful of cutlery. He turns around to face me again. 'This is all going way too fast, Jess.'

'Too fast for who? Because I'm enjoying the ride.'

'And nought to sixty in nine seconds isn't a sensible way to drive.'

'What is this? The *Top Gear* parenting manual?'

Dad sighs and puts down the tea towel hanging over his arm. 'This isn't what you wanted, Jess. What about your dreams? All the amazing artwork you did at college?'

'I grew up, Dad. I got real.'

'And you got a boyfriend.'

I feel my eyes narrow as I look at him. 'What's that supposed to mean?'

'Don't let him change you too much, Jess.'

'He's not changing me. I'm changing myself, OK?'

I head for the door.

'Good luck, love,' he calls after me. But my legs have carried me out of the door before I have the chance to reply.

The building where Lee works is old and a bit grotty from the outside, but as soon as you walk inside it's all uber trendy with stylish displays of their PR campaigns and a squishy purple sofa in the corner of the reception. The woman behind the front desk looks up and smiles at me.

'Hi,' she says. 'How can we help you?'

'Hi. I'm Jess Mount,' I reply. 'I'm here for an interview.'

To her credit, the brightness of her smile doesn't dim, even when she realises I am her possible replacement.

'That's great, do take a seat, Jess,' she says, gesturing towards the sofa. 'Can I get you a tea or coffee?'

I am already feeling inferior to her and I've only been here two minutes.

'Er, coffee would be great, thanks. Milk, no sugar.'

I sit down on the sofa. It's only when she steps out from behind the desk that I remember why I'm replacing her. The bump emerges several seconds before the rest of her. To be fair, it is a neat bump. I've seen women who look like they're about to explode by the time they're seven months pregnant. And she is still slim, apart from the bump. Pretty, too – dark brown, shoulder-length hair, nice make-up, long legs. I notice she's wearing stilettos. She must be dead uncomfortable in them. It suddenly occurs to me that if I get this job I will presumably be working here when I am pregnant. Will they expect me to dress like that when I'm about to drop? I think I'll probably want to come to work in my onesie at that stage. I bet I'll have fat ankles too. Mum said she had fat ankles when she was pregnant with me. And her feet went up a size. She hoped they'd go back after she had me, but they didn't, so she had to give all her size four shoes to Auntie Sarah.

The receptionist comes over with my coffee. I glance down at her ankles. They look fine to me.

'Thanks,' I say as she hands it to me. 'Your feet must be killing you by the end of the day. I can't walk in shoes like that and I'm not even pregnant.'

'I know, it's company policy. It's not written down or anything, but I came in wearing flats one day and I got a look and a few comments.'

It must have been Carl. Lee would never do that.

My brain races forward and starts joining the dots in my future timeline. They will have to get someone to replace me when I go on maternity leave, just like they've done with her. People will probably make jokes about how you've only got to stand behind the front desk to get pregnant, or that there is something in the water. I will greet the young women who come here to be interviewed to be my replacement. All the time knowing that, unless I manage to change my fate, I will be dead in a few months.

I sip my coffee, trying to stop my hands from shaking. Another woman comes downstairs, followed by a tall, well-built man in a grey suit, who must be Carl. I see him shake her hand. She gives me a little smile as she walks past. I feel like a complete cow as I smile back. I am going out with one of the fucking bosses. She's not going to get the job. She's probably desperate for it. I hope she goes for it next time, when I'm being replaced. I won't feel such a cow then because I'll know it's hers for keeps.

'And you must be Jess,' says the man in the grey suit. 'Carl

Walker. Pleased to meet you. I've heard a lot about you.' He winks at me as he holds his hand out. I wonder what Lee has said about me. Whether he's told him we've slept together. I hate the thought of Carl knowing stuff like that. I should never have agreed to this. I should be coming into work on the train with Sadie. I shouldn't be trying to be someone I'm not. It's too late to change my mind now, though. Lee would be disappointed with me if I backed out at this stage. It would make him look stupid. He'd have every right to dump me. I stand up.

'Hi, pleased to meet you,' I say, shaking his hand. He holds on to it a bit longer than seems acceptable.

'Let's get started then. After you.' I swear I feel his eyes on my arse as I walk up the stairs. I'm conscious of how tight my skirt is, how see-through the blouse is at the back. I wish I knew how much men talk about personal stuff at work, whether Lee told Carl as much about our weekend as I told Sadie. I feel dirty. Like a prostitute who wants to get this over with as quickly as possible so she can go home and shower.

I pause on the landing at the top of the stairs and let Carl go past me, brushing against me as he does so. I'd like to think he didn't do it on purpose, but I'm pretty sure he did.

'Come in and have a seat,' he says, holding open a door on the left. I go through into a large office with a big black swivel chair behind the desk. I sit on the chair in front of it and cross my legs, still quite surprised to see them on display instead of under leggings.

When I look up, Carl's eyes are on them too.

'Good to see you dressed for the part. We always like our front office staff to be well turned out, keeps the punters happy.'

He winks again and sits down heavily in his chair. I try to keep the fact that he is making me want to vomit from showing on my face.

'Right, thanks for the CV,' he says.

I did it yesterday with one of those templates you can get online, hoping the professional design made up for the lack of content – though I had embellished it slightly.

'So, Jess, you work on reception at the cinema in the shopping centre.'

'Yeah. I deal with internet and phone bookings and all the usual meeting and greeting. We're only a small cinema so we can't compete with the multiplexes on size, but we like to offer a personal, friendly service.'

I'd read one of those online articles too, about how to bullshit your way through interviews. It's all about pressing the right buttons, apparently. From the look on Carl's face it appears I've managed it.

'Absolutely. It's so important to a small company like ours that our clients and prospective clients are made to feel welcome from the second they arrive.'

'Well, I'd make sure they were. I like to put people at ease, make them feel comfortable, so that by the time they get to you, they are already feeling positive about the company.'

Carl is smiling. And repeatedly glancing down at my boobs. I am going to get this job, whether I still want it or not. My future is rushing at me so fast I am in danger of being knocked off my feet. I can't work out if I am giddy with excitement or if I am actually going to be sick.

I am sorting out the cutlery later, back in my usual work gear with my interview outfit safely stored away in the staffroom, when I get the text from Lee.

Congratulations. Carl was blown away. The job's yours. How about I take you out for lunch tomorrow to celebrate?

I did it. I got what I wanted. I just wish I felt a little bit happier about it. Sadie walks into the kitchen. I have two choices: I can tell her now and get it over with; or I can put it off as long as possible and crap myself about what she's going to say when she finds out. It isn't much of a choice, to be honest.

'Hey,' I say. 'Got a minute?'

'Yeah, sure,' she says, a slight frown on her face. I lead her out of the kitchen, down the corridor beyond and check that no one is in earshot before I say anything.

'I've, er, I've got a new job,' I say.

'What?'

'I went for an interview at lunchtime. I got the job.'

She is staring at me, a look of complete and utter disbelief on her face.

'Where? What doing?'

'At Lee's company. As a receptionist.'

She pulls a face and turns her nose up. 'Why the hell would you want to do that?'

'It's the only way I'm going to get to see Lee. If I stay here it's not going to work.'

'Fucking hell, Jess.'

'What?'

'You're letting him take over your whole life.'

I stare at her. I think it's the first time I've ever seen her jealous. That's why she's lashing out like this, saying stuff that isn't true.

'No, I'm not! They happened to have a job going, so I applied for it. Lee didn't even interview me.'

'But you'd never have gone for it if you hadn't been going out with him.'

'No, I probably wouldn't have. But if I wasn't going out with him, I wouldn't be fed up with working evenings and never seeing him, would I?'

Sadie shakes her head. 'So you're going to jack in a job you love for him?'

'Come on, it's not exactly a dream place to work.'

'We have a laugh, don't we?'

'Well, yeah. But it doesn't mean I'm going to work here for the rest of my life, does it? Look. It's only covering maternity leave. If I don't like it, I can always come back.'

'So it's not even a permanent job?'

'No. But Lee doesn't think the current receptionist will come back after she has the kid.'

'You always said you couldn't hack working in an office.'

Sadie looks close to tears. I feel awful about doing this to her but I don't see that I had a choice. Not if I want to carry on seeing Lee.

I shrug. 'I need a nine-to-five job. It's as simple as that.'

Sadie shakes her head. 'What about us?'

'What do you mean?'

'Well, if you're working there office hours and seeing him in the evenings, when are we going to see each other?'

'We can get together at weekends.'

'Don't be daft, you'll be too busy shagging lover boy.'

I look away. 'Sadie, please don't be like this.'

'What did you expect?'

'I know it's a shock, but I thought you'd at least be happy for me.'

'How can I be, when you're selling out like this?'

My skin prickles. She's gone too far now. 'That's out of order.'

'Why? Because it's true? You've never wanted to be a receptionist. You've never wanted to have a nine-to-five job and you've never wanted to be the little woman, doing everything her boyfriend asks her to.'

I go to say something back but the lump in my throat is too big for me to get the words out. I turn on my heels instead and head off in the direction of the toilets. I can't believe Sadie would say that. It's so not true. It's because she's jealous. She thinks Lee is taking me away from her, that's why she's lashing out and saying stupid things.

I shut the cubicle door and lean back against it, telling myself over and over again that I am doing the right thing.

When it doesn't work, I get out my phone and log on to Facebook. Dad has posted another photo of Harrison. He says he is being a brave boy for his mummy. I put my head back against the door and start to cry.

Sadie Ward
03/08/2017 11:20pm

They wouldn't listen, Jess. They said they would, but they didn't even ask me to make a formal statement. They just nodded a lot and took my details and said they'd be in touch if they needed any further information.

I kept hoping they would postpone the funeral, but they didn't. They buried you along with any evidence and left me standing there bawling my eyes out, wanting to shout and scream at all the other people bawling their eyes out that they didn't know the half of it, that it wasn't an accident. That everything they had read or heard about it was wrong. I couldn't even look at your dad, he was in such a state.

Lee wasn't though. Lee was about the only one there who managed to hold himself together through the service. People are saying he's still in shock. He isn't though. I know that. The only thing he's in shock about is the fact that he has got away with it.

PART TWO

JESS

Friday, 4 March 2016

I still can't get over the fact that Sadie thinks Lee killed me. It is plainly ridiculous. I thought I was the one with mental health problems. All I can think is that it's jealousy. That's all it can be; she's usually so clear-headed. But, thinking about it, her whole reaction to me saying I was leaving work was so over the top. And she's been off with me for the past month. She blames Lee for taking me away from her. And somewhere down the line she lets that eat away at her so much that she actually believes he killed me.

I've tried to get her to see that this is about her, not Lee. She clearly feels like she's being left behind. I've suggested that she start applying for jobs, but she doesn't want to know. Which is a shame, because if she stays there, at the cinema, without me, this is obviously going to fester. I need to find a way to get her to see sense. It'll be too late once I'm gone. When someone you love dies, you don't think straight. I, of all people, know that only too well. I need to nip this in the bud now.

'Hey,' I say, when I arrive on the platform later to find Sadie already there.

'Hi,' she replies, not even bothering to hide her feelings as she says it. It's my last day at the cinema. The last day we will share the train journey in. It feels like the end of an era. It feels dead weird. By the end of today, after everything we have gone through together, Jessadie will be no more. She will never return, I know that already. I simply wish it could have ended on a positive note, instead of with this horrible atmosphere.

'Have you changed your mind about a leaving do? There's still time to organise something if you want to,' says Sadie.

'No, thanks. I don't want a big fuss. And Lee's meeting me after work now, anyway.'

She makes a face and looks at the ground, scraping her left boot along an imaginary line.

'Why don't you give him a chance, Sadie?'

'A chance for what? We're hardly going to become best mates, are we?'

'You don't know that. You've never properly met him.'

I'm aware this is as much my fault as hers. I get to see Lee so rarely that, when I do, I want him all to myself. I have mentioned the idea of going for a drink with her to Lee, too, but, to be honest, he hasn't seemed that keen either.

'I'm not sure we'd get on,' says Sadie. 'We haven't exactly got anything in common.'

'You've got me in common.'

'So we just talk about you all night?'

'Look, come for a drink with us after work tonight.'

She hesitates before answering. 'I'll think about it, OK?'

I guess it's the best I can hope for.

'No regrets about leaving then?' she asks.

'Nope. It's what I need to do.'

'You won't be saying that when you've had a week of getting up at seven in the morning.'

'Maybe not,' I say. 'But I'll stay over at Lee's some nights, that'll make things easier.'

'And your dad's fine with that now, is he?'

It's my turn to look at the ground. 'He'll come round,' I say, more in hope than certainty.

'So, when are we going to see each other then?'

'Lunchtimes. If you don't mind coming in early for a shift.'

'You buying, are you?' For the first time there is a hint of a smile on her face.

'Might be.'

'It won't be the same though, will it?'

'No,' I say. 'But that doesn't mean it's a bad thing. Just that things are changing.'

Sadie looks away as the train pulls in. When I sit down opposite her, she is still wiping the tears away.

We don't really say anything on the walk from Leeds station. There is nothing left to say. As soon as we get to work, Sadie dumps her stuff and goes off to the kitchen to get started. She isn't normally this keen.

'Hello, sweetie,' says Adrian, coming into the staffroom and giving me a hug. 'I can't believe it's your last day.'

'I know. I'll still come and watch films here, though. You can't escape me that easily.'

'Well, just make sure you don't spill your popcorn. You might be all gorgeous receptionist in your new job but I know what a slob you are, remember.'

I dig him in the ribs, unable to say anything, and walk out of the staffroom, immediately coming face to face with Nina in the corridor.

'No slacking because it's your last day, OK?' she says. I'm not sure if she means it seriously or not.

'You'll miss me when I'm gone,' I reply, before walking off down the corridor.

Lee is standing outside the front entrance when I walk out with Sadie that night. She's going to stay for one drink. I haven't told Lee she's coming with us. I figured it would go down better as a spur-of-the-moment thing.

'Hey, how's it feel to be a woman of leisure?' He steps forward and kisses me.

'Only for a weekend,' I reply.

'That's what you think.' He puts his hand into his jacket pocket, produces an envelope and hands it to me.

'What's this?' I ask.

'Open it and see.'

I look at him, and then at Sadie, who is hovering behind me.

'Sorry, this is Sadie,' I say to him. 'Sadie, Lee.'

'Hi,' says Lee, flashing her a smile and then looking straight back at me. I open the envelope and pull out two tickets from inside. It takes my brain a moment to register that they are flight tickets to Italy. It takes another moment to notice that the date on them is tomorrow.

'Oh my God. Are we going for the weekend?'

'A week, actually.'

'I don't understand. What about work?'

'I've got a temp in to cover. Thought you deserved a proper holiday before you start. So it's a week in Venice – if you can put up with me for that long.'

I stand there staring at him. He has done this for me. Thought of it and organised it and paid for it. No one has ever done anything like that for me before. If this is what being with him all the time is going to be like, I can't wait to get started.

'Have I finally succeeded in making you speechless?' Lee asks.

'I can't believe it,' I say eventually, rushing forward to throw my arms around him. 'Thank you so much!'

'You're welcome. I'll run you home now so you can pack and then I'll bring you back to mine so we can get to Leeds Bradford Airport for eight thirty tomorrow.'

'Oh wow. This is amazing. Thank you so much.'

I suddenly remember Sadie is still standing behind me,

expecting to go for a farewell drink. I turn around. 'I'm so sorry,' I say. 'I had no idea this was going to happen.'

'It's OK,' she says. 'You go. You've got stuff to do.'

I look at her, trying to work out if she really means it or if she's simply being nice.

'Do you want a lift home with us? I'm sure Lee won't mind.'

'No, you two go on,' she says. 'I'll get the train. I don't fancy playing gooseberry.'

She's doing a good job of trying to hide it, but I can still hear the note of resentment in her voice. This is what she'll remember one day in the future. How Lee always came between us. Always spoilt everything. The seeds of her hating him are probably being sown right at this moment, and there's nothing I can do about it. She has seen him make this amazing gesture and still she can't be happy for me.

'OK.' I shrug.

'Right, well. I'll see you after your holiday, I guess. Have fun.'

'Thanks,' I say, even though she said it through gritted teeth. She starts to walk away but I go after her. 'Sadie, at least be happy for me.'

'I am,' she replies. 'You and Cinder-fuckin'-rella.'

I let her go, remembering for a moment how we used to do that whole scene from *Pretty Woman* together, before turning back to Lee.

'What's up with her?' he asks.

'I guess it's hard for her being the one left behind.'

'Right. Well, we'd better go. We have a plane to catch in less than twelve hours.'

I take his hand and walk with him. Walk towards a future that no longer scares me. Because nothing can hurt me when I am with this man. Nothing at all.

We pull up outside my house. I know I should ask Lee in while I pack, but I still can't bring myself to do it. It's as if I think the bubble will burst if I allow him to step into my real life. And my carriage will turn back into a pumpkin.

'I'll be as quick as I can,' I say, unfastening my seat belt.

'Sure. We're travelling light, remember. Anything you haven't got to hand, I'll get it for you there. Leave some room in your suitcase.'

'Thanks,' I say before sliding out and shutting the door behind me. Maybe Sadie is right – maybe things like this don't happen to people like me. Not in real life, anyway. It crosses my mind that she could have something to do with the Facebook posts. The first one was from her, after all. And they started on the day I met Lee. I hate myself almost the second I think it, because I know she wouldn't do that to me, wouldn't be so cruel. Not when she knows everything I've been through.

I let myself in. Dad is making himself an espresso.

'Hello,' he says. 'Didn't expect to see you yet. Thought you were going for a farewell drink.'

'No,' I say. 'There's been a change of plan.'

'Oh?'

I can't stop the grin from spreading across my face. 'Lee's taking me on holiday to Venice. We're flying tomorrow morning. I've just come home to pack then I'm going to his place. We've got an early start.'

'Woah,' says Dad, taking the cup of steaming coffee from the machine. 'That's a bit sudden.'

'It was a leaving work surprise. He's got a temp to cover at work next week.'

'You're going for a week?'

'Yeah. He's booked the hotel and everything.'

'But you hardly know him.'

I feel the pin puncture my balloon and the first of the air start to escape. 'Jesus, don't start this, Dad.'

'Well, he can't expect you to drop everything and just go with him. There are things to think about.'

'Like what?'

'Like whether it's a sensible thing to do.'

'Sensible?' I stare at him, not quite believing I am hearing this. 'When have I ever done anything sensible? I don't want sensible. I want spontaneous and exciting and that's what this is. Now, if you'll excuse me, I've got a case to pack. I don't want to keep Lee waiting.'

'Is he outside?'

'Yeah.'

'You should have asked him in.'

'And you've just demonstrated exactly why I didn't.'

His face crashes into pieces on the kitchen floor. I hurry upstairs, trying not to think of the mess I am leaving behind, and get my case out from under my bed. I haven't used it since the end of last summer, when Sadie and I went to Amsterdam for a long weekend. We went by train. We didn't have any choice, really. I couldn't risk getting on a plane and having another meltdown. It suddenly occurs to me that tomorrow morning I am going to have to get on a plane with Lee and hold myself together for the entire flight. I have to. Because I don't want him to know anything about what happened. I don't want to be that Jess Mount anymore, so I need to bury her past with her.

I open my wardrobe. I have no idea what people wear in Venice, but I'm pretty sure the only things I have in here that are suitable are the evening dress, the mustard tunic and the boots Lee bought me. I pack them and add a couple of pairs of skinny jeans, black leggings and a few long shirts. I chuck in my best underwear and some shorts and cami sets before rushing through to the bathroom and emptying half the contents of the cabinet. I grab my make-up bag and go back to my room for a quick check around. I spot Mum's shoes, which are still in the bottom of my wardrobe. I know I should ask Dad first, really, but I'm sure he'd say yes, so I put them in and close the case.

I hurry back downstairs. Dad is sitting at the kitchen table, seemingly resigned to the fact that I am going.

'Are you sure you've got everything?' he asks.

'Yeah. I think so.'

'Passport?'

I groan, run back upstairs and rifle around in the chest of drawers until I find it.

'Thanks,' I say, when I return downstairs. 'Saved my life

there.' I realise what I've said as soon as the words are out of my mouth and have to bite my lip hard.

'Look,' he says, getting to his feet, 'I'm sorry if I went off on one. I worry about you.'

'I know. But you have to let go a bit now, let me live my life.'

'I'll do my best.'

'Do I have permission to enjoy myself?'

'Of course you do.'

'Good. Because I intend to.'

'As long as you give me permission to worry. Because I will do, whether you like it or not.'

'I'll be fine. I'll be having the time of my life.'

Dad nods and steps forward. I know he is going to hug me and I have to try really hard to get that image of him crying at my funeral out of my head.

'Text me when you get there,' he says. The hug arrives on cue. I suck my breath in hard in an effort to stop the whimper that's threatening to emerge.

'I'd better get going,' I say.

'Sure. Let me carry your case out and meet this young man of yours.'

I hesitate. I don't really want to spoil the magic by letting him intrude on it right now. But I also know that I don't want to go off on holiday with an atmosphere hanging over us.

'OK,' I say. I follow Dad outside. Lee gets out of the car when he sees us and steps forward.

'Hi, Mr Mount,' he says, offering his hand. 'I'm Lee. Pleased to meet you.'

Dad shakes it firmly. 'And you. But call me Joe, please.'

'Sure.'

We stand awkwardly on the pavement for a moment.

'Good choice to go to Italy, anyway,' says Dad.

'You can't go wrong there, can you? Whereabouts are your family?'

'In the south, near Naples. We get over to see them when we can.'

The truth is that we used to stay with them for most of the summer holidays when I was younger, but the summer after Mum died I wasn't able to get on the plane and we've only been twice since. Partly because it's such a hassle to get there and back by train.

I look at Dad. I can tell from his face that he's suddenly remembered about the flying too.

'Will you be OK with the—'

'Yeah. Fine,' I say quickly. 'We'd better be off.'

'Right,' says Dad. 'Well, have a great time, both of you.'

'We will,' says Lee. 'And don't worry, I intend to take very good care of your daughter.'

Dad nods, seemingly reassured. We get into the car and Lee starts the engine. I wave at Dad as we pull away.

'He seems like a lovely guy,' says Lee.

'Yeah, he is. And you do a very good line in impressing a girl's father. I think he liked you.'

'That's because I didn't tell him the bit about planning to ravish you every day.'

'Probably a good move.'

'I will show you the sights too,' he says. 'In between all that.'

'I should hope so. We can't go home without any photos. People will know what we've been up to.'

My phone beeps. It's a text from Dad.

I like him. I think your mum would too. Have a great time. Love you xx

He always does that – puts a kiss from both of them, as if Mum is still here. I look out of the window as a single tear falls down my cheek.

Joe Mount
4/09/2017 7:11am

I went to your grave last night. I went with a shovel because I had decided I couldn't bear it any longer and I was going to dig you up so I could be with you again. It was crazy, I know that. But, as you told me once, when you're in love you do crazy things. And I am still in love with you, Jess. I have been in love with you ever since I first heard your heartbeat through the midwife's stethoscope. Since I first felt you kick my hand through your mum's tummy. Since the second you came out, screaming your heart out, and I had to catch my breath because I knew at that second that you would always be the most important thing in my life.

So I took the shovel. You probably don't even remember I had one. I kept it in the tool shed in the backyard. I used it for clearing snow more than anything else. I can't remember ever actually digging with it, but I always felt a man should have a shovel.

I took it with me in the car. And when I got there I took it down to your grave with me. Only then did it first occur to me that it was a crazy thing to do. It was dark, two in the morning (I don't sleep very well these days), so I didn't have to worry about there being anyone else around, not even dog walkers at that time. And I just stood there, my foot on the top of the shovel, poised for action. I did at least manage to break the surface, and I dug like a man possessed for a few minutes, but then I realised I couldn't do it. I didn't want to hurt you, Jess. I got you one of those biodegradable willow coffins because you always liked the trees, and it suddenly occurred to me that if I did manage to dig that far down, my spade might go through it. It might have rotted away by now, in which case there would be nothing to protect you. Or maybe it would be so soft that my shovel would go right through it. And I couldn't bring myself to hurt you, Jess. I couldn't risk that, however much I wanted to bring you back, to be near to you again.

I dropped the shovel and fell into a crumpled heap on the ground and sobbed. Sobbed like I've never sobbed before, not even at your funeral. Because I miss you, Jess. More than you can ever believe. And it finally sunk in, at that moment, that I can never get you back. It hurt when your mother died. It hurt like crazy. But I got through it because of you. But now I don't have you, there doesn't really seem any point. It's like I'm grieving for both of you. So I sat there between your two graves and talked to you. Talked about every single thing I could remember about you. I was still there at dawn. And still there when the first of the dog walkers turned up. A cocker spaniel ran up to me and licked my face.

The owner came over and apologised. He asked me if I was OK. He probably thought I was bloody dangerous, sitting in a graveyard at seven in the morning with a spade. And I just looked at him and nodded. He nodded back, even though he could see I wasn't, and walked on, calling the dog to follow him.

And I came home, Jess. And I put the spade back in the tool shed. And I'll probably never use it again. Not even to clear snow. Because every time I look at it I will think of you. And how I will never be able to see you again.

JESS

Saturday, 5 March 2016

I stand in a toilet cubicle at Leeds Bradford Airport, tears streaming down my face as I read Dad's post. My dad. The sane, sensible one who has never done anything crazy in his life. Only now he is taking a spade out in the middle of the night to try to dig me up. My death is clearly sending him round the bend. He'll probably end up having a breakdown. I mean, it's more than anyone can take, isn't it? Your wife dying and then your daughter. And he's got no one left to talk to. He hasn't got any friends. Not what I'd call friends, anyway. Only man friends, which means they're just guys he works with. He doesn't go out with any of them, he doesn't call any of them. The only person he has left in his life is Harrison, and he's not much use to talk to. And I'm not sure how much he even sees him if Lee and Angela are taking care of him. The thought of Angela bringing up my son makes me feel uncomfortable. It isn't the life I want for him. But if I'm not around, I don't suppose there's much I can do about it.

I shake my head and put my phone away. I can't deal with this now. Lee is waiting outside, probably wondering what the hell I'm doing in here. I blow my nose on the loo roll, wipe my eyes and step outside. The reflection that greets me in the mirrors above the sinks is not a good one.

I was stupid to check Facebook before the flight. So incredibly stupid. My boyfriend is about to whisk me off on the holiday of a lifetime and I'm now standing in the bogs looking a complete mess. I splash water over my eyes, get my make-up bag out and attempt a quick repair job.

When I arrive back outside, Lee is leaning against the wall.

'Hi,' he says, looking up. 'Everything OK?'

The question suggests that he suspects not.

'Yeah, fine thanks. Just doing some deep breathing. I haven't flown for a while. I get a bit nervous before take-off.'

It sounds better that way. I mean, plenty of people are nervous flyers. It's not a big deal.

'Hey. You should have said before,' he says, wrapping his arms around me. 'I'll hold your hand all the way. And it's a quick flight. You'll be there before you know it. There is one stop in Amsterdam, though.'

He kisses me on the forehead. I hadn't realised it wasn't a direct flight. My stomach clenches again. I ball my hands up so he can't see my fingers shaking.

'I'll be fine once we're in the air. It's the take-offs and landings I'm not keen on.'

'Well, I shall do my best to distract you during both.'

He takes my hand and leads me over to the departure

lounge. Our luggage has already been checked in. The other people are mainly older couples, maybe trying to rekindle a bit of romance with a trip to one of the most romantic cities in the world. I catch a few sideways glances from the women. Mum told me once that you never stop fancying younger guys when you get older, but you can get away with looking because you know they aren't going to be checking you out.

I squeeze Lee's hand and lean in to his body. If David Attenborough were narrating, he'd say something about the female letting everyone know that the male is taken and not to come any nearer.

'It's going to be fine,' Lee whispers into my ear. And I believe him.

It is fine, too. Not brilliant, but OK. I think I behave like any other nervous flyer, rather than a woman who is in danger of completely losing it. And the thing I think of to stop myself freaking out is Harrison. I know I'm not going to die on this flight, because if I did, Harrison would not exist. And he does exist. I have seen photos of him. So I am able to convince myself I must make it to Venice and back safely.

And Lee does his bit by kissing me during take-offs and landings as promised. I am pretty sure other people look and mutter about it, but I don't give a toss.

I let out a long sigh as I unbuckle my seat belt.

'It wasn't too bad, was it?' asks Lee.

'No, thanks to you.'

'I can cancel the flight back and we'll go home by train, if you'd rather.'

'Don't be daft. I'll be fine.'

'Good. I don't want you worrying about it, that's all. I want you to enjoy every second of the holiday.'

'I will. I promise.'

We get a water bus from the airport. An orange line one. Lee seems to know exactly where we are going without asking or stopping to look at maps. He must have been here before and I can't help wondering who with. Obviously there will have been girlfriends before me. Plenty, I would imagine. You don't look like that and end up going on holiday on your own. I wonder how many of them he brought to Venice. Because as much as I'd like to think I am the first, I am not stupid enough to believe it.

I sit nearest the window and gaze out at the old buildings lining the canal. Lee drapes his arm around my shoulder.

'So this is the Grand Canal. It's a bit shabby here but it'll get better as we head towards the centre.'

'Well, it beats the outskirts of Leeds on a Monday morning. How many times have you been here?'

'Oh God. Quite a few. It's one of my favourite places.'

Maybe he's brought every girlfriend he's ever had here. It could be some kind of initiation test, like when Richard Gere takes Julia Roberts to the opera in *Pretty Woman*. Maybe I'm supposed to say something about the architecture or the history. Or maybe, like in the film, it's enough just to appreciate it as a first-timer.

'I love it already.'

'Good. And we're going to do the whole works while we're here. No expense spared.'

I smile up at him and rest my head on his shoulder. I suppose, if I really am going to die, I should at least give thanks that I will die happy.

'Next stop's ours,' says Lee after a while. He picks up our cases and gives me his hand as I step off the water bus, unable to suppress a shiver.

'First thing we'll do is buy you a proper coat,' Lee says. 'I told you it would be chilly.'

'I know. I just didn't think it would be colder than Leeds.'

'Don't worry,' he says. 'The hotel's only five minutes' walk away.'

He leads me along the street; we take a left, then cross a small bridge before turning right.

'There you go,' says Lee, pointing across the street. A uniformed doorman greets us in Italian and calls a porter to take our cases. I hear Lee tell him we're in the junior suite before I follow him through into the reception. There is a grand piano there. A fucking grand piano. Talk about being out of my depth. It's all I can do to stop my mouth gaping open.

My boots squeak slightly on the marble floor. I look across at Lee; he smiles and takes my hand. 'Wait till you see the room,' he whispers.

The woman on reception smiles at us and Lee gives her his name. A few moments later, the porter returns to take us up a flight of stairs, and then opens a wooden door. Lee holds his arm out for me to go first. I step inside. The first thing I see is a huge, round bed in the middle of the room, draped in white sheets and with gold cushions scattered on it and a low, red lampshade above it. The ceiling has dark wooden beams. The wall behind the bed is painted a mottled gold with empty gold picture frames dotted over it. Across the other side of the marbled floor are ornate glass and gold doors leading onto a terrace overlooking the canal.

'Oh my God,' I whisper. 'Is this for real?'

'Yep. Your home for a week.'

'Wow. I'd have been happy with a Travelodge.'

'Well, you deserve better than that.' Lee smiles. 'Besides, if you're going to do Venice for the first time, you have to do it in style.'

The porter leaves, though not before Lee has tipped him.

I notice the iPad on the desk. 'If this were Leeds, someone would nick that in the first five minutes,' I say.

'They do have my address, remember,' Lee replies. 'Anyway, you won't be needing that this week. It's a computer- and phone-free holiday, remember?'

He'd told me on the plane that that was his only rule for holidays. I'd agreed. I'd been quite relieved, to be honest.

'Yeah. I've turned mine off already.'

'Good.' Lee sits down on the bed and pats it. 'Come on. Time to unwind.'

'You said you were going to show me the sights.'

'Not on the first afternoon, I didn't.'

I smile and sit down on the bed next to him. He takes hold of my left boot and pulls it off, followed by the right, and starts kissing me.

'I've never done it on a circular bed,' I whisper. 'I'll probably fall off.'

'Well, if you do, I'll be going down with you.' He kisses my neck and starts unbuttoning my shirt. He has that intensity in his eyes again. He always looks at me like that when we are about to have sex. I don't care whether he looked at other girlfriends in the same way. Maybe even other girlfriends who he brought here. All I care about is that, in the short time I am going to be with him, he never stops looking at me like that.

He slips the shirt off my shoulders and bends to kiss my belly, his hand rubbing between my legs. I raise my hips and let him peel off my leggings. He pulls at the top of my thong with his teeth. I laugh and help him ease it down. I go to pull up his T-shirt but he shakes his head.

'Not so fast,' he says. 'I haven't finished looking at you yet.' He sits me up enough to unclasp my bra, then tosses it onto the floor before laying me back down again and parting my legs. He walks around the bed as he takes his T-shirt off and removes his trousers and boxer shorts.

'Make yourself come,' he whispers.

I am unsure at first but move my hand down and do as he says, conscious of his eyes boring into me as he watches. He continues to circle me, encouraging me, waiting until I am moaning out loud with my eyes screwed shut before finally joining me on the bed.

'You are so fucking hot,' he says as he straddles me. 'My turn now.'

Afterwards, when we are lying on the bed, our bodies stuck together with sweat, I feel a single tear escape from the corner of my eye onto his shoulder.

'Hey, what's up?' he asks.

'Nothing,' I say, shaking my head. 'Just a bit emotional.'

'Good, because I love you.'

I swallow hard, trying to hold back the rest of the tears, which are already rushing towards the surface. I have been waiting for him to say that. Even though I know I am going to marry him and have his baby, I still needed to hear it.

'I love you too.'

'That's OK, then,' he replies. 'We're all square.'

Lee orders breakfast to our room when we're finally ready to get up the next morning. We have both freshened up in the bathroom and put on the robes provided by the time there is a gentle knock at the door.

'Come in,' Lee calls. I am sitting on the edge of the bed as the young woman walks in. She has dark hair tied back in a ponytail and pretty rosebud lips. She is carrying a brass tray laden with a cafetière, cups and saucers and a selection of croissants. She keeps her eyes down, goes straight to the table and is about to put the tray down when I see her glance across at Lee. Her eyes widen, there is a sharp intake of breath and she drops one side of the tray. The cups fall off and smash onto the floor. I hear her mutter something in Italian, swiftly followed by 'So sorry' in English.

Lee is striding towards her before I have even moved from the bed.

'What the hell do you think you're doing?' he shouts at her. I see her cower back against the balcony doors, plainly terrified.

'Lee, stop it!' I shout at him, jumping up from the bed and launching myself between them. The girl looks at me and back to Lee before making a run for it, tears streaming down her face. It is only then that I look up and see Lee's face. His eyes are dark. Darker than I have ever seen them before, his brows knitted heavily across them. His breath is coming in short, sharp gasps.

'What on earth were you doing?' I ask, my voice as shaky as my legs.

'Nothing,' he replies.

'What do you mean, nothing? You shouted at her. You scared the hell out of her.'

He scared me too. He is scaring me right now, standing there motionless like that. He shuts his eyes. I hear a deep sigh as his hands go up to his head.

'Look, I'm sorry, OK? I lost it for a moment.'

'She only dropped a tea tray, there was no need for any of that.' My heart is still pounding. I don't understand what just went on. It was not the Lee I know. It was such a complete overreaction.

He walks over to the bed and sits down heavily on it, his head still in his hands.

'I'm sorry,' he says again. 'I know I overreacted. It's just that I want everything to be perfect for you. It felt like she was spoiling it.'

'She could drop a three-course meal on the floor, for all I care – it wouldn't matter. It was an accident. I drop things at work all the time. No one ever bawled me out like that.'

He brings his hands down from his head and reaches out to me. I flinch. I can't help myself. He is staring at me. The thing I can't get out of my head, the thing that's freaking me out, is that flicker of recognition in her eyes when she first saw him. She knows him. She must do. Why would she react like that otherwise?

'Do you . . . have you ever seen her before?' I ask.

Lee looks up at me. 'No,' he says sharply.

'But have you stayed here before?'

'Look, I've said sorry. Let's just leave it, shall we?'

He stands up and goes into the bathroom. My hands are still shaking. She had seen him before, I'm pretty sure of it. But what I can't understand is why she looked so scared when she saw him, and why he responded the way he did. When Lee comes out of the bathroom, I try to pluck up the courage to say something, but then there is another knock at the door and a uniformed man arrives with replacement cups and a dustpan and brush. He apologises profusely as he places the cups on the tray and sweeps up the broken crockery on the floor. As he goes to leave, Lee follows. I see him reach into the pocket of his jacket, which is hanging on the back of the door, and take out some money before slipping outside and speaking to him in a hushed voice. Lee is smiling when he comes back in. Acting as if nothing ever happened.

'Right,' he says. 'Breakfast.' He pushes the plunger down on the cafetière and pours the coffees, placing them on the bedside table before climbing back into bed with the plate of croissants.

I am still sitting there, unable to move. Lee passes me the plate but I can't even begin to think of eating at the moment.

We are silent for a minute or two. I want to say something but I don't want to upset him or make him feel like I don't believe him.

'Look,' he says eventually. 'The waiter said I reminded the girl of an ex-boyfriend. And not a very nice one at that. That's why she freaked out when she saw me.'

'So she'd never seen you before?'

'No. She just thought she had.'

I nod. I want to believe him. I really do. I want everything to go back to how it was before. I wish I could erase what I have just seen from my head, but it's not that easy.

'Why did you give the waiter money?'

'To buy the girl some flowers. I would have done it myself but I don't want to freak her out again.'

I nod. Relieved that the Lee I thought I knew has re-appeared. It must be like he said – all a big misunderstanding. I feel bad for doubting him. I pick up the croissant and take a bite.

Lee strokes my arm, looking massively relieved. 'So,' he says. 'Where do you want to go today?'

We go to St Mark's Square. It wasn't the first thing on my list – the gondola ride was, but somehow I don't think it's the right time for that. Besides, I want to be with people. Lots of other people. I want to hear their chatter and smell the coffee and be distracted by the busyness of it all. We find a table right in the centre of the square. The guide book I picked up at the airport said those ones are the most expensive, that it pays to go down one of the side streets off the square, but Lee doesn't seem to care.

He orders coffee and two slices of chocolate torte. A pigeon lands on our table and Lee shoos it away. He does it gently, mind. As if he doesn't want to scare it too much. It's hard to believe he is the same person who shouted at the girl a couple of hours ago. He reaches out across the table and takes my hand. The waiter returns with our coffees and tortes. Lee thanks him in Italian and squeezes my hand. Everything is fine. It was just some kind of blip. He really does want this holiday to be perfect, I can sense that. And I know what it's like to want something so badly that it can make you behave weirdly. I should give him the benefit of the doubt. I let out a long, deep breath.

'When we're finished,' I say. 'Can we climb up the tower?'

'We can do whatever you want,' says Lee.

We don't see the girl again for the rest of the week, even though we order breakfast in bed every day. I wonder if she is avoiding Lee on purpose. I remember once I saw Callum waiting to order food at the cinema, a few months after we'd split up, and I got Adrian to serve him instead (Adrian said I was well shot of him because he had bad skin which, apparently, is always a sign of poor character).

It is the man who came in to clean up after her who brings us breakfast on our final morning. He puts the tray down in the usual place. I notice there is something extra on it; one of those silver domes with a handle that they put over food. I wonder if Lee has asked them to cook us something special for our final day. He goes over to tip the waiter before he leaves.

'Right then,' Lee says, as he returns. 'Where would signorina like to eat her breakfast today?'

'I'm still not going outside, if that's what you're thinking. It's freezing.'

'Oh, come on. It's the last chance we'll have. I didn't pay for a room with a balcony with canal views for nothing, did I?'

'OK, I'll do it. But it will have to be a quick one, before the coffee goes cold.'

Lee smiles and opens the doors onto the balcony before picking up the tray and taking it out there. It is only when I follow him that I see the single red rose in a vase, a small bottle of champagne and two glasses on the table.

'When did you do that?' I ask.

'Well, if you will spend ages in the bathroom, you might just miss something important.'

I shake my head and smile at him.

'Do take a seat,' he says. I do as I am told. Lee goes to

the other side of the table and lifts up the large silver dome. Underneath is a box. A small, red, square box. I look up at him, not quite daring to believe it. Lee smiles and picks up the box, going down on one knee on the balcony as he opens it and holds it out to me, revealing an engagement ring with a single diamond, perched on top of a twisted antique gold band.

'Jess Mount, the craziest, most beautiful, sexiest, funniest woman I've ever met, will you marry me?'

I stare at him. The tears come before any words do. Lee lifts up my chin and brushes one away. 'It wasn't that bad, was it?'

I laugh and shake my head.

'Do I get an answer then?' I don't even hesitate. The biggest decision of my life and I know exactly what to say. Some people say they've seen their future written in the stars. I've seen mine on Facebook. It may not be quite as romantic, but at least when you know what's coming, you have an answer ready.

'Yes,' I say. 'The answer's yes.'

Lee lets out a little sigh, as if he is actually relieved. As if he had some element of doubt.

'Why would I have said anything else?' I ask, stroking his face.

'I don't know. I guess you can never be one hundred per cent sure.'

'You do all this for me,' I say, waving my hand across the table and back into our room, 'and you actually thought I might have said no?'

'I'm aware it's a bit quick, that's all. I thought you might be worried about what your dad will say.'

I shake my head, and look out across the canal for a second so he can't see the fresh round of tears. I still feel like a fraud. Perhaps I should tell him the truth, let him be the one to make the call once he knows what he is marrying. I can't though, because I can't risk losing him. I need him. Harrison needs a father.

'When you know that someone is the one,' I say as I turn back to him, 'there's no point waiting any longer.'

'Thank you,' he says. 'I can't tell you how happy that makes me.'

'Good. So can we go back inside now before this weather freezes my tits off?'

Lee laughs. Only when you've put this on,' he says, holding out the ring.

'Go on, then,' I say. 'I'll let you do the honours.'

He slips it onto my finger. It's a tiny bit big, but not so much that it will slip off.

'I can always get it adjusted,' he says.

'It's fine,' I reply. 'It's better than fine. It's perfect.'

We go inside and drink the champagne in bed before having sex one last time. It is different this time. Slower, more tender. Deeper, somehow. And afterwards, as I lie next to him, gazing down at the ring, I realise that it is unstoppable now. This force propelling me towards my future. All I can do is buckle up and enjoy the ride, and hope that at some point before this perfect life of mine goes so horribly wrong, I work out where the hell the ejector button is.

*

It is later that morning, when I am doing a final check of my case while Lee is in the bathroom, that I find the note, folded up and pushed down the side next to my cream camisole. It has two words written on it, in shaky black lettering. 'Be careful.'

JESS

July 2008

I sit and stare at the woman opposite me. She is an educational psychologist called Paula. She seems nice enough, but I don't want to be here with her. I am here because school referred me due to their 'concerns', and Dad said he thought it might help me. I shouted at him and said that the only thing that would help me was if Mum walked through the door and it had all been some horrible nightmare.

Paula is talking, explaining how this is supposed to work. She is saying all the 'right' things, except they are not the right things for me. They are the things that do my head in. In a minute she's going to start talking about the five stages of grief, as if that's something I've never heard of. I want to shout at her that I am capable of using Google. I know that there is no time limit on grief, that everybody goes through it at a different pace. But it turns out that, in real life, it isn't like that. People make their own minds up about whether you are doing it right, without even talking to you.

Paula is looking at me now and I realise I am supposed to say something, although I have no idea what. So I just start talking.

'Last Saturday,' I say, 'I was waiting for a train to Halifax and a guy on the platform took one look at me and said, "Cheer up, love. It might never happen." So I said, "It has actually. My mum died of bowel cancer." And it shut him up and he walked away without saying anything and I wish I could say that to everyone, or have it tattooed on my forehead or something, because then people would understand that bad things do happen and they can happen to anyone, at any time. I could walk home tonight and be run over by a bus. And cars sometimes mount pavements and hit people. There was a story in the newspaper about a man who died when that happened. The driver was changing the CD at the time.

'People die in train crashes – not very often, but they do. They are usually the ones in the end carriages. I've learnt that from reading about the inquests. Just going to school or college or work can kill you.

'One of my teachers is in hospital because she fell down the stairs and broke her back. No one tells you not to walk down the stairs, do they? No one says it's dangerous and you'd better take care or get a fucking stairlift installed, even if you're only in your twenties. Turns out everything is dangerous, even walking downstairs. You could be a hermit and not go out and you could still die falling down the stairs.

'I don't care about the people who die climbing Mount Everest or sailing across the Atlantic in some little rubber dinghy. They knew the risks and they still did it. They're professional thrill seekers who get off on that stuff. They probably go bungee jumping in their spare time just for a laugh.

'No, the people I feel sorry for are the ones who don't do anything stupid. Who have a weird allergic reaction to a wasp sting and die from it. Who are standing in the wrong place when a sign falls down and kills them. Who are driving along when an idiot throws a brick off a motorway bridge.

'But when I talk about stuff like this, people say I am being ridiculous. Actually, the ridiculous people are those who stick their fingers in their ears and pretend stuff like this never happens.

'And before you say it, it's not being morbid, OK? It's just stuff that happens, but people don't want to talk about it or even think about it because it scares them, so they make everyone around them put on a happy face and talk about nice things because that doesn't feel so scary. Well, I'd rather be scared than stupid, and I think everyone else should be scared too. And if that makes me weird then that's fine by me.'

I look at Paula and she nods and writes something down. I wonder if she too thinks I'm not coping.

ANGELA

Sunday, 13 March 2016

I have a feeling about it before they even arrive. I mean, Venice is such a romantic city, isn't it? I have never been there – Simon wasn't one for romance or culture – but from everything I've seen and heard, it's the perfect place for it.

Even by the way she holds herself when she gets out of Lee's car, I can tell she is feeling special. She is not some silly little girl anymore – she's a woman. And it shows.

I try to keep my face together as I go to greet them at the door. To not look down at her left hand as soon as they walk in. But they are practically falling over themselves to tell me, they are so giddy with it.

Lee takes her hand and holds it up for me to see. 'We've got some news,' he says.

I let the excitement that has been bubbling under the surface break out as I hug Lee and Jess in turn.

'Oh, that's marvellous! Congratulations! I'm so pleased for

you both. I had a feeling, you know, the last time you came. I didn't think it would be long.'

I look at Jess. Her hair is falling across her face as she looks up at Lee but I can still see how smitten she is. You can tell that a mile off.

'Let's have a proper look then, love,' I say, holding my hand out for hers. I gasp as I see the ring. It really is that beautiful. Elegant and understated, but clearly not cheap.

'It's gorgeous,' I say. 'I'm glad he's got such good taste.'

'What do you mean? It was the only one they had under fifty quid,' says Lee.

We all laugh. I usher them into the kitchen.

'I wish you'd warned me, Lee. I'd have got some bubbly in for the occasion if I'd known. I'm afraid I've only got wine.'

'That's fine. We had champagne for breakfast yesterday, didn't we?' he says, turning to Jess.

'Well, I'm glad you celebrated in style,' I say. 'Sit down and tell me all about it, then. Where did you propose?'

'On the hotel balcony.'

'I'd have thought you'd have done it in a gondola,' I say, looking at Lee.

'No, it's a bit cheesy, isn't it?'

'Is it?'

'Yeah. I didn't want to do one of those touristy proposals people post online. I wanted it to be personal. Besides, it's not easy to go down on one knee in a gondola.'

'He did take you for a ride on one, though, didn't he?' I ask Jess.

'Oh yeah. The gondolier was really funny, kept pulling weird faces. I'm glad Lee didn't ask me there, to be honest. I don't think I could have taken it seriously.'

'And you did go down on one knee?' I ask Lee.

'Of course. It was all legit and above board.'

'Glad to hear it. We can't have Jess thinking she's marrying into a family that doesn't do things properly. Let's see the photos then.'

'What of?' asks Lee.

'The holiday, you daft thing.'

'They're all on my camera back at my place.'

'This is the trouble with our Lee not being on Facebook,' I say to Jess. 'I'll never get to see those photos, you know. Why he can't just take them on his mobile and share them like everyone else, I don't know.'

'Because I don't want everyone else seeing them,' says Lee.

'Are you on Facebook?' I ask Jess.

'Er, yeah. But I don't really post much.'

'You'll be posting a photo of your ring, though, won't you? And updating your status.'

'I don't know,' she says, giving a sideways look at Lee. 'I'll probably just tell people myself. The important ones, anyway.'

'Have you told your dad yet?'

'No. I'm going to tell him in person later.'

'I expect he'll be thrilled.'

She nods without saying anything.

'Have you met him yet, Lee? Jess's dad.'

'Briefly, before we went away.'

'I'll have to invite him over here soon to discuss the wedding plans.'

Jess looks down. I think she feels a bit overwhelmed by the whole thing. She is only young, after all. I was a good five years older than her when I got married. And even then, Mum did most of the organising. It's then that I remember: she hasn't got a mum to help her with it.

'Now, don't you go worrying about it all,' I say. 'I'm very happy to take on all the organising. I mean, it's the least I can do in the circumstances.'

They exchange looks again. I hope I haven't overstepped the mark. I was simply trying to do the right thing.

'Say if you'd rather I butt out,' I continue. 'I don't want to put myself where I'm not wanted, but with so much to do, I expect you could do with a hand.'

'Thanks. That would be great,' she says, though she still sounds unsure.

'Have you sorted a date yet?' I ask Lee.

'Give us a chance, I only proposed yesterday.'

'Yes, but I know what you're like. You don't do owt on the spur of the moment. I bet you've got it all planned out.'

'We want a summer wedding,' he says.

'This summer?'

'Neither of us sees the point in waiting now we've made the decision. And it will be a civil ceremony, probably in a hotel or somewhere like that.'

'Well, I'd better start looking for hats then, hadn't I? And Jess, why don't we go wedding dress shopping together?'

'No, it's OK. You don't have to do that,' she says. 'I'll go with my best friend.'

'Best friends don't always tell you what you need to hear,' I say. 'You need someone older, someone with a bit more experience.'

Her mouth opens but nothing comes out. She looks across at Lee. I see him give a little nod.

'Er, yeah. That would be great, thanks,' she says.

'Right, well, you let me know the first Saturday you're free and I'll draw up a list of shops and make appointments. We've got no time to lose.'

I'm so glad she's got me to do this with her. The thing is, I know Lee better than anyone. She may think she knows him, but she doesn't. Not as well as his own mother, anyway. I know exactly the sort of look he'll want. Classy and timeless. *Think Grace Kelly*, that's what I'll tell them in the shops. You can't go wrong with Grace Kelly.

We sit down and tuck into our Yorkshires as they tell me more about their holiday. Jess seems very taken with the hotel. I'm pretty sure it's the same one he took Emma to, but I don't say anything. I don't want her thinking she's second-hand goods. Anyway, there's no point in bringing any of that up now. It's water under the bridge. It's Jess who matters now. Jess who is going to be my daughter-in-law. And, more importantly, the mother of my first grandchild.

She eats well again. Though it doesn't seem to make any difference to her size, which is good as far as the wedding dress is concerned. There's nothing worse than seeing a bride squeezed into a dress that's a size too small for her. I still don't understand how that happens. My dress had to be taken in on the run-up to my big day. Pre-wedding nerves are very good for weight loss.

'And did you get to the opera house, dear?' I ask her. 'Our Lee's told me all about it. It sounds wonderful.'

'Yep. It was so good I almost peed my pants.' I put my fork down and look at her. 'It's a line from *Pretty Woman*,' she adds quickly, when she sees my face.

'Oh yes,' I say. 'I liked that one. Richard Gere was very charming, wasn't he?'

'Yeah, but his eyes are too small for his head,' she replies.

I glance at Lee. He is looking at her and smiling. She makes him laugh. That's a good thing. He can be rather too intense sometimes. Hopefully she will be able to help with that.

'Right, we need to get going if Jess is to make it over to her dad's,' Lee says later that afternoon. 'And she's got to get ready for her big day tomorrow.'

'Of course,' I reply, turning to Jess. 'I'd almost forgotten about your new job, what with all the excitement.'

'Yeah,' she says. 'So had I.'

'Although fortunately I hadn't,' says Lee. 'Which is why she's got a whole new wardrobe for the occasion.'

'Ooh, how lovely.'

'I know,' says Jess, gazing up at him. 'He spoils me rotten.'

'Well, it's important to look the part,' says Lee. 'Though I still can't persuade her to wear her hair up. Don't you think Jess'd look great with her hair up, Mum?'

'I'm sure she would, but it is a bit of a faff to do that every morning. Have it up for your wedding, Jess. I always think brides look lovely with their hair up.'

She stares at me, her eyes almost popping out of her head. It's odd how every now and again she seems to react rather strangely to something completely harmless.

'Anyway,' says Lee, standing up and kissing me on both cheeks. 'We're going to have to love you and leave you.'

'Yes, you get off, love. You must be tired after all that travelling. And congratulations again, best news I've had in ages.'

I kiss Jess and she thanks me for lunch. 'I'll have a ring round of the bridal shops,' I say. 'Get an idea of timings and that.'

She nods, although she still appears rather stunned. Perhaps she's just overwhelmed with it all.

'And don't you worry about a thing,' I continue. 'I'll organise everything for you. All you need to do is turn up and look gorgeous.'

'Jess always looks gorgeous,' says Lee.

'There you go then,' I say. 'All you need to do is turn up.'

Afterwards, when they have gone, it suddenly occurs to me that Lee might invite Simon to the wedding. I don't think he will – as far as I know, they haven't been in contact for years – but he could do. And that is enough to turn me cold inside. I'm not sure I could bear to see him again. To have him stand next to me in the wedding photos as if everything was fine between us. He was always very good at that, pretending everything was fine. Keeping up appearances, as they say. Everything was kept within these four walls.

We've never really talked about what happened. Lee was a bit too young at the time, and it's not something I've ever wanted to bring up since. I'm not sure how much he remembers or was even aware of. Probably more than I realise, but the past is best kept in the past. No point in dragging it all up now. We need to concentrate on the future. That's all I am interested in. A future that involves a wedding and, hopefully, a family to follow. I don't think they'll wait long. In fact, I'm sure of it. When Lee sets his heart on something, nothing gets in his way. And he clearly wants Jess. Jess and everything that she can provide for him. It will be the making of him, becoming a father. He will not make the same mistakes as Simon. He is better than Simon. Always has been and always will be.

Sadie Ward
13/09/2017 10:45am

The police have been in touch. They've said Lee's ex-girlfriend has come forward and made an allegation. It sounds pretty serious. They've interviewed her and she's told them about a possible witness, who they're going to interview. Obviously, none of it is about your case, but the thing is it's not just me anymore. Other people are saying the same thing. It means they're taking it seriously now. They're not just going to sweep the whole thing under the carpet. I'll not give up fighting, Jess. I don't care if I make myself unpopular – I've got to make sure the truth comes out.

I know it's going to upset your dad, but it's for the best, I wouldn't do it otherwise. He's too nice, your dad. Always sees the best in people. That's why Lee won him round. I'm not going to say anything in public on here, because I know he'll see it, but I'm sure the police will contact him at some point. They're on to it now. The detective who called me, a Scottish woman, was dead serious about this, I could tell that. Not like the guy who took my statement, who didn't want to know. She's going to leave no stone unturned. That's what she told me. I'll keep fighting, Jess. For you and for Harrison. That's what best friends do.

JESS

Sunday, 13 March 2016

I put my phone away as Lee comes back to the car after paying for the petrol. My hands are still shaking. It's the first time I've checked Facebook since we went on holiday and I'm already regretting it. It can't be true. I can't believe Lee would attack a girlfriend. He's been nothing but kind and considerate to me: holding my hand when I was nervous on the plane, complimenting me, buying me all those clothes. But I also know how he reacted to that waitress at the hotel. I saw the flash of temper, the darkness in his eyes. She was scared of him. He is clearly capable of scaring other women. Maybe he snapped, maybe he went too far. There's a big difference between shouting at someone and attacking them, though. And I still don't think Lee would hurt anyone. Perhaps the ex-girlfriend is exaggerating. Maybe she's jealous that he married me and not her, and Sadie has stirred this whole thing up by going to the police and now they're digging for dirt on him. It's easy to find dirt when you're looking for it. We've all done things we regret. Things we wouldn't want anyone else to know about.

'You OK?' Lee asks as he gets back in. I'm aware that I'm sitting rigidly clenching my hands, my knuckles white.

'Yeah, just a bit nervous about telling my dad.'

'Are you sure you don't want me to come in with you?'

'I think it's better if I tell him on my own.'

'Because you reckon he's going to go apeshit?'

'He won't be expecting it, that's all. He'll say we're rushing into it.'

'If you want to put the wedding back to next year, I don't mind. Not if it makes it easier for you.'

I shake my head, thinking of Harrison. He must have been conceived just after we got married. Lee's still using condoms. I guess he must only stop using them once we're married. If we put the wedding back, there will be no Harrison before I die. Our son will not exist. Nothing is worth that.

'Thanks, but no. I want to do it in July, like we agreed. Everyone else is just going to have to get used to the idea.'

'Well, if you need backup, let me know. And if your dad wants to meet me properly, that's fine by me. I can have a man-to-man talk with him. Assure him of my good intentions.'

I glance at him with raised eyebrows.

'Hey, cheeky.' Lee smiles as he pulls away. 'I'm ideal son-in-law material, me. Clean-cut, solvent, butter wouldn't melt in my mouth.'

I clench my hands tighter and look out of the window, trying not to think about Sadie's post.

*

Dad gives me a massive hug as soon as I walk through the door.

'Hey, the wanderer returns. How was Venice?' He is like some daft Labrador who has been left home alone and now finds his owner has returned. It is almost painful to watch, especially bearing in mind what I am about to tell him.

'Amazing. It's so beautiful.'

He goes to shut the door. 'Has Lee gone?'

'Yeah. We're both pretty shattered to be honest. Think he wanted to get back home.'

'How about a hot chocolate to welcome you home?'

'That would be great, thanks,' I say, sitting down at the kitchen table.

'So, did you do all the touristy stuff then?'

'Yep. Lee took me pretty much everywhere. Rialto Bridge, the opera house and the top of that tower thingy in St Mark's Square.'

'The Campanile,' he replies. 'And the opera house is called the Teatro La Fenice.' He says it in his best Italian accent, which makes me smile.

'Whatever,' I say. 'We had a fantastic time.'

'That's great,' he says, pouring the milk into the saucepan. I'm keeping my left hand under the table because I want to tell him before he sees the ring. Now seems as good a time as any.

'Actually,' I go on, 'I've got some news for you.'

Dad turns around. I realise my best hope is that he thinks I'm up the duff, in which case the wedding will come as something of a relief.

'Lee proposed to me,' I say, taking my hand out and holding it out to him. If he is relieved about me not being pregnant, he doesn't show it. The expression on his face suggests he wasn't expecting this at all.

'You're getting married?' he says, his face twisting into some strange contortion.

'I know it probably seems a bit fast, but I love him, Dad, and he loves me. It's the real deal. I'm sure of it.'

'Everyone always thinks it is, Jess.'

'You said you liked him, Dad.'

'I did. I do. Though I've hardly met him.'

'So what's the problem?'

He turns the milk off and slowly pours it into my mug, whisking as he goes.

'The problem,' he says, turning and handing the hot chocolate to me, 'is that I love you so much – I don't want to see you get hurt.'

'So – what? I never go out with anyone in case they dump me?'

'No. But like you said, it is a bit quick.'

'Some people wait for years and they still get it wrong. Look at Auntie Sarah.'

'Yes, I know,' he says, sitting down opposite me. 'But that wasn't her fault. She didn't know he was going to go off with someone else within a year of them getting married, did she?'

'No, and she'd been with him for nine years. That's my point. You never really know someone, do you?'

'Maybe not, but you've got a better chance of getting through things if you've got a few years behind you.'

I thump the table. Dad almost jumps in surprise. I want to scream at him that I don't have a few years. That it's now or never for me.

'Listen, I don't want to screw up my life any more than you want me to, but you've got to let me live it. That's what Mum said to me, before she died. She said I had to be true to myself and live the life I'd always dreamed of.'

It's low, quoting Mum, I know that. But I have to pull out all the stops to get Dad on board. I want him to be happy about this. I think it will make it easier for him afterwards.

Dad's eyes are doing that Bambi thing. He stands up and comes over to me and hugs my head to his chest. 'And she was right, of course. Your mother was always right. It's just hard letting go of my little girl.'

I stand up and give him a proper hug, wiping my tears on the shoulder of his cardigan. 'I'm never going to stop being your daughter.'

'And I'm never going to stop worrying about you. I couldn't bear to see you hurt again.'

I can't help the sob that comes out this time. Dad reaches over to the kitchen counter and passes me a tissue from the box.

'Are you sure about him, Jess? You've not just been swept off your feet by a good-looking guy with a fancy job and a nice car?'

I shake my head. 'Come on, you know me better than that.'

'He has bought you a lot of things. And taken you on a very expensive holiday.'

'Yeah, but that's not why I'm marrying him, is it? Prince fucking Harry could ask me to marry him and I'd say no – because I don't love him and he's got ginger hair.'

Dad smiles and wipes a tear from the corner of his eye.

'Anyway, what I'm trying to say is that Lee's the one. No one's ever treated me like he does. Made me feel so special.'

Dad nods slowly. 'Have you set a date then?'

'July.'

'This year?'

'Yep.'

'You're not—'

'No. I told you, he's responsible. We just don't see any point in hanging around.'

Dad is silent for a moment. I know what he's doing. He's trying to work out what Mum would have said at this point.

'Well, let me know what you need. I mean, I'll pay for it all, obviously.'

'You don't have to do that. Lee's going to pay for it.'

'It's supposed to be the father of the bride.'

'Dad, that is a bit last century, you know.'

'What? A man can't pay for his own daughter's wedding anymore?'

'It just makes sense. Lee earns a lot more than you do. And it'll cost a fair whack.'

'So it's not going to be at the church down the road?'

'Nope. Lee wants to hire a hotel somewhere around Leeds. Angela's going to help organise it.'

Dad looks as if he's been kicked in the teeth.

'She offered because Mum's not around to do it. I didn't want to offend her by saying no.'

'Sure.'

'Maybe you can sort out the catering for us? Help put together a menu or something?'

He walks over to the sink and begins to rinse out the milk pan. I know he's hurting but I don't know what more I can say.

'Anyway. I'd better go up and get myself sorted out for tomorrow.'

'Yeah,' replies Dad. 'Big day. Seems like there's going to be a lot of them this year.'

It feels wrong, being on the platform at Mytholmroyd station without Sadie. It feels wrong to even be out the house at seven thirty in the morning, let alone dressed up like some girl behind the make-up counter at Boots.

Lee said to make sure I was well turned out on my first day. I'd only really heard that term used about horses before. But I figured he meant for me to do my hair and make-up, rather than impersonate a show pony.

I feel a bit like a show pony, mind. I don't usually do make-up at all before eleven, and certainly not this much. I did forget the lippy, probably because I'm not used to wearing it, but I'll do it when I get to Leeds. I don't want to be one of those women who does their make-up on the train.

A guy in a grey suit gives me a quick once-over as I walk down the platform. I am about to shout out, 'What you looking at, arsehole?' when I realise that it's probably not very receptionist-like. To be honest, none of me is very receptionist-like. I may as well be acting a part in a play: stage make-up, wig, costume, learning to walk differently, talk differently, be someone else. All in a desperate attempt for audience approval.

On that level, I'm quite glad Sadie isn't here. She'd be the heckler. She'd ask me what the fuck I'm playing at. I've no idea what I'd say in response.

The train pulls into the station and people shuffle towards the edge of the platform. I had forgotten about this jostling for position thing. I might not even be able to get a seat. A lot of people get on at Hebden Bridge at this time in the morning. The train doors open. I feel someone nudging me in the back from behind. I go cold inside. My brain races ahead, thinking of the journey to come, the bodies pushed against one another, people stumbling slightly when the train jolts. I start to use one of the techniques I was taught by the therapist. I need to bring myself back to centre. To not let myself get derailed. That's the last thing I need on my first day in a new job.

I head towards a spare seat between an older woman and a middle-aged guy in a trench coat. I look at the woman and then down at her bag, which is on the empty seat. I wonder if she's one of those people who makes you ask them to move it. But she sighs and gives me a look as she puts it on her lap instead, as if sympathising with the bag for the massive inconvenience.

I get my phone out. It's what everyone does on a train when they haven't got anyone to talk to. I click on Facebook, just on my main feed rather than my timeline. I'm aware that, for the first time in forever, I actually have something newsworthy to post: my engagement. I'm not going to do it though. I don't think Lee would approve, for a start. And besides, there's no way I'm going to let Sadie find out like that. However strained things are between us, no one deserves to find out on Facebook that their best friend is getting married.

I scroll down, looking for anything vaguely interesting or amusing. Mostly it's just stupid selfies and posts full of OMGs about nothing that really matters. No one puts anything serious on Facebook. No one puts anything bad or sad on about their lives. It's basically a bunch of people trying to look like they're having a great time. Maybe Lee's right – maybe it is for losers. I imagine it was better when it started, before everyone's parents went on. That's why I'm hoping Angela doesn't try to look me up on Facebook. I won't ever be able to say anything again if I accept a friend request from my future mother-in-law.

I go to a few film websites to pass the time. I always used to say they should have one screen at work just showing trailers. I'd sit there for hours. I remember watching the *Fantastic Beasts and Where to Find Them* trailer with Sadie. We said we were going to go to the first screening. We won't be able to do that now. I wonder if Lee will take me. He doesn't like Eddie Redmayne, though. So I guess not.

The train pulls into Leeds on time. I let everyone else get off first. I don't fancy the stampede to get through the ticket gates. When the train is empty, I get my little mirror out and put on my new lipstick. I'm not overly keen on the colour, but I guess I'll have to go with it now as I assume I won't be considered 'well turned out' without it.

It feels weird, turning in the opposite direction than usual when I get out of the station. Lee did offer to walk into work with me on the first day, but I said no. I already feel a bit weird that I am going out with one of my bosses – walking in together like some loved-up couple who can't be parted would be too much.

I wonder if he will introduce me to anyone as his fiancée. I've always hated that word, it sounds so old-fashioned. And now I am one, I think I hate it even more.

I take a deep breath as I round the corner and see the Eclipse PR sign. *I can do this*, I tell myself. I can be anyone I want to be. A second later my phone beeps, it is a message from Lee.

I hear the new receptionist is well fit. Enjoy your first day. Love you. X

It is all I need. I step inside the main door, a ready-made smile on my face. Even when I see the front desk and remember the pregnant woman standing behind it the last time I was there, I manage to hold myself together.

Lee comes down the stairs. 'Wow,' he says. 'Don't you look the part.'

'Did I scrub up OK then?'

'Better than OK. I think the rest of us will have to raise our game.'

'If anyone asks, what shall I tell them? About us, I mean.'

'Let's keep things professional at work. They'll all know soon enough.'

'OK,' I reply. I thought he would have told them all by now, actually. Maybe it's for the best, though. I don't want everyone to think I only got the job because I'm going out with him. I'm aware that they'll probably think that anyway, once they find out, but it would be nice if they could get to know me a little bit first.

Lee goes back upstairs. I take my coat off and hang it on the stand. I pop my bag behind the front desk and switch my computer on. I need a password. I'd forgotten how much I hate the first day of anything. Carl comes downstairs. I wonder if Lee has at least told him about the engagement. I hide my ring in case not. I don't want to be the one who blows it.

'Hi, Jess, looking good. It's great to have you with us.' His eyes are wandering up and down my body as he says it. I wonder if Lee knows he does that or if he has never noticed.

'If you can give me five minutes, I'll pop back with your password, go through the ropes with you and give you a quick tour of the building.'

'Sure,' I say. He disappears back upstairs. The phone rings. It makes it to the third ring before I pluck up the courage to answer it.

'Good morning, Eclipse PR, how may I help you?'

I try to put the image of Sadie pissing herself laughing out of my head as I listen to the caller. He asks to speak to Lee. He's already told me what his extension is, so I put the call through. And then I stand there like some Barbie receptionist doll, wondering what the hell I've done.

Joe Mount
14/09/2017 9:58pm

Jess, I want you to know that I'm sorry if I let you down. The police have been round today, asking lots of questions about Lee. That's why I'm telling you this in a message instead of posting it for everyone to see. I didn't believe them. I told them I thought someone was making mischief and they should leave well alone. But when they'd gone, when I was left on my own, thinking about what they'd said, I started to panic that they might have been right. What if I have made the biggest mistake of my life? What if I only saw what I wanted to see? And didn't see the rest? People do that, don't they? And I started going back through everything and thinking about what I might have missed and now I'm worried sick that I might be the one who got it wrong. That I didn't do my job of protecting you. If I failed you, Jess, if I wasn't there for you when you truly needed me, please forgive me. I'm truly sorry.

JESS

Friday, 18 March 2016

I stop on the stairs and do a few deep breaths before I go into the kitchen. I need to hold it together when I see Dad. If I crack, he'll want to know what's wrong, and I can't tell him. I can't breathe a word of what I've just read. I'm still trying to get my head around it, to be honest. It's the fact that the police are taking it seriously that has thrown me. Presumably, they know what they're doing. They wouldn't waste time investigating something unless they thought it was true, or at least might be. They wouldn't go and speak to Dad unless they thought these allegations were genuine.

And yet, at the same time, I can't reconcile the man they are investigating with the one I am engaged to. They are not the same person. They can't be. I wouldn't be stupid enough to fall for a guy who hits women. I'd see right through him. I don't have time for arseholes like that, I never have done. All I can think is that, somewhere along the line, someone got it wrong. Maybe his ex-girlfriend said something about him snapping at her and they read too much into it and she then started saying other stuff that wasn't true. And I know that Sadie was jealous of Lee to start with. It wouldn't have taken much for her to jump to the wrong conclusion. People believe what they want to believe. Only now Dad thinks it might be true too.

'Morning!' I say as I go into the kitchen. Dad looks up from his coffee, immediately suspicious because I never say good morning. In fact, I don't normally say anything in a bright and breezy voice before eight in the morning.

'Morning, love. Are we all set for tonight then?'

He's got the night off work. I'm taking him for a meal with Lee, hoping they do a bit of male bonding.

'Yeah, I'll come home after work and we'll go over to the restaurant together. Lee's going to meet us there.'

I walk over and kiss him on the cheek.

'What's that in aid of?'

'Nothing. I just want you to remember I mean it. That's all.'

Meeting Sadie for lunch is pretty much the last thing I want to do right now. She'd texted me on Monday, asking if I fancied meeting up this week, and I hadn't had the heart to say no. Besides, I know I've got to tell her at some point. The last thing I'd want is for her to find out from someone else.

I walk into Pret. She'd said she didn't want to go anywhere fancy. I see her clock me straight away, although she does a double take.

'Hey,' I say, going over to her. 'How you doing?'

'I'm good. Have you seen Jess Mount at all? She appears to have gone AWOL.'

'Very funny.'

'Well what's with the get-up?'

'I can hardly turn up for work in leggings and DMs, can I?'

'Jeez, you'll be carrying a designer Tote bag next.'

'Nope. Still got my trusty backpack,' I say, patting it. 'There are some things that are non-negotiable.'

She continues staring at me incredulously.

'What do you want then?' I ask. 'I'm buying.'

'The whole works, in that case.'

'Seriously.'

'A warm wrap, a chocolate brownie and a hot chocolate, please. And I'll get them next time.'

I nod, grab the same things for me, pay for them and go back to the table. I try to unload the tray solely with my right hand. Sadie could have a wedding ring and a veil on and I wouldn't notice but she's always been much more observant than me.

'So, how's the job going?' she asks.

'Yeah. It's OK.'

'Only OK?'

'It'll take a bit of getting used to, that's all.'

'Are they all up-their-own-arses PR types?'

'I hope you're not including Lee in that.'

'You know what I mean.'

'They're a bit straight. They don't seem to have much of a laugh, but the job's a piece of piss, to be honest. I just have to stand there and smile a lot. And no one expects you to crawl on the floor to pick up popcorn.'

'I guess that's something.'

'Yeah. How're things at work?'

'Oh, you know. Same old, same old. How was the holiday?'

I wait until Sadie takes a big bite of her wrap before I reply. I want to have a few seconds of her being unable to speak before the onslaught begins.

'Great, thanks. And I've got some news. I wanted to tell you face-to-face.'

I hold out my left hand. She looks at the ring and back at me. She stops chewing for a moment. When she resumes, she does it very slowly. I think I would have preferred the onslaught straight away instead of having to wait for it.

'What the hell are you playing at?'

'I'm getting married.'

'Yeah, at twenty-two, to some guy you've only known a couple of months.'

'Jeez, you sound like my dad.'

'Well, it's not surprising, is it? I'd have thought everyone would say the same thing. Everyone who cares about you, anyway.'

'I knew you'd be like this.'

'Yeah, because you're doing something stupid. You're throwing your life away, Jess. And I'm not going to stand by and watch it happen without saying something.'

I put down my wrap. 'Have you quite finished?'

'I haven't even started yet.'

I glance around, aware that other people are looking at us.

'Look, I'm sorry for being happy. For getting a new boy-friend and a new job and leaving you in your old one.'

'You think I'm jealous?'

'Well, it sure looks like that from where I'm sitting.'

Sadie shakes her head. 'How do I get through to you, Jess? I am not jealous. You pulled a good-looking guy and I was really pleased for you. But this' – she gestures down towards the ring – 'this is crazy. Look at you! You've changed so much in a few months, I don't recognise you anymore. It's like you're just turning into whatever he wants you to be and you're so far gone on him you can't even see it.'

I look down, mainly to hide the tears welling in my eyes. 'After all the stuff I've been through, something good has finally happened to me, and you react like I've lost it again.'

'You can't see sense because you're so gone on Lee.'

'Why do you hate him so much?'

'I don't hate him. I just want you to wake up to what's happening.'

'You have no idea what he's like. He makes me feel like the most special person in the world. He loves me, Sadie. No one's ever loved me like he does.'

She shakes her head. 'If he really loved you, he wouldn't ask you to change.'

'He hasn't.'

'Oh right. And these new clothes and the new job and wearing fucking lipstick – they're nothing to do with him are they?'

The tears come now, I'm unable to stop them. For a moment, Sadie looks as if she is going to reach out for my hand, but then she thinks better of it.

'You've got to stop this,' I say. 'People are going to get hurt.'

'What are you on about?'

'If you can't be happy for me, you've got to butt out of my life. Because if you carry on like this you're going to end up spoiling things for everyone.'

'Fine,' she says, standing up, stuffing the food in her bag and picking up her hot chocolate. 'It'll be lunch on the go then. And consider me officially butted out.'

I fight back a fresh round of tears as I watch her go, and the realisation hits. It was me who drove her to do this. Me who made her so mad that she told the police my husband killed me.

Dad and I are sitting in the one decent restaurant in Mytholmroyd (if you exclude the chippy, which is seriously good). I would have preferred to go to Leeds but it's full of pissheads on a Friday night and I don't want anything to spoil this for Dad. I want everything about it to be positive. He has put a suit on for the occasion. He looks pretty good, actually. Well, for someone of his age, anyway. One of the good things about Italian genes is that you can carry off a receding hairline.

'So, did you catch up with Sadie today?' Dad asks, as we sip the table water.

'Yeah.'

'Am I right in thinking she didn't take it too well?'

LINDA GREEN | 217

'Bit of an understatement.'

'Come on, you've been best friends forever, Jess. It must be really tough for her.'

'I'd be happy for her if it was the other way around.'

'Would you? It would leave a massive hole in your life.'

'Well, I certainly wouldn't make her feel bad about it. She's like this seething mass of resentment.'

'She'll come round.'

'She doesn't,' I say, then catch myself. 'I mean, she won't. She's really got it in for Lee.'

'Why?'

'Because she blames him for taking me away from her. If she ever says anything against Lee, remember that.'

Dad puts his glass down. 'Why would she say anything against Lee?'

'Just remember, that's all I'm saying.'

Right on cue, the door opens and Lee walks in. I saw him only a few hours ago but I still get that feeling, like my insides are about to explode.

'Hi,' I say, standing up and smiling at him. He kisses me on the lips, just the right amount to be acceptable in front of family, but still enough to make me wish that Dad wasn't there.

'You're looking as gorgeous as ever,' he says, before turning to Dad. 'Good to see you again, Joe.'

Dad stands up and offers his hand. 'And you, Lee. Congratulations. You move quickly, I'll say that for you.'

'Thanks,' replies Lee. 'You've got a pretty amazing daughter.

I wasn't going to wait around until somebody else snapped her up.'

I watch as the approval-ometer on Dad's face moves up another notch. We all sit down again. It feels like Lee's charm has won the first bout. Dad appears to be on the verge of throwing the towel in. The waiter comes over to take our drinks order.

'I think a bottle of champagne is in order,' says Dad. Lee's charm offensive has won out. Dad is back onside, where I need him. The two men I love most in the world are going to be there for me, whatever the future holds.

Sadie Ward
01/10/2017 11:22pm

I met her yesterday – Lee's ex-girlfriend. Emma, her name is. Emma McKinley. Although you probably knew that. She's an actress. Not a dead famous one, she does soaps and extra parts on TV and touring theatre stuff. She was in *Emmerdale* for a while a few years ago. Not that either of us ever watched it. I probably shouldn't have met her, I know that. But I tracked her down online and got in touch after the police told me she'd given her statement.

She's very pretty. Or rather, she used to be. I googled her to see what she looked like when she was in *Emmerdale*. She looks very different now, of course. It's like someone sucked the air out of her, she's that gaunt. Not surprising really, when you consider what happened. He beat her, Jess. He beat her really badly. Not at the beginning. She said he was all sweetness and light at the beginning. But later, when they moved in together. It started with a slap. Just one slap. And he was dead sorry afterwards and promised her it would never happen again. But, of course, it did. Time and time again. And every time, she let him off because he was so upset by what he'd done. She thought she could help him to stop, to become a better person.

Until they went to Venice on holiday. He broke her jaw, Jess. He broke her fucking jaw. She never reported it – she was too embarrassed in case it ended up in the papers. But she did at least dump him afterwards. She moved back to London. That's where she lives now. And she didn't have any further contact with him. She didn't know he'd married or that you'd died until she came back to Leeds to visit and a friend told her. That's when she decided to go to the police. She's got photos, Jess. Photos of what he did to her. And records of her treatment in the hospital in Italy. There was a witness too, at the hotel where they were staying. A maid who came in just afterwards and saw the blood and everything.

And all the time she was telling me this, all I could think of was what he must have done to you. The times you didn't show up when you were supposed to and you said it was because you'd had a bad night with H. The time when you explained away a bruise as an accident. I thought about them all, Jess, and I cried big fat tears for you. For what he did to you and the way you must have suffered.

But we are not going to let him get away with it, Jess. Emma is prepared to go to court if necessary and so am I. The truth will come out. I just wish it had been in time to save you. X

JESS

No! Although I scream the word, I do it silently in my head. Which is fortunate, because I am in bed at Lee's and he is in the kitchen cooking a late breakfast.

My heart is hammering against my chest, as if trying to alert me of the impending danger. My eyes, when I see them reflected in the wardrobe mirrors, are wild and staring. My whole body is trembling. I do not want to believe this. I do not want my happiness spoilt. Whoever is doing this, and however they are doing it, they are doing it on purpose to hurt me. I know that.

But what I can't deny now is that they know stuff. Stuff that I don't even know yet. But stuff that, if I allow myself to consider it for a moment, makes perfect sense.

The waitress in the hotel in Venice. The one who dropped the tray. What if she did recognise Lee? What if she recognised him because she had seen him before, in the same room but with a different woman? One who was lying on the floor with blood on her face when she unexpectedly came into the room.

It seems too implausible to make up. That is what's unnerving me. I didn't tell anyone about her. No one apart from Lee and the waiter who cleared up know what happened. So how the hell am I reading about this in a post Sadie supposedly writes eighteen months from now?

I turn off my phone – completely off this time. I get up and put it in my backpack in the corner of the room. It is not a case of out of sight, out of mind, though. How can it be? How can you read something like that and simply forget about it?

Because if, for a moment, I accept that it is true, then I am engaged to a man who attacked his ex-girlfriend so violently he broke her jaw.

It can't be true. This is not happening to me. I have an amazing new life and I am not going to let anyone trample all over it by trying to scare the shit out of me.

I put my silk wrap on, the one Lee bought me in Venice, and walk through to the bathroom. The kitchen door is shut but I can hear the bacon sizzling in the pan and the radio in the background. Lee is singing along to the Kaiser Chiefs. I want to smile but the muscles in my mouth won't allow it.

I go into the bathroom and shut the door behind me. I refuse to be scared by this. I refuse to let them mess with my head. No one is going to screw with me.

I turn the shower on and take off my robe. I look at my body in the mirror. The smooth, unblemished skin. It is lies, all of it. I would know by now if he was like that. He has never even lost his temper with me. I have a shorter fuse than he does. One incident in a hotel room in Venice does not turn him into a wife murderer. He has never hurt me and I have never seen him hurt anyone else. That is what I need to stay focused on.

I step into the bath and shuffle behind the shower screen. It's slippery. He needs a bathmat really. But you don't suggest getting a bathmat to a man like Lee. He would just laugh and say I'll be buying knitted toilet-roll covers next.

I reach out and turn up the temperature. It needs to be hot today. Hot enough to take my mind off things. I shut my eyes and let the water hit my face, then begin to shampoo my hair. But all I can see is the face of the girl in the hotel room in Venice. Her look of shock and unmistakable fear. That is why she put the note in my case. Because she saw what happened to the woman before.

I realise I am shaking. I run through it one more time, the way Lee told it. Maybe he did look like her ex-boyfriend. Perhaps the fear in her eyes was to do with her ex. And the note? *Be careful.* Maybe she was simply warning me off getting serious. If she'd been treated badly, she might have a problem with all men. I felt like that after Callum dumped me. I could easily have screamed a warning at any woman who had gone anywhere near a man.

I turn off the shower and reach out for the towel. It is only then I realise I have left it on the back of the door. I step out of the bath with my hair over my eyes and reach for the towel – but touch Lee's shoulder instead. I jump and let out a gasp. I hadn't even heard the door open.

'Hey,' he says. 'It's only me. I was going to tell you that breakfast's ready, but now it'll have to wait.' He starts kissing my shoulders. 'When you go wedding dress shopping later,' he says, 'make sure you get an off-the-shoulder one. I want everyone to see what gorgeous shoulders you've got.'

His hands cup my breasts. He kisses me hard on the neck. I want him so badly. I want him to make me forget about everything I have just read. To be the Lee I know. The one who worships the ground I walk on. Who would never hurt me. Not in a million years. I let out a moan as his hand moves between my legs. My body wants this. My body wants him inside me. And there is no reason that my body would lie to me.

He takes his dressing gown off and pushes me back against the tiles. I bite down on my lip as he slips inside me. And I let him fuck me up against the bathroom wall. Fuck me so hard that for a few moments I can barely remember what my name is, let alone what I just read.

I walk into the city centre to meet Angela later. My brain is still aching, my body still tingling, like they have had a fight with each other and won't let it go.

Angela has arranged this, made appointments with all the bridal shops. She told me that all I had to do was turn up. Normally, I'd hate having other people telling me what to do and where to go. Today, I'm quite relieved. I'm not sure I'm capable of organising a trip to the toilet at the moment, let alone an entire wedding.

I arrive outside the first bridal shop on the list. It looks a bit traditional for my liking. Angela waves at me through the window. I manage to assemble a smile and what I hope is something at least bordering on excitement as I enter the shop. She rushes over and kisses me. It is apparent that she can barely contain herself.

'Hi, Jess. Oh, they've got some lovely dresses here. I couldn't resist having a quick look while I was waiting. I've seen at least three which Lee would love already.'

A tall woman wearing a shift dress comes over to us. 'Hello, I'm Julia. And you must be Jess – or, rather, the future Mrs Griffiths.'

If Sadie were here she would probably punch her. To be fair, she'd be quite entitled to. I resist the temptation and nod politely instead.

'And how lovely to come shopping with your future mother-in-law. I'm sure you'll be able to find something your fiancé will absolutely adore.'

Everyone seems particularly keen that Lee likes the dress – less so that I do.

'Right,' she continues. 'Let's go through a few basics to narrow things down. White or ivory?'

I am tempted to say red, but I don't think for a minute that she would appreciate my sense of humour.

'White would be lovely,' says Angela.

'Actually, I was thinking ivory,' I say.

Julia looks between the two of us but Angela offers no resistance.

'Right. And have we got a particular style in mind?' Julia asks.

The fact is I could describe the dress I will wear to marry Lee in minute detail. I have seen it. I know every inch of it because I have looked at it so many times on my timeline. But I can't possibly tell her that.

'I'll know it when I see it,' I say.

'Well, that's good to hear,' Julia replies.

'I think we're looking for timeless and classy,' says Angela. 'Think Grace Kelly and you won't go far wrong.'

'But off the shoulder,' I add, remembering what Lee said. 'I'd like it to be off the shoulder.'

Julia smiles. 'Lovely. Let me go and see what I can find. I'll be back in a moment.'

'This feels really weird,' I say to Angela as we wait. 'I can't believe I'm about to try on a wedding dress. What if I don't suit wedding dresses?'

'I wouldn't worry. You'd look gorgeous in a bin bag.'

'Do they do them in ivory?' I ask.

Angela laughs. 'I'm so glad our Lee is marrying a girl with a sense of humour. Between you and me, his last girlfriend seemed to have lost hers. If she ever had one, that is.'

Everything clenches inside me. I do my best to keep my face neutral. 'Did he go out with her for long?'

'About a year. I thought she was going to be the one at the time. Though I can't say I was keen. She was an actress. I'm not sure she was the settling-down type. And Lee wants a family. He's quite definite about that.'

I nod and fiddle with my engagement ring, trying desperately to stop my hands from shaking.

'Is that why they split up then?' I ask.

She looks down at her hands. 'I imagine so. It was certainly our Lee's decision. He came back from a holiday they'd taken together and said he'd ended it. I never saw her again. Not even on the TV. Emma Mc-something, her name was. I'd know her if I saw her. Pretty enough – long red hair. Not a patch on you, mind.'

I feel as if I might throw up. Julia returns with an armful of dresses, but I don't want to do this anymore. I want to run away and lock myself in somewhere and sing 'La, la, la!' very loudly as I clap my hands over my ears.

'Here we go,' Julia says. 'How about we start with this one?'

She holds one of them up. It has a satin bodice and a fishtail skirt. I am not really looking at it. I am staring at the one behind. The dress I marry Lee in. I feel as if the four walls are closing in on me. I can't escape now, even if I decide that I want to. Unless . . . unless I change things. Mix them up a little bit. Maybe if I don't wear that dress I can change what happens. It might be like the film *Sliding Doors,* only instead of which tube train I get on, it is which dress I wear that will decide my future.

'Yes,' I say, taking the dress with the fishtail skirt from her. 'I love it. I'll go and try it on.'

Julia hovers outside the changing room and pokes her head around the curtain a couple of times. 'Are you OK in here? Let me know if you need a hand.'

I let her come in to do up the clasps at the back of the bodice. She thinks it's because it's awkward to get to them, but actually it's because my hands are shaking too much. I step out of the changing room and look at my reflection in the mirror. I look completely different to my wedding photo. And I could wear my hair long, maybe curl it a little?

'I love it,' I say, turning around.

'You don't think it's a little too revealing, do you?' asks Angela, eyeing the bodice. I look up to see she is asking Julia, not me.

'If you've got a fantastic figure, you may as well show it off,' says Julia. 'Especially if it's your wedding day.'

'Right. Well, that's me sorted,' I say.

'But aren't you going to try anything else?' Angela appears horrified. Clearly this dress is well wide of the Grace Kelly mark.

'I don't need to. I love it.'

'It is useful to compare styles,' says Julia. 'You never know, you might find something you like even better than that one. Maybe try two more?' I suspect she has a degree in mother-and-daughter bridal dress negotiations.

'OK,' I say, deciding it will probably be the easiest way of placating Angela. 'I'll try the one with the full skirt.'

'The taffeta, yes,' replies Julia, holding it up.

'And this one,' says Angela, taking hold of the real wedding dress. 'I think you'd look gorgeous in this one.'

I may as well do it to keep her happy. It doesn't really matter because I am not going to change my mind. I follow

Julia back into the changing room. I try the taffeta one first. I actually laugh when I see myself in the mirror. I look like an oversized fairy with an attitude problem.

'Maybe not,' says Julia.

'Definitely not,' I reply.

I try not to look while I am putting on the other dress. I'm simply doing it to placate Angela. I will get it on and off as quickly as possible and buy the first dress I tried on.

It is only when I step outside and see the look on Angela and Julia's faces that I realise it might not be so easy.

'Oh, Jess,' says Angela. 'You look absolutely beautiful.'

'That lace top does look adorable on you,' says Julia.

'I still prefer the first one,' I say.

'I do think this one is more demure,' says Angela. 'I'm sure Lee would love it – and your father, too.'

It's a low-down trick, but I'm not going to fall for it. Dad will be happy whatever I wear. As long as I'm happy, that's what he always says.

'Thank you. It is nice, but I definitely prefer the first one. I said I'd know it when I see it and I did.'

Julia glances at Angela, like an auctioneer checking if there is going to be a final bid. There isn't though, only a shrug of resignation.

'Right,' says Julia. 'I do believe we are sorted – and in record time too.'

I go to the changing room and take off the dress, hoping I am shedding not just the outfit but everything that came with it. Freeing myself to map out a new future – one where

I can shape the ending, can take back some sort of control of my life.

Angela takes me to a cafe further along the arcade afterwards. We order coffee and cake and sit down at a table by the window.

She gets her mobile phone out of her bag; I get the impression she is still pissed off with me. 'I'm just going to ring the other bridal shops to let them know we shan't be needing them.'

But before she can make a call her phone rings.

'Hello, Julia,' she says, a note of surprise in her voice. She is quiet, listening intently and offering the occasional 'I see'. I'm straining to make out what is being said on the other end of the line, but I can't hear it above the din of the coffee shop.

'I'll ask her,' Angela says, after a while. 'I'll give you a call back to let you know one way or the other. No – no worries. These things happen.'

She puts the phone down and looks at me. 'That was Julia,' she says. 'The dress you chose was actually bought by someone else this morning. Her assistant should have put a reserved tag on it but she forgot. She's new, you see, and it was very busy. Anyway, Julia rang the company but unfortunately it's out of stock and they won't be getting any more in till August at the earliest. She was very apologetic and she said she'd give us a ten per cent discount on the other one you tried on – if you'd like it, that is. We can go to the other shops if not. It's up to you.'

I look down at my hands, which are shaking beneath the table. It doesn't matter what I do; I can't change anything. However hard I try, I will be thwarted somewhere along the line. Resistance is futile. I may as well accept my fate.

'I'll take the other one then,' I say quietly.

'Are you sure?' It's almost as if she feels sorry for me now that she's got what she wanted. Almost. For all I know she cooked this up with Julia while I was getting changed. It doesn't matter how it happened, though. Not really. All that matters is that it did.

'Yeah,' I reply.

'I'll ring Julia right back and let her know.'

I listen to Angela's end of the conversation, trying hard to blink back the tears.

'For what it's worth,' says Angela, when she's finished the call, 'I think that's worked out for the best. That dress was perfect for you, Jess. Absolutely perfect. It must be fate, eh?'

I nod and take a sip of my coffee.

'Now, before I put my phone away, you must help me find you on Facebook so we can become friends. All we need to do then is try to persuade our Lee to join. You're a better woman than me if you manage it, mind.'

I try to say something in response but am unable to form any words. I take a bite of the chocolate brownie she has bought for me instead. I no longer know if I am able to control my own future or if all I can do is go along with it. I'm beginning to feel like a passenger in my own life, and I'm not sure I can stop the train and get off, even if I want to.

Angela Griffiths ▸ Jess Mount
3 October 2017

I know it's daft to think you can see this, but I wanted to show you the latest photo. He's nearly six months old now, our Harrison. Looking more like his father every day too. He's even trying to crawl, doing a sort of commando-style thing on his elbows and dragging his legs after him. He doesn't want to be still, you see. Always likes to be on the move. I'm going to have my work cut out once he's walking, I can see that. It won't be long, either. He'll be an early walker like our Lee was. Determined, see. And chunky thighs too.

Anyway, he's happy as Larry. He misses you, obviously. But it's such a blessing that he's too young to actually remember you or to properly understand what happened. We will show him photos as he gets older, of course. And tell him all about you. You may be gone but you will not be forgotten. And you have left me with the most precious gift of all. My first grandchild.

JESS

Sunday, 3 April 2016

I am back home when I see it. I usually stay at Lee's on Sunday nights but I made my excuses when we left Angela's after lunch and said I would come home to see Dad and get an early night.

And now there is no chance of any sleep at all. My son is staring back at me from the computer screen. He has the most gorgeous big brown eyes and little dimples. And Angela is right – he does look like Lee. So much so that I can't see any of me in him at all. I wonder for a second if he is actually my child, but deep down I know he is. It's weird – I give birth to this baby and yet he is a complete stranger to me.

I reach out and touch the screen. For a moment I think I see his smile broaden and hear him gurgle back at me. I wonder if it would be possible to print out the photo. I suspect not, but it is worth a go. I save it to my pictures folder, but when I go there to find it, there's nothing there. I can't even have a photo of him. One single, lousy photo for his mother to keep.

I wish I had one of those 3D printers. Maybe that would work and I could somehow print him out whole. Have him appear on the floor in front of me, laughing and crawling around and smelling of whatever it is babies smell of, a mixture of poo and vomit and milk, I suppose.

As it is, I will just have to bide my time. Because I will get to meet him. In a few months' time he will be growing inside of me. And I will feel him kick, just like other mothers do with their babies. And I will get to give birth to him and hold him and feed him and all the other stuff new mums do.

The only difference will be that I'll be saying goodbye to him very soon afterwards.

And the saddest thing, the thing I am really struggling with, is that he will never remember our short time together. At least when Mum died I had fifteen years of memories and happy times to cling on to. He will have nothing. Although perhaps, as Angela said, that will make it easier for him. I hope so. It is a horrible thing to hope for, though. That your son will be able to cope better with your death because he doesn't remember anything about you at all.

'I love you,' I whisper to him. And I know at that moment that I do. And that I must stick by Lee whatever happens, because without Lee there will be no Harrison. And I don't think I could bear that, I really don't.

I am not going to read any more of these posts and messages. I mean it this time. I will stay away from Facebook. I will not let it get the better of me.

I smile again at H. 'Night, night,' I say. 'I'm not going to look at you for a while, but it doesn't mean I won't be thinking about you.' I kiss the screen, shutting my eyes and imagining one day kissing him for real.

My phone rings the next morning while I'm waiting for the train. I pick it up and am surprised to see Sadie's name on the screen. I wonder whether to answer it or not, but pick it up on the next ring.

'Hi,' I say. 'Bit early for you, isn't it?'

'I got up especially early to tell you what an arsehole I am.'

'What do you mean?'

'The other day, at Pret. I behaved like a real jerk.'

I don't say anything for a moment. I am stunned, to be honest. I thought I had lost her, I really did. I did not expect to be given another chance.

'And I should have realised how hard it would be for you,' I say, my voice quivering.

'I wasn't expecting it, that's all. I mean, no one gets married nowadays, do they? If you'd said you were moving in with him, I would have half expected that. Given the choice of a tiny bedroom in a terraced house in Mytholmroyd or a swanky apartment in Leeds, I know which one I'd take.'

'I'm not marrying him for his flat. I really do love him, you know.'

'I get that. I just don't want you turning into a middle-aged housewife on me, that's all. If you're not careful, you'll be smelling of baby sick and complaining about sleepless nights before you know it.'

I have to hold the phone away from me while I take a couple of deep breaths. She doesn't know what she's saying, I understand that, but I am beginning to see how fraught this relationship is going to be, if it does survive.

'Listen, I can't talk long,' I say. 'My train's due in a minute.'

'Are you not at his place?'

'No. I came home to see Dad. I was pretty knackered, to be honest. I went wedding dress shopping with Lee's mum at the weekend.'

'Oh wow. That really is serious. Did you get one?'

'Yep.'

'Would I like it?'

'It's not black and it doesn't involve leather, if that's what you mean. And before you ask, no, I will not be wearing my DMs underneath.'

'Shame. Would have been a good look.'

'I don't think Lee's mum would approve.'

'Does she approve of you?'

'I guess so. We're friends on Facebook now, anyway.'

'I'd better be careful what I tag you in then. Don't want you getting into trouble with your mother-in-law.'

My train pulls into the platform.

'Anyway. I've got to go,' I say.

'Look, how about we try that lunch again this week? Only I'm paying this time, to make up for being such an eejit.'

I hesitate, unsure whether it's a good thing to start this up again, bearing in mind what I was reading last night. But I have already decided not to read it anymore. And maybe it would be a good idea to get her onside again. Maybe if I make her see what Lee is really like, it'll stop her doing all the shit stirring later.

'You're on. Just let me know when.'

I feel it as soon as I wake up on Wednesday morning. It is the same every year. The ache. The hurt. The pain. People are lying when they say that time heals. It doesn't. It means you have more days in between where the pain is numbed and you aren't conscious of it all of the time, but every year, on the anniversary of her death, it's like the anaesthetic wears off and you realise that the wound is still there, as deep and painful as ever, and you have just been masking it all year in order to get by. And the whole day just becomes one long, silent scream while you wait for it to pass and for the anaesthetic to kick in again.

I dress quickly and go downstairs. Dad looks up as I enter. He has been crying already, I can tell. I go over and hug him. We don't need any words. Just the comfort of knowing we are both feeling it as bad as each other. After a while, he takes my head in his hands and kisses me on the forehead.

'It doesn't get any easier, does it?' he says.

'No.'

'Do you want any breakfast or shall we just go?'

'Let's go.'

We get in Dad's car and make the ten-minute journey in silence. All I can think of on the way is Dad doing this same journey with his spade in the boot. Of how desperate he must have been to try to dig me up.

I fiddle with the stems of the daffodils I have in my lap. Daffodils were Mum's favourite flower. Actually, I don't know if that was true or she simply said it because I always gave her daffodils on Mother's Day. I wonder what flowers Harrison will bring for me when he is old enough. I don't have a favourite flower. I guess I need to pick one, tell Dad and Lee what it is. Anything to make it easier for them.

As cemeteries go, it's a nice one. There's a gorgeous view over Luddenden Valley – a few chimneys from the old mills and fields and trees and little winding lanes with dry-stone walls. It's peaceful, too. We used to walk up here as a family when I was little. Me complaining about my legs being tired, even back then.

I follow Dad over to the far corner where the newer graves are. The trees behind them screen us off from the church beyond. There are a few splashes of colour around – flowers wrapped in cellophane with handwritten messages in wobbly writing.

Mum's grave is in the corner. Dad got a family plot. He told me it meant that we would all be back together one day. That Mum would be waiting for us. But I know from his post that it is me who is buried here first. It is our two graves that he sits between and where he sobs.

I watch as he lays his single red rose down. His hand is shaking, his bottom lip trembling. I go over and squeeze his hand, lay my flowers down next to his. But as I do so, the noise that has been brewing deep inside me comes out, like something primeval. I sink to my knees and gasp the air back in to fill the hole it has left inside. Dad crouches down next to me, grabbing my arm.

'It's OK,' he says.

'It's not. It's not going to be OK. Not for you. Not for either of us.'

'Jess, come on. We've made it this far. We can do this together.'

I shake my head and start scrabbling at the earth with my hands.

Dad tries to pull my hands away, to haul me up to my feet. 'Jess, stop it, please.'

'I can't,' I shout. 'I can't stop any of it. It's all going to happen anyway, whatever I do.'

'Come on, you're not making sense. We need to get you home.'

I realise he is going to think I am ill. That it is starting again. I take my fingers out of the earth and look at them, bring them closer to me and sniff the soil in case I can get a faint trace of Mum.

Dad's hands reach under my arms and he hauls me to my feet. My legs are still shaking. I cling on to him, not daring to let go.

'When I die, you'll bury me here,' I say. 'Next to Mum.'

Dad wipes the tears from his face. 'No, you'll bury me here. But there's a space for you too, when the time comes.'

'What about Lee?'

'I don't know if there's enough space. Maybe I can ring up and ask, if it bothers you.'

'And any children we have,' I say. 'I want them to be here too.'

Dad nods. 'Let's not worry about it now, eh? We've got a wedding to look forward to.'

He is gripping my shoulders hard. I can sense the worry in his fingers. I nod back at him.

'Do you need to see someone, Jess? Are things troubling you?'

I hesitate. I wish I could tell him, but I can't. He will only worry. And I'll get put away again and the wedding won't happen. And if the wedding doesn't happen, Harrison won't exist and I couldn't bear that. I couldn't bear to not have my baby boy.

'No. I'm fine. But I want you to know that my favourite flowers are daffodils too.'

JESS

August 2008

I stand with Sadie on the platform, waiting for the train to come in. Stations are very difficult for me now. I think about the people who throw themselves in front of trains. I don't think about doing it myself – I have never thought about that – but I do wonder what they might be thinking about just before they do it. What it feels like, the moment they step off the platform, the moment when they hit the track or the train hits them, whichever happens first.

I think about other people too. The people on the trains that crash. Whether anyone ever actually manages to break the safety glass. Whether it's better to be in an aisle or a window seat. What would happen to the person who was in the loo at the time?

The train is coming in. My fingers curl up. I dig my nails into my palms. I can do this, I can. I count the carriages but there are only two, which means I can't get in the middle carriage. I don't like being in the end ones. You are much more likely to die in a crash if you are in the end ones. Sadie reaches out and presses the button, and the doors hiss back. I can see her looking at me, looking and waiting.

'Come on,' she says. 'Let's see if we can grab a seat.'

I force my legs to move, to follow her onto the train. But once I do, they seize up completely. There are only two seats together in the carriage. They are the two nearest the driver's cab. Sadie has already got the window seat; she is looking at me, a frown creasing her brow.

I shake my head. It is all I can do.

She picks up her bag and comes over to me. 'What is it? What's the matter?'

I can't tell her the real reason – that I don't want to sit there in case there's a train crash. I can't explain that you are statistically more likely to die in a train crash if you are sitting at the front of the train. People don't think about it. They just hear that three people died in a train crash. They might know that one was the driver, but they don't ask where the other two were sitting. People don't ask because they don't want to know. They want to be blissfully ignorant.

I look at Sadie. She is still waiting for an answer. I move my mouth but no words come out.

'Would you rather stand?' she asks.

I nod. She gives a little shrug and grabs hold of the rail as the train sets off. I can see it in her eyes though. She has crossed to the other side. She is one of them now. She thinks I am cracking up.

PART THREE

ANGELA

I get to the bridal shop for the final fitting before Jess. She is not as punctual as Lee and me, I've noticed. But if that is her worst fault, it's not such a bad one. I get my to-do list out of my handbag and start to go through it. As fast as I cross one thing off, it seems there is another one to add. Not that I am complaining. It has been lovely to be so involved in the wedding. Some of my friends felt completely shut out when their sons got married. I suppose, in a way, I am the mother of the bride and the groom for this wedding. That is certainly what it feels like.

At least it's been a fairly smooth process so far. There have only been one or two sticking points since the whole business with the dress. Jess was adamant that she didn't want any bridesmaids, and I accepted that, even though the hotel was prepared to be incredibly accommodating about matching the colour of the napkins to the bridesmaids' dresses.

And she did insist that her father be allowed to organise

the menu with the hotel's chef, even though I'd have been perfectly capable of doing it.

I look up as the doorbell tinkles and Jess rushes in.

'Hi, Angela. Sorry to keep you.'

Her hair is still damp at the ends, as if she has just got out of the shower.

'That's OK. I'm just glad you didn't go for a morning wedding.'

'I'm always so knackered at the end of the week. I don't think my body clock's got used to the early starts yet.'

'Well, only one more week to go and then you can spend a fortnight in bed if you want to.'

She flushes slightly. I do too, when I realise what I've said. It's not something you like to think about – your son's sexual appetite. Though I should imagine it is quite a healthy one.

'And here's the bride-to-be!' says Julia, bursting through from the back of the shop. 'How are we this morning?'

'Fine, thanks,' Jess replies. She is not as excited as I thought she would be by now. Maybe a touch of last-minute nerves? It's hardly surprising, really, especially without her mother around to support her.

'Right, let's go through,' says Julia, beckoning her towards the changing rooms. 'We've got the dress ready for you. And if any minor adjustments are needed, we can still get them done in plenty of time for the big day.'

Jess nods and disappears into the changing rooms with Julia. I take my phone out and scroll down my Facebook page.

Jess hasn't put anything on about the wedding preparations. I asked her about it once – I wondered if it might be because she was superstitious – but she just said she didn't really go on Facebook anymore. I had a look through her timeline when we became friends. There were quite a lot of posts from last year – all those silly selfies with pouting lips that the girls do. Lots of things she was tagged in by her friend Sadie, the one who's going to be her witness. But it all seemed to stop around the point she started going out with Lee. I guess she hasn't had so much time on her hands, and I know he doesn't like people being on their phones when he's with them. It was the one thing about Emma that used to really wind him up. It was the only time I ever heard him snap at her, when he caught her on the phone.

The curtain of the changing room is drawn back and Jess steps out. I actually gasp when I see her, she looks that beautiful. The dress fits perfectly – she could have been sewn into it. And she really does have such pretty shoulders.

'Oh, Jess,' I say. 'You look absolutely wonderful. I'm so glad you ended up with that one in the end.'

She manages a little smile. It is one of the things I like best about her, that she appears to have no idea how attractive she actually is. I never got that impression with Emma. But then I don't suppose you end up as an actress if you're low on self-confidence.

Julia fusses about her for a moment or two, tweaking the sash and adjusting the skirt, before standing back and sighing.

'I have to agree with Angela. It really is perfect for you.

And once you have your hair up, the tiara will top things off beautifully.'

The tiara had been Julia's idea. Jess had gone along with it, though with what appeared to be an air of resignation.

'And we're doing a hair and make-up practice on Wednesday with the stylist you recommended,' I tell her.

'Goodness, won't you look a treat. You have one very lucky young man.' Julia smiles.

'Oh, don't worry, he knows it,' I say. 'And I shan't let him forget it. It's the first rule of being a mother-in-law, make sure your son treats his wife as you would want to be treated.'

I look down and shuffle my feet, aware that my own words are making me feel uncomfortable.

'Can I take it off now?' asks Jess.

'Yes, that's fine. Let me come and give you a hand.'

Julia reappears from the changing room after a couple of minutes and comes up to me. 'I think she could do with some quality ivory stockings,' she whispers. 'I did ask her to bring some for today but she appears to have forgotten.'

'Thank you,' I say. 'Leave it with me.' I get out my piece of paper and add it to the list. I will take her to the lingerie section of one of the department stores afterwards. The poor girl probably isn't thinking straight at the moment.

She emerges from the changing rooms, still looking in a bit of a daze.

'You're in no rush to get back, are you?' I ask.

She shakes her head. 'Lee has gone on his stag weekend.

He's flying to Dublin about now. I did ask Jess if she wanted me to organise a hen weekend for her but she didn't seem keen. Said she'd probably just go for a night out with Sadie.

'Right. Well, let me take you for elevenses and then we'll pop into the shops and get a few last-minute bits. I've told Julia we'll pick up the dress on the way back.'

'OK,' she says.

We go to the same cafe as last time and she orders a chocolate brownie and a hot chocolate again.

'I do wish you'd tell me your secret, Jess,' I say as she tucks in. 'I'd only have to look at that and I'd put on a couple of pounds. You must be burning it off with lots of nervous energy or something.'

She looks down at her hands. I can't help feeling she's a bit tense today.

'Are you OK, love? A bit of pre-wedding nerves creeping in?'

She shrugs. 'I guess so. I can't quite believe I'm getting married next week.'

'Well, that's understandable. As long as it's just that and nothing Lee's said or done.'

She looks up, her eyes boring into me. It's the first time she has made me feel uncomfortable. It is almost as if she suspects me of holding something back.

'He's a good man, Jess. He'll take good care of you.'

She fiddles with her ring and looks out of the window, blinking hard.

'Is your dad looking forward to it?' I ask.

'Yeah. Though it'll be tough for him afterwards, being on his own and that.'

'He'll be fine. I found it hard when Lee flew the nest, but you get used to it. And it's not like you'll be far away. And you never know, it might not be long before he's got a new addition to the family to welcome.'

She puts her mug down with a clatter on the table and stares at me.

It suddenly occurs to me that the reason she's so quiet might be because she's keeping something to herself.

'You're not . . . I mean, there's nothing you need to tell me?'

'No. No, of course not.'

'That's fine, just thought I'd better check. It wouldn't have been a problem, of course. Not for me, anyway. And I'm sure not for Lee, either. You know how keen he is to start a family.'

She looks down again, shifts a little in her seat.

'And when the time comes,' I continue, 'I don't want you worrying about having to cope on your own. I'll be round every day to give you a hand. All those sleepless nights can take their toll, you know. I'll do the washing or take the baby out for a walk, whatever I can to give you a break.'

Jess gets to her feet. 'Excuse me,' she mumbles, before hurrying off towards the ladies. I hadn't expected her to be like this. She's never struck me as the sensitive kind. I expect it's simply the pressure of the whole thing getting to her. I wonder if I should go after her, but think better of it. I really don't know her well enough for that.

I drink my coffee and get out my phone. I send a text to Lee.

Jess looks a treat in the dress. Have a good time and behave yourself! X

He will do. He knows where to draw the line. He won't spoil anything now. And it's not like he's gone with a big group of young lads. Only three of them from work, and the others are all older than him. I daresay there'll be a fair few pints of Guinness downed but nothing worse than that.

Jess comes back out after a few minutes. She looks like she's been crying.

'I'm sorry,' I say as she sits down. 'There's you with the jitters about next Saturday and I'm going on about babies and the like. I must sound like I'm wishing your life away.'

She looks up at me with wide, staring eyes. 'I think I'm going to catch the train home,' she says after a moment. 'I'm not feeling too good.'

'What about the dress?'

'Would you mind collecting it and taking it home with you in the car? I'll get it from you at the rehearsal on Thursday. It'll be easier than taking it on the train anyway.'

'Yes. Yes, of course. No trouble at all. Are you sure you're feeling well enough to walk? I can drop you off at the station, if you like.'

'I'm fine, thanks,' she says, putting on her jacket and picking up her backpack. 'I think the fresh air will do me good.'

I hang the dress up on the outside of the wardrobe in the spare room when I get home. It is nice to have it in the house, actually. Makes the whole thing seem real. I've managed to keep myself busy with all the arrangements, but most of it has been done online or over the phone. Now I've got the dress here, it feels like it's actually happening. I put my hand inside the plastic cover and stroke the skirt, remembering the excitement I felt on my big day. How I was so full of hopes and dreams for the future. And trying not to think about what came afterwards.

I sigh. At least it won't be long now. Lee will waste no time at all once they're married. And she's so young, she'll probably get pregnant straight away – it's not like she's one of these women in her thirties with her eggs dwindling by the day.

I kneel down next to the bed and pull open the bottom drawer. It is rather more crowded than it was. Since they announced the engagement I haven't seen any reason to hold back.

I take out the little cream and beige sleeping bag. Apparently, no one bothers with cot blankets anymore. I got three of them, identical. I'm sure there'll be plenty of nights when the baby will be sleeping here and I want to make sure I have everything ready for grandma duty. I shall be one of those hands-on grandmothers. That's the beauty of living so close to them. I can pop by any time and take the baby off her hands for a while, give her a well-deserved break. And they can have date nights, like couples do these days, without having to worry about waking the baby when they get home. I'll get the crib later, once the pregnancy has been confirmed. Just in case she's a bit funny about things like that. I wouldn't want her seeing it and feeling under any pressure.

And the good thing about her not having a mother around is that there won't be any interfering from her family's end. I mean, her father's hardly going to want to be knee-deep in nappies, is he?

No. My first grandchild really will be all my own. He or she will want for nothing. And, once it is here, I will want for nothing either. It will be a happy family home, like it once was, a long time ago. Before he tore the whole thing apart.

JESS

Saturday, 2 July 2016

Sadie is organising the hen night. I wasn't going to bother with one, but when I told her Lee was going away for a stag weekend she insisted. I agreed on one condition: that it was just me and her. And definitely no Angela.

The invitation, which she'd emailed, had simply said to arrive at hers at 7.30 p.m. – 'dressed to impress' and with an overnight bag.

It feels weird, walking round to Sadie's house, like I've regressed to being fourteen again. Jessadie is back, although probably for one night only. I ring the doorbell and, shortly afterwards, hear footsteps charging down the stairs. Her mum always used to call her a fairy elephant. In an affectionate way, of course.

Sadie throws open the door, wearing what appears to be a chicken onesie.

'Sadie!' I say. 'Here I am on time for once and you're not even dressed.'

'Ahh, that's where you're wrong. This is what I'm wearing.'

'Very funny. Can I remind you it said "dress to impress".'

'That was a decoy. Believe me, I am dressed entirely appropriately.'

'For what?'

'Come upstairs and I'll show you.'

I follow her upstairs, feeling a bit pissed off that I have gone to the trouble of getting done up for no reason. She opens the door of her bedroom. Inside there is a pile of pillows and cushions spread over her bed and the floor. The curtains are drawn and the lamps are on. On the bedside table is the biggest supply of popcorn and chocolate I have ever seen, with a bottle of wine and two glasses. And in front of the curtains is a giant projector screen, linked to a laptop.

I turn to look at Sadie and grin. 'Our own private cinema.'

'Yep,' she said. 'Just what you always wanted.'

She is right, as well. We used to talk about it all the time, searching Rightmove for houses with a home cinema.

'It's brilliant,' I say, my voice catching. 'Thank you.'

'Well. I couldn't run to hiring the screen at work as the tight bastards wouldn't give me much of a discount, so this was the next best thing. One of Dad's friends lent me the screen. You'll need to get changed, of course. Here.'

She hands me a large gift bag. Inside is a chicken onesie just like hers.

'Have a look at the back,' she says.

I do as I am told. It says 'Jess's hen night, July 2016'. Underneath there is a big heart with 'J. M. loves L. G.', with stupid arrows through it, like we used to do on our pencil cases at school. She got that done. Despite how she feels about Lee, she did it for me. I feel such a cow for hating her future self. I go over and give her a hug.

'Thank you. It's perfect. All of it.'

'Good. I figured it was our last chance to have a proper girls' night in. You're sleeping over as well. We've got a fair few films to get through.'

She points towards the pile of DVDs on the floor. I can see at least two *Harry Potters* and *Pretty Woman* in there. 'Starting with this one,' she says, holding up a copy of *Chicken Run*.

'Oh my god, I love Ginger the chicken.'

'Yep, perfect hen night material. And we've got a pizza delivery coming soon. Plus, I promise not to make you scramble on the floor to clean up the popcorn afterwards.'

I grin and give her another hug.

'I'm going to miss you so much,' she says.

I swallow hard. She has no idea just how much she will miss me.

'Hey, I'm only getting married, not emigrating.'

'I know. But it won't be the same, will it? I already miss you at work and on the train. Now I'm going to see you even less with you living in Leeds.'

'We can still meet up at lunchtimes.'

'I know. But like I said, it won't be the same.'

I get changed into my onesie while Sadie gets the first DVD set up.

'Fucking hell,' she says, when she turns to see me.

'What?'

'You even manage to look sexy in a chicken onesie. I really do hate you.'

'Maybe I should take it on honeymoon.'

'Ew,' she says, screwing her face up.

'What now?'

'You going on honeymoon. That sounds even weirder than you getting married.'

I shrug. 'I guess it's been a weird year.'

Sadie looks sideways at me as we plonk ourselves down on the bed and the opening credits of *Chicken Run* come on. 'Did you ever see any more of those Facebook posts?' she asks.

I notice she says 'see', as if it was something that only existed inside my head.

'I haven't been on Facebook for ages,' I reply.

She passes me the popcorn.

'I was worried for a bit,' she says. 'I thought the whole thing might be starting up again.'

'It just threw me, that's all.'

'You do know that can't happen? That people can't send posts from the future.'

She is testing me. Trying to work out my state of mind without directly accusing me of anything. I take another handful of popcorn and watch Ginger's latest escape bid from the chicken farm being thwarted before I answer.

'Yeah, course I do.'

'So you have all the time in the world to get married if you really want to. You don't have to rush into anything.'

'What is this? The is-my-friend-mentally-unstable questionnaire? Only I think you might have missed out number five.'

'Hey, come on. I'm just looking out for you.'

'Well you don't need to, OK? I'm fine. I know what I'm doing.'

It's not true, of course. I have no fucking idea what I'm doing anymore. All I know is that I have to go through with it, for H's sake.

It is later, much later, when the pizza has been and gone and we are one *Harry Potter* film down and halfway through *Pretty Woman*, that Sadie turns to me and says, 'You were right, you know. I was jealous. Just a little bit. I always knew you were Vivian and I was Kit, but I guess I never thought Edward would actually come along until Lee asked you out.'

'You're way better than Kit.'

'I like Kit.'

'I know. I do too. But you're still way better than her. She may have had potential but you're the real article.'

'Just tell me Lee's not turning up in a white limo on Saturday and shimmying up the drainpipe to get you.'

I smile and shake my head.

'And tell him he'd better look after you properly because he'll have me to answer to if he doesn't. He has no idea how mad I will get if he ever hurts you.'

I throw my arms around her, tears streaming down my face. He may not, but I certainly do.

*

The hotel looks even bigger than I remembered. To be honest, I don't really see why we need a rehearsal. You don't rehearse for any of life's other big events, do you? Your death, for instance. What's so important about your wedding day that it must go precisely to plan? Surely it's what happens afterwards that's more important?

Anyway, Angela said we had to do it. Like Angela said the hotel was ideally situated between Leeds and the airport. And that the rooms were tastefully decorated and spacious. Personally, I think Angela might have swallowed the hotel website whole, but who am I to question her?

'Wow, impressive,' remarks Dad as we get out of the car.

'Yeah,' I reply. 'I guess it is.'

'Don't you like it?' he asks.

'I'd have been happy with the registry office, to be honest.'

'So why did you agree to it?'

'I didn't. She'd already booked it when she first showed me.'

Dad sighs and makes a face. 'You can say no to her, you know.'

'I have done, on quite a few things. This just wasn't one I was bothered enough to argue about.'

We walk past the tree with the twisty stump that's in the background of the wedding photograph on Facebook. I recognised it the first time we came here. It was too late then to do anything about it; Lee had already paid the deposit. And bearing in mind what happened with the dress, I suspected that if I had gone out and booked a new venue, it would have burnt down overnight.

Lee and Angela are already in the hotel reception. Angela has a notebook and pen in her hand. Lee comes over and kisses me, and I think of Harrison as he does so. Think of what an amazing father Lee is going to be to him.

'Good to see you again, Joe,' Lee says, shaking Dad's hand. 'I've just been reading your menu. Sounds amazing.'

'Thanks. Let's hope it tastes great,' says Dad. 'Otherwise there will be words.'

'Are you the Gordon Ramsay of West Yorkshire?' asks Lee.

'No, he's a big softie,' I reply. 'He doesn't even shout, let alone swear.'

'I have a look,' says Dad. 'If you are respected in the kitchen, all you have to do is give a look.'

He turns to Angela and kisses her on each cheek. I think she likes it that he is half Italian. She is the sort of woman who, if she invited him round for a meal, would do a whole Italian theme and think that no one had ever thought of that before.

'Hello again, Angela,' he says. 'Thanks for all your hard work on this.'

'Not at all,' she says. 'I want to make sure everything is perfect on the day.'

Marie, the hotel's wedding coordinator, appears. 'So, how are we all feeling?' she asks.

'Raring to go,' replies Angela. Marie turns to look at me. I decide it's best not to mention that I was up half the night and am feeling sick with nerves.

'Yes,' I say, with as much of a smile as I can muster.

'Right, if you follow me, I'll walk you around the hotel

and show you everything you need to know. Then we'll go through the whole ceremony step by step and I'll answer any questions you may have.'

We follow her as she sets off. Lee takes my hand and gives it a squeeze.

'Just focus on the honeymoon,' he whispers into my ear. 'None of this will matter once we're there.'

I look up at him. This is the Lee I fell in love with. The kind, caring, playful man who is going to be my husband and the father of my baby. But if that is the case, why do I still feel so uneasy in his presence? Why do I have to try to stop myself flinching whenever he touches me? I need to put the other Lee out of my mind. The other Lee is merely a figment of my – or someone else's – imagination. He does not actually exist. There is nothing to be scared of. Nothing to worry about at all.

It is when we get to the room where the ceremony is going to be held that it hits me. In two days' time I am going to be married. This is going to happen, and I have two options: to worry myself sick as to whether I am doing the right thing, or to go ahead and enjoy it. And Mum always used to tell me not to spend my life worrying about stuff that might never happen.

I walk down the aisle between the chairs and stand next to Lee.

'Wow, you look incredible,' he says.

'How do you know? You haven't seen the dress yet.'

'I can see you in my head,' he replies. 'And I reckon you're going to look even better than that.'

*

Dad is quiet on the drive home. I think it started to sink in tonight that on Sunday he is going to come home from a wedding to an empty house. He parks in the only space available on our road. I get out and go to the boot to get my dress. It's covered in a white bag so he can't see anything of it.

'Am I allowed a peek?' he asks.

'Absolutely not. You haven't got long to wait, though.'

He smiles at me, a rather sad sort of smile, and goes into the house. I take the dress straight upstairs to my room and hang it in the wardrobe. When I come down again he is sitting at the kitchen table. There is a present on it, a flat square box wrapped in silver paper and tied up with blue ribbon.

'What's this?' I ask.

'Something for you.'

'Am I allowed to open it now?'

'Yes, but you've got to read this first. I should warn you, it's from your mum.'

He hands me an envelope. My name is written on it in Mum's handwriting. I stare at it, my hand trembling.

'She wrote it for you before she died,' Dad says. 'Asked me to give it to you when the time came. If you want to take it to your room, I don't mind. Or I can read it to you.'

I shake my head, open the envelope and pull out the two pieces of writing paper inside.

Dear Jess,

I'm sorry if this has come as a bit of a shock. It probably feels a bit creepy now, me contacting you from beyond the grave, but at the time it seemed like a good idea. One of the hardest things about saying goodbye has been knowing that I won't be around for all the big moments in your life. Dad's a good man, a very good man, one of the best, but there are times when a girl just needs her mum and I thought this might be one of them.

You're getting married! I have to say it feels odd even thinking about it because right now you are a feisty fifteen-year-old who lives in ripped jeans and DMs and who would no doubt roll her eyes at me if I even suggested such a thing.

And it's possible you're not getting married, because I told Dad to give this to you when you find a partner for life, so maybe you're just moving in with them and that's fine too. It doesn't really matter to me about the piece of paper, what matters to me is that you're happy.

But anyway, congratulations! I don't know how old you will be when you read this – eighteen (doubtful, I know), twenty-five, forty-five or whatever – but I am so pleased you have found someone you want to spend the rest of your life with. It's not easy, life. And getting married doesn't make it any easier, but it does mean you've got somebody by your side to help when things get tough. I hope that person deserves you and I hope they love you almost as much as I do (I don't think it's possible for anyone else to love you as much as I do).

Most of all, I hope they will love and cherish and care for you in the way you deserve. Always remember that you are amazing, and to be worthy of you, they need to be amazing too.

As I used to say to you, I don't care how gorgeous the guy on your bedroom wall is to look at (and I do admit Robert Pattison is quite cute), if they don't treat you right, you need to get shot of them.

Dad is not perfect (none of us are) and he may have lost a bit more hair since I've gone, and he's probably still wearing the same bloody cardigan, but none of that matters, because he has a heart of gold and has been a complete rock for me these past few years.

When you were born, Jess, I tore really badly. Not just the usual stuff, but you perforated my bowel as you came out (you had your arm over your head – it's OK, I forgave you a long time ago). I had to have it stitched back together again in the operating theatre. Loads of stitches – they didn't even tell me how many because there were so many of them. And they told me when they discharged me from hospital that the first time I had a bowel movement afterwards, there was a chance they could burst. So when the time came, I was so bloody scared that I was going to split open again that your dad came into the bathroom with me and held my hand. It might not sound very romantic, I know that, but that is what real love is, Jess. Not all that silly stuff you see in Disney films.

So I hope the person you have chosen to spend the rest of your life with is that person. The one who is there for you when you most need it. The one who will never leave you to go through difficult stuff on your own.

I've left a present for you. Something borrowed, which I wore when I married your father. I hope you will be as happy as we were, Jess. And know that I am happy for you too.

Love always,

Mum X

I put the letter down on the table and burst into tears. Dad kneels down next to me and hugs me. He pulls me into him and rocks me, smoothing my hair with his hand. And right now I don't care that I am twenty-three years old. I like feeling like a kid again, and I wish that he could hold me like this forever and make all the bad things go away.

'She really loved you,' I manage to say eventually, between sobs.

'I know,' he replies, brushing a damp strand of hair from my face, 'but not as much as she loved you.'

Dad hands me the present from the table. I remove the blue ribbon, my fingers still shaking, peel back the Sellotape and pull out the box inside. When I lift the lid, I see a beautiful pearl choker. It is the one from my wedding photo. I had been wondering where it came from; it was the only thing missing. I thought maybe Angela was going to give it to me on the wedding morning, but it wasn't Angela, it was Mum. I hadn't even realised it was the same one as in her wedding photo. A fresh round of tears start to fall. Dad takes the choker out of the box and fastens it around my neck. I touch it lightly. I can feel her. She is going to be with me on Saturday. She is going to help me through. Because she understands that nobody can love someone as much as a mother loves her child.

Joe Mount
08/01/2018 at 9:39pm

They have charged him, Jess. Lee has been charged with your manslaughter. The police say they can't charge him with murder because they can't prove intent, but it doesn't change the fact that he killed you. My beautiful, precious daughter, killed by her own husband. And I did nothing because I didn't know he was hurting you. I didn't know because you didn't tell me. Why, Jess? Why couldn't you have confided in me? Perhaps you didn't want to worry me, but I wish you had.

The woman detective who came to see me said that sometimes women are embarrassed to come forward, that they feel it must be somehow their fault. Well, it wasn't, Jess. No one deserves to be hurt like that. I'm sorry I didn't protect you. I'm sorry I didn't see the signs. Maybe I didn't want to. Maybe I was trying too hard to be approving of my son-in-law, thinking that was what you wanted. I wish your mum had been here. She would have seen through it. She would have realised what was going on. And I know you would have talked to her.

I still can't get my head around what has happened. It's like you lived a secret life. I can't quite take it all in. But in the meantime, I'm going to try to get Harrison. Angela will not want to let him go, I know that. But I am going to find a way to get him back where he belongs – because I know it's what you would have wanted.

JESS

Saturday, 9 July 2016

I don't scream when I read it. I don't make any sound at all. Maybe because it is four o'clock in the morning and I don't want to wake Dad up. Or maybe because I am no longer capable of making a sound. My body appears to have gone into some kind of convulsion. I am lying here shaking uncontrollably, my head lolling from side to side. My phone is lying on the bed, the post still showing. Lee does kill me. The man who I am due to marry today is the one who will end my life. Exactly how, I don't know. But it doesn't really matter. What matters is that he does it.

I only checked Facebook because I wanted to see a photo of H. I had been so good, not clicking on my timeline for weeks. But I couldn't sleep because I was nervous and the only thing I could think of that would make me feel better was seeing H again. It was a stupid, stupid thing to do. But now I know and I can't undo it. I can try to convince myself it is rubbish; more lies from a dumped ex-girlfriend and a jealous best friend. But I can't un-see it. It is there, in my dad's own words.

I close my eyes, trying to shut it out, but it is imprinted on the inside of my eyelids. I will never get rid of this now. The seed of doubt has been planted. And even if I try not to water it, it will look for cracks of light and seize upon them, finding a way to force itself to the surface. And as I walk up the aisle later today, that is what I will be thinking of. Instead of bursting with happiness at marrying the man I want to spend the rest of my life with, I will be wondering how he kills me. Wondering if it is true.

The shaking slows slightly and I regain limited control of my body. I am acutely aware that I still have a choice here. I could decide not to go through with the wedding. I wouldn't even need to say why, I just wouldn't turn up. Angela would go mental. Dad might secretly be relieved. Sadie certainly would.

But I could never explain my decision to anyone and would be left forever wondering if I'd thrown away my best chance of happiness because of something that might never have happened. And I'd have to quit my job, of course. Though that wouldn't matter too much, because I'm sure I could get my old one back.

But there is one major reason not to call it off. One that stands out above all others. I pick up my phone, close Dad's last private message and scroll back to an earlier post. A new photo of H. He is smiling, dimples on full, and I can see a couple of teeth. I didn't even know my baby had cut his first tooth. That's what I've missed, these past few months. Missed seeing him grow up. He has a bit more hair as well, though still not a lot. I look at the date of the post and Dad's 'Eight months today' comment. I don't even register the number of likes or all the comments underneath it. I am too busy doing the maths. It is only then that I know for sure: it is going to happen any time now. H is a honeymoon baby.

I start to shake again. The mercury is rising inside, so much so that I feel I may explode. If I don't marry Lee today, H won't exist. He will never get to cut his first tooth or smile at his grandad or be held by people who love him – people like me. How can I rob him of that? How can I rob him of the life he could live? He deserves to live; he deserves that chance. But I also know that if Mum were here, she would tell me I don't deserve to have my own life cut short, like she did.

I sit bolt upright as I remember Sadie saying that she had read my letter. That she was going to make sure H was safe. I realise what I have to do. I can't tell anyone now because they will not believe me, but I can leave a note for a time when they will. It might not save *my* life but it will maybe ensure that if – when – anything does happen to me, H is safe. Because, clearly, leaving him in the care of the person who supposedly kills me is not a satisfactory option.

I get out of bed, all thoughts of sleep having disappeared. I am wired now. I rummage through the cupboard in the corner of my room in search of some paper and an envelope. Then I grab a pen, sit down on the edge of my bed and start to write.

*

When dawn breaks, I am lying in bed, eyes wide open. I have decided. Or rather, I know what I must do. I feel like some figure from history; a young queen resigned to her fate. I get up slowly, wondering if it is the world that's spinning or simply the inside of my head. The sealed envelope is propped up on top of my chest of drawers. It will be delivered today, no questions asked. Well, they might be asked but they will not be answered. I take three deep breaths before standing. I walk regally to the door, take my bathrobe from the hook, wrap it around me and open the door, prepared to face whatever the day should bring.

It is my turn to make breakfast for Dad. So often it has been the other way around, and I am painfully aware that from tomorrow I will no longer be able to do this simple thing for him. I wonder if all children are this crap or if it's just me. Was I so busy wallowing in grief after Mum died that I never noticed his grief? Never noticed him running himself ragged on my account? It is not even a very good breakfast – poached egg on toast and a cup of tea. If I'd thought about it, I could have got something in specially. I didn't think about it, though. That is the kind of half-arsed daughter I am.

Dad looks surprised when he opens the door and finds me with everything set out on the table. 'Are you OK?' he asks.

'Yeah. Couldn't get back to sleep. Thought I may as well get up and make myself useful.'

'Big-day nerves?' he asks.

'I guess so.'

He comes over and gives me a hug. It takes all I have to hold my composure. 'Thanks,' I say. 'I needed that.'

'You haven't got to worry about anything, you know. Angela really has taken care of it all.'

'I know.'

'She was right. All you've got to do is turn up.'

I manage half a smile. 'I've made you poached eggs on toast,' I say, going over to the cooker. Dad gives a sad kind of laugh.

'What?' I ask.

'It doesn't matter, you've made it now, but I'd got you something special in.'

It's the waiting that does me in. If I had gone for a morning wedding, it would have been much easier. Simply a case of getting up, getting ready and leaving the house. There wouldn't have been time to think about what I was doing.

Instead, there is this excruciating void. It's too early to get into my dress. I still have a couple of hours before the hair and make-up lady comes.

My room is not the sanctuary it once was. My room is where the truth unfolds or the lies are spun, depending on how you want to look at it. There is nothing much left in there anyway. Most of my stuff has already gone over to Lee's flat, including the case packed for the honeymoon. The room reeks of empty. Of saying goodbye. Of memories already fading. My phone beeps with a message. It is Lee.

I love you. Can't wait to see you later Mrs Griffiths X

The two competing elements within me collide with such force that my whole body shudders. I need to deliver my letter. I pick up the envelope, run down the stairs and head towards the back door.

'Where are you off to?' asks Dad.

'I need some fresh air.'

'Are you OK?'

'I'm fine. I won't be long.'

I suspect Dad is about to ask if he can come with me, which is why I run out before he has the chance. I don't want to offend him by saying no. I head straight for the canal. The same place I went to when Mum died. I like the fact that you can walk in either direction and be able to get back without having to think about it. I take out my phone and call Sadie. I am crying even as she answers.

'Hey, what's up?'

'Can you come and meet me?' I sob.

'Are you still at home?'

'No. Down by the canal.'

'What the fuck are you doing there?'

I go to answer but nothing comes out.

'Look, stay there,' says Sadie. 'I'm on my way, OK?'

I note the sound of panic in her voice. She probably thinks I'm going to do something stupid. Which, I suppose, I am. Just not the sort of stupid she probably has in mind.

She arrives within five minutes. I can tell from her face and her breathlessness that she has run all the way. She throws her arms around me, seemingly relieved to find me still here. I start crying again.

'What is it?' she asks.

I shake my head. Still incapable of words.

'Do you not want to do this?'

I shrug. 'It's hard,' is all I manage.

'What's hard? Have you been pressured into it?'

'I have no choice.'

'Of course you have a choice. You can walk away right this minute. I'll come with you if you want.'

'No, you don't understand.'

'Then help me to.'

I look up at the sky, realising for the first time that it is a beautiful day. A lovely day for getting married.

'I have to do this. It's the only way.'

'You're still not making sense.'

'If I don't marry him, good things won't happen.'

'How do you know?'

'I just do.'

I see the realisation on her face, can hear the click somewhere inside her head.

'Are you seeing the posts again?'

She thinks I'm ill. It's what everyone will think if I don't go through with it. *Jess Mount, she's not right in the head. Never has been. Well, not since . . .*

'No,' I say sharply.

'Do you love him?'

'Yes.'

'Does he love you?'

'Yes.'

'So what's the problem?'

I swallow hard. She doesn't realise I am talking about Harrison. 'It's hard. That's all.'

'Is it pre-wedding nerves getting to you?'

'Yeah. I guess so. I'll be fine.'

'Are you sure?'

I nod as I wipe my eyes. Sadie squeezes my shoulders one last time and lets go.

'Well, thank fuck for that, because I've bought a new outfit and everything.'

I manage to smile through the tears.

'I've even got a hat,' she adds.

'But you don't suit hats. You said so yourself.'

'I know. But I figured it wouldn't matter because everyone will be looking at you anyway so I may as well go a bit crazy.'

I shake my head. 'I love you, crazy lady.'

'Don't get emotional on me, either. I'm saving my tears for later.'

I take the envelope out of my pocket and hand it to her.

'What's this?'

'Keep it somewhere safe. Only open it if something bad happens to me.'

'Come on, Jess. I thought we'd just gone through this?'

'It's all I'm asking of you. It will make me feel better if you take it. Please.'

She takes it and puts it in her jacket pocket.

'Thank you. Just remember that this is my choice and you couldn't have talked me out of it, OK?'

She shrugs. We walk back along the canal together in silence.

I can't say I don't recognise the person who stares back at me from the mirror, because I do. I recognise her from the photograph on Facebook. She has the same hair and make-up, the same dress, the same uncertainty in her eyes. I know her now. I understand that she is doing what she has to do. I take a last look around my bedroom. So many memories, good and bad. But I am burying Jess Mount along with them. Today is a fresh start. It's about new beginnings. A new life.

Dad starts crying pretty much the second he sees me on the stairs.

'Oh, come on,' I say. 'You're going to mess up my make-up if you do that.'

He smiles and wipes his face. 'You look so beautiful.'

'I've got my DMs on underneath.'

'You better not have.'

I lift my dress to show him I'm joking – I am wearing proper bridal shoes. Why anyone bothers with such things I do not know, but Angela insisted.

He kisses me on both cheeks when I get to the bottom of the stairs. His eyes drop to my choker.

'It's perfect,' he says.

'I know,' I reply, touching it gently.

'If you feel you need her at any point, just remember she is with you.'

I nod. A car pulls up outside. A white limo, to be precise. I look at Dad.

'Honestly, it would have been fine to go in your car,' I say.

'No,' he replies. 'This is your day, I wanted to make this bit extra special.'

'Thank you,' I say. He paid for this. I know because Lee told me. He paid for the food too. I asked Lee to let him, not wanting to dent a father's pride.

When Dad opens the door there are other people outside in the street. Old ladies who used to say hello to Mum when we were walking to and from school. Kids on their bikes. The guy from the chippy. A few people I vaguely remember from Mum's funeral. They break into a round of applause. I smile because I don't know what else to do.

The driver comes round and opens the door. I gather up my dress and get inside, like I do this every day, like I know what I'm doing. Dad sits down next to me and holds my hand. He gives it a little squeeze.

'I wish she was here for you today,' he whispers.

'I know,' I reply. 'I do too.'

The car sweeps around the little roundabout with the fountain in the middle and comes to a halt outside the main entrance of the hotel. This is it. There is no going back. If I step onto the red carpet which runs up to the entrance, my life will go in one direction; if I ask the driver to take me back home, it will go in another. One without H in it.

Dad gives my hand another squeeze.

'Ready?' he asks.

I nod. I fix the photo of Harrison in my head. I am doing this for him. I cannot bear the thought of him not existing, of losing my child before he is even conceived, let alone born. And if that means I am risking my life in the process, then so be it. I choose him. I choose my son. And I trust Sadie to fight to get him back to my Dad if she needs to.

I step out of the car. My legs are a little shaky. Dad comes around and takes hold of my arm, for which I am grateful. Marie, the wedding coordinator, is hovering at the top of the steps, beaming at me.

'Hello,' she says. 'You look amazing. Everyone's in the room waiting.'

'I'm not late am I?'

'No, bang on time. If you follow me, I'll take you through to the room and let the registrar know you're here.'

I sweep through the hotel behind her, my dress rustling, my toes clinging desperately to my bridal shoes, which are half a size too big for me. I have taken this path now. I can't deviate from it. Maybe I am effectively walking to the gallows. Or maybe it is still possible to get a last-minute reprieve. The fact that so much of it has proved true so far doesn't mean it all will. Perhaps I do still have the power to change the ending . . .

We stop outside the doors to the room. I can hear the murmur of voices inside before the music starts up. The doors open. It is my cue to enter. My feet don't move, though. I am paralysed from the neck down. Only my head is working; my eyes see the man I love standing at the front of the room, my ears hear my screams as he kills me, and my brain aches as it tries to work out which one to believe.

I start to shake again.

'Are you OK?' Dad whispers.

I nod as a tear rolls slowly down my cheek.

'I've got you. I'm not going to let you fall.'

Dad's grip on my arm tightens. I lift my other hand to touch my choker. She is here. She is with me. She understands what I must do. And she will be waiting for me at the other side.

I start walking. When I glance sideways, I see that Dad is crying too. His grip on my arm never falters, though. I am aware of heads turning, but I don't see the faces of the guests – only a hat, which I presume to be Sadie's because she is the only person I know who would wear a huge black hat to a wedding. I hear vague, murmured oohs and aahs, but I am not sure who they're coming from. My eyes are fixed on the man standing at the front of the room. The man who is growing nearer and nearer. My fate. My destiny. My lover. My killer. And soon to be my husband. He turns his head as I reach him and smiles. He mouths the word 'beautiful' to me. My heart judders, careering between love and hate. I feel myself falling. I put my hand out to save myself. He takes it and holds it. The registrar begins talking. Sand is running out of the bottom of my shoes. Just a trickle, but it has begun.

Marriage in this country is the union of two people, voluntarily entered into.

I am doing this voluntarily. I am offering myself up for slaughter. I am Aslan at the Stone Table in Narnia.

. . . solemn and binding character of the vows you are about to make.

I am brave and I am strong. It is my turn to speak now. My turn to roar.

I do solemnly declare that I know not of any legal impediment, why I, Jessica Mount, may not be joined in matrimony to Lee Griffiths.

It is a lie, of course. I know of one very good reason. But I cannot speak it here. I must accept my death with dignity.

I call upon these persons here present to witness that I, Jessica Mount, do take thee, Lee Griffiths, to be my lawful wedded husband.

There, I have done it. It wasn't too bad. It didn't hurt at all. I am still here, still breathing – just. We are pronounced husband and wife. Lee is leaning in to kiss me. I close my eyes. I see H's face smiling back at me. It won't be long now until he is inside me. Not long at all.

Angela Griffiths
09/01/2018 10:34am

He did not do it. Although I don't need to tell you that because you know it already. It's the others who need to hear it. The ones who will listen to the lies and swallow them whole. It is innocent until proven guilty in this country. At least, it is supposed to be. But people are talking already. Pointing and whispering. Making such a silly fuss about nothing.

It is their fault, of course. Emma and that silly friend of yours. Cooking up a story between them like a couple of modern-day witches. I have no idea why the police have taken them so seriously. They will get found out, of course, when we have our day in court. When all of these claims are proved to be a tissue of lies.

You know exactly what happened, Jess. Because, unlike them, you were there.

JESS

Sunday, 10 July 2016

I put my phone down quickly as Lee comes back in from the en suite, hoping he doesn't notice the confusion in my eyes.

'Hey, I told you, no phones on honeymoon.' I am taken aback by the sharpness in his voice.

'I didn't know it had started yet.'

'It started from the moment I put the ring on your finger. Here, please.' I am still not sure if he is being serious or not. I hand it over anyway. He turns it off and packs it away in one of the cases, one that will not be going with us.

'That's a bit much.'

There is a steeliness in Lee's eyes, but it softens slightly when he sees me frowning at him. He comes over and sits on the bed.

'I don't want anything getting in the way of spending time with you, that's all.'

'When are you going to tell me where we're going?'

'When we check in. But wherever it is, you won't be needing your phone.'

'Your mum's been posting wedding photos on Facebook already.'

'Doesn't surprise me. She needs to get a life.'

'Your dad won't find out, will he? Through anyone else, I mean.'

'Nah. And if he does, it doesn't matter. It's too late now.'

'Do you not get on at all?'

Lee shakes his head. 'He spoilt everything he touched. We had nothing in common. Nothing at all.'

He comes over and kisses me on the lips. 'Anyway, Mrs Griffiths, you'd better get your arse in gear. There's a massive breakfast to eat downstairs and then a plane to catch.'

It's weird, going into the hotel dining room and seeing everyone again. My grandparents, aunts and cousins from Italy are still here. I feel bad because I hardly got the chance to talk to them last night. Lee kept whisking me off to dance or introduce me to one of his family or friends. They will be staying on for a few days though, so at least Dad will have them around after I've left. It should make things easier for him. And Mum's sister Sarah is still here too. She'd been hoping to bring Grandma Mary up from the nursing home in Devon, but she'd been too poorly to travel in the end.

Auntie Sarah comes over to me and takes hold of my hands.

'What a wonderful day it was yesterday. I've taken lots of photos to show your grandma.'

'Thank you,' I say, giving her a hug. I turn to introduce Lee properly to her, but he's gone over to talk to Angela.

'You seem to have got yourself quite a catch there,' Auntie Sarah says. 'And he's obviously besotted with you.'

I swallow hard and look down at my feet. All I can think of are the sad emojis she puts on all of Dad's posts after I've gone. No doubt she will feel guilty, too. She'll think she should have been looking after me on Mum's behalf. I see Dad waving and beckoning me over to the Italian enclave.

'Anyway, I'd better go and see Dad,' I say.

'You had. He's really going to miss you.'

'I know.'

Lee and I leave straight after breakfast in a blur of tears and hugs and shouts of 'Have a great time!' Sadie comes up and gives me a massive hug.

'Have fun. I'll miss you,' she says.

'I'd do the chucking the flowers over my shoulder thing,' I say. 'But I know you hate stuff like that.'

'Too right,' she says.

'I'd have thrown them in your direction if I had, though,' I tell her.

I save Dad until last. He's hanging back, probably dreading it as much as I am. I can't see his eyes because he has shades on, but I suspect he's blinking furiously. Finally, the people around him step back and part, leaving him standing there, seemingly unable to look me in the eye. I throw my arms around him as he sobs into my hair. He smells so familiar, so unquestionably good. His grip loosens eventually, and he takes my head in his hands.

'Be happy,' is all he manages to say, before the tears overcome him again. I see Nonna put her arm around him; she's crying too. I try not to think about how they will be at my funeral.

I feel a hand on my shoulder.

'Ready?' asks Lee. The same question I was asked yesterday. Only this time I am asked by my husband instead of my father. I nod and get into the car.

It is only once we are on the plane that I confess I'm not even totally sure where the Seychelles are. Lee laughs and asks the air hostess for a napkin so he can draw me a map.

'We're stopping over in an airport hotel in Abu Dhabi tonight. Do you know what the main difference is between Dubai and Abu Dhabi?'

'No,' I reply.

'The people in Dubai don't watch *The Flintstones* but the people in Abu Dhabi do.'

It takes a second for it to click, but when it does my face breaks into a smile, quickly followed by a full-blown laugh.

I elbow him in the ribs. 'I thought you were being serious,' I say. 'I was feeling all inferior in the geography department again.'

'You should know me better than that by now.'

'Yeah,' I reply, gazing up at him. 'I should.'

'Anyway, it's fourteen hours flying time in total and we'll get there tomorrow morning. But it'll be worth it, I promise.'

I'm not so sure. It is way further than I have ever flown before. I try not to let him see I am gripping the side of my seat with my other hand.

He notices though, and squeezes my palm more tightly. 'You'll be fine. I won't let go all the way. I promise.'

'Even when they bring the food?'

'Even then. However messy it gets.'

I smile at him, feeling myself soften inside. I did do the right thing. It's hard to believe how close I was to screwing it all up.

'Thank you,' I whisper.

'For what?'

'For caring.'

He kisses the top of my head. 'That's OK. It's my job.'

I gaze out of the aeroplane window the next morning as we descend onto a landing strip that juts out from the edge of the island into the sea, with heavily wooded hills on the other side. I am so taken by the beauty of the place that I don't even feel anxious about the landing. It is only as we touch down that Lee finally lets go of my hand.

'See, it wasn't too bad, was it?'

'No. No, it wasn't.'

A boat is waiting to take us to Silhouette Island, where we are staying. It makes sense that I am no longer Jess Mount. Jess Mount didn't do things like this. Jess Mount lived in Mytholmroyd, scrabbled around for popcorn on the cinema floor and sometimes ate cold pizza for breakfast on a Sunday morning. Jess Griffiths appears to live in an entirely different universe – one where she jets around the world to an island where the sea is so blue it doesn't actually look real, and the man who is holding her hand looks like a cut-out-and-keep husband from some teenage magazine.

Lee kisses me on the back of my neck; a warm breeze caresses my face. I choose this life. And maybe, if I can learn to relax and simply enjoy it, it will turn out to be a long and happy one.

The boat glides into a small jetty. A barefoot man jumps out and ties it up. Somebody else is unloading our luggage and Lee is taking my hand and leading me up the jetty onto a beach so white it dazzles my eyes. In front of us are clusters of holiday villas nestled amongst the trees. We follow the man with our luggage up some steep steps to a villa on its own, with a waterfall cascading into a pool at one end and two sun loungers looking out across the sea at the other. I turn to Lee in disbelief. He smiles. The man leads us on through two sliding doors into a room so big they've fitted a lounge into it as well. The huge canopied bed has lace curtains tied at each bedpost. I look around me, still unable to speak.

As soon as the porter leaves I start to cry. I sit on the end of the bed with tears streaming down my face and I feel such a cow for doubting Lee because everything he's actually done for me has been fucking amazing and it's only inside my head that he's turned into this monster. I think it's because, on some level, I don't think I deserve him. I think he is way too good for me, and I'm doing that thing of sabotaging my own happiness because, hey, woe is me and all that.

'Listen,' says Lee, 'if you don't like it, we can always try somewhere else.' He is smiling as he says it. I shake my head, about twenty little shakes, before I am finally able to say something.

'I love it,' I say. 'And I love you. And I kind of feel not worthy of all this.'

'Don't be daft,' says Lee, kneeling down on the floor in front of me. 'Or you're going to get me quoting L'Oréal adverts in a minute.'

I stroke his face. 'This is how it's going to be, right?'

'Well, I can't really afford for us to stay here more than a fortnight.'

'No, not this – us. This is how we're going to be. We're always going to be this happy.'

Lee nods. 'Yeah. Only I don't want it to be just us. I want to start a family and I don't want to wait. Or to stop at one, or even two. I want to have a whole bloody football team with you.'

'Woah, give a girl a break. Can't we just adopt like Brad Pitt and Angelina Jolie?'

'No, because I want them to be ours – yours and mine. I don't know about you, but I hated being an only child. I don't want them to be lonely growing up.'

'OK, but if I turn into some big, bloated mamma who permanently smells of sick, you will still love me, won't you?'

'Of course.' He smiles. 'But you won't. You're going to be an amazing mum. Like you're an amazing wife.'

He starts kissing me. I let his words seep in, let his hands caress my warm skin, and I wonder what the hell I've been playing at these past few months. This is my life. This is my reality. This is everything I ever wanted.

Lee is unbuttoning my shirt. All I see in my head is the photo of H. And he is smiling, his teeth poking out from shiny pink gums. And for the first time I hear him gurgling, doing all those happy baby sounds. And I know then that this is it. This is where and how he is created. It couldn't be any more perfect. And that is all I want for him. For everything to be perfect. Lee lays me down on the bed, and I tell H silently, in my head, that I will do anything in the world for him. Anything at all.

PART FOUR

JESS

I know the exact moment H was conceived, which is maybe why I am in no rush to do the pregnancy test. It is three days since my period was due. But it's not as if I'm waiting on tenterhooks – it's more like printing out an official confirmation slip. Even so, I know as I sit and wee on a stick in the bathroom at home that it will be good to see the blue line appear.

I say 'at home', although, if I'm honest, it still doesn't feel like home. It feels like I'm house-sitting for someone and a little part of me is expecting them to come home from holiday at any point and kick me out. At which point I'll have to pack my bags and go back to my old life. I wonder if I'll ever get used to it, or if it'll only be when we move somewhere new that I feel like I belong. And we will need to, of course. An apartment like this really isn't a place to bring a baby up in. I want H to have a garden he can run around in. Nothing big or fancy. Just a little patch of grass and enough room to kick a ball about.

I take the stick out and put the cap back on before flushing and washing my hands. I've heard some women say they feel different once they know. Even though they can't possibly feel a cluster of cells inside them. I've felt different since the moment he was conceived. The reason I got up and went swimming every morning before breakfast was so that I could talk to him without Lee hearing. It felt like I was spending time with him already. I even heard him gurgle as I lay on my back in the water. He liked it, I know he did. And I love him. I am absolutely besotted with him. I love having someone more important than me to think about. Someone who I would lay down my life for. Though maybe I already have.

I slap the thought down as soon as it comes to me. I have not been allowing those thoughts into my head since the honeymoon. I have not gone on Facebook since I've been back either. Because last time I did, I ended up nearly walking out on my own wedding. I am not going to be that stupid again – I have too much to lose now. And I don't want to drive myself half crazy by reading that stuff.

I take the lid off the stick and find the blue line there. It is bluer even than the example on the diagram. Blue and strong and true. H is here. He is right inside me. I knew it already but now I have proof for the rest of the world. No one can doubt me. No one can say it is simply inside my head. It is here, in blue and white. He exists.

I hadn't planned on telling Lee straight away. I'd thought I might want to keep it to myself for a little longer. But, actually, I've been keeping it to myself for so long that I am fit to burst.

I come out of the bathroom and go through to the kitchen where Lee is making us coffee. I have put the cap back on but I am still holding the test in my hand. He turns and looks at me. His eyes fall to the test and dart back to my face. His eyebrows rise questioningly. I nod, unable to stop a smile from creeping onto my face.

Lee comes towards me, grinning broadly, and picks me up.

'Bloody hell, you don't waste any time, do you?'

'You were the one who said you wanted to start trying straight away.'

'I know, and I did. I do. I just didn't expect it to happen quite so fast.'

'Well, it did. You haven't changed your mind, have you?'

Tears well up in Lee's eyes. The man who I have never seen shed a tear, who took great pride in telling me he didn't even cry when Simba's dad died in *The Lion King*, is shedding them now for his son.

'I love you, Mrs Griffiths.'

'I love you too.'

'And him,' Lee says, placing his left hand on my stomach. I'm taken aback for a second.

'Why do you say him?'

'Just a feeling, that's all. I told you I wanted a football team.'

'It could be a women's football team.'

'Could be, but I don't think so. Not the first one anyway.'

It's all I can do to stop myself from telling him that he's right. The temptation to blurt out the whole thing is overwhelming. Well, not the whole thing, obviously, but part of it. I want to run and get my phone and show him the photos. Only he wouldn't be able to see them. And then he'd think I'd lost it. At which point he would leave me.

Instead, I simply smile and say, 'Let's wait and see.'

Lee beams at me and shakes his head and looks for all the world like a little kid who's just got the best Christmas present ever. And I love the fact that I gave it to him.

'Are you feeling OK?' he asks. 'I mean, you're not feeling sick or anything?'

'No. I'm fine. I feel great, actually.'

'Good. Wow, I'm going to be a dad. I still can't quite get my head round that.'

'I know. I don't feel old enough to be a parent. All that responsibility.'

He looks at me. He still looks like a little kid, although this time a scared one. 'We'll be OK, though, won't we? We won't screw our kids up.'

'No. We'll be fine. We'll muddle through like everyone else does, I guess.'

He shakes his head again. 'Wait till I tell Carl he's going to need another new receptionist.'

'I don't want to tell anyone yet. People usually wait three months. Just in case, you know, anything happens.'

'Yeah, sure. Anyway, he did say one of the other girls he interviewed was good. Maybe he can go back to her. See if she'd like a permanent job.'

'Permanent?'

'Well, yeah. You're not going to need to go back to work afterwards, are you?'

I look at him, unable to hide my irritation at that. 'I might want to.'

'Of course you won't. You'll be bringing up our kid – that's much more important, isn't it?'

I turn and walk away as I blow out.

'What?' he asks, his jaw tightening.

'Er, that sounded a little bit 1950s.'

His expression darkens. He stuffs his hands in his dressing gown pockets. 'Well, it wasn't meant to be. I don't want our kid being looked after by someone else, that's all.'

'Your mum does it.'

'What?' he says, frowning.

'I mean, she'll help out when the baby's born. She's already said she'd like to.'

'When?'

'She talked about it before the wedding. Said she'd be happy to come round every day to give me a break.'

'Well, you still don't need to go to work.'

I shake my head, trying to work out how we got from being elated about me being pregnant to having our first row.

'I might go stir-crazy, staying here with a baby all day. Anyway, we might need the cash.'

Lee does a little laugh.

'What?'

'Well, you coming back to work a couple of days a week is hardly going to make much difference, isn't it?'

His words sting me. It almost feels as if he has actually hit me.

'We might need a bit extra. I mean, we're not going to be able to stay here, are we? We haven't even got a nursery.'

Lee turns his back on me and walks over to the window. 'They have two-bedroom apartments here. There are some on the next floor down. And it won't cost much more. I can certainly cover the difference without you having to go out to work.'

He has riled me now. I am not going to let it drop, even though I know that's what he wants.

'Shouldn't we be getting a house? You know, something with a garden?'

'We don't need a garden. There are parks and stuff. Besides, if we have a garden we'll only end up with one of those crappy red and yellow plastic playhouses. That's what happened to Carl and his wife and I'm not ready to go there just yet.'

Lee stomps out of the kitchen. I was going to say I don't fancy lugging a buggy up the stairs if the apartment lifts are ever broken, but I don't see the point of arguing any further. He is clearly not in the mood to listen. Besides, I can't tell him what I'm really thinking, which is that H won't want to be cooped up in an apartment all day. He'll want a garden to play in. He'll need fresh air. I want him to be able to play in the street with other kids. There are no kids here. I put my hand on where my bump will be in a few months. My bubble has been well and truly burst.

*

I stand behind the desk at work, wondering if anyone else can tell. I feel so different that I can't help thinking I must look different too. I remember the pregnant receptionist who was here when I came for my interview, how uncomfortable she looked in her high heels. I still don't know who gave her 'the look' about wearing flats. At the time, I assumed it was Carl, but after the row I had with Lee on Saturday, I am not so sure.

I can't imagine my colleagues will be very impressed when they find out. One or two of them were a bit sniffy when they found out we were getting married. I can imagine what they're saying behind my back. I mean, one of the directors gets his girlfriend a job with the company, marries her, knocks her up and she's off again, all within the space of a year. They'll probably make jokes about me in the bar after work. Not that I'll ever hear about it. I'll be long gone by then.

The door opens and a young man with floppy blonde hair comes in, flashing me a toothpaste-advert smile as he approaches the desk.

'Hi, how can I help you?' I ask.

'Hi. I'm here to see Lee Griffiths. It's Dan Templeton.'

'Thanks,' I say. 'Do take a seat. I'll let Lee know you're here.'

He sits down, crosses his legs and loosens his tie slightly. I call Lee, but his line is engaged. I put the phone down for a second.

'Can I get you a coffee?' I ask.

'That would be great, thanks. Black, no sugar.'

I try Lee once more but the line is still engaged. I make the coffee and take it over to Dan. 'Here you go,' I say, handing it to him.

'Thanks,' he says, frowning slightly. 'Do I know you from somewhere?'

Although on paper it's an obvious chat-up line, it honestly isn't said like one.

'Um, I don't think so. I'm fairly new here.'

'Where were you before?'

'Not a PR firm. I actually worked at the independent cinema in town.'

'That's where I know you from,' he says, jabbing the air with his finger. 'I go there all the time. I've seen you on the front desk and I think you've served me a couple of times.'

'Wow, I'm impressed you remember me. I looked a bit different then.'

'I never forget a pretty face,' he says.

I smile, flushing slightly. I am suddenly aware of footsteps behind me. I turn to see Lee standing at the bottom of the stairs, looking quizzically at me.

'Oh, er, Dan Templeton's here to see you.'

'I can see that.'

'I did try you but you were on the phone.'

He nods, stony-faced, and turns to his client. 'Hi, Dan, sorry to keep you. Please do come straight up.'

Dan picks up his coffee, flashing me another smile as he goes past. I scuttle back behind my desk like an animal running for cover. I don't know why I am reacting like this – it's not as if I've done anything wrong. It was simply the look on Lee's face.

I busy myself for half an hour or so, though, in truth, I really haven't got much to do. But I make sure I'm tapping away on the computer when I hear two sets of footsteps coming down the stairs.

'Thanks again for coming in, Dan,' I hear Lee say from behind me. 'I'll be in touch soon.'

'Great. Thanks for your time,' Dan replies. I glance up as he walks past – I was told always to smile at clients as they left the building.

'Good to see you again,' Dan says with a grin.

'You too,' I reply.

He pulls the door behind him. Lee walks up to me. His face is like thunder. I can feel his hot breath on my face.

'Where do you know him from?' he asks.

'He used to go to the cinema, that's all. He remembered me.'

'That's a bit weird, isn't it?'

'I don't know. He said he was a regular.'

Lee raises an eyebrow. 'Well, I'll arrange to meet him somewhere else next time.'

'There's no need for that.'

'You want him to come here, do you?' he snaps at me.

My whole body tenses. 'I didn't say that.'

'That's what it sounded like.'

'I was just saying he wasn't bothering me, that's all.'

'Yeah, well, he was bothering me.'

Lee turns and heads back upstairs. I stand there for a second, still not quite sure what I have been accused of. I have never seen Lee like this before; he has never struck me as the jealous type. Then again, I don't suppose I've been around many other men when I've been with him. The only male friend I invited to the wedding was Adrian and his male partner. I wasn't even flirting with Dan. It was such a massive overreaction. I sigh and go back to my computer screen, hoping he'll have a very good explanation.

Lee doesn't mention it again until that evening, when we get into bed.

'Look, I'm sorry about earlier. I realise I probably came over as a bit heavy.'

I shrug. I don't want him to know how much it upset me. I couldn't concentrate on my work for the rest of the day. 'He really wasn't causing a problem, you know.'

'I get a bit overprotective, sometimes,' says Lee. 'I think you being pregnant has made things worse. I kind of feel like it's my duty to protect you. Both of you.'

'I can handle myself, you know. I thought you might remember that.'

'Yeah, well. That was before.'

'Before what?'

'Before you were married to me. Before you were carrying my child.'

'I'm still capable of calling out an arsehole when I see one.'

'Well, you shouldn't have to. Not now. I'm looking after you, OK?'

I give a little nod, simply because it's easier than continuing the argument. I'm tired. It's been a long day. I'd rather get to sleep, to be honest.

Lee pulls me into him and kisses me. A proper kiss, rather than a goodnight one. I think for a moment about telling him I'm too tired, but I find myself worrying about what his reaction will be. Besides, Mum always used to say that couples should never go to bed on an argument. We need this. We need to reconnect again. Then everything will be OK.

JESS

September 2008

'How often do you think about death, Jess?' Edward asks. He told me to call him Edward, although his official name is Professor Jenkins. Paula, the educational psychologist, referred me to him because she thought I needed more specialist help. Which is a polite way of saying I am cracking up.

'Do you want the honest answer, or the one I should give you if I don't want you to think I'm a fruit loop?'

'Honest is usually best.' He smiles.

'Then I think about it a lot. But that's just being sensible, isn't it?'

'What do you mean?'

'Well, if you think about death you've got a better chance of avoiding it, haven't you? I mean, we tell kids to cross the road safely so they don't get run over. That's thinking about death, isn't it? It's just that people say that's sensible.'

'Is that how you see it? As a safety device?'

'Yeah. You're careful when you cross the road, so why not be careful

when you get on a train, or careful where you go out? I don't see the difference.'

'Is that why you won't go to Manchester?'

'People get shot in Manchester.'

'So you don't think it's safe to go there?'

'No. Clearly it's not.'

'And what if I said the young men who were shot in Manchester last year – and they were all young men – were deliberately targeted, not random victims?'

I shrug. 'People get caught in crossfire, don't they? You can't be too careful.'

Edward nods and writes something down. They must have a lot of notes on me now. All the things Paula wrote and now all the things Edward is writing. It doesn't mean they know me or understand me. It just means they think they do.

'You didn't think like this before your mother died, though, did you?'

'No. But it's like people don't stop smoking until they're told they have lung cancer. It's a wake-up call, isn't it?'

'So you see your mother's death as a wake-up call? Only she didn't die in an accident, did she? She died from bowel cancer. She couldn't have prevented that.'

'Yes, she could. She could have avoided meat. I don't eat red meat anymore because too much of it gives you bowel cancer.'

'Well, we can't say that for certain, only that there are studies linking red meat with an increased risk.'

'Exactly. That's what it's all about – risk. I'm cutting down my risk. Doctors tell you to do that all the time, don't they? Don't smoke. Don't drink. Don't eat fatty foods. Exercise more. Lose weight. It's all about* *cutting down your risk of dying. Except when they say it, they're being sensible, and when I say it about other things, I'm considered a nutter.'*

I cross my arms as I finish. Edward doesn't say anything. I think I might have convinced him that I am right.

ANGELA

Sunday, 28 August 2016

It is when she hardly touches her dinner that I know. She just about manages her Yorkshire pudding, but even as I put the beef in front of her, she looks close to retching. She is pale, too, and slightly gaunt in the face. She has never looked gaunt before. I thought she looked a bit peaky last week, and she didn't eat as much as usual, but nothing like this. She cuts things up and pushes them around her plate for a bit before finally looking up. I see Lee catch her eye and raise an eyebrow; she gives a tiny shake of her head.

I decide it is kindest to put her out of her misery.

'Oh, Jess, why ever didn't you tell me?' I put down my knife and fork and rush around to her side of the table to whisk the plate from under her nose. I return and look down at both of them in turn before bursting into tears.

'I'm so, so happy for you both,' I say, bending to give Jess a hug before planting a huge kiss on Lee's cheek. 'You must be absolutely delighted.'

They look at each other again. Jess shrugs and Lee looks up at me.

'Thanks,' he says. 'We are. Jess wanted to wait until she was three months before telling anyone, but I guess you worked it out anyway.'

'I was exactly the same with our Lee,' I say, turning back to Jess. 'I couldn't look at a cooked meal without feeling like I was going to throw up. Horrible, it was. And it wasn't just in the mornings either, it was pretty much twenty-four hours.'

'I know. Mine's the same. It's got much worse since last week. I've hardly been able to eat.'

'Can I get you summat else? Soup and a roll? Or even dry crackers? I remember eating a lot of crackers when I was pregnant.'

'Yeah, maybe I'll try crackers, thanks.'

I pop a couple of Jacobs on a plate and bring them over. She nibbles around the edges first, then takes a few larger bites.

'Well, at least there's summat you can eat. You can take that packet home with you, love. Little and often, that's what my mum used to say. So, when's it due?'

'Around the second week in April, but I haven't had a scan yet so I haven't got an exact date.'

'Oh, a spring baby will be lovely, you'll have all the summer stretching in front of you. I remember it always being so dark in January when I was up early in the mornings with Lee.'

'I guess it'll be nice to be able to go out for walks with the buggy.'

'Well, I insist that I buy you the buggy. I want to get

something practical for you. As long as I get a turn pushing it, of course.'

Jess looks at Lee.

'Thanks,' he says, when he's finished his mouthful. 'That would be great. But don't go mad getting stuff. We've got plenty of time yet.'

'Jess doesn't want to be traipsing around looking at buggies when she's seven months pregnant. Now's the time to do it.'

'Maybe once the sickness has gone,' says Jess.

'Yes, of course. Though it didn't go until sixteen weeks for me, but let's hope you're luckier than that. Anyway, we can start looking online, can't we? Makes the whole thing a lot easier.'

Jess takes another bite of her cracker. Lee gets back to his beef. I suspect he's a bit nervous about it all. It's a big responsibility, fatherhood. I stand by what I said, though. It will be the making of him. It'll be good for him to have a wife and baby to come home to – stop him being too career-obsessed.

'Ooh,' I say out loud as I realise. 'And you'll be moving, too, of course.'

Jess looks at Lee again.

'We're probably just going to get a bigger apartment in the same block.'

I frown at him, not sure I've heard right. 'You'll need a proper family home, though,' I say.

'It'll be fine while the baby's small. We can get something bigger later.'

'But it's no place to be living with a baby, is it? What if

the lift breaks? There's no way she can get a buggy up those stairs.'

Lee gives a little roll of his eyes. He used to do it all the time as a teenager. There is a steeliness in his eyes when he speaks. One I remember only too well.

'The lift's never been out of order since I moved there. We don't have to move to a semi-detached in suburbia just because Jess is pregnant.'

I suppose the dig is aimed at me. Lee loved our garden as a little boy. He was always out there, kicking a ball around or digging in the flower beds. But as soon as he became a teenager, he decided that he hated Horsforth. Said it was boring and there was nothing going on. He always said he was going to move to the city centre as soon as he could, and that's what he did. Rented first when he came back from uni and bought when he started earning good money. The city centre isn't a place to bring up a child, though. It really isn't.

I want to say something, but I know I have to be careful. I don't want him snapping in front of Jess. It's not pretty and I don't want her to see him like that.

'Well, maybe it's fine for now, but you'll have to move eventually for the schools, won't you? Can't imagine there are any nice ones in the city centre.'

'We'll probably go private,' he replies.

'What, waste your money on fancy uniforms when there are perfectly good state schools around here? The primary up the road is outstanding. I've seen the banner on its railings as I've driven past.'

Lee puts his cutlery down on the side of his plate with a clank. 'I said we're fine for now, thank you.'

His tone tells me I have said enough. I glance up and see Jess frowning at him. I will change the subject. I don't want things getting any more heated than they already are. I am good at changing the subject. I have had to be.

'Did you see *Bake Off* this week? A girl from Leeds is on it. Ever so good, she is. Her choux pastry looked amazing.'

I wait till we've finished dinner and Lee is loading up the dishwasher before going back into the lounge to see Jess.

'Come upstairs for a bit, love. We can start having a look for buggies on the internet.'

Jess follows me up the stairs and into the guest room. I turn the computer on and wait. It always takes a minute or two to start up. Lee tells me it's because it's old and I need to upgrade, but I don't see what the big hurry is.

'Here we are,' I say, bringing up the Mamas & Papas page. 'There's one of these in Leeds we can go to. Let's have a look at what they've got.'

The page comes up with a bewildering array of options, including travel systems, buggies, pushchairs and prams.

'I suppose you need a travel system, don't you?'

'I have no idea,' says Jess.

'I think they're the ones where you just pick up the car seat and attach it to the frame of the buggy, so you don't have to worry about waking up the baby.'

I glance across at Jess as I say it. She has tears in her eyes.

'Oh, love,' I say, reaching across and giving her hand a squeeze. 'There's no need to get upset about it.'

'I haven't got a clue,' she says. 'I don't know what I need. I don't know anything about babies. How the hell am I going to be able to look after one?'

The tears fall properly now. I put my arm around her and pat her shoulder.

'Don't you worry,' I say. 'Everyone feels a bit like that at the beginning. I certainly did. We were all learner drivers once, you know. No one's expecting you to be an expert.'

'You honestly didn't have a clue either?'

'Not really.'

'Then how did you know what to do?'

'Instinct, I suppose. And my mum was a huge help.'

I realise as soon as I have said it. She lets out another sob.

'I'm sorry, I didn't mean to make things worse. I know it's going to be tough without your mum, but I want you to remember I'll be there for you every step of the way. You can call me any time, day or night, and no question will be too daft, OK?'

She nods and wipes her nose with her hand. I go and get a tissue from the box and hand it to her.

'And I'll come over every day to help out, especially at the beginning. I'll make sure you're not on your own when Lee goes back to work.'

'Thanks,' she mumbles. 'That's really kind of you.'

'Don't be daft. This is my first grandchild. I want to spend every second I can with them. It will be a pleasure to be on hand. Consider me hired.'

She manages a little smile before blowing her nose.

'Look,' I say, shutting down the computer. 'Why don't we do this another day, when you're feeling up to it. There's summat else I want to show you before you go.'

I bend down, pull out the bottom drawer and take out the christening robe wrapped in tissue paper.

'This was Lee's. I want you to have it for your baby's christening.'

She starts crying again – if she even stopped, that is. She barely looks at it, to be honest, before she wraps it back up in the tissue paper.

'Thanks,' she whispers. 'It's beautiful. Can you keep it here until nearer the time? At least until we've moved.'

'Of course,' I say, taking it from her and putting it back in the drawer. I catch her expression as I stand up. She's frowning.

'What are all those other things?' she asks.

'Oh, just some bits and bobs I've got in ready.'

'But you've only just found out.'

'Well, yes. But it was only a matter of timing, wasn't it?'

She walks towards the door. I think she's still worried about what Lee said earlier.

'Listen,' I say, going over to her. 'Don't you worry about our Lee. I'll work on him. I expect he's just a bit uptight about becoming a father, thinking about providing for the baby. As soon as it's born I'll keep an eye out for summat local. A nice house with a garden. I'm sure he'll come round once the baby's here.'

She looks at me and says nothing before heading back down the stairs.

Angela Griffiths ▸ **Jess Mount**
15 April 2018

Here he is. Little Harrison, one year old today. He's doing a special smile for his mummy, but he wants you to know that grandma's taking very good care of him. He loves playing in my garden (we always said he'd like to live in a house with a garden, didn't we?) and now he's taken his first steps, he'll soon be kicking a football around, just like his daddy did. Daddy will be back home soon, but in the meantime Harrison is here with me and we are both loving spending time together. He is the most special grandson I could ever have been given. Thank you.

JESS

Saturday, 15 October 2016

I only went on Facebook because it was his birthday. I have managed to stay away for three months, but I was so desperate to see a photo of him that I broke my vow not to go on again. It wasn't as if I didn't know what to expect, but still the sight of H is enough to reduce me to a blubbering mound of tears. He has changed so much. He is a proper little boy now, with so many teeth I can't even count them. He has a lot more hair too. Dark and quite thick. And although he is still unmistakably Lee's son, I think I can see a tiny little bit of me, or even Mum, around the mouth.

'Hello, you,' I whisper, holding the phone to my chest as if I am holding him, letting him know that I am here. The fear that I will never see this version of H in real life, that I will be gone by the time he's three months old, grips me. I don't want to believe it is true, but everything else has come true so far, even when I have fought against it, so why should this part be any different? And I don't understand why H is still living with Angela. Surely Dad should have him now that Lee has been arrested? I suppose he's still considered to be not guilty at the moment ... once he's been convicted and Lee has gone to jail, Dad must get him back then. Surely my letter would count for something? I know it's not a will but they are my final wishes. And I made it very clear to Sadie in that letter who I wanted to look after H – and why it wasn't safe to leave him with Lee.

I will fight to stay here with H, because the last thing in the world I want is to leave him. I will not have him being brought up by anyone else – and certainly not Angela.

I go into the bathroom and wash my face. Lee is out. He's gone to the Leeds match with Scott from work. I've arranged to go and see Dad and Sadie this afternoon. I haven't told them about being pregnant yet, but it's time now. I'm three months gone and it'll soon be hard to cover up that I'm starting to show. It feels like an incredibly big, grown-up thing to do, to tell your father you're pregnant. And I don't feel big or grown up at the moment. I feel small and tired and still a bit sick. But I know it's got to be done.

Dad is cooking me lunch when I get there. It feels weird, walking into my own home when it's not my home anymore. Everything looks the same but it already feels smaller and more distant.

'Hi,' he says, hugging me and kissing me on both cheeks. 'Lovely to see you.' I know he means it too. I can tell by the way his eyes have lit up. I try not to think about how lonely he must be without me here.

'Hi. How've you been?'

'Yeah, fine. Keeping busy, you know.'

I nod, even though I suspect he hasn't been fine at all. The smell of whatever he's cooking is already making me feel slightly nauseous. I couldn't think of a way to tell him I wouldn't be able to eat some foods without him guessing, and I so wanted to tell him in person.

'I've got some news,' I say, deciding not to keep it any longer. 'You're going to be a grandad.'

He stares at me for a second, as if waiting for me to start laughing and tell him I'm having him on. When I don't, he appears to shake a little before he starts tearing up.

'Hey,' I say, going over and giving him a hug. 'I thought you'd be pleased.'

It is a moment or two before he can speak. When he finally does, he simply says, 'I am. I'm more than pleased. Overwhelmed, to be honest. How far gone are you?'

'Three months. It's due on April the ninth.'

He looks at me.

'Yeah,' I say. 'I know. It's kind of like she sent him so we'd have something happy going on to dull the pain.'

Dad wipes his eyes. 'She'd have loved it, Jess. She'd have been overjoyed.'

'She'd probably have started knitting, wouldn't she?'

'God, yeah. She'd be knitting from now until the baby comes. You'd be under six foot of booties and hats by the time it arrived.'

'And she'd have told me loads of stuff about what to do and not to do, what to eat and not to eat. She'd have issued a new advice notice every day.'

Dad smiles before his face drops slightly. 'I've cooked fish, is that OK?'

'It's fine, thanks. Although I haven't got a very big appetite at the moment. I've had pretty bad morning sickness, to be honest.'

'Oh love, I'm sorry. I remember what your mum was like. I wish I'd known.'

'I didn't want to tell people before three months. You know what it's like.'

'Sure. Are you telling Angela tomorrow?'

I wonder for a second whether to lie but decide against it. 'She guessed, actually. Because I couldn't eat Sunday lunch. It kind of gave the game away.'

'Oh, right,' he says, obviously trying very hard not to be offended. 'I bet she was pleased.'

'Yeah. She was. A bit over the top, to be honest.'

'What do you mean?'

'Oh, she wanted to start looking at buggies straight away. And she's got a drawer of baby clothes put by. No pressure there, then.'

'Wow. Well I can't compete with that. We might have a few of your old things in the attic, but probably nothing useful.'

'These aren't Lee's old things. They're brand new. She bought them for her grandchild before he was even conceived.'

'That's a bit odd.'

'She gave me a christening gown, too. Lee's old one. She wants the baby to wear it.'

'I wouldn't have thought you'd want a christening.'

'I don't. I'll have to save that argument for later. I told her to hang on to it for now.'

Dad seems thoughtful for a moment. He shakes his head a couple of times.

'What?'

'I'm still trying to take it all in. A year ago you hadn't even met Lee, and now you're going to be parents. I take it he's happy about it?'

'Yeah. He was the one who wanted to try.'

'Oh, you mean it was actually planned?'

'Great,' I say, laughing, 'you think I'm just one big disaster area, don't you?'

'No, I didn't mean to . . . It just hadn't occurred to me that you'd want to start a family so soon, that's all.'

I look down and twiddle my wedding ring.

'Well, you never know what's around the corner, do you?'

'Hey, come on. You know what Mum would say to that.'

'Yeah, and she'd also tell me you never regret the things you do, only the things you don't do.'

Dad is quiet for a moment. 'You'll be a brilliant mum.'

'Will I? I can't imagine it, somehow. I totally expect to leave the baby on the train and put nappies on backwards and do loads of stupid things like that.'

'You'll love your child to pieces,' says Dad. 'And that's all that matters.'

*

I've arranged to meet Sadie by the canal. I thought the fresh air would do me good, and I didn't want to tell her in a cafe in case she has another public meltdown. I suspect her reaction won't be as positive as Dad's. I mean, she's not gaining a grandchild, is she? She isn't gaining anything from it. Just losing a little bit more of her best friend. A best friend she's hardly seen for the past two months.

'Hey,' she says, giving me a hug as she arrives. 'How you doing, stranger?'

'Yeah, OK, thanks.'

She looks at me. 'Why only OK?'

I decide I may as well go for it now. 'Well, I've spent most of the past six weeks chucking my guts up.'

Her mouth falls open as the penny drops. 'Oh my god. You're pregnant?'

I nod, giving a little smile as I do so in the hope that it will make her see it's a good thing, at least as far as I'm concerned.

'Fucking hell.'

I shake my head. 'That's great. Maybe they should start doing cards like that in the shops. "Fucking hell, you're pregnant."'

'Sorry. I'm shocked, that's all.'

'Yeah, woman gets married, has baby. Never really been done before, has it?'

'But it's you, Jess. Not some random woman. My best friend who, until recently, still slobbed about in her PJs until eleven every morning. I haven't even got my head around the fact that you're married yet. Now I've got to start going shopping for maternity clothes with you.'

'Well, that's how it is. I'm sorry if you're not pleased for me.' I start walking up the towpath. I hear Sadie groan and run to catch up with me.

'Hey, I wasn't saying that. Of course I'm pleased. As long as you're happy about it. Are you?'

'Yeah,' I say.

'And Lee?'

'Big time. It was his idea.'

'So it was planned?'

'You sound like my dad. I did make it to the sex ed classes, you know.'

'You never told me you were going to try.'

'Yeah, well, you made it pretty clear it was the last thing you wanted.'

We stand to the side as a kid goes past us on a bike, then walk on in silence. I know that Sadie will be the first to crack.

'Look, I'm sorry, OK?' she says after a bit. 'But if this is what you really want, and you haven't been pressured into it, then of course I'm happy for you.'

'Really?'

'Yeah. I mean, it'll be like being an auntie, right? I'll get to do all the good bits and give the baby back to you when it throws up or needs its nappy changing.'

'Good to know I can count on you.'

'You can, though. Seriously. I'm here for you. I'll even be there for the birth if you want me to.'

'Don't be stupid. Do you not remember what happened

when you held my hand while I had my Deathly Hallows tattoo done?'

'What, you screaming the place down and drawing blood from my palm with your fingernails, you mean? No, I've forgotten that entirely.'

'Maybe I should go for a caesarean.'

'Just get yourself knocked out with drugs. Take everything you can get your hands on.'

'Anyway, you haven't got to worry about that bit. Lee will be there with me.'

'Are you sure you want that? Remember what Robbie Williams said about it being like watching your favourite pub burn down?'

'Oh cheers.'

'What? You always say you like the fact that I give it to you straight.'

'Yeah, maybe not that straight, though. So when I blow up like a hippopotamus, don't start calling me Gloria.'

'OK, I'll send you *Madagascar* gifs instead.'

'I can't wait.'

'Anyway, you haven't got to worry. I bet you'll have one of those neat little bumps where people will hardly notice you're pregnant.'

'What I'd really like would be one of those pregnancies where the woman doesn't even realise she's up the duff until she sits on the loo and a baby pops out.'

'I never believe those stories,' says Sadie, as a big dog stops to sniff at her boots before bounding on.

'I don't now. I've never felt so tired and sick in my entire life.'

'You should have told me.'

I shrug. 'I was keeping shtum until I was three months gone.'

She hesitates. I know what she is thinking. I can see the concerned look gathering on her face.

'But nothing bad happened, did it?' she says softly, trying to reassure me.

'No,' I say. 'Not yet.'

We stand to one side for a moment as three men in Lycra cycle past.

'Everything will be fine,' says Sadie.

'Yeah,' I reply. 'Let's hope so.'

Lee is already back when I get home. The TV is on – Sky Sports.

'Hi. Did they win?' I ask, going over to the sofa and giving him a kiss.

'Yeah. Two–nil.'

'Good.'

'How was your dad?'

'Dead chuffed. Said to say congratulations.'

'I told you he'd be fine.'

'I know. Cheeky sod thought it was an accident, mind. Sadie said the same.'

Lee frowns at me. 'When did you see her?'

'Afterwards. We went for a walk along the canal.'

'I don't know why you still bother with her.'

I take a step back, surprised that he's being so rude. 'What do you mean? She's my best friend.'

'Was. You hardly see her now. You've moved on.'

'We've been friends since we were four, Lee.'

'It doesn't matter. People grow apart. You'll have nothing in common soon. You'll be bringing up a kid and she'll be going out with her other single mates. You may as well let it go. It's not like she'll be a great loss.'

I feel myself bristling. I can't believe he has just said that. 'I don't tell you who you should be mates with.'

Lee sits upright on the sofa and jabs his finger at me. 'I don't appreciate your tone,' he says.

'And I don't appreciate you telling me to stop seeing my best mate.'

I know as soon as I say it that I shouldn't have. He picks up the TV remote and hurls it across the room at me. I duck and it hits the wall behind me. I burst into tears.

'I'm sorry,' he says straight away, his eyes wide and staring.

'What the hell do you think you're playing at?' I sob. He jumps up off the sofa and comes towards me but I push him away.

'Look, I overreacted. I'm sorry.'

'You could have hurt me, or the baby.'

He sinks down to his knees on the floor, holds his head in his hands. 'That is the last thing I would ever want to do,' he says.

'So why the hell did you do it?'

He looks up at me and sighs, his big eyes pleading for

forgiveness. 'My mum and dad used to row a lot,' he says. 'It scares me sometimes when we start to argue. I worry we're going to end up like them.'

I find myself putting my hand on his shoulder. It's instinctive – he is upset, and I've gone to comfort him. Yet I'm aware that he should be the one comforting me.

'I'm sorry about that,' I say. 'But that's still no excuse for what you did.'

'I know. It's you being pregnant. It's brought it all back. Started me worrying about what sort of dad I'll be.'

I don't know what to say. I want to tell him he'll be a great dad, but I don't know if that's true. I have no idea what's true at the moment.

Lee gets to his feet. He holds out his hands to me. I shut my eyes and take them, wanting it all to go away. Wanting to pretend it never happened.

'It won't happen again,' he says.

'Good.'

'I didn't mean to upset you. I was just suggesting that it might be a good idea to ease things off a little with Sadie. Bit of a green-eyed monster thing going on there, if you ask me.'

'It's not easy when your best mate gets married.'

'Like I said, maybe it's time for you to move on without her.'

He pats the sofa next to him, but it feels kind of disloyal to Sadie to sit down next to him. And I don't want him to realise that I am still shaking.

'I'll go and make us a tea,' I say.

Sadie Ward
28/05/2018 9:05am

They've got another witness. Your cleaner, Farah. The woman you told me about. The detective said she hadn't told them everything before, because she was scared she would lose her job and get deported. Something about her discretionary leave being due to expire and her not wanting to do anything which might affect it being renewed. But she's been told she can stay for good now, which is why she came forward and made a new statement. She knew, Jess. Knew about what he was doing to you. You might not have realised it at the time, but they don't miss a thing, cleaners. They're in your bedroom, your bathroom. They see your rubbish, they flush your toilet. They clear up your mess.

The detective said Farah saw bruises on you. Always in places that could be covered up when you left the house. She saw something else, too. The detective won't tell me what but she says it's important. That it strengthens our case enormously. He's going down, Jess. We're going to put the bastard away for good. And your dad's got a solicitor to try to get H back. Lee's mum's hanging on to him for now, but she won't be able to if Lee's found guilty. We'll get him back for you, Jess. If it's the last thing we do.

JESS

Monday, 28 November 2016

I am shaking in the bathroom as I read it. Our cleaner, who I have never even met, is going to testify against Lee. Why? What reason could she have? Other than telling the truth, that is.

Maybe Lee complains about her and she loses her job and wants to get her revenge? But he's always said she's a great cleaner. She is. We get back from work every Monday and the place is spotless. It really does feel like we're living in a hotel. And she's reliable, too – never fails to turn up.

I put my phone in my dressing gown pocket and open the pedal bin, peering at the contents inside. What does she see? Does she find something in there? Something hidden?

A knock at the bathroom door makes me jump. The bin clangs shut. The door opens and Lee's face peers around it. 'Are you nearly ready? We need to leave at ten past.'

'Yeah, I'll be out in a few minutes.'

He glances at my maternity bra and knickers hanging up behind the door.

'On with the passion killers then,' he says. 'I don't want to be late.'

I breathe out as he shuts the door behind him. I'd tried to tell him I'd be fine to go to the scan on my own. I wasn't sure it would be a good idea to have him around when I saw the image of H on the screen. I don't think I'll react like other mums, seeing their babies for the first time. Because it won't be the first time I've seen him.

But Lee has insisted on coming. Said he's not going to miss out on the opportunity of seeing his child for the first time. And now I can't decide whether to be pleased about that or terrified. Because the signs are there now – the flashes of temper, losing control. And it's making me think he may, after all, be capable of the terrible things I have been reading about.

We sit down in the clinic waiting room. It's the first time I have been surrounded by other pregnant women. As much as I don't want to compare myself to them, it's hard not to. Several have bigger bumps than me. One smaller. Almost all of them are older. Most are a lot older. I wonder if they're looking at me and thinking I'm too young to be a mum. The song 'Teenage Dirtbag' starts going around in my head. I'm glad Lee is here with me, otherwise they'd probably have me down as a single mum as well. I feel like getting a 'planned pregnancy' sign to put on my bump. Everyone we've told so far seems to think it must have been a mistake, a case of getting carried away on our honeymoon. People have no idea that this baby was more than planned. It already exists, out there in the future. All we were doing was making sure it arrived on time.

'Mrs Griffiths?' calls a woman in a blue uniform. Lee has to give me a nudge. I still haven't got used to the new name yet.

'Yes,' I say, standing up.

'Would you like to come through?'

'Can my husband come too?' I ask.

'Yes, of course.' She smiles.

We follow her through to a dimly lit room with a couch in the centre, surrounded by various hospital machines and screens.

'Right,' she says, looking at my notes, 'if you could just pop yourself up there and pull your leggings down a little and your top up so I can get a good look at your bump.'

I do as I am told. She puts paper towels inside the waist of my leggings and under my top.

'That's just to stop the gel from getting on your clothes,' she says. 'It might feel a bit cold when I put it on, but we need it to get clear pictures.'

Lee takes my hand. His palm is clammy in mine. Or maybe it is mine that is clammy, I'm not sure. I look at his face staring at the screen, desperate for something recognisable to appear. I try to imagine what this would be like if I didn't know everything was fine. If I was worried about all the usual things people are worried about, instead of being worried about what my husband might do to me when this baby is three months old.

She rolls the device around for a minute.

'Someone's very active this morning.' She smiles again.

'Is he?' I ask.

Lee looks around at me quizzically, as does the sonographer.

'My husband thinks it's a boy,' I say quickly.

'Well, if it keeps still for a moment, I might be able to let you know. I take it you'd like to?'

We both nod. Something comes into focus on the screen. He is lying with his head to the left, his little nose sticking up in the air. It looks like he's blowing bubbles. The sonographer twists the screen so we can see more clearly. Lee squeezes my hand, a smile lighting up his face. 'Well, everything's looking fine there,' she says after a while. 'And your husband's right. You have a little boy.'

Lee starts to cry. Proper man tears. He buries his head against my shoulder and I hold him to me. 'It's OK,' I whisper. 'Everything's going to be OK.'

I am telling him and I'm telling H, and most of all, I am telling myself.

We sit in Lee's car afterwards, staring at the black and white printout of the scan. Angela had suggested we have a 3D one. She showed me what the images look like on her iPad, but I thought they all looked like Dobby from *Harry Potter*, to be honest. Which is why I said the 2D one would be fine.

And it is. It is still quite clearly H. It's weird, but I actually recognise him from the photos. It's like going back in time. I wish I could erase the future from my head and simply be happy in this moment.

'He's perfect,' says Lee. 'Absolutely perfect.'

'I know. I love his little nose.'

'That must be your nose.'

'No. He looks like you. He's going to look just like you.'

'Now we know it's a boy,' says Lee. 'Am I allowed to start suggesting names?'

I feel my hand clenching the piece of paper tighter.

'You can suggest,' I say. 'Whether I'll agree to any of them is another matter.'

'I've only got one,' he says. 'I think you might remember. It's Harrison.'

I nod, swallowing hard. This is another chance. Maybe I can still change things. But I'm worried that if I do suggest a different name, and Lee agrees to it, Harrison will never exist. Maybe something will happen to this baby and I will lose him. At least I know now that Harrison is alive out there in the future, even if I'm not.

'Harrison's great. But why don't we just call him H for now? I don't want people to know his full name until he's born.'

'Fine by me.' Lee shrugs. 'I guess it's nice to keep something a secret until the birth.'

I smile at him. I feel like I have bought myself some more time. All I need to do now is use it wisely.

Lee drops me off back at the flat. He'd arranged for me to have a half-day off work, just in case the appointment ran late. And because I said I'd like to go home afterwards and get myself cleaned up and changed for work.

He waves as he drives off. He is going straight to meet a client in Harrogate. I go through the main door and press the button for the lift. It comes straight away. I step inside and the doors close in front of me. I put my hand on my bump and stroke it.

'I saw you, H,' I say. 'So I know you're in there now. And I can't wait to meet you. But, in the meantime, I'm going to take such good care of you. I promise.'

The doors open. I step out and get the key from my pocket, jiggling it in the lock until it turns. I dump my backpack in the hallway, still holding the scan of H in my other hand. I walk towards the kitchen, intending to stick it on the fridge with a magnet. I am going to be like every other pregnant woman in the country. I am going to be normal and this is going to be a normal pregnancy and I am going to do all that soppy stuff that other women do, because all I want right now is to be normal.

The bathroom door opens. I feel myself go cold inside. A dark figure comes out carrying something and I scream. I scream so loudly that I can hear it vibrating inside me long after it has come out. There is a gasp and a clatter and a young woman is staring back at me. A slight woman wearing a hijab, with dark, scared eyes.

'I am sorry,' she says, in slightly broken English. 'It is me, your cleaner. I did not mean to scare you.'

I nod at her, gasping, waiting until I am able to speak.

'It's OK,' I say, bending to pick up the bathroom cleaner she has dropped and passing it to her. 'I forgot you would be here.'

'Thank you,' she says, taking it from me. 'You are Mrs Griffiths. I have seen you in the photo.' She points towards the living room. 'Forgive me looking, but it is such a beautiful dress.'

'Thank you,' I reply, my breathing starting to return to normal. 'Please call me Jess.'

She wipes her hand on her apron and holds it out to me. 'Pleased to meet you. I am Farah.'

JESS

November 2008

The carriage is packed with commuters as the train pulls out of Leeds station. I went over after school to get a birthday present for Sadie and now I'm wishing I'd waited until the weekend. I don't normally travel at rush hour. I don't like the sensation of someone else's body pressed up against mine. I don't want to breathe in as they breathe out. I want my own air, my own space.

I should shuffle further down inside the carriage, where there is a little more space, but I do not want to be that far away from the emergency pull handle. If anything were to happen, that is where I would need to be. Ideally between that and the thing you can use to break the glass. I try to find a spot where I can see both. I plot my route towards them: past the woman with the pink tote bag and stopping just before the middle-aged man with a beard and glasses. They won't do it, you see. People freeze in an emergency. Well, some people do anyway, I have read about it. Paralysed by fear. That is why you always have to stay alert and have your wits about you. You can't rely on other people to be good in a crisis, which is why I spend the first part of every journey working out my exit strategy. Sometimes I move away from fat people, fearing they could fall on top of me. It would be no good if the only person in the carriage who knew what to do was trapped underneath some lard arse.

Today I am OK – the people around me all happen to be lightweights. No bulky luggage either, which is good. The last thing you want is to be trapped underneath one of those giant suitcases.

The train starts to gather pace as we head out of Leeds. I clutch the pole I am holding more tightly, watching as my knuckles whiten. I didn't manage to get a proper look at the driver because I ran onto the train a minute before it was due to leave. Usually, if I'm waiting on the platform, I will have a good look as it comes in. The middle-aged drivers are the best; if they're too young they might be inexperienced. Too old and they might have a heart attack or be more likely to fall asleep.

We take a bend at speed and the man next to me steps backwards and bumps into me. He mumbles an apology. I slide my hand down the pole a little, aware that my palm is sweating. I try looking out of the window, but things are starting to rush past too quickly. I bring my attention back inside the carriage, look down at the floor and try to guess what shoe size people are. I notice one woman with tiny feet, maybe a size three or less. It is harder to tell with the men, particularly between nine and eleven. A young man opposite me has pointy shoes on, perhaps a size twelve, although the points always make their feet look bigger than they are.

I glance up as the train jolts. Something isn't right, I know it. I take a step towards the emergency alarm. He's going too fast. It doesn't usually feel this bumpy. Maybe the driver is young and doing it for a dare. Some of the lads at school are stupid enough to do things like *that. Either that or he's older and he's falling asleep, unaware that the train is gathering pace.*

My top is damp against my back. I can hear my breath, fast and shallow. If the guard comes past I will ask him what the problem is. Maybe he can go and have a word. I look in both directions but there is no sign of a guard. He is probably at the other end of the train, checking tickets. Paying no attention to what is happening. It will be ages before he gets to me. Too late, in fact. I let go of the pole and take another step towards the alarm. Nobody around me seems bothered. They are too busy looking at their phones to notice, of course. The train jolts again, and seems to get faster still. No one else is going to do this. It is going to have to be me. I wipe the sweat from my brow then wipe my hand on my skirt. I can hear the wheels grating on the tracks, they're out of control. We will derail any moment if I don't do it.

I lunge forward, grab the emergency handle and pull. The brakes screech and the carriage jolts forward before the train judders to a halt. People look up from their phones and stare at me. A man calls out, 'Hey! What the hell do you think you're doing?' I smile at him, knowing I have saved him, saved myself, saved everyone. Other people start shouting and swearing and pointing. I sink down onto my heels, shaking at the thought of how close we came to disaster. I am still squatting like that on the floor when the guard arrives. Squatting and calling out for my mummy.

ANGELA

Sunday, 25 December 2016

I have always loved Christmas. So many memories of Lee waking up at three in the morning to dive to the bottom of Santa's sack. He always started at the bottom for some reason, never the top. Simon didn't even bother coming in to watch him sometimes, but I wouldn't have missed it for the world. They grow up so quickly, you see. Before you know it, they're grumpy teens who don't even get out of bed on Christmas morning.

To be honest, it's not been the same for many years now. I've busied myself preparing lunch for Lee, having a little bop in the kitchen to all the Christmas songs while I work. And don't get me wrong, it's been lovely having him to dinner. But at the end of the day, Christmas is about children. And next year there will be a child in this house again. Granted, he will be a bit young to know what it's all about, but that won't stop us making an enormous fuss of him. Christmas is on again. A proper family Christmas. Even this year I have Jess and her dad coming. That is two more than last year. It made sense to invite her father. They might have left early to go to his place otherwise and it would have been such a shame for the day to end there.

I am glad it's a little boy they're having. I think Lee will like it, having a lad he can play football with and take to matches when he's older. There's plenty of time for them to try for a girl later. That's why it's good they have started so early. And why I'm glad he didn't settle down with one of these career women who wait until their mid-thirties before they even think about starting a family. Talk about leaving it to the last minute. No, have them young and enjoy them, I say. And the bonus is you get grandparents young enough to be able to help out with them too.

They won't tell me the name they have chosen. They insist on only calling him H, and although I have been through every boy's name beginning with H in the baby books, they remain tight-lipped. My money is on Harley; it's modern enough to appeal to them and Lee used to like his bikes when he was younger. Either that or Hilton, after the hotel they stayed in on their honeymoon. The celebrities do that, don't they? Name their child after the place where they were conceived. The Beckhams did it with Brooklyn, anyway. It's a shame he wasn't conceived in Horsforth, although I don't suppose they'd have gone for it if he was.

At least knowing his initials has helped. I have embroidered them on the baby blankets already. And knowing it is a boy means I have been able to start buying blue things. There is only so far you can go with lemon or beige before it starts to get a bit much.

I check the turkey, then the veg and roasties. Everything is under control. I cook a good Christmas dinner. Even Simon used to say so, albeit somewhat grudgingly. Jess's father did offer to cook for us. I told Jess to thank him and suggested he brought the Christmas pudding, so he felt he had contributed something. To be honest, I wouldn't have wanted a chef running around cooking in my kitchen. From what I've seen on the TV, they're not the tidiest of people. This way, he'll simply turn up with one bowl to warm up and I won't have to worry about all of the mess.

I go upstairs to freshen up before they arrive. The whole house is decorated. Lee always jokes that it's like stepping into Santa's grotto. It's nice though, to make a bit of an effort. It cheers everyone up. It cheers me up, anyway.

Jess's father arrives first. It feels quite strange, having a man kiss me on both cheeks on my doorstep and wish me a happy Christmas. He hands me a bottle of wine; I don't really know anything about wine, but I suspect it is a good one because I've never heard of it.

He smells nice as well. I noticed that about him at the wedding. Something to do with the Italian blood, I expect. I always think Mediterranean types take more pride in their personal grooming. Although having said that, Lee always smells nice too.

'Hello, Joe. And a happy Christmas to you too. Our Lee

and Jess aren't here yet, but come in and make yourself at home.'

'Thanks. I've got the pudding in here,' he says, holding up a bag. 'It'll just need warming up.'

I take his coat and hang it up before he follows me through to the kitchen. The table is already laid; the crackers are from the Pound Shop, because no one will know the difference, and I've added a bit of holly from the market to give it the finishing touch.

'This all looks very festive,' says Joe, putting the bag down on the counter and rubbing his hands together.

'Well, we haven't had guests for Christmas for a while. I don't know about you, but I can't wait till next year – it will be so lovely to have the little one here. I'm counting down the days already.'

'I think Jess is too. It's been a tough pregnancy for her.'

'I know, but it'll all be forgotten once he arrives. Her whole world will change then. I know mine did.'

'Yeah. Mine too.'

'She is looking forward to it, isn't she? Only she's seemed a bit quiet lately.'

'Just a bit anxious about how she'll manage, I think. It'll be tough for her without her mum around.'

'Yes, of course, but I've already told her I'll do whatever I can to help out. I'll pop round every day.'

'Thank you. I know she really appreciates that.'

'And our Lee will be a very hands-on dad, I'm sure. It'll be the making of them both, being parents. There's nothing in the world better than it, is there?'

'No. No there's not.'

Lee and Jess arrive shortly afterwards. She's wearing a baggy beige tunic. There are shadows under her eyes and her hair isn't as shiny as usual.

'Happy Christmas to you both,' I say, giving them each a hug. 'And to this little one.' I put my hand on Jess's bump. She flinches and steps back. I don't know why, because I've done it before and she has never said anything.

Lee looks at her and back to me. 'I think she's trying to make sure he doesn't kick you,' he says.

'Is he moving? Can you feel him kick now?'

Jess nods.

'Oh, how lovely. It makes such a difference, doesn't it? When you can actually feel them moving about inside you.'

'Yeah.'

Joe comes out into the hall. Jess throws her arms around him. I see her bottom lip trembling.

'Did you take them?' she asks quietly.

'Yes. They're in the vase next to mine. It's all neat and tidy down there.'

He looks up and catches my eye. Whatever they're talking about, they clearly don't want to share it.

'Now, come in and sit down, love,' I say.' Take the weight off your feet.'

She zips off her boots, follows me through to the kitchen and sits down next to her dad at the table.

'Can you give me a hand with the wine, please, Lee?' I ask. He comes over. 'Is she OK?' I whisper as I pass him the bottle opener.

'Yeah. Just a bit upset about her mum. It's the first year she hadn't been to the grave on Christmas day, but I told her she should take it easy. Put the baby first.'

'Absolutely. You did right, love. I expect it's just her hormones playing up.'

Lee opens the wine and takes it over to the table while I get the warmed plates out of the oven.

'Right, time to get the turkey out, I think.'

'Can I give you a hand at all?' Joe asks.

'No need, thanks. Our Lee will take care of it. He's the chief carver in this house.'

I hand Lee the carving knife. I suggested getting one of those electric ones in the sale one year but he wasn't keen. Said he was perfectly capable of doing it without. I wonder if he remembers how we had to look away when Simon did it. How he hated us watching in case it went wrong.

I dish up the roasties, carrots and parsnips as Lee passes the plates along. I take the gravy jug over to the table along with the cranberry sauce, which I've got in specially this year. Lee brings the first two plates over while I go back for the others.

'Right we are then,' I say, sitting myself down and picking up my wine glass. 'I think this calls for a toast.' I look at Lee.

'To next Christmas,' he says, raising his glass. 'Which I am sure will be a lot noisier than this one.'

'And to absent loved ones,' adds Joe, raising his.

I look at Jess and realise she still has an empty glass.

'Oh, I'm sorry love. What can I get you?'

I see Joe glance at Lee and then back to Jess.

'You can have a spot of wine, love,' her father says. 'A little bit won't hurt.'

She shakes her head. 'Water will be fine, thanks.'

'I've got orange juice, if you'd prefer? Or Coke, if you can handle the fizzy stuff.'

'Honestly, water will be great.'

I take her glass and go and fill it. The Christmas CD finishes, so I press play again and sit back down at the table having given her the water.

'Last Christmas' by Wham! comes on. I always liked the sleigh bells in it, proper little Christmas classic it is. I usually sing along, but not when we have guests.

'Right. Where were we?' I say. 'Jess, did you want to make a toast?'

Her mouth opens but nothing comes out. Tears start spilling out of her eyes. 'Sorry,' she says, standing up. 'You start without me.'

She pushes her chair back and hurries out of the kitchen. I look at the others, not quite sure what to do. 'You'd better go after her, Lee,' I say. 'See what's the matter.'

Lee stands up, but Joe reaches out and puts a hand on his arm.

'Give her a few minutes,' he says. 'It's always a tough day for her. She'll need a bit of time to get herself together.'

'Yes, of course,' I say. 'She was so young when she lost her, too. I was fifty when I lost my mum and that was hard enough.'

'Do start, though,' says Joe. 'Like she said.'

'You're right. It would be a shame to let it all go cold. Shall I put hers back in the oven to keep warm, do you think?'

'I'll do it,' says Lee, standing up and taking it over. 'Though she hasn't got much of an appetite at the moment anyway, to be honest.'

'Did she take it badly?' I ask Joe. 'When her mum died, I mean.'

'She had a tough time,' replies Joe.

Lee sits back down at the table and we all start eating.

'And did she get any help?' I ask between mouthfuls. 'Only it's never too late for it, you know. I was listening to someone talking about it on Radio 2 last week, how losses like that can affect you for years to come.'

Joe looks at me. He seems to be struggling for words.

'We were all there for her,' he says.

'Oh, I'm not saying you didn't support her. I'm sure you did. I mean professional help, all the counselling and stuff you can get nowadays.'

Joe looks at Lee. Neither of them say anything.

'What is it?' I ask.

'Look. Lee obviously hasn't told you, and I appreciate his discretion, but perhaps it's best you know that Jess was put under psychiatric care for a while after her mum died.'

'Oh. Oh, I see. You mean she had some sort of breakdown?'

Joe nods and looks down. 'I think it's important that everyone who's going to be supporting her after the birth is aware of that. Just so we can all keep an eye on her.'

'Yes, of course. Does this mean she's going to be one of those girls who gets postnatal depression? Only I've heard them talk about that on the radio as well and there's a lot of help they can give for that nowadays too.'

'No, I'm not saying that at all. I just want us all to be looking out for her. I want to make sure we don't miss any of the warning signs. I'm sure Lee would agree.'

I look at Lee. His eyes are dark, his face contorted. I know that face. I know it all too well. He didn't know. Jess must have kept it from him. And now there is going to be a terrible scene.

'Oh, look,' I say. 'We haven't pulled the crackers. Here you are, Joe, grab the end of this!'

Joe and I have just put our paper hats on when Jess comes back in.

'Are you OK, love?' I ask.

'Yeah, I'm fine, thanks.'

'I'll get your dinner out of the oven. Our Lee popped it in to keep it warm for you.'

I put it down on the table in front of her. 'Don't worry if you can't manage it all, just do the best you can.'

She looks up and sees Lee. He is staring at her, his jaw set, his brows heavy. She frowns and looks straight back down again. Fiddles with the napkin in her lap.

I have to do something. I have to lighten the mood. I don't

want everything spoilt again. Too many Christmases have been spoilt over the years.

'Anyway. Happy Christmas,' I say, raising my glass. 'To new beginnings.'

The glasses clink softly against each other. There are a collection of mumbled happy Christmases. No one says anything for a while after that. We eat quietly, accompanied only by the CD. It is when Johnny Mathis gets going with 'When a Child is Born' that I look up and see that Jess and her father both have tears in their eyes.

'There's more stuffing in the oven if anyone wants it,' I say. Nobody says anything. I get up anyway and bring it over. On the way past, I press skip on the CD player and Paul McCartney's 'Wonderful Christmastime' comes on. Somehow I don't feel it would be appropriate to sing along.

Joe Mount
25/06/2018 8:05pm

I should have seen the signs. That's what I keep torturing myself about. When I look back, they were there, I just didn't want to see them. Like when you didn't come to your mum's grave that Christmas and I put it down to you being tired. Or when Lee didn't pour you any wine, without even asking you. I thought it was your decision. I thought everything was your decision. I didn't believe any man could make my daughter do something she didn't want to. I mean, it's not like you were one of those delicate little things, is it? You always gave as good as you got. I should know, I was on the receiving end of it enough times.

I suppose I did notice that you'd changed, but I simply thought it was you growing up. That marriage and motherhood had calmed you down, made you less fiery. My little girl had become a mum – of course she'd be different. That's what I told myself.

And now I know what was going on – well, some of what was going on, I'm steeling myself to hear the rest of it at the trial – I realise that it was all part of it. And I am sorry, so sorry, that I didn't realise and step in to help you. If I'd known, I would have come round there straight away and got you, brought you back home. Barricaded the bloody doors and windows to keep him from ever getting to you again. But I didn't know. And you didn't tell me. And that is why I will be visiting your grave in a few weeks' time, on the anniversary of your death. And why I will be sitting in a courtroom in September, listening to how that bastard destroyed you and took your life. I trusted him, Jess. The stupid fool that I am trusted him, because he was always so polite and well turned out. And even when Sadie came to talk to me, my first thought was that you were on the verge of a breakdown again, not that he was pushing you to the brink.

I am dreading the court case, Jess. At times I don't know how I will possibly get through it. But I will be there every single day and I will listen to every single word, because no one is ever going to pull the wool over my eyes again.

JESS

We sit in silence during the short journey home. It makes it worse, the knowledge that whatever he has got to say to me cannot be said in the car. Something happened while I was out of the room, I knew it by the tone of Angela's voice when I came back in and the way my dad squeezed my hand when we left, as if he was trying to say sorry for something that I didn't even know about yet. And, most of all, I know it because of the way Lee looked at me at the table and has barely spoken to me since.

I think Dad must have said something about Mum, about what happened to me after she died. I don't know exactly what, but anything was too much. I chose not to tell Lee about it because I was scared it would put him off me, to be honest. And I know that if Dad did say something, it's only because he worries about me, but I am still bloody furious with him. It is something that happened to Jess Mount and I am not Jess Mount now. I am Jess Griffiths, and it's got nothing to do with her. Nothing at all.

We pull up outside the apartments. Lee gets out, slamming the door behind him. He comes round and opens the door for me. Usually, he would give me a hand, as I now find it difficult to get out of a car in anything resembling a ladylike fashion, but he doesn't tonight. He stands there and watches me struggle. As soon as I am out he locks the car and strides off towards the front door. I think for a moment that he won't let me get in the lift with him, that I will either have to wait for it to come back down or drag myself up the stairs, but he holds the button for me until I am in.

To be honest, I wish he hadn't. I've never seen him like this before and I have no idea if it's safe for me to be in there with him. It's like standing next to a volcano just before it erupts. My body is preparing itself for a fight-or-flight response, but my brain keeps reminding me that, at five months pregnant, I am hardly in a condition to do either. I stare straight ahead, avoiding even glancing at his reflection in the mirror in case it tips him over the edge. I sigh as the lift doors open, then I step out and wait for Lee to let us in. I can almost hear the steam hissing out of him. I realise that this could be it, the point where he blows his top and hits me for the first time. Maybe it is all about to start, and here I am walking into the apartment after him. There will be nothing I can do at all once I am inside. If I scream, no one will hear me. I will be on my own.

The door shuts behind us. I try to brace myself for whatever is about to happen. He turns and looks at me, as if waiting for me to say something.

'Tell me what's happened. Please tell me,' I say.

'I think you're the one who needs to tell me a few things. Starting with the truth.'

'Is it about what happened after Mum died?'

'I don't know, Jess, you tell me. I don't seem to know anything about you.'

'I had to go into hospital for a bit.'

'A psychiatric hospital, apparently.'

'Yeah. I had a bit of a meltdown, that's all. I wasn't thinking straight.'

'So why the hell didn't you tell me about it?' He screams it at me.

I cower back against the wall. 'I didn't think it mattered. I was fifteen. I don't know anything about you when you were fifteen.'

'You know that I wasn't in a psychiatric hospital.'

'It wouldn't matter if you had been. It wouldn't change anything.'

'You made me look stupid.' He practically spits it out. His face is only a couple of inches from mine. I feel his breath against my face. If he is going to hit me, I wish he would just get it over with. Instinctively, I put my hands over my bump.

'Look, I'm sorry, OK? I didn't know my dad was going to say anything. He had no right to tell you.'

Lee grabs hold of my left wrist, squeezing it so hard it hurts.

'So is there anything else you need to tell me, while we're about it? Any more little secrets? Ex-boyfriends who are now in Broadmoor?'

'Lee. Don't.'

'Why not? Scared I might not like what I hear?'

I start to cry.

'Oh, that's right, turn on the waterworks.'

'What's that supposed to mean?'

'It's what women do when they want to get off the hook, isn't it?'

'I'm five months pregnant, Lee. It's another Christmas Day without my mum and my husband is shouting at me. Perhaps that might have something to do with it?'

He puts his face right up against mine. 'You lied to me, Jess. You made me look stupid. And I am telling you now that you will never do that again, do you hear me?'

I gulp and nod. He lets go of my wrist and heads for the bedroom, pulling the door shut behind him.

I slump to the floor in the hallway, sobbing and shaking. It is happening. He is turning into the monster I told myself he could never be. This is where it starts, where it changes. And maybe it is possible to get from here to murder in six months. If that's true, then what the hell am I doing still here? H gives me a little kick, as if to remind me of the reason.

If I run now, Lee will find me, I am sure of it. And if he does, I have no idea what he will do to me or my baby. No. I need to stay here. It's the safest place for H to be. I don't think Lee will hurt him while I am here.

And maybe it will be better once H is born. Maybe Lee will change. People say parenthood changes them. Perhaps I can still stop this. All I have to do right now is protect H.

He is all that matters. As long as he is OK, then everything is fine.

I drag myself up off the floor, take my boots off and hang my jacket on the hook, removing my phone from the pocket as I do so. I head for the bathroom. The tiredness is crushing me but there is no way I am going to bed until I know Lee is asleep. I will not risk him starting up on me again.

I have a wee. Still, even now, I am surprised when I see my bump in front of me. It is not neat like Sadie said it would be. It makes me look like I am massively bloated. I can't see past it anymore when I look down. I am not the girl Lee fell for. Maybe that is why he's being like this to me. I wear maternity knickers and bras. I change into leggings and baggy jumpers as soon as I get home. I am too tired to go out and too tired for sex, though sometimes that doesn't seem to bother him. Mostly we have sex at night with the light off, as if he can't even bear to look at me anymore.

I wash and dry my hands, put the toilet lid down and sit heavily on it before picking up my phone. I read Dad's post with tears running down my cheeks. I wish I could call him right now. Tell him everything and have him come and pick me up. Have him chase the monsters away like he used to do when I had nightmares as a kid. But I also know I can't go back home. It is the first place Lee would come looking for me. And I will not put Dad through any more trauma. He has had enough to last a lifetime.

I flip back to my normal Facebook page. People are posting tributes to George Michael. For a minute I'm not sure if this is somehow in the future as well. I check on the BBC news website. It is real. He is dead. He was only fifty-three. Mum liked him. She used to play his CDs in the car and sing along to them. Apparently I used to do a really cute version of 'Wake Me Up Before You Go-Go' from my car seat.

I switch back to Facebook. Someone has posted a joke about it being George Michael's last Christmas. It is not funny. None of it is funny. Everyone is fucking dying and it is starting to creep me out. I sit there for a long time, clicking on the links to George Michael songs to keep me awake. When I am sure that Lee must be asleep, I brush my teeth, remove my make-up and go to the bedroom. I push the door as gently as possible but it still makes a clicking noise as I enter. Lee has his back to me. If he is awake, he clearly doesn't want me to know it. I get undressed and squeeze under the duvet. I lie on my side with my back to him; it is the only way that's comfortable for me to lie now anyway. I put my right hand on my bump and whisper, 'Night, H, love you.' And with the other hand, I cling desperately to the bed sheet.

The first thing I see in the morning is Lee's face smiling down at me. He has already drawn the curtains and the sun is streaming in so brightly that I have to squint to see him clearly.

'Morning,' he says. 'I thought a Boxing Day breakfast in bed was in order.'

I look down and see that he is holding a tray with a coffee pot, mugs and a pile of croissants. I rub my eyes and sit up in bed, not sure that I am even awake. He is still smiling at me expectantly, as if last night never happened.

'Here,' he says, putting the tray down on my bedside table, taking another pillow and propping it behind me. He picks up a plate from the tray.

'Chocolate or plain?' he asks.

'Er, plain, please.'

He puts a croissant on the plate and hands it to me, before picking up the tray and taking it round to his side of the bed. He gets back in bed next to me, still smiling.

I don't know what to say or do. I'm scared that if I mention what happened he will flare up again. He looks over and sees me still staring at him.

'Look, let's just forget about last night,' he says. 'I think we were both tired and I know you'd had a tough day. How about we start Christmas again, from now, just the two of us? Well, three of us,' he says, correcting himself.

'But—'

He puts his finger to my lips. 'Not another word. I don't want you to worry about anything. Just take it easy. I'm going to be looking after you all day. You don't even have to get out of bed if you don't want to.'

He picks up his croissant and takes a bite. I am too stunned to say anything so I simply stare out of the window.

We are supposed to be going out for New Year's Eve. Some bar in town with a whole crowd of people from work and their partners. I can't think of anything worse, to be honest. I have never liked New Year's Eve. I remember, as a child, begging Mum to let me stay up to see in the New Year. When, finally, she relented, I sat there listening to the bongs from Big Ben on television, expecting something amazing to happen afterwards. When it didn't, when it was just a few people, one of them in a kilt, hugging each other, I turned to her and said, 'Is that it?'

She nodded. 'Afraid so,' she replied. 'Bit of a disappointment, isn't it?'

I never really bothered after that. The last few years, Sadie and I have had film nights in. That's where I'd rather be tonight, to be honest. Although I couldn't possibly tell Lee that.

He comes into the bedroom looking every bit as good as he always has done.

'Best get a move on,' he says, seeing me still sitting on the bed in the leggings and jumper I have been wearing all day.

'I don't really feel up to it, to be honest,' I say.

'Why? What's wrong?'

'Nothing. I'm tired, that's all. And if I go I'll be half asleep by ten o'clock and I don't want to drag you back early.'

'OK,' he says. It is the worst kind of OK, said in a tone that makes it plain it isn't OK at all. 'We won't go.'

'No, you go. I don't want to spoil your fun.'

'Are you sure?'

'Yeah. I'll be fine. I'll get an early night.'

'I won't stay much after midnight.'

'Stay as long as you like.'

'Right. I may as well make a move then, as I'm all ready.'

'Yeah. Have a good time. Say hi to everyone.'

I don't mean the last bit. I'm not really friends with any of them. They are not my type of people. Sadie was right – they are all up-their-own-arses PR types. None of them say anything more than hello or goodbye to me. They treat me like I'm inferior to them, just because I'm working on the front desk.

'Will do. Happy New Year then.'

He leans down and kisses me on the top of the head. This wasn't how I had imagined our first New Year's Eve together would be. Not in a million years.

As soon as he has left, I pick up my phone to call Sadie. There's a chance she might not be doing anything. Maybe she could even come over. She hasn't been here yet. I didn't see how I could invite her, after what Lee said about her. Even if I'd picked a time when he was out, I'd have been worried that he'd come back and find her here and the whole thing would kick off again. The phone rings a couple of times before she answers. I can hear a lot of noise in the background.

'Hey, you,' she says. 'How you doing?'

'Yeah, OK. A bit knackered, that's all. Where are you?'

'Work. I volunteered to come in, seeing as I didn't have any better offers. How about you?'

'At home. Lee's, I mean. We were supposed to be going out but I didn't feel up to it.'

'So you're having a quiet night in together instead?'

'No. He's gone. It was a work thing. I said I didn't mind.'

'Right.'

'What time do you finish? Only I wondered if you fancied coming over for a bit.'

'Not till eleven, I'm afraid. And Adrian's got tickets for some gig in town, so I said I'd go with him.'

'Sure. No problem.'

'I can cancel and come round to yours instead? It doesn't matter.'

'No. I don't want to mess up your plans. I'll probably be asleep by then anyway, to be honest.'

'Well, if you're sure.'

'Yeah. I'll catch up with you soon. Have a good one.'

'And you. Well, a good kip anyway.'

I hang up, biting hard on my bottom lip. A few moments later my phone beeps. It is Sadie, sending a whole load of emojis that I haven't got the energy to look through. I click on to Facebook. People are still talking about Carrie Fisher dying and posting *Star Wars* links. Lee didn't seem that bothered about it, which surprised me. When I asked him why, he said it was only really the male characters he'd been into.

Everybody is saying how they are going to be pleased to see the back of 2016. And doing loads of RIPs for all the celebrities who have died. And all I can think is that next year, all these people will be saying how truly awful 2017 was. And remembering me.

I go to my timeline and scroll back to the most recent photo of H.

'Can't wait to meet you,' I say, kissing the screen. I go to bed then, knowing that when I wake up, it will be the year I meet him and the year I say goodbye.

Sadie Ward ▸ **Jess Mount**
11 July 2018

A year ago today I lost my best friend. I still can't believe you're gone, Jess. I still look for you on the station platform, I still expect to hear you having a laugh at work and I still miss you more than words can ever express.

Not everyone has a best friend like I did. My first memory is of playing with you at school. I don't remember life before you. It's been like starting over for me, learning to live my life without you. And most of the time I can get by, I can just about manage to function and hold down my job and be civil to people. But sometimes I wake up in the morning and all I can think about is what happened to you, then I lie in bed at night, unable to sleep because I feel so bad about it all, and in between those two points all I have is a huge fucking great void in my life which is the space you used to fill. I miss you, Jess. I love you, and although I'm not allowed to say anything on here about what happened, I want you and everyone to know that when the court case starts, I will tell the truth, the whole truth and nothing but the truth. And I will do it for you.

JESS

Tuesday, 14 February 2017

Last year there were roses. Two dozen of them. I remember them being delivered to work and Nina muttering about some people having more money than sense. I remember feeling special, spoilt, adored even.

This year, there is a card on the breakfast bar in the kitchen.

'Happy Valentine's Day,' Lee says, coming over and giving me a kiss. I do not feel worthy of even this. I am standing there in my grubby dressing gown, the belt tied loosely under my bump. My hair is straggly, there are dark circles under my eyes. I don't know who the hell these women are, the ones who are supposed to bloom in pregnancy, because it is certainly not me. I am wilting and dying in front of his eyes.

'Thanks,' I say, taking a card from my dressing gown pocket and handing it to him.

We open them at the same time. Lee has written 'To the mother of my son' inside. I wonder again what has happened to Jess, the girl he fell in love with. I am not sure she even exists anymore. We both make the appropriate noises; I don't know what to say after that. I put the radio on to cover the awkward atmosphere while we eat breakfast. Lee loads the dishwasher while I get ready for work. I have finally relented and bought maternity clothes. I was trying to avoid them – the term 'maternity wear' makes me feel queasy – but I have got to the point where I can no longer get away with simply wearing clothes a size or two bigger. I put on my maternity leggings and pull the new charcoal-grey jersey tunic down over them. I turn to look in the mirror. All I can think is that Sadie would piss herself laughing if she could see me now. I run a brush through my hair and tuck it behind one ear in the vain hope that it will somehow salvage a tiny amount of respectability. It doesn't. I step out into the hallway, where Lee is waiting. He looks me up and down, a frown on his face.

'Are you planning to wear that to work?'

'I know it's rank. Nothing else fits anymore.'

'Well, you can't go like that. You're a receptionist, Jess. You've got to look the part.'

'What part? I'm pregnant. This is what you look like when you're pregnant, unless you're Beyoncé, which I'm not.'

'There's no need for that.' His tone has sharpened. He looks at me with utter disdain.

I feel myself shrinking back against the wall. 'What do you suggest I do, then?'

'Go into town and get yourself something more appropriate to wear. I'll tell Carl you've got a doctor's appointment. And make sure, when you do come in, you look like you're coming to an office, not a mums and toddlers' coffee morning.'

He turns and leaves, pulling the door shut behind him.

I close my eyes. The sad thing is that my first response is not anger that he talked to me that way, but relief that he didn't hit me. 'Happy bloody Valentine's Day,' I mutter, as I slump back against the wall.

I'm not convinced the new outfit's made much of a difference, to be honest, but I arrive at work an hour later in a sleeveless black maternity dress from H&M, tights and ankle boots. I've put more make-up on too, in the hope that it will at least signify that I've made 'an effort'. I take my coat off and squeeze behind the front desk. It's not so bad when I am here, top half only and all that.

I remember Beth, the receptionist who I replaced, struggling in her stilettos at eight months pregnant. I don't think I'll actually fit behind the desk at eight months.

Carl comes down shortly afterwards. He stands at the side of the desk. I see his gaze fall to my boots and back up again.

'Jess,' he says. 'I understand you're struggling a bit with work now, so I was going to suggest we bring your maternity leave forward so you can finish at the end of the month. Hopefully that will work better all round.'

I stare at him. There is only one person that could have possibly come from. Lee told him to do this. Lee is so embarrassed at the way I look that he no longer wants to work with me. I try to push the hurt down inside of me so I am capable of speaking.

'No, thanks. That won't be necessary,' I reply.

Carl's eyebrows rise. Clearly he is not used to women answering him back.

'Well, I'm your boss and I think it is. That's not a look we want to greet our clients with. I suggest you stay behind the desk as much as possible until you leave in two weeks.'

I am so stunned it is difficult to know what to say. 'Fuck you' would be the obvious response. That is what Jess Mount would have said. But Jess Mount doesn't exist anymore.

'Fine,' I say. 'And just so you know, I shan't be coming back.'

Carl smiles in a way that suggests he is very pleased to hear it.

'Oh, and in the meantime, if we could stick to the office dress code with regard to heels, that would be great.'

He disappears before I have the chance to say anything, which is probably just as well.

It is about an hour later when the flowers arrive for me. Two dozen red roses, tied with a massive red bow. Amy, one of the account executives, is in reception when they are delivered.

'Wow,' she says. 'Lucky lady. Go on, take a photo of them for Facebook, show the world how much he loves you.'

I smile at her before she goes back upstairs. I suspect she knows as well as I do that it is all about keeping up appearances.

It had been Sadie's idea to meet up for lunch on Valentine's Day. She said it was the only way she would get taken out for a meal, even if it was just a sandwich at Caffè Nero. I'm just relieved to have escaped the office, to be honest.

She is grinning as I approach her.

'What's up with you?' I ask.

'You, looking like a properly pregnant woman, that's what.'

'You should have seen what I looked like this morning before I changed.'

'You'll be updating your profile pic to one of you holding your naked bump next.'

'Don't hold your breath.'

'It is weird, though, how things have changed. I was just remembering that thing we did a few years ago of booking a table for two at a restaurant on Valentine's night and then turning up and being loud and drunk just to piss all the couples off.'

'I'm sure they remember you fondly, too.'

'Well, someone's got to cut through all the romantic crap, haven't they? Talking of which, what did he get you?'

'Red roses,' I reply. 'Like last year.'

'See, he's trapped now, isn't he? Once he's set the bar high like that, he'll have to do it every year or you'll think he's going off you. I'd start with a single rose, me. Then, if I did go off them, it would still look romantic but it wouldn't be nearly as expensive.'

I laugh, even though I do not feel like laughing inside. Just being in Sadie's company is the best therapy I can have right now. 'Come on,' I say, fiddling with my wedding ring. 'Let's go and get our slap-up Valentine's sarnie.'

Sadie tells me all the news from work while we queue. The usual stuff about what Nina said, and another chef quitting, and some guy on the double sofa at the back of screen two having to be told to zip himself back up. I miss it. All of it. I miss Sadie, I miss having a laugh, I miss Jess.

'So, how's things with you?' she asks as we sit down with our lunch.

'Yeah, fine. Knackered, as usual.'

'How long before you finish work? Another month or so?'

'No, just a couple of weeks actually. I'm leaving at the end of the month.'

'Oh, right. Won't you go stir-crazy sitting around for six weeks doing nothing?'

'Yeah, well. I wasn't given much choice in the matter. Carl has decided I do not meet the image requirements of a receptionist now that I resemble Gloria from *Madagascar*.'

'Are you serious? That's fucking illegal.'

'I know. Wouldn't look good to take my husband's company to court, mind.'

'What does Lee think about this?'

I finish my mouthful slowly in order to ensure that I have composed myself enough to answer.

'Don't know. We haven't had a chance to talk about it yet.'

Sadie looks at me. I can't get anything past her.

'Is everything OK?' she asks.

I shrug. 'It's just a difficult time all round, I guess. Everything will be better once the baby comes.'

She doesn't appear convinced, but I don't think she's going to push it in a public place like this.

'Well, until then, you can come and have lunch with me any time you want,' she says, wiping the crumbs from her mouth.

'That's if I can still waddle into town by then.'

'It will be fun watching you try.'

'And once we've got the move out of the way.'

'I'd forgotten about that. I've still never heard of anyone moving house one floor down.'

'It'll be more like moving hotel rooms, to be honest. I can practically pack all my things in a suitcase.'

'Where's all your other stuff then?'

'At home. I mean Dad's. Lee doesn't like clutter. And most of it is crap – old books and photos and mementoes and that.'

'That's not crap, that's the important stuff.'

I take a sip of my hot chocolate.

'So what's the new place like?' she continues.

'Exactly the same as the current one but with an extra bedroom.' I stop myself as I realise Sadie has never seen our apartment. 'You'll have to come round one morning before work to see it – when I'm on maternity leave, I mean.'

'Yeah,' she says. 'I'd like that.'

'But we'd better wait until Angela's finished decorating the nursery. Sounds like she'll be practically living with us while she does it.'

'Won't that do your head in?'

I shrug. 'I guess it's nice that she's so excited about it.'

'Sounds a bit OTT to me.'

'She means well.'

'You won't be saying that when she's stencilling fucking rocking horses and teddy bears on your walls.'

I laugh. A proper laugh. Like the ones Jess Mount used to do.

JESS

November 2008

I am lying in a hospital bed. Everything has gone inside out and upside down. It got worse after the train thing. Much worse. There was an episode at school where I was screaming at one of the teachers and refusing to go on a school trip because the coach wasn't safe. And another one where I pulled a boy off his bike on the tow-path because I could tell he was going to hurt someone.

Edward said I had ceased to be able to function effectively in society, that I needed to be under twenty-four-hour psychiatric care while they assessed me and sorted out my medication. So now I am on the inside with all the crazies. I have been locked up by the people who really are crazy, and they are on the outside. They say they're only trying to help me, they're doing what is best for me. But that is because they want to carry on being crazy and they don't want people to realise that I am right.

Dad is sitting in the chair next to my bed. He has been crying a lot. And staring out of the window. When I look at him, I see the fear in his eyes. He thinks I am going mad and he doesn't know what to do and he's beating himself up about it, but it's not his fault that Mum died. It's nobody's fault. It just happened. Like it could happen to any of us at any time. And that's the whole problem.

The nurse comes round with my medication. I do not want to take it. They are trying to turn me into a zombie who thinks the same way as everyone else. And the pills have side effects. I have read all about them. They are trying to kill me from the inside now. I put the tablets in the side of my mouth behind my teeth, drink some water, open my mouth and the nurse thinks they have gone. She says something to me but I do not hear the words properly. It is like I am underwater and the people above the surface are talking but I can't hear the words. Dad smiles and nods. Later, when they are not looking, I will go to the toilet and spit them out and flush them down the loo. And everyone will smile and say I am going to get better soon and I will start telling them what they want to hear and then they will have to let me go home and get off my back. And nothing will have changed and I will still think the same but they will be happy and say that they have cured me and that is what it is all about at the end of the day. They want to be proved right and say that I have been proved wrong, and then they will be satisfied. And I am going to give them that satisfaction because I have the far greater satisfaction of knowing they are complete idiots. I just have to keep that information to myself and I will be OK.

ANGELA

Wednesday, 1 March 2017

It is, as I warned Lee all those months ago, not a home at all. Certainly not a home to bring up a baby in. Jess and Lee only moved in a few days ago but they have already unpacked, so it should feel at least a tiny bit homely. It doesn't though. It still looks like a hotel and they don't have any knick-knacks or personal things to give it that homely feel. I gave them a framed embroidery for their wedding day, with their names and the date on and everything, but I have never seen it put out anywhere. It's certainly not here. There is only one photo on display: a black and white one of their wedding in a black frame. I know Lee likes this minimalist look, but I think he takes it a bit far, to be honest. Still, it will have to change once the baby arrives. You can't have a baby and expect your home to be spotless and clutter-free. Everything is about to change, and to change for the better.

'So', I say, turning to Jess, 'are you absolutely sure about the colour?'

She nods. I'd spent a long time looking at paint charts with her. I hadn't quite realised how many shades of blue there are these days. We've gone for a sort of soft turquoise, which is brighter than traditional baby blue. Jess seemed to like it better. Lee didn't seem too bothered, to be honest. He's left the whole nursery to us, said it could be our project. Although he is paying for it, of course.

I dip the roller into the tray. I have never actually done this before. Simon always did the painting and decorating at our house. Well, apart from the wallpaper that I stripped in our bedroom. And after he left, I got an odd-job man in to do it. But a nursery is different. A nursery needs to be decorated with love. And it's only a small room, so I'm quite sure we can do it between us in a day.

I place the roller on the wall and move it back and forth.

'There,' I say to Jess. 'It's going on lovely. The colour looks a treat, too.'

'Yeah,' she replies, looking up from her own roller. She seems quieter these days. Like someone has sucked the spirit out of her. I suppose she's tired, which is understandable. But I do worry about her, especially after what Joe said about her going to that mental hospital. I mean, she must have been in quite a state to be admitted. Clearly, she wouldn't be fit to look after a baby if that happened again. It's a good job I'm around. I have told Lee I will pop in every day once the baby is here, just to keep an eye on her. I wouldn't want him worrying while he's at work. I know it must have been tough on her, losing her mum so young, but lots of other people go through things like that without cracking up, don't they? And if she had a screw loose then, who's to say it won't come loose again?

Also, I don't like the fact that she obviously hadn't told Lee about it. It's as if she was trying to hide things from him before they got married. Edit her past so he would think she was marriage material. Who knows what else she's concealing? I don't think he liked it either, although when I tried to talk to him about it he changed the subject pretty sharpish.

I get the sense that all is not well between them. All the smiles and handholding and whispered jokes, that all seems to have gone out of the window. It worries me, of course, particularly because of what happened with Emma. I do hope he realises that this relationship has got to work. She's carrying his child. If it all went wrong, goodness knows when I'd get to see my grandson. No, I need to ensure they get things back on track. That is why I've booked them on the antenatal course. I figured that if they were more confident about becoming parents, and met some other young couples in the same position, it would give them a bit of a boost.

'Ooh, Jess, remind me before I go, to email you the details of the course I told you about. You know, this NCT thingy. It starts in a couple of weeks.'

'Oh, right. I'm still not sure it's a good idea, you know. Lee didn't seem very keen.'

'Sometimes, Jess, he just needs a gentle push. He doesn't always know what's best for him.'

'Yeah, but it's not his sort of thing. Bit out of his comfort zone.'

'Well, he's got no choice now. I've booked you on.'

She puts her roller down and stares at me. 'What, without asking him?'

'The lady said you were ever so lucky to get a place. They'd had a cancellation, you see. Usually these things are booked up months in advance.'

She is shaking her head, doing that rabbit in the headlights thing with her eyes again.

'No, it's a bad idea. You know he hates being told what to do.'

I purse my lips. I don't need her being difficult like this. Telling me what Lee is like as if I don't know my own son. And when she has only known him for five minutes.

'Don't fret about it, Jess. I know what's best for him. I'll talk him round.'

'Yeah, but you won't be there afterwards,' she says, her voice rising to a pitch I haven't heard before. 'You won't see what he's like when we're alone.'

She puts some more paint on the roller, bashing it repeatedly into the tray. As she holds it up against the wall, I see that her hand is shaking.

'Jess,' I say, putting my roller down. 'What on earth's the matter?'

'He'll go mad. He'll be so angry.'

'No, he won't.'

'He will, and then he might—'

She breaks off and starts sobbing. I put my arms around her and feel her body shaking next to mine.

'He might what?'

'It doesn't matter. I think he might be cross with me, that's all.'

'But he's got nothing to get cross with you about. I'm the one who booked the course. I'll make that clear to him.'

She wipes her nose with her sleeve. I'm not sure she's seeing things straight. She appears to be a bit hysterical, to be honest. I wonder if it's starting again. The mental thing.

'Is it all getting a bit much for you?' I ask. 'Are you struggling to cope, dear?'

'No. I'm fine. Just a bit nervous about the baby, that's all.'

'Because if you are struggling, we can get help for you.'

'There's nothing wrong with me.'

Her tone has changed. There is a sharpness in her voice I haven't heard before. Maybe this is what Lee has to deal with. Maybe this is why things seem a bit strained between them.

'I know, but we need to make sure we keep an eye on you, that's what your father said. We don't want things to get to the point where—'

'Angela, I said there's nothing wrong with me, OK?'

'Well maybe you need to go for a lie-down then, dear. I can finish this on my own.'

'I'm fine.'

'You're clearly not fine, Jess. But I'm sure you'll feel a whole lot better after a little nap. Go on, I'll finish this. Don't you worry about it.'

She wipes her nose again and looks up at the ceiling. For a moment, I think she is going to argue with me, but she doesn't. She simply gets to her feet and walks out of the room. A few seconds later, I hear her bedroom door shut. I let out a long sigh. Clearly things are worse than I'd feared. I'm really not sure she is going to be up to caring for a baby – not if her current state of mind is anything to go by.

I can see I am going to be needed even more than I thought. Before the baby arrives as well as after. I will pop round on a regular basis and perhaps not give her any advance warning. That way, she won't be able to cover it up if she really isn't coping.

I'll need to check she's looking after herself and going to all her antenatal classes. I get the sense that she needs a mother figure to take care of her right now. I can do that. I can be mother and grandmother rolled into one. I will not let this family fall apart. I have stood back and allowed that to happen once and I will not do it again.

I pick the roller up again and carry on painting the wall. I'll have it done by the time she wakes up. That should perk her up a bit. And then I can show her the stencils I brought with me and see which one she likes best.

Joe Mount
12/09/2018 6:53pm

I don't want to believe it, Jess. I don't want to believe that was your life. At least when his ex-girlfriend took the stand I could tell myself it wasn't you. I heard what she said about how Lee had flipped when he'd caught her checking her mobile while they were on holiday. I saw the faces of the jurors as they looked at the X-rays of her jaw from the hospital in Italy. But I could tell myself it was not you. It was appalling, what he did to her, and sick that he would then take you to stay in the same hotel room a year or so later, but it still was not you. Even when Sadie started giving evidence, and said about seeing bruises and marks on you in the last few months and you always explaining it away, I thought, maybe it's an overactive imagination. Maybe, like the defence claimed, she was jealous of him taking you away from her. But then they read out the letter you wrote to Sadie, asking her to make sure I got custody of any children you had if anything happened to you, because it wouldn't be safe to leave them with Lee. That's when I knew something was wrong. Of course, the defence made out that you were not right in the head when you wrote it, but I knew that wasn't the case.

And when that cleaner took the stand today, just a scrap of a girl herself really, and when she started talking about seeing bloody tissues in the bathroom bin on more than one occasion, that is when my stomach started to turn. And I listened as she told them about how she'd been emptying the bin when she found it. Something hard and white that fell out of a piece of toilet paper. And she'd held it up to the light and realised that it was a tooth – well, part of a front tooth. Part of the tooth that he'd knocked out when he'd hit you. That was when I put my head down and started crying. Because I couldn't deny it any longer, not even to myself. He beat you Jess. He slapped you and punched you and God knows what else. And some of it was probably in front of Harrison and I give thanks that that little boy won't be able to remember that when he's older. But I will always remember it, Jess. I can see it in my head now. And I can't imagine a time when I will ever stop seeing it. I will never forgive myself, Jess, for allowing that to happen to you.

I can still remember holding you in my arms for the first time when you were a tiny, red, wrinkled thing, and turning to your mum and telling her I would never let anything bad happen to you. Turns out I let her down as well as you. I'm sorry, Jess. Truly sorry and truly heartbroken.

JESS

Monday, 20 March 2017

I wake up and instinctively run my finger over my top teeth, just to make sure they are still there. I have done the same thing every morning for the past week, since I read it. I wonder which one it is that he knocks out. And how the hell I get it repaired without anyone noticing. I'm still registered with the dentist in Mytholmroyd, but Lee is with a private one in Leeds. Perhaps it's the sort of place that would be able to stick a crown on with short notice. I suppose if they do ask questions, I will simply lie. If I lie to my best friend and my father, I see no reason why I wouldn't lie to a dentist.

I put my hands on my bump. H does a little wriggle. Not that there can be much room to wriggle in there now.

'I'm doing this for you,' I say. But even as I say it, I know it doesn't make sense. He won't have a mother in four months' time, how can that be good for him?

The truth is that I'm doing it because I don't know what

else to do. If I run and hide I may still die anyway. I don't know where I am killed yet. It might not be here. Then there is the tiny bit of me that still thinks I can change Lee. That even if he did hit Emma, he might have learnt his lesson and have no intention of doing it to me.

And if I can't change him, then perhaps H will. Perhaps the second he is born, Lee will look at him and soften inside and know that he can never hurt me.

I haul myself up out of bed. I have decided I quite like maternity leave. Not the being huge and having heartburn and needing to get up three times a night to go for a wee bit, but the having a lie-in in the morning and having the place to myself part of it. It gives me space and time and they are two things I am in need of at the moment.

I am on my way to the kitchen to put the kettle on when I notice that the nursery door is open slightly. I go inside and turn the light on. It's like something out of one of those baby magazines Angela keeps bringing over, which is not surprising given that she got most of the ideas from them.

Everything is colour-coordinated in turquoise and cream. I managed to talk her out of stencils on the walls, mainly because I knew Lee would hate them, but she did get away with stars, moons and space rockets on the curtains, lampshade and rug, and a stars and moon mobile hanging above H's cot, together with an 'I Love You to the Moon and Back' framed embroidery on the wall. I go over to the cot, put the side down and stroke the mattress. He will be lying here soon. My little boy. I can see him already, of course. I see him all the time. But I will be able to touch him and hold him and he will finally be real instead of a photo on my phone.

Farah arrives at ten thirty. I made sure I was out for the past two weeks, took myself off for a walk along the canal, because I could not bear to face this person who will soon know things about me that I do not want anyone to know. But today I am here. Today I feel I ought to say hello to the young woman who speaks up on my behalf.

'Hi, Farah,' I call out when I hear the key in the door, not wanting to startle her, like she did me. She pops her head around the kitchen door.

'Hello.' She smiles. She has a pretty face, and dark brown almond-shaped eyes with beautiful eyelashes, the sort that don't need mascara.

'I've just made a coffee, would you like one?'

'No, thank you,' she replies. 'We are not supposed to stop for coffee while we are working.'

'Well, I won't tell anyone.'

She looks unsure for a second before her smile widens. 'If you are sure that is OK. I will make up the time at the end.'

'Don't be daft. Everyone should be allowed a coffee break. How do you take it?'

'Black please, with no sugar.'

I nod. 'How long have you been working for the agency?'

'Nearly a year, almost since I arrived in this country.'

'And where did you come from?'

'From Afghanistan, my home.'

I nod, but I feel stupid because I don't really know anything about Afghanistan. Only bits and pieces that I have seen on the news.

'Did you come with your family?' I ask as I hand her the coffee.

She shakes her head. 'No. My family, they are all dead.'

'I'm sorry,' I say, looking down. 'I didn't realise. My mother's dead too, I know how hard it is.'

'It is OK. I am used to talking about it. I had to tell the authorities about them when I arrived here.'

'So you're a refugee?'

'No. My asylum application was refused. They say it is safe for me to return there. Even when I told them what they did to my mother and father and brother, they say it is different now, it is safe. They do not really understand.'

'So how come you're still here?'

'I was given discretionary leave to remain, because I am under eighteen and I have no one left there to look after me.'

'How old are you?'

'I will be seventeen next month.'

I blow out. I had no idea. I can't imagine what it must be like to lose your entire family when you are the age I was when I lost Mum.

'I didn't realise you were so young.'

She shrugs. 'I think when you live a difficult life, you do not look your age.'

'So you were just sixteen when you came? You made that journey on your own?'

'Yes, although I was with many others. We had all paid the same man.'

'Weren't you scared?'

'I was, but not as scared as I was in Afghanistan. They would have come back for me, you see. Because my family did not live the way they told us to live. Because my father spoke out.'

'It was still very brave of you,' I say. She takes a sip of the coffee.

'It is easy to be brave when the alternative is to die.'

'And will they let you stay for good when your leave runs out?'

'I do not know. When I am seventeen and a half they will decide.'

'But you can't go back!'

'I know that. But I will have to wait and see what they say.' She finishes her coffee. I remember Sadie's post, how she said Farah hadn't come forward at first because she had been scared. I understand now, at least a little, what it is like to be scared.

'I hope they let you stay.'

'Thank you,' she says. 'I hope so too.' She comes over to the sink, about to wash up her mug.

'It's OK,' I say, taking it from her. 'Please let me do that. It's one of the few things left I can do.'

'Thank you,' she says, turning to leave and then turning back. 'The nursery for your baby, it is so beautiful. He is going to be a very lucky little boy.'

I smile at her, knowing that very soon she will know the truth about our family too.

Lee is not happy about these classes. Not happy at all. I still remember the face he pulled last week when he was confronted with a nappy coated with a mixture of marmite and peanut butter. I was surprised he didn't walk out there and then, to be honest. Playing mummies and daddies is clearly not his idea of fun. I am still surprised he even agreed to come at all. I don't know what Angela said to him or how she talked him round, but I'm pretty sure he's regretting it at the moment.

We pull up outside the college where the classes are held. Lee slams the car door and comes around to my side. Another car pulls up next to us. I see the man get out as Lee opens my door. I recognise him from the classes, although I can't remember his name.

'Maybe they should allow two parking bays for pregnant women,' the man jokes. 'It's a wonder the supermarkets don't have "Mum and bump" parking spaces.'

Lee smiles at him, I suspect more because he feels he has to than because he finds it funny. He helps me out of the car and shuts the door behind me. The woman from the other car emerges with a small grunt.

'Hi, Jess,' she says. 'It doesn't get any easier, does it?'

'No,' I reply. 'It doesn't.' I can't remember her name, although I think it is Rachel. Either that or Charlotte. Half of them seem to be called Rachel or Charlotte. They are all older than me, of course. Most of them at least ten years older. And they all seem to have proper careers, unlike me.

'I wonder what they'll get us doing this evening,' she says, as we waddle up to the entrance together. Her partner holds the door open for us, and I thank him as I go through.

Lee takes my hand as soon as we're inside. It's like the opposite of when you're a kid and you suddenly let go of your mum's hand when you see people you know. I don't know whether to feel happy or sad about it.

'I have to say, you made a much better job of the nappies than I did,' her partner says to Lee.

'Yeah, but when we have to deal with the real ones they won't be covered with marmite, will they?' replies Lee.

They both laugh. They seem to like him. They will probably recount this episode when they hear that he's been charged with my manslaughter. Say things like, 'He seemed to have a great sense of humour,' and, 'He always helped her out of the car and held her hand.'

We walk into the room. The chairs are laid out in a semi-circle. It's pregnant woman, dad-to-be, pregnant woman, dad-to-be all the way around. We sit down at the end. The NCT teacher, whose name is Cath, comes over.

'Hi, Jess. How's the heartburn?'

'Still as bad.'

'Did you try the little and often eating?'

'Yeah, still no difference.'

'Oh dear, at least you've not got long to go now. Three weeks, is it?'

'Yeah, about that.' I don't tell her he's going to be six days late. It's not the sort of thing you can say.

Cath moves to the front of the class once everyone is assembled. 'I hope everyone's well and comfortable, or as comfortable as they can be in the circumstances.'

I look around. Lee is the only one not smiling. His jaw is set firm. He is hating this, I know.

'Well, having dealt with some of the practicalities of life with a new baby last week, we're going to deal more with the emotional side this evening, both for you and your partner.'

I think I hear the groan that Lee lets out, even if no one else does. We are split into two groups, the mums and dads-to-be, and are asked to make a list, in order of priority, of our personal, emotional and physical needs after childbirth. I don't say much; I don't need to. There are a couple of women in the group who seem to do most of the talking. It is easiest simply to nod and agree with them when they look at me. I glance over at Lee a couple of times. He doesn't appear to be joining in much either, apart from once when I hear him do a deep, throaty laugh. I suspect they've got on to talking about sex, as we have.

Once Cath has spoken with both groups, she calls us back together again.

'Right, there's a lot of common ground,' she says, 'and some areas where you're quite a way apart. We're going to start by discussing sex after childbirth. Now, before any of you women groan, I understand that it's probably the last thing you are thinking about right now, but I can assure you from looking at the charts that not everyone in the room feels that way.'

There are a couple of laughs from the men. Lee is staring straight ahead.

'I'm going to ask you all to go out into the corridor and place a coloured counter somewhere along it to signify when you expect to have sex again after your baby is born. I've put markers down along it from one day to one year.'

There are more sniggers, from both the men and women this time.

'Oh, believe me, I've heard of both,' she says. 'Now, ladies, off you go first. Here are your red counters. Write your initials on the back and put it down where you think. When you come back in, I'll send the lads out with their blue ones.'

I take the counter she hands me and follow the other women out into the corridor. To be honest, I haven't really thought about this until now. We haven't had sex for about a month. I'd assumed it's because I'm not exactly looking hot right now. Although the fact that I am going to bed an hour or two before him every night probably doesn't help.

The other women are laughing as they place their counters down, mostly somewhere between three weeks and three months. I head towards the three-month point. I am aware that I can't go beyond it because I will be dead by then, so I put it down exactly on three months.

We go back into the room and the men go out to the corridor. There are a lot of laughs and mutterings before they come back in again.

'Right, folks. I'd like you all to go and stand next to your counters,' says Cath.

I shut my eyes. Lee is going to hate being put on the spot like this. We troop back into the corridor, there is more laughter and exclamations as we see the blue counters all clustered up at one end. I go and stand next to mine. There are a couple of other women with me, but their partners are standing fairly close. Lee isn't. He's right at the other end, on three days, from what I can see.

The others start laughing when they notice.

'Er, Lee and Jess,' says Cath, 'I think there might be a little chat about your differing expectations on the way home tonight.'

There isn't a chat, of course. Simply a crushing silence. I'm struggling to know what to say but I desperately want to say something, anything to avert what I suspect is about to happen.

'Look, we don't have to go next week if you don't want to. I won't tell your mum.'

It was meant to lighten the mood, but his mood doesn't appear to want to be lightened. Not in the car, or the lift or even outside our front door. He opens it and I step inside, aware that I am already starting to shake. He shuts it behind him quietly. Incredibly quietly. And then turns around and slaps me hard across the face.

I scream and put my hand up to my cheek, but he grabs my wrist before it gets there.

'Don't you ever, ever humiliate me like that again, do you understand?'

I nod, gulping back the tears.

'Good. We are not going back there, and you are going to remove all the numbers of those women from your phone and if they call or text you're not to reply to them. I will email Cath next week and tell her that you're not well and we won't be coming back. Understood?'

I nod again.

'Good. Now get in the bathroom and clean your fucking face up.'

Sadie Ward
20/09/2018 6:45pm

He got off, Jess. I am so sorry, but they found him not guilty. I think the judge did it in his summing up. He told them to remember that Lee Griffiths wasn't on trial for assaulting Emma McKinley, or for what he may or may not have done to you in the run-up to your death. The only question they had to answer was whether it was beyond reasonable doubt that he struck you while you were in the shower that morning, causing you to fall and hit your head on the basin and the tiled floor. Two blows that were serious enough to knock you unconscious and cause the raised intracranial pressure that led to your death.

He said that it was only actual evidence they had to concern themselves with, not conjecture. I thought Farah's evidence may have been enough, especially when the dentist confirmed that he had treated you and put a crown on your front tooth that day. But still the defence said that it could have been an accident, as you'd told the dentist and Lee had maintained was the truth. There was no proof that Lee had knocked your tooth out. And even if he did, it didn't prove he'd laid a finger on you on the day you died. They tried to discredit Farah too, of course, about the fact that she hadn't told the full truth when you'd died. That when the police interviewed her after she'd found you lying on the bathroom floor, she hadn't mentioned anything about the tooth or the blood she'd seen before. She tried to explain about how frightened she had been of being sent back home. About how finding you lying there with blood all over the place had brought back the trauma of what had happened to her family. But in the end, the jury didn't buy it.

They preferred to believe Angela. Angela, who reckoned butter wouldn't melt in her precious son's mouth. Who claimed she knew nothing about what had happened to Emma. And who crucially claimed that she'd arrived at the apartment after Lee had gone to work and that you'd been fine but tired because you'd been up a lot in the night. And that was why she'd taken H home with her and told you to go back to bed. Only you'd said you didn't think you'd be able to sleep and you might just take a shower instead to try to wake yourself up. She even said she'd told Lee to get a bathmat for the shower, but that he hadn't wanted one because he said they were naff and only went mouldy.

I know Angela was lying, Jess. I watched her as she was giving evidence. I didn't take my eyes off her for one second. All that stuff about how she was worried for your mental health and thought you had postnatal depression. She said she had started to come round every morning because she was worried that you weren't fit to look after H, that you might crack up at any moment. She even had the gall to claim you hadn't bonded with your baby, that she didn't feel comfortable leaving you alone with him for long periods. It was bollocks, all of it. I nearly shouted that from the public gallery at one point. I wish they could have called me again because if they had done I would have told them the truth: how I had never seen anyone so besotted with their baby in my life. And that was from the moment you told me you were pregnant, let alone the moment he was born. But instead, I had to listen to her lying through her teeth. Of course she was lying, I could see it in her eyes, though she tried to hide under her stupid fringe. Well, she would do, wouldn't she? Lee's her own flesh and blood. I bet she collected Harrison before Lee left for work and they concocted that story together afterwards. Because if she hadn't have covered up for him, not only would Lee have gone down but she'd have lost H too. But now Lee has got off, she has her son back and she can keep her grandson. And she'll be the one looking after him when Lee goes back to work.

They showed him on the news, walking out of court a free man. Making some pathetic statement about how it had been such a nightmare for him to be accused of killing you, that the case should never have been brought to court and that all he wanted to do now was go home to his son.

And that's the thing that really gets me, Jess. The fact that he's going to bring H up now and he'll tell him his version of the story and he'll never know the truth. And your precious little boy will grow up believing that his mummy died in a tragic accident.

Lee knows the truth, though. And Angela does. And they will have to live with it for the rest of their lives X

JESS

Tuesday, 21 March 2017

That's it then. That is how I go. Killed in my own bathroom by my own husband. A husband who gets off because there is not a shred of actual evidence against him. The only witness to the crime is me, and I am dead. Lee will get on with his life and will probably do the same thing to his next girlfriend. And H will grow up being looked after by his mum's murderer and a grandma who lied to save him.

What kind of life is that? What kind of death? Not one I want for either of us, I know that much. I put my phone down and try to stretch, aware of a dull ache in my lower back, worse than the usual pregnancy ache. My whole body is cramped and stiff. I have spent the night on the sofa. I couldn't bear to get into the same bed as Lee last night, so I lay down here with my dressing gown over me. I think I managed a little sleep at some point, but mostly I stared at the ceiling, my hands gripping my dressing gown, waiting for morning to come.

And now what? I lie back and wait for it to happen? I don't think so. Not anymore. I know now that he does hit me. I can't pretend it is a figment of my imagination any longer. All the times I told myself it might not be true, he might not ever lay a finger on me, well, I know now that it isn't the case. I am reminded of something Farah said to me. That it is not brave to leave when the only other option is death. She is right, I see that now. I know that if I stay I will become a statistic and I don't want to do that. It is not about being brave. I simply need to do the sensible thing. For me and, more importantly, for H.

I turn on my side and manage to ease my legs down onto the floor and sit myself up, my back propped up against the cushions. That is when the door opens. I am half-expecting to see a tea tray full of coffee and croissants. I don't though. I see a man whose face is contrite, who looks as if he has had as little sleep as I have. He walks over to me, still unable to look me in the eye. When he reaches me, he kneels down on the floor, head bowed, and starts to cry.

I am not prepared for this. I do not know what to say or do. He reaches out a hand towards me and sobs. 'I'm sorry. I'm so sorry.'

I take his hand, I don't know what else to do. He looks up at me with those bloody huge eyes of his.

'I never meant to hurt you,' he says.

'But you did.'

'I know. That's why I've come to say sorry.'

'And is that supposed to make it all OK?'

He shakes his head. 'Sometimes,' he says falteringly, 'I scare myself. I really scare the shit out of myself. Last night was one of those times.'

'You scared me too.'

He nods, and his gaze falls to my bump. 'And to think that I did it when you . . .' His voice trails off. He holds his head in his hands again.

'What I told you about my mum and dad,' he says, 'it was only part of the story. It was much worse than rows. I've never told anyone this, but my dad . . .' He breaks off again, shuts his eyes and takes a moment to compose himself. 'My dad beat my mum,' he says. 'I can only remember bits – I was little and I think she tried to keep it from me – but I saw him hit her once, smash her in the face with his fist in the bedroom. He hit her so hard that she rocked back on her feet and fell against the wall. Her nose was bleeding. There was blood splattered all over the wallpaper. They hadn't realised I was watching. I'd come out of my room to see what all the shouting was about. He didn't even help her to her feet afterwards. He walked over and spat on her. What I said to you last night, "Go and get your fucking face cleaned up", that's what he said to her.'

He starts crying again. I don't know what to say or do. I am still trying to reconcile the Angela I know with the woman he has just described, lying battered and bloody on the floor. I had no idea. No idea at all of what she has been through.

'I'm sorry,' I say, my hand on his shoulder. 'I'm sorry that you had to see that, but it doesn't mean that it's OK to do it to me.' My voice is not even cracking. I have found a strength from somewhere. A strength I didn't even know I had.

'I know,' says Lee. 'That's why I feel so bad. I'm scared that I'm turning into my dad.'

I get that. I get what it's like to be losing control. I decide to give him a chance. One chance to be honest with me.

'Have you done it before?' I ask. 'To other girlfriends?'

He hesitates, then looks up at me. 'No. Never. This was the first time.'

I swallow hard, knowing that he is lying. Picturing Emma's face after he broke her jaw. There were probably others, too. Others who were too scared to come forward.

'You need to get help, Lee.'

'Then I'll get it. I'll do anything to make it right. I don't want our son to grow up seeing the things I did.'

'He won't,' I reply calmly.

Lee looks up, his face a little less crumpled than it was. 'We'll talk later, when I get home from work. And I'll take you out for a meal, or get a takeaway if you're too tired, whatever you'd prefer.'

I nod without saying anything. He stands up and kisses me on the top of my head.

'It will never happen again,' he says. 'You have my word.'

I wait until I hear the front door shut behind him to move. I can't do anything quickly anymore, but I do at least move with more speed than usual. I go into our bedroom and take my case out of the wardrobe. I gave him a chance and he blew it. He lied to me that it had never happened before and then he promised me it would never happen again. I bet he said that to Emma too. And to the girls he went out with before. For the first time, I am glad about the Facebook posts. They have shown me a future that I do not want to stay for. They have shown me that his word counts for nothing.

I don't pack any of the clothes he bought for me. It is the comfortable things I pack – the leggings and sweatshirts, the things that Jess Mount used to wear. Because it is Jess Griffiths I am leaving behind. I zip up the case and roll it out into the hallway. I take one last look in the nursery. It is calm and peaceful, waiting patiently to welcome its new arrival. Its beauty is a pretence, though. What lies beneath the surface, that is what matters.

I go through to the bathroom. I will grab a quick shower and go. I need to scrub away the hurt in order to start afresh. I take off my dressing gown. My bump is so huge now that it is difficult to get in and out of the bath. I wish for the hundredth time that we had a walk-in shower. I guess the extra bedroom meant they had to skimp on space in the bathroom. I hold on to the corner of the sink to steady myself. All I can think is that this is where it happens. I am in the murder scene, effectively re-enacting the murder, except that it doesn't happen for another four months. And H is still inside me, where he is safe. Where no one can take him away from me.

He kicks, as if to remind me of that fact. I put my face up to meet the warm jet of water. I wonder what I would have done if I didn't know how the story ends. It is pretty clear, though. I would have stayed. I would have believed him when he said it had never happened before and would never happen again. I have the benefit of foresight, which is why I need to act on it. I do not want to become the woman in the story. As much as I do still love Lee – well, part of me does, at least – I know that if I stay I will lose my life. That I will lie in a pool of blood down there and be found by the cleaner, a poor girl who has already seen enough death in her young life. And that Lee will get away with it and get to bring up H.

And that is why I am able to ignore the voices inside my head, the ones telling me to believe him, to understand that he is a victim too. That maybe, just maybe, I have made this whole thing up in my head because I am intent on destroying any shred of happiness that comes my way.

I hear a noise from outside the bathroom. The front door banging shut. I turn off the shower, grab the towel from the rail and wrap it around me. What if Lee has come back? What if he has realised I'm going to leave and is going to stop me? I hear footsteps on the laminated floor in the hallway. But they are not Lee's footsteps. They belong to a woman. The footsteps stop. I remember that my case is out there. All packed and ready to go.

Silence for a moment. And then a voice. A woman's voice, calling out my name with a sense of urgency.

I stand frozen in the bath, clinging on to the towel. I watch the door handle turn down and see Angela step into the bathroom. Her face is hard and bitter.

'Get out,' I shout.

She shakes her head. 'I won't get out until you tell me what your case is doing in the hall.' Her voice is low and urgent. I have never heard her speak like that before. I am about to lie to her, tell her it's my overnight bag for hospital, but I realise it is not a time for lies. It is a time for the truth.

'I'm leaving,' I say.

'What do you mean? You're eight months pregnant.'

'I know. That's why I'm leaving. To protect my son.'

'Now, Jess, I think you'd better calm down. You're getting yourself in a state again.'

'No, I'm not. There's nothing wrong with me. It's your son who's got the problem.'

She frowns at me. 'What's our Lee got to do with this?'

'He hit me, Angela. Last night he hit me hard across the face, outside in the hallway.'

I see her shudder. Her body appears to contract. 'No. You're lying.'

'I wish I was, believe me. It's your son who's lying. But maybe you know that already.'

'I have no idea what you're talking about.' Her voice is higher. She is avoiding eye contact with me.

'Oh, I think you do. He didn't dump Emma after their holiday in Italy, did he? He flew back on his own because she was in hospital there, recovering from the broken jaw he'd given her.'

'No.' She shakes her head vehemently. She does not want to admit it, even to herself.

'And there were probably others before. Dozens, for all I know. And every time you just pretended that it wasn't happening and put the baby clothes back in the bottom drawer, ready for next time. And finally he found a girl stupid enough to trust him. To fall in love with him so hard that she was blind to what he was doing to her, how he was controlling her, moulding her into what he wanted her to be.'

'Jess, I think you'd better go and lie down. I don't think you're well. I don't think you've been well for some time now.'

'Oh, I'm fine,' I say, my voice strong and clear. 'I've never seen things more clearly, believe me.'

'You're making this up. It's all inside your head. It's another one of your episodes.'

'Like the fact that your husband hit you?' I say, raising my voice. 'I'm making that up, am I? That he used to hit you and scream at you to go and clean your fucking face up.'

She crumples before me. I see her put one hand on the basin.

'Your husband did it to you, Angela, and Lee is doing it to me. It's time to stop all the deceit.'

She looks up at me. 'He told you that? He remembers?'

I nod. 'He's the one who needs help, Angela. Him, and maybe you.'

'You mustn't go,' she pleads. 'It will destroy him.'

'And if I stay, he'll destroy me.'

'He won't. I promise. I'll see to it that he gets help.'

I shake my head. 'No, that's not what happens. He carries on, see. It gets worse. He punches my tooth out after H is born. And he ends up killing me, here, in this bathroom.'

Angela shakes her head. Her whole body is shaking. 'No. You're talking nonsense now. How can you know that's what happens?'

'It doesn't matter. I just do. Lee is charged with my manslaughter. Only he gets off because you lie for him. You say you came here and took H after Lee went to work, but you didn't. You cover up for him killing me because you cannot bear to lose your precious grandson.'

I raise my leg, ready to step out of the bath. As I do so she lunges at me, screaming hysterically, 'You are not going, you are not going to take my grandson away!' She grabs hold of my arm, her fingers digging into my flesh, pulling me, yanking me down. I scream, lose my footing and start to fall. I see the basin rushing towards me. It is going to happen now, here, before H is even born. I am going to die and lose my baby. I try to twist, desperate to protect my baby. I feel myself falling. I look up at the ceiling; I can hear Angela screaming. Or maybe it is me screaming, it is hard to tell. And then there is a thud as I hit the cold, hard tiles of the bathroom floor.

JESS

June 2009

Sadie knocks on my bedroom door and comes in. It's weird, seeing her in her school uniform. I can't remember the last time I wore mine. I haven't been to school for a long time and I can't imagine going back there.

'How did it go?' I ask.

'Yeah, OK, I think, but you never really know with English, do you? I might have written a whole pile of crap.'

'Nah. You'll have done really well.'

Sadie smiles and sits down on my bed. She didn't come to visit when I was in hospital. Dad said the psychiatric unit wasn't a nice place for a girl her age to visit. He seemed to forget that it wasn't a nice place for a girl my age to be in either.

'How're you doing?' she says.

'Oh. You know.'

'Are you still off the medication?'

'Yeah. They say I don't need it anymore. They're going to see how it goes.'

She nods. She knows that I lied about taking it in hospital. They all found out in the end. Some smart-arsed nurse thought she'd get the better of me. I still didn't take their tablets for long, though. Just long enough for them to be convinced they had worked.

'So, what now then?'

'I dunno. It's too late to go back to school now. Dad says I can do retakes next year when I'm better. Not there, though. Maybe at college. I want to make a fresh start. I don't want everyone knowing.'

She nods. 'You could go to Calderdale? Just tell the other students you flunked your exams. No one will know any different.'

She's right. But I'm also aware that any friends I make there, or at any point afterwards, will be different to the ones I had before. There will be those who know me and those who only know the bits I want them to know.

My gaze rests on the photo of Mum and me on the bedside table. The one where we have our arms around each other and are laughing. I can't even remember what we were laughing about now. I wish I could.

'She'd be proud of you, Jess,' Sadie says.

'What, of me going gaga and freaking you all out?'

'No. Of you getting through stuff so horrible that the rest of us can't begin to imagine what it must have been like.'

I shrug. 'I might not be through it yet.'

'You've got through the shittiest year possible. There's nothing life can throw at you now that could bring you down. You're stronger than all of us, Jess. You just don't realise it yet.'

I lean across and give her a hug, like the ones we used to share before all this happened. Except it's not like those ones at all. It is so much more than that.

'Thanks,' I say. 'For being there, I mean. For not giving up on me.'

'It's what friends do,' she says.

'No, it's what you did.'

She smiles at me, wipes at the corner of her eyes with her long fingers. 'Do you want to come into town on Saturday?' she asks.

I hesitate before answering. It's been a long time since I've been anywhere apart from home and hospital.

'Yeah,' I say. 'Yeah, that would be good.'

Dad will be happy, I know that. He'll think it means I'm better. Back to normal. I have no idea what normal is anymore. When people ask if I am better, I don't know what I'll say. Better than what? Better than I was a few months ago, yes. Better than I was before Mum died, no way. I don't think of myself as better. The doctor said that there is no such thing as sane and insane. That mental health is a continuum, a line on which we all move up and down at different points in our lives. And most of the time we manage to keep out of trouble. Only sometimes we hit the buffers at one end. And just because we might eventually get off them, it doesn't mean to say we are always going to be OK. But it doesn't mean to say we are always going to be crazy either. Simply that we are back on that line, jostling for position with everyone else who claims to be normal.

ANGELA

Tuesday, 21 March 2017

She lies there in a heap on the floor. For a moment I dare not touch her in case she is dead. Because if she is, I will have killed her – and my grandson too. Fear surges through me. How will I ever explain this to Lee? I start shaking uncontrollably. She makes a sound. Only a faint one, but I know that she is still alive.

'Oh, thank God,' I say, kneeling down on the bathroom floor next to her. The towel has fallen open. Her huge bump is sticking out of it. She turned somehow as she fell, twisted onto her back. I did nothing. I was rooted to the spot. Paralysed by fear – not that I was about to witness her death, but that I was about to lose my grandchild.

I look for blood but I can't see any. I rack my brain to try and remember what you are supposed to do in a situation like this. I think I should try to turn her on her side, but I'm not sure I can actually move her. And I'm scared that it might not be the right thing to do, that I might make it worse. She moves her head a little. A second later her body contorts as she lets out a high-pitched cry. She opens her eyes, the first time I know she is properly conscious. 'H,' she breathes. 'He's coming.'

I get up and run into the hallway, where I left my bag when I saw her case. I get my phone out and dial 999. I have never done this before. My hand is shaking as they answer.

'Ambulance,' I say, when they ask which service I need. As I wait to be put through there is another cry from the bathroom.

'It's my daughter-in-law,' I say, as soon as I am put through. 'She's eight months pregnant and she's had a bad fall. She says the baby is coming.'

I give them the address and rush back into the bathroom as she screams again.

'It's OK,' I tell her. 'The ambulance is on its way.'

'Dad,' she says. 'Call Dad! Tell him to come to the hospital.'

'What about Lee?'

She shakes her head. 'Dad.'

I go back out into the hallway and do as I am told. Joe sounds surprised when he answers the phone.

'Hello, Angela. Everything OK?'

'It's Jess,' I say. 'She's gone into labour.'

'But she's not due till next month.'

'She had a fall,' I say. 'She slipped in the bathroom. The ambulance is on its way. They'll take her to Jimmy's, you know, St James's Hospital. She wants you to meet her there.'

'Is she OK?' Joe asks.

'I don't know,' I say. 'We're waiting for the paramedics to arrive. Just go straight to Jimmy's, to the maternity unit.'

He hangs up. I can picture his face now, can imagine him running out to the car. She is his daughter. She is all he's got left, her and the baby. I know how that feels.

I go back into the bathroom, take the dressing gown from behind the door and put it over her.

'He's on his way to the hospital,' I say.

She nods before her face contorts again as she screams. I take hold of her hand but she pulls it away.

'Try to breathe,' I say. 'Try to slow things down.' She screws her face up. I wonder whether I should try to lift her, but decide it's better to leave it to the paramedics. I'm still not sure if she's injured. I do not want to make things any worse. I have made them bad enough already.

I hear the buzzer going. I run out to the hallway and pick it up. I tell them to use the lift and press the button to let them in. I wait for them to reach our floor.

'Here,' I call out. 'She's in here.'

They run in; one of them has a wheelchair, which he leaves in the hallway. I hold the bathroom door open for them; Jess lets out another scream as they go in.

'It's OK, love,' the older one says as he bends to examine her. 'We're going to get you to hospital in a jiffy. I just need to make sure there's nothing broken and no serious damage done.'

He lifts her side slightly and puts his hand beneath her, feeling along her spine, pressing around her lower back. He asks her to move her toes and she does it.

'Was she unconscious at any point?' he asks, turning to me.

'No. No, I don't think so.'

He shines a light in her eyes, gets her to follow his finger. Feels around her neck and collarbone. Then he takes a stethoscope out.

'This might be a bit cold,' he says.

He puts it onto her bump and moves it around slightly before stopping and listening.

'Is he all right?' she whimpers.

'Yeah,' he replies. 'He's fine. We're going to get you up and put you in the wheelchair and get you to hospital, OK?'

She nods and clutches at her bump as she moans again. The paramedics move to either side of her and lift her up. The towel falls off. I dash in and put her dressing gown around her, trying to protect her modesty. They put their arms under her shoulders and shuffle her out into the hall sideways. I bring the wheelchair over and watch as they lower her gently into it.

'Right, are you coming with her?' the older paramedic asks. Before I can say anything, I see Jess shake her head.

'No,' I say quietly. 'Her father's going to meet her there. She'll need her overnight case. It's there,' I say, pointing.

The other paramedic takes hold of it. 'Oh, and this,' I say, running into the nursery and returning with the car seat.

'Do you want me to give you a hand?' I ask.

'No, thanks,' he says, taking it from me. 'I can manage.'

Jess screams again.

'Right,' says the older one. 'Let's get you to hospital.' I watch them wheel her out of the apartment and into the lift before I shut the door, turn around and walk straight into the nursery. It is only there that I start crying, slumping down on the floor and clutching the teddy that I bought for my grandson. The grandson I have no idea if I will ever see.

Angela Griffiths
21 September 2017

I always knew Lee didn't do it, Jess. They didn't have any evidence to pin on him because he didn't do it. It's as simple as that. I also knew it might look like he did do it, though. Which is why I acted the way I did. I am not proud of what I did, Jess. I simply panicked when I arrived and saw your case in the hall. Because I packed a case once, Jess. I left it standing in the hall, too. The only difference was that I couldn't bring myself to go through with it because of the little boy who spotted it there. Who started asking questions. Painful questions, which I didn't have answers for. And so the case was unpacked by the time his father came home from work, and that little boy was told not to say any more about it. I stayed; for weeks, for months, for years, afterwards. Taking everything that was thrown my way because I could not bear to leave my little boy and I knew that I could not take him with me. Could not afford to look after him on my own. In the end, it was his father's case that ended up packed in the hallway, when he left me for another woman, a woman who may have been younger than me but who is probably old now. As old and damaged and broken as I am.

So that is why I went to pieces. That is why I ran into the bathroom to beg you to stay. And when I saw you lying there motionless on the tiles, blood oozing from the wounds on your head, I knew that you were either dead, or dying. In that split second, I had to make a decision as to whether to stay and help you or pick up Harrison and leave. Pretend I had arrived before the accident and taken my grandson for the morning as usual, allowing you to have a shower in peace.

So I chose Harrison. All I could think about was that little boy, screaming his heart out. And I knew I had to get him out of there. That if I stayed for another second, even to dial 999, it was more likely that the police would think it wasn't an accident at all, that Lee had done that to you. And then Harrison would have lost his father, as well as his mother. And no child deserves that.

So yes, I took him, and I shut the door behind me, leaving you there to die. Because I could not bear to do that to my grandson. And while I may have sacrificed your life in the process, I tell myself that that is what you would have wanted. Because you, of all people, know that a mother will do anything to save her little boy.

And, of course, the police believed me when I said I arrived at the apartment after Lee left for work. Nobody thought to question that. I mean, what kind of woman would leave her daughter-in-law dying on the bathroom floor? They believed me in court, too. Even after those women had come forward and said all those nasty things about Lee.

What's done is done and I will have to live with it for the rest of my life. No one will ever know the truth now, because I am not going to tell anyone. Lee may know, of course. But only if he did kill you, and I still don't believe he did. And I can't ask him, even if I wanted to, because if I do, he will know that I found you, know that I left you dying on the floor. We have never spoken of it. I don't suppose we ever will. There is a special bond between a mother and her son. And some things are best left unsaid.

JESS

Tuesday, 21 March 2017

I am so convinced that I am going to give birth in the ambulance that I am surprised when we pull up and they begin wheeling me out backwards.

'Are we here?' I ask the older paramedic. The one who told me his name was Terry.

'Yep, we'll get you straight inside now. There are people waiting to take over.'

'Is he going to be OK?'

'He'll be fine,' he says, smiling at me. 'He's got a tough cookie for a mum, hasn't he?'

I nod and moan simultaneously as the contractions come again. Terry pushes me into the maternity unit reception. A doctor and a midwife are waiting for me with a trolley. I hear Terry talking to them very quickly as I am lifted onto it. I can only hear snatches of what he says, the timing of my contractions, the fact that I will need a thorough check after the birth. The other paramedic hands over my case and the car seat. And then we are off, straight into the lift. The midwife takes my hand and tells me her name is Gloria. I try not to think about the hippo in *Madagascar*.

'Is Dad on his way?' she asks.

I am about to say yes when I realise she means my baby's dad.

'No,' I reply. 'I've just left him.'

Her eyebrows rise slightly. 'Girl, you certainly pick your moments.'

It makes me smile. It is the first thing that has made me smile for days. Maybe weeks.

'*My* dad's coming, though,' I say. 'He's the only family I've got. Well, him and this little fella.'

She grips my hand tighter as another contraction comes.

'He's not due for three weeks,' I say. 'I had a fall. I'm worried it's hurt him.'

'The paramedic says he's fine. You woke him up, that's all. And now he thinks it's time to put in an appearance.'

The lift doors open. I am wheeled out and turned left.

'We're going to do a quick assessment,' says Gloria.

'I told you, I'm having the baby,' I shriek.

'I know.' She smiles. 'We need to check how far along you are.'

'OK,' she says a few moments later, reappearing from between my legs. 'Looks like we're going to get you down to the delivery suite. No panic, but he seems to be keen to meet his mum.'

'You won't let anyone else in, will you?' I ask, sure that

Angela will have phoned Lee by now. That he could be on his way. 'I only want to see my dad.'

'That's fine. No one else is going to get in. You're safe here.' Gloria squeezes my hand as she says it. I wonder if she's guessed that it's not the giving birth I'm worried about now, it's what happens afterwards.

I am wheeled into the delivery suite room and put on the bed. I remember it vaguely from the tour Lee and I did of the maternity unit. Lee made some joke that at least he could have a bath while I got on with it. I didn't even find it funny at the time.

'You don't have to stay here,' says Gloria. 'I can run the bath for you, or there's a birthing ball through there, or you can squat on the floor if you want to.'

'I'll stay here,' I say. She picks up a hospital gown and helps me into it, wires me up to a machine next to the bed to monitor the baby's heartbeat.

'Is he still OK?' I ask.

'He's fine.'

I shut my eyes. All I see is H's face, the little dimples, the smiling eyes. And all I can think, as another contraction hits, is how I can't wait to meet my little boy.

I'm not sure how much later it is when there is a knock on the door. All I do know is that I am somehow on all fours on the bed, sweat dripping from my face, my arse sticking up while I am howling like a bloody wolf.

'Who is it?' I ask her. 'I don't want him in here. I don't want him anywhere near me.'

'Your father?' Gloria asks.

'No,' I say. 'I'm not talking about him.'

'OK,' she says. 'I'll go and see who it is. Ain't no one getting past me.'

She goes to the door. It is not Lee's voice I hear. It is not Dad's either. It is Sadie's.

'It's your girlfriend,' Gloria calls out, turning to do another raised eyebrow look at me. 'Girl, you really do waste no time.'

I start laughing, more out of relief than anything.

'She's my best friend,' I call out.

'You want her in here?'

'Yes,' I say.

Sadie hurries over to me. 'Hey, you,' she says, rubbing my shoulders.

'Why did you say you were my girlfriend?'

'Had to get past the woman on reception, didn't I? Your dad's waiting there. He thought you might want me with you rather than him. That's why he picked me up on the way past.'

I nod and let out another howl.

'Is she usually this noisy?' asks Gloria.

'Worse,' says Sadie. 'Where's Lee?'

'I've left him,' I say.

'What? Why?'

'Can I tell you later? I'm kind of busy right now.'

She nods and grabs my hand.

'Go and tell Dad I'm OK and that the baby is fine,' I say,

breathlessly. 'And then come back and be prepared to be screamed at.'

Sadie doesn't ask any more about Lee when she comes back. And she manages not to laugh out loud when I introduce Gloria to her, just gives me a knowing smile and whispers '*Madagascar* baby' to me when Gloria is out of earshot. She is, in fact, the perfect birth partner. I am glad she's here. Glad, when I start swearing, that I have someone other than Gloria to swear at. Glad when I am pushing, scared that I'm going to split in half, that she reassures me I haven't crapped myself by accident. And glad when she puts her hands on my shoulders as I squeeze a slithering, wrinkled little object out into the world.

'He's fine,' says Gloria, giving H a quick check over before she passes him to me. And I cry as I hold him. My baby. The baby I would have died for, but found I didn't have to in the end.

'Oh my God,' says Sadie, sniffing loudly and wiping her eyes. 'That's your baby. That's your son.'

I nod. 'His name's Harry,' I say. 'Because he's the boy who lived.'

It is a little while later, after they have checked Harry over and examined me too, that they wheel me down to the transitional care unit. Gloria has told me it's a precaution, just because Harry was three weeks early and they want to keep an eye on him. Not because there is anything wrong with him.

Dad is waiting for me by the bed, a huge bouquet of flowers in his hand, tears coursing down his cheeks before I even get to him.

He bends down to kiss me. His hand is shaking as he holds mine. 'I was so worried when Angela phoned,' he whispers.

'We're fine,' I reply. 'We're both fine.'

I see his eyes move to my baby. He bites his bottom lip before a smile breaks over his face.

'Meet your grandson,' I say. 'His name is Harry Joe Mount.'

'He's gorgeous,' he says. 'Absolutely perfect. Thank you.'

He is silent for a second. I know what he is going to ask me before he even opens his mouth.

'What's happened? With you and Lee, I mean. Why isn't he here? Why hasn't Harry got his surname?'

'I've left him, Dad. I'm going to tell you why and I'm going to explain everything, and I know when I do that you'll understand, but I'd rather not do it right away, if you don't mind. I don't want anything to spoil things right now. All you need to know is that I'm fine and Harry is fine and we're going to be coming home to live with you when we get out of here, if that's OK?'

'Of course it is,' he says, swallowing hard. 'Your mum would have been so proud of you, you know.'

I nod. Dad slips his hand inside his coat pocket and hands me an envelope with my name on it. I recognise the handwriting at once.

'I told you she wrote a few of them,' he says. 'For major events and emergencies.'

'Thank you,' I say. 'I guess I'm getting through them more quickly than she expected.'

I wait till later to read it. Until Dad and Sadie have gone and Harry is sleeping next to me and the midwives have reassured me again that no one will be allowed in to see me without my permission. I am sore down below and aching all over and so tired that I am desperate to sleep. But I know I am not going to be able to until I have read what it says.

I open the envelope, pull out the piece of paper and start to read.

Dear Jess,

No one prepares you for this moment, you know. You can go on all the courses and read all the baby books in the world, but nothing prepares you for holding your baby for the first time.

And I know what you will be thinking, because it's the same thing I felt when I first held you. The same thing all mothers think when they hold their baby for the first time. But you will cope, Jess. And you will know what to do. Not because you have read books or listened to what other people have told you, but simply because it's your baby and you will know instinctively what to do. And there may be people around you who tell you otherwise, who try to get you to do things differently. Maybe if I was still around, I would be one of them. But you don't need to listen to them, Jess. You just need to learn to trust yourself. It won't happen at first because you'll be so anxious, but gradually that will lessen and you will start to trust your own judgement.

And I tell you why you will always be right, Jess. Because you love that baby more than anyone else in the world. You're its mum and you'll fight for it the same way I fought for you. All you have to do is love it, Jess. It's as easy as that. And please give your baby a kiss from Grandma and tell my grandchild every day that, although I'll never meet them, I love them too. And I'll be looking out for them, like I'll always be watching over you.

ANGELA

Tuesday, 21 March 2017

I am waiting for Lee when he gets home from work. Sitting in the nursery, surrounded by everything I had got ready for my grandson.

'Jeez,' says Lee, jumping as he catches sight of me. 'What are you doing in there?'

'Remembering,' I say. 'Remembering when you were born.'

'Where's Jess?' he asks, putting down his briefcase and loosening his tie. 'Is she having a nap?'

'No,' I say. 'She's not here.'

'What do you mean?'

'She left, Lee. She left this morning.'

He stares at me. I can see the panic in his face. 'You'd better start making sense,' he says.

I get to my feet. 'She told me what happened last night, Lee. She had to tell me, because her suitcase was packed in the hall and I was screaming at her not to go.'

Lee looks down. He doesn't say anything.

'I tried to stop her leaving,' I continue, surprised by how calm my voice sounds. 'I went into the bathroom where she was having a shower and pleaded with her not to go. That's when she told me everything. She knows, you see. Somehow she knows about Emma and the others.'

'Don't be ridiculous,' says Lee. 'She can't do.'

'Well, she does. She also told me what she thought would happen if she stayed. She thought you would kill her and that I would lie in court to cover your back.'

'Jesus Christ. She's lost it, hasn't she? Finally flipped her lid.'

'No. I don't think she has. I've been sitting here all day, thinking about what she said, and I can see how that would happen. I mean, we both know how things can escalate, don't we? We know how, when a man has hit a woman once and got away with it, he is likely to do it again and again.

'And if I covered up for all the other times you did it, I don't see why it would be any different if you killed her. I love you, you see. You're my son, so it's unconditional love. I'd do anything for you. Even lie and perjure myself in court. Only I've realised this afternoon that it wouldn't be real love, just a sort of blind devotion. And I did that for years, Lee, put up with everything that was thrown my way, and look where it got me.'

'I'm not as bad as him,' Lee says.

'You will be if I let you carry on like this. You'll be worse than him. That's why it's got to stop.'

'What do you mean?'

'I'm not going to cover for you anymore, Lee. I'm not going to pretend I don't know what's going on. You're going to face up to what you've become and I'm going to as well. You haven't got any choice.'

His face is pale. He looks somehow smaller than he usually does. 'I don't understand,' he says.

'Jess has had the baby. She fell when I tried to stop her leaving, and then the contractions started. The paramedics came and took her to hospital. Her friend has just posted on her timeline. Said he was born this afternoon and that mum and baby are doing well.'

Lee turns and heads towards the door.

'Where are you going?' I ask.

'To the hospital,' he says. 'To see my son.'

'No, you're not,' I reply. 'Because Jess doesn't want you there. And if you go, I will post what you've done on Facebook. I'll tell everyone what you've done to her and all the others.'

'You wouldn't dare,' Lee snarls.

'Not before,' I say. 'But I would now.'

Lee starts to come at me, his fist raised. I hold up my hand. The hand that held him as a baby. The hand that calmed him when he was crying. The hand that waved him goodbye on his first day at big school.

He stops just short of me. Puts his own hand down and turns and kicks his briefcase across the nursery. It flies into the teddy bear music box on the dresser. It plays a few notes of 'Rock-a-bye Baby' before it falls to the floor.

Lee does the same, sinking to his knees on the rug. Sobbing

uncontrollably. I put my hand on his shoulder. My hand is stronger than his now. Because I have found a stronger love.

I don't put my usual brave face on in the morning. I am not hiding behind a mask anymore. It feels strange, looking at my barefaced reflection in the mirror. My eyes seem so much smaller without the eyeliner. But although they may appear like that to others, I know that for the first time in years they are open wide.

I sent her a message on Facebook, asking if I could visit. I told her Lee would not be with me. That I would be coming alone. It was a while before she replied. I suppose she was busy with the baby. Though maybe she was simply wondering what to say.

She said yes, though. Which surprised me, to be honest. I thanked her and told her I would not stay long. I am well aware that she won't be looking forward to it, that she would much rather be alone with her baby.

I catch the bus into town. It is always difficult to find parking at the hospital and I do not want to arrive flustered. I manage to find the transitional care unit easily enough.

I give my name to the lady on reception. She asks what relation I am to the baby.

'Grandmother,' I say, my voice firm and proud. A midwife swipes me through the door and takes me to her room.

'She's in there.' She smiles. 'The baby's feeding on her at the moment. They're both doing fine.'

I open the door and step gingerly into the room. Jess looks up. She doesn't smile but she doesn't scowl at me either. She has a look of pure contentment on her face. My gaze falls to the baby feeding at her breast. He is red and tiny. His little fingers are gripping her chest.

'Congratulations,' I say. 'He's gorgeous.'

'Thank you,' she replies. Then her face drops. 'Does Lee know?'

I nod. 'I told him last night,' I say. 'After I'd seen your friend's post on Facebook.'

She frowns at me. 'So why didn't he come?'

'I told him not to.'

Her frown deepens.

'I told him a lot of other things, too. Things I should have told him a long time ago. He won't be bothering you, Jess. I've told him he needs to get some help before he comes anywhere near either of you.'

She starts crying.

'I'm sorry,' I say, sitting down next to the bed. 'Sorry for everything I didn't say and didn't do. I didn't think I had the courage to stand up to him, you see. All the years my husband beat me and I put up with it, I thought it was because I was weak.'

Jess shakes her head. 'You loved him,' she says quietly.

'Yes,' I reply. 'Yes, I did.'

'It blinds you, doesn't it?'

I nod, wipe a tear from my own eye. 'And when he started doing it, when the girls he brought home ended up looking the same way I did, by the end, I didn't want to believe it. I couldn't bear to think that he was going the same way.'

'So what changed?'

'You,' I say. 'You changed him and you changed me.'

'He still hit me.'

'Yes, but he hated himself for it. And I got my strength from you. God, I wish I'd had half of your strength at your age.'

We fall silent for a moment, listening to the sound of the baby feeding.

'Will he change? Can he?'

'I don't know,' I reply. 'All I know is that he can't go on as he is.'

She looks down at the baby as he stops feeding. His eyes are shut. She pulls him closer to her.

'The midwife said he was doing fine,' I say.

'Yeah, he is. He was lucky. We both were.'

'I'm sorry. I don't know what came over me.'

'It's OK,' she says. I know it isn't though. Know that I can never take away what happened.

'Anyway,' I say, standing up. 'You must be tired. I'll let you get some rest.' She glances down at the big shopping bag in my hand.

'Oh,' I said. 'I nearly forgot. These are the new clothes I got in for him. You don't have to take them if you don't want to.'

'Thank you,' she says.

I put the bag down in the corner of the room, next to the car seat, and turn back to her.

'I didn't put the christening robe in there,' I say. 'It has a blood spot on it, you see. Lee's dad hit me when we got home from the christening. Said I should have been able to stop him crying in church. I was still holding him, in his gown, when he did it.'

She looks down and fiddles with the blanket around the baby.

'Do you want to hold your grandson?'

I look at her. I hadn't dared to ask. 'Thank you,' I say.

I go and stand next to her and she passes him over, this precious bundle of hope. I gaze at him and bite my lip as the tears fall. Because I love him so much. And because I so nearly lost him.

Jess Mount
11 July 2017 at 8:33pm

I wasn't supposed to see this day. It doesn't matter why or how now, but I wasn't supposed to be here. But I am, which is why I want to thank you all today, for being there for me when I needed you, even if you didn't realise it at the time.

The last few months haven't been easy, but they have also been the best four months of my life. Yes, being a single mum is hard. Yes, I'm still crap at sleep deprivation and yes, sometimes I collapse in a heap at the end of the day and cry. And it's important I tell you that, which is why I've posted stuff on the tough days too. Because for every glowing, smiling Facebook post there's another one that doesn't get posted. One that shows the other side of life – the tough times, the tears, the terror of getting through another day.

But today I'm doing a positive post, which is why I've got a smiley photo of me and Harry to go with it. Because today I am simply happy to be alive.

ABOUT THIS BOOK

Warning: Spoiler Alert!

Sadly, it was the deaths of two friends that led to me writing this book. I had been playing around with the idea of writing a novel about a young woman who finds pages of her life story and has to choose between keeping every detail the same or changing it all. I was interested in how, when we say we'd like to change the past, we often forget that the thing that we'd like to change may have had a positive consequence as well as a negative one. However, it wasn't hanging together as a novel and didn't seem to have much modern relevance.

When a friend died from breast cancer, it was my first experience of losing someone who I was friends with on Facebook, as well as in real life. Before her death, her family and friends used social media in a positive way to help raise money for her children, giving her huge peace of mind in her final days. What I also discovered was that reading the messages that her friends posted on her timeline after her death was enormously comforting and built a new community of friends (many of whom had never met before).

My second friend died in very different circumstances. She had documented her mental health problems on Facebook, and when she sadly took her own life, there was an outpouring of grief on her timeline from people whose names and photos I recognised as those who had, like me, tried to offer support to her on Facebook during her troubled life.

Again, there was comfort in reading other people's memories of her and piecing together the areas of her life I hadn't known much about. When I attended her funeral, I got talking with some of the people whose tributes I had read on her Facebook timeline.

Since their deaths, friends of both have continued to post thoughts and memories of them on their timelines, particularly on significant dates. As I write this, I have been reminded by Facebook that one of them will be celebrating her birthday this week. She won't, of course, but what will happen is that loved ones will post tributes on her Facebook page as part of this new phenomenon of social mourning.

That is how the premise of this novel developed, from the idea that if someone saw the outpouring of grief on social media after their future death, it may impact on the way they lived their life.

Look away now if you haven't already read the novel, but the obvious situation for this was one of domestic violence. As a journalist, I had covered so many appalling cases and interviewed many women about their experiences of domestic violence, as well as spoken to men about how they had become a perpetrator (and I'd like to make it clear at this point that although Lee witnessed domestic violence as a child, I am in no way saying that all boys who do so will become abusers. Many boys in this situation do not go on to become perpetrators and are often vocal in opposing male violence against women).

I particularly had in mind the statistic that, on average, women are assaulted thirty-five times before their first call to the police. I have often heard people questioning why they stay so long, people who don't understand the complexities involved in such cases – the controlling behaviour, the way women are often psychologically and emotionally abused, their self-esteem eroded, not to mention the worries surrounding any children involved and whether they will be able to care for them if they leave the family home.

But I wanted to give my central character the ability to see into the future, and explore how the knowledge that the abuse would continue and ultimately lead to her death would impact on her. I also wanted to highlight the fact that thirty per cent of domestic violence starts or gets worse when a woman is pregnant. When, twenty years ago, I relayed the findings of a survey on this from a local women's refuge, my news editor said, 'Yeah, that's because the men have got more to aim for.' When I objected to this 'joke', I was told that feminists lack a sense of humour. Sadly, these attitudes still exist today; we need to go on challenging them in an effort to ensure that violence against women is one day eradicated. I will be making donations to the following charities, all of which do brilliant work in this area, from the royalties of this book. I would be hugely grateful if you could support them too – or pass on the helpline number to anyone you know who may need support. Thank you.

The White Ribbon Campaign – men working to end violence against women
www.whiteribboncampaign.co.uk

Women's Aid – national charity working to end domestic abuse against women and children
www.womensaid.org.uk

Refuge – the country's largest single provider of specialist domestic violence services
www.refuge.org.uk

National Domestic Violence Helpline – run by Women's Aid and Refuge
Freephone 0808 2000 247,
available twenty-four hours a day

BOOK CLUB QUESTIONS

1. Does it matter that we never discover the truth about if, why or how the Facebook posts are sent from the future?

2. How do the Facebook posts colour your view of what is happening in the present-day storyline?

3. Does Jess's history of mental health issues impact whether we believe what she is seeing?

4. Does the fact that Jess is so feisty at the beginning of the story mean that her future demise has more impact?

5. What was your response to Angela, both in the future storyline and in the present?

6. How do your feelings towards Lee change throughout the novel?

7. The theme of parental love is a strong one. Contrast the love shown to Jess by her father and late mother to the love shown to Lee by Angela.

8. How does Jess's love for her son, H, influence her decisions during the story?

9. How does Jess and Sadie's friendship change during the novel?

10. Do you think you would live your life differently if you could read the tributes paid to you at your death?

11. How has social media affected the way we discuss the deaths of loved ones or celebrities?

12. Did you feel the novel gave you a greater insight into the reasons why women may stay in abusive relationships?

ACKNOWLEDGEMENTS

I thought I'd do the acknowledgements Oscars-acceptance-speech style this time – hoping I haven't muddled any envelopes! Writing a novel is a solitary process but an awful lot of people are still involved in bringing that novel out into the world and ensuring it gets read. Huge thanks to my editor, Kathryn Taussig, for helping me knock the story into shape (it's a better book because of her) and championing it everywhere – and to the whole team at Quercus for all their hard work. My agent, Anthony Goff, has been there for me since the beginning and his expertise and wisdom are invaluable, as is the support from all at David Higham Associates.

Thanks to Emily and Mylo for braving the camera for the book trailer, and Julia and Karen for providing a location; Lance Little for again giving my website a fantastic new novel makeover; and to David Earl for answering yet more police questions. Thanks to all the authors who read early copies and provided quotes; the book bloggers who reviewed and helped spread the word; and independent bookshops and libraries for still being there to support readers and writers – the book community is a truly lovely one.

Thanks to my family and friends for their ongoing support and for putting up with the anti-social periods. And a special thanks to the four of you who loaned your Facebook photos to Jess, Angela, Sadie and Joe – you know who you are!

To my husband, Ian (camera cuts to long-suffering man with grey hair in the third row), thanks for filming the brilliant book trailer, taking the author photos, doing all the housework and accompanying me on all those walks where I thrash out the plot and, somewhat annoyingly, for suggesting the Facebook idea. To my son, Rohan (eyes tear up), thanks for all your technical help, ideas and enthusiasm, and for being such an 'overrated actor' (cut to a laughing Meryl Streep) and getting cast in shows on stage and screen to allow me the extra time needed to finish writing this book. I promise to wear a 'proper dress' for your future award ceremonies!

To the survivors of domestic violence whom I interviewed during my years as a journalist, thank you for sharing your experiences to try to help others – your strength is my inspiration (full-blown tears).

And to you, my wonderful readers, for borrowing, buying, recommending and reviewing, and whose appreciation, feedback and comments constantly remind me what an honour it is to do this job, thank you. Please do get in touch on Twitter @lindagreenisms, Facebook at Fans of Author Linda Green and via my website (www.linda-green.com) to let me know what you think of this one – all apart from the person who reviewed my previous novel on Amazon by saying, 'this is the first book I have read by Linda Green – and it will be the last'. I hope you've found something better to read!